The MONGOLIAD
Book One

ERIK BEAR, GREG BEAR, JOSEPH BRASSEY,
NICOLE GALLAND, COOPER MOO,
NEAL STEPHENSON & MARK TEPPO

47N⬤RTH

Published by 47North
P.O. Box 400818
Las Vegas, NV 89140

ISBN-13: 9781612182360
ISBN-10: 1612182364

TO MICHAEL "TINKER" PEARCE,
ANGUS TRIM & GUY WINDSOR

✦ ✦ ✦

THEY PUT SWORDS IN
OUR HANDS AND TAUGHT
US HOW TO USE THEM.

1241

MID~SUMMER

CHAPTER 1:

⁓

NEW GROWTH AMONGST OLD STONES

C nán halted just outside the clearing surrounding the stone monastery and dropped to a crouch. She knew how to move silently in the dense woods of the North, and she had approached the isolated ruins more quietly than the breeze in the branches or the insects scuttling under last year's leaves.

Through the uneven morning mist, she could make out the ruin of the monastery on the northern verge. The broken, roofless walls of outbuildings stretched south of the main ruins in a broken curve. Birches and a few young oaks had grown up where monks had likely once raised vegetables. The rest of the clearing was filled with grass and brambles cut through with newly blazed paths. Four lean-tos had been erected just beyond the stone fence of an overgrown graveyard.

She had found a camp—that much was certain. But whose camp?

From far away came the rattle of a woodpecker gathering breakfast, interrupted by a closer and louder clash of steel— the unnatural sound that had drawn her attention. This close, she could hear men talking—many men—but she had yet to see the monastery's new guests.

Two days before, a band of black bone Mongols had chased her like a deer to the edge of the thick forest, where they had jerked up short, cursing in bastard Turkic and peppering the trees with arrows. Steppe-bred warriors loathed thrashing through cluttered groves where they could neither gallop freely nor swivel quickly on their powerful ponies. The deep woods were still safe, though traveling through them was slow.

It was just after the solstice: three months since the dissolute Khan known as Onghwe had defeated the armies of Christendom at Legnica, just a few miles from here, and a bit more than one month since he had issued his challenge.

She shifted to her left, darting behind the trunk of an elder oak. She stroked the bark lightly as if to ask the oak for guidance, then passed her fingers over her eyes in an old Binder prayer. The mist was clearing already; she could wait. In these lands, a well-trained adept knew to be patient.

Snatches of a conversation came to her, a back-and-forth argument that sounded like it hadn't started this morning, nor would it be finished anytime soon. Cnán recognized the cadences of Latin, which she had not heard in a while and had not spoken since childhood.

"—relax your vision. You know where the blade is. Stop looking at it—"

"—don't close your eyes! You might as well throw down your sword altogether. Are you a dumb lamb?"

"—if you watch his blade, it is too late. You can't see his eyes, so why are you—"

Less than a stone's throw away, a young man, no more than twenty years of age and crowned with hair so blond it was almost white, was facing an older man—a bulky, battle-scarred redhead. Both were carrying great swords of war, and their repetitive exercises were being observed by a man dressed like a monk.

These men were likely knights of the Shield-Brethren—the ones she had been instructed to find. If there were anything to their reputation, they would have responded within days to the Khan's unlikely invitation. The Shield-Brethren were scattered all about, but their closest branch was in Petraathen, an ancient crag-fort in the mountains south of Kraków, just a few days' journey from here. Their instinct—the reverse of the Mongols—was to camp in the woods, and their scouts had spied this old monastery, long since abandoned. To her, it had the look of a pagan temple, reminding her of the subterranean *mithraeum*, the hidden temple wherein her people had once held their arcane rites. This ruin, whatever its original purpose, had been converted into an impromptu chapter house, a sanctuary where these knights could wait and train while they reconnoitered the territory around the blood-soaked battlefield of Legnica and the great, stinking tent city that Onghwe had built there.

A horseman emerged from behind the graveyard wall riding a big blue roan stallion. Cnán flinched at the sight of a Mongol-style bow, striped and jointed like the leg of an insect, held out in the man's hands. But this was no Mongol: his hair was brown, long and full, and below his sharp nose drooped a luxuriant mustache. He pivoted his mount and galloped along the curve of outbuildings, then pivoted again and rode back and forth through the grass. His apparently aimless movements made no sense until she understood that he was practicing archery. When his eye fell on something that looked like it might serve as a target, he loosed an arrow from the bow, sometimes galloping past, sometimes away, or jerking his horse up short and shooting from a standstill.

She did not know these knights other than by reputation, but she saw the rider as one who had suffered under the power of the Mongols and had learned from them, adopting and adapting their weapons.

Farther back in the clearing, visible through dispersing curtains of fog and over the tumbled walls of a refectory, a young man was striking at an upright log with a sword, repeating the same attack over and over again. Near him, two others sparred with carved wooden sticks while another paced around them, sidestepping as necessary. To her left, in the green shade of a sapling oak, two men sat at a table assembled from half-rotted lumber, sharing refreshment from battered brass cups. Both wore trim dark hair. One sported a dark beard and had black eyes to match—*a kind of Saracen*, she thought—his Syrian heritage apparent also in the cut of his clothes.

The other, rounder of face and lively, flashed pale eyes as his nervous fingers fidgeted, and he whispered in short bursts as if laying out plans he knew the dark-eyed one would not approve.

Nine that she could see, then. A strong crew, but mostly young—and not the sorts of men usually found in close company. This was either good and expected or very bad indeed— for in the Land of Skulls, this region that had been devastated by the passage of the Mongol hordes, desperation and evil intent often united the most diverse stragglers.

Still, they seemed to be the ones she had been sent to find. *Ordo Militum Vindicis Intactae* now claimed to be Christian, so hiding near a monastery would come naturally to them. There were stories, however, of how, in older days, the knights of Petraathen had practiced a cult of death, harboring strange ideas about the benefits accruing in the afterlife to warriors who went down bloody and swinging. These brethren then might also take comfort from sharing quarters with the heroic and blessed warrior dead. From where she squatted, she counted seven big granite Crusader crosses in the monastery's overgrown graveyard, erected perhaps a century and a half before.

Cnán picked at her teeth with a twig, then shifted on her knees, practicing quiet breath, quiet heart—confident in her stealth, contented to watch unobserved.

Or so she told herself until she heard a flicking noise behind her head. A twang, a hiss, and something jerked her off her feet, slamming her head against a tree with a thunk that rang her skull like a bell.

She reached around desperately and felt a smooth, long shaft. A broad-headed arrow had snagged the hood of her cloak and pinned it to the bole of an aged birch. She struggled to yank herself free. Two years of running from Mongols had taught her that another arrow, better aimed, would soon fly, and she had best leave the garment behind and make a run for it.

But a voice—like the voice of her mother, only far away and sad—spoke as if in her ear: "*First arrow perfectly timed, perfectly aimed.*"

Cnán understood immediately. She lowered her hand. The archer had accomplished precisely what he had intended. Likely he had left camp even before she arrived, to circle around, guard, and observe.

Running was useless. She was dealing not with Mongols or their jackals, nor with ill-trained bandits, but with men born and raised in the woods. At any false move, that second arrow could strip through the green branches and split her spine.

Cnán quieted herself. Her eyes twitched at more rustling, faint, very close. She had been tracked through the trees by at least *two* men: the archer, still unseen, off to her right, and the stalker, now approaching from behind. Both were almost certainly from the camp, posted in the woods as sentries.

The hunter behind her began to move freely, making plenty of noise, but she could not yet see his face, nor he hers, because of the pinned-up hood and the dense cowl of mud-crusted black hair falling from the part in the middle of her head. He circled her warily, and when he finally came into full view, they spent a few moments gauging each other.

Cnán had seen some wild-looking men during her long trek across the lands of the Ruthenians, but this fellow—clothed entirely in things he'd killed, sporting a matted beard thick as a bear's pelt—looked half animal. Nothing woven—no womanly arts for him. Green eyes, sun-wrinkled at the corners, lent him a glimmer of youthful amusement.

No need to guess what he saw in her, since he announced it. His language was unfamiliar, but some of the words came from familiar roots. She recognized "woman" and "Mongol" and "spy"—the last a word very like her real name, in Tocharian.

She could have framed a denial in words he might vaguely recognize, but there were more effective languages that did not involve words.

Cnán shrugged out of her cloak, drew herself up, made a derisive snort, and fixed him with a glare.

It was better than slapping him in the face. The hunter recoiled half a step, then recovered with a mock stagger. Now the green eyes really were laughing. He glanced to his right, gathering a third party into the unspoken conversation: the archer, using the end of his bow to push a branch out of his way and step closer.

This was the tallest man Cnán had seen in years, possibly in her whole life. She knew that the men of Christendom were of greater stature than those of the steppes, but this one was likely a giant—even among his own kind. His hair and beard were red-blond. He was not handsome, but there was a strength in his face that demanded respect. He examined her for a few moments, then faced the hunter, who was still chuckling. They exchanged some halting banter that included a few more repetitions of the words "Mongol" and "spy." Their languages sounded the same to Cnán, but must, in fact, have differed, since they were not communicating very well.

After a few misunderstandings, the archer broke into Latin. But the hunter only shook his head and held up his hands.

Time to take charge, clearly.

"I am Vaetha," she lied—in Latin. The words from her mother's second tongue rolled forth with surprising ease. "I come from lands far to the East with tidings for Christendom. I would deliver this news to the master of your Order. Please take me to him."

The hunter shook his head again, grinned, then heeled about and sauntered back to the compound.

"Don't move," said the archer. He unsheathed his knife and warily moved in and around her, eyes narrow and glittering. He roughly cut the hood from the arrow, ripping the fabric in the process. Apparently the iron head of the arrow was more important, as he then carved away bark and pried it from the tree with the delicacy of a surgeon.

"I am Rædwulf," he said, tossing the cloak to her feet. "What manner of person are you, and why do you speak Latin?"

"She is of the Bindings," said a new voice, hollow and deep between the trees.

Cnán spun to discover that the older man had come upon them silently. He wore the robes of a Christian monk. His face was creased and rugged, counting at least threescore years, but age had not brought frailty. As he solemnly inspected her, he held his hand to his chest and drummed his sternum with his fingers. A chingle of mail suggested a hauberk under his travel-worn tunic.

All the activity had drawn the attention of the others in the clearing, even the younger ones busy hacking each other with sticks. They called a halt to the mock combat and took time to salute each other and shake hands before turning to amble in Cnán's direction.

The horseman cantered past them and drew his horse up short, just at the edge of the woods, then sidled close behind the older man. He looked down on her, his huge mustache flicking in disgust, as if she were an engorged tick just plucked from his inner thigh.

"Mongol!" he proclaimed.

Without turning, the older man countered, "No, Istvan. She has the cheekbones, it's true, but take a closer look at her eyes."

"Bandit or corpse robber, then. Either way, kill her." The horseman, Istvan, spat on the ground near her feet, expertly swung the stallion around, and cantered away.

The older man came closer and bent before her to pick up the torn cloak. Unafraid, polite, but far from humble, he handed it to her.

"I am Feronantus," he introduced himself, "of the *Skjaldbrædur*." He used not their newer Christian name, but an older one, in the tongue of the Northmen: *Shield-Brethren.*

"I am Vaetha," she said. "As you judged, I am a messenger."

"'One who sees,'" Feronantus translated. "From the Tocharian. Wordplay for 'spy.' Of course, you are lying about your name—we expect that. But *Vaetha* will serve until you trust me well enough to tell me who you really are."

She tried to best his steady gaze but could not.

"Come," said Feronantus. He turned his back on her and walked away. She followed him into the compound. The giant archer Rædwulf trailed after them both, clutching his precious arrow and smoothing the fletches as if it were a living thing in need of the master's comforting touch.

The young blond watched with dumfounded amazement as she passed, then whirled on the others. They laughed at his astonishment.

The pell fighter leaned forward and stretched out a clutching hand toward the blond's crotch. "She could have cut your balls off," he chided. "No great loss!"

"Did *you* see her?" the boy asked sharply. He tagged along after Feronantus, his sidewise gait that of a whelp. "I'm called Haakon," he said to her. "How do you say your name again?" Clearly he had never seen a dark woman before.

"Don't bother," Feronantus said. "She'll be gone before you glean any truth from her. And remember your vows."

The boy's feckless astonishment disgusted Cnán. This Feronantus might be of the ancient school, but the others—the Saracen-looking fellow, the men still clutching their cups of country beer, the stick-swinging, rowdy youngsters, this rudely staring blond—appeared far more raggle-taggle than her mother's tales of steel and glory had led her to expect. Clearly the warrior monks of Petraathen had fallen on hard times.

Perhaps her news would change all that.

✦ ✦ ✦

Before they reached the tumbledown monastery they were using as their chapter house, Feronantus's attention was drawn to the skin-clad hunter. He, for no obvious reason, crouched, then performed a clownish flop to the ground, and with eyes closed, pressed his ear against a settled and moss-covered tombstone.

Not his ear, actually, but the heavy skull bone behind it. He was listening for something.

"What comes, Finn?" said Feronantus, or something like that in the rough tongue Finn favored.

Finn held up four fingers. Then he dropped his hand to the ground and made it prance along like a cantering horse.

*Many steppe ponies...*Finn opened his eyes and shook his head. He held his hands close and then drew them farther apart. *One very big,* he judged.

"Destrier," Feronantus said.

All of the men in the compound, save Feronantus and Finn, seemed to have disappeared. Looking around, Cnán was able to see where they had gone to ground. Boys who had been brandishing wooden swords a moment ago were suddenly armed with long steel. Istvan and Rædwulf had their bows out and arrows nocked, and as soon as Finn rolled back to his feet, he did too.

It was an embarrassingly long time before Cnán could hear anything at all. But finally a heavy clop of hooves and jingle of steel penetrated the dense swath of greenery that surrounded the compound, and two riders came up the forest road abreast, each leading a spare horse.

Now here, Cnán thought, *was a knight worthy of her mother's tales.* He was tall, with long brown hair swept back from a high forehead, hazel eyes, and the clean-shaven face of an angel. He was armored in a shirt of mail, which she was accustomed to, but over that, guarding his shoulder and his breast, he wore segmented plates of polished steel. Slung over his back was a shield shaped, she sourly guessed, like the teardrops that must have rained from the faces of all the fancy ladies in his castle on the day he had gone prancing off to fight the Mongols. On his hip was a sword made for use in one hand, but straight, double-edged, longer and finer than most such weapons.

The other man was smaller, thick-muscled, and with a head more square than round. At first she assumed he was a squire, but as the pair rode into the compound, she saw he was at least as old as the knight. His clothes, though travel-worn, were more in keeping with courtly life than this forest camp. Something like a hatchet dangled from his waist, and he was festooned with daggers. Across his back was slung a crossbow, drawn and cocked. In his posture and the way he related to the beautiful knight, there was no deference, only equal regard and camaraderie. Coupled with a wry awareness of how people favored his handsome friend.

The knight had eyes only for Feronantus and a courteous greeting seemed ready on his lips, but the courtier with an excess of daggers broke in and was first to speak. He swept his arm ceremonially and announced in a booming voice to the compound: "Christendom is saved! Brother Percival has made a quest of it."

Laughter from all around, partly at the jest, but partly, Cnán thought, out of relief that these men were on their side.

The knight Percival drew up near Feronantus and dismounted with practiced grace. Finn had been right about his horse. It was a rare, beautiful brute with a white blaze on its forehead and a silky gray mane, barrel-chested, bigger than Istvan's stallion, and easily twice the size of a Mongol pony.

She had heard tales from her kin-sisters of an altercation between certain brothers of the Teutonic Knights and a party of Mongols who had gone astray and gotten lost in enemy territory. Trapped between river and woods, unable to maneuver as they were wont to, the Mongols had crowded together and the warhorses of the Teutons had slammed their smaller mounts around like bowling pins. Seeing this huge destrier, it was easy to believe. A horse worthy of the man...

Percival bowed low to Feronantus. Cnán was not at all amused at how much pleasure she felt, studying his face. She did her best to make sure it didn't show.

"Brother Percival, Brother Roger, welcome," Feronantus said. "It is very good to see you both. Thank God for your safe arrival."

Percival's companion, Roger, was only a step behind him. "Truth be told, God was surprisingly unhelpful," he began. Percival shot him an exasperated look. Side by side, the difference in height between the pair was not as great as she had thought at first; Percival had seemed larger because of his mount.

"We will listen to your stories while we sup," Feronantus said, holding up a hand to stay further discourse between the two.

"And listen, and listen some more—and listen again!" cracked the big man who had been training Haakon.

Percival turned to look at the source of the jest, and unfeigned delight spread over his face. "Taran! I hoped you'd be here."

"I heard you might come," said Taran, "and knew you'd need whipping into shape before the contests begin."

"Taran you know," said Feronantus, "and this dark, splendid fellow is Raphael, our physician. There is much we might speak of greetings and tales, but, Roger and Percival, you have interrupted me en route to a meeting, one I'm assured is too important to be delayed."

Eyes went to Cnán, then back to Feronantus.

"This is our swift-footed guide and messenger," Feronantus said. "Her name is not important—for now."

Taran muttered something about *Bindings*, and then wary interest chased the confusion out of their faces.

◆ ◆ ◆

"Where did I come from? Places of which you have never heard the names. So there would be little point in my reciting them," Cnán said, in answer to Feronantus's first question.

Amusement around the table, only a little strained. She was nervous that the one named Raphael, with the close-cropped black beard and the Syrian look, might call her bluff. A Crusader, she guessed, born and bred in one of the few surviving fortress-cities that the armies of the West still garrisoned in the flyblown hellhole that they styled the Holy Land. But such a man might know the deep parts of Asia better than, say, Taran, who was Irish and probably considered Dublin to be part of the exotic Orient.

Or perhaps she was being unkind. Hunger, and being hunted like an animal, had a way of shortening her temper. She tore into a piece of bread while the three senior knights enjoyed a chuckle.

"But most recently," she went on, chewing and talking at the same time, "in the last few days, I have traveled from Czeszow. East of here." She swallowed. "In the forest." And again. "Where Mongols don't like to go. There is a man there, a Ruthenian of noble birth, from the city of Volodymyr-Volynskyi—you probably know it as Lodomeria. He says he knows you."

A serious, pained look came over Feronantus's face. "Illarion," he said.

"A member of your Order?"

"No," said Feronantus, "but he could have been, were it not for...religious controversy."

"Wrong kind of Christian?" Cnán asked, still chewing.

"Yes. Please go on. Illarion is alive, you say?"

"You seem surprised," Cnán observed, "which tells me that you must have heard tell of what happened at Lodomeria."

Feronantus's silence implied assent. But Taran only looked provoked. "I have *not* heard," said the Irishman.

"Briefly, the same as happened to all other cities that stand in the way of the Mongols. Perhaps worse than usual."

"How did Illarion escape? He is not the sort to run away."

"Aye, your judgment of his character is sound," Cnán said. "He stood and fought. Was captured, along with many others of that city's noble class, as well as clergy, merchants, and so forth. Mongols do not like to shed the blood of captives. It's fine on the battlefield, of necessity, but they prefer to put prisoners to death bloodlessly. If it's only one, or a few, they bring out a wrestler who breaks the spine. But that's too slow for large numbers. So they bind their captives and force them to lie down in an open field, like a human carpet. While the poor people moan and plead, over this the Mongols throw planks, making a heaving floor. Then they ride their horses up onto the floor—though the ponies like it not a whit—and ride them back and forth…over and over…until the crying and moaning stops. The Mongols bray and babble and toast each other with their foul milk. Their young watch and dance like imps in hell. It's a *fine* party," she spat, and her eyes darted around the astonished circle. She put down her bread. "By the time the party's over, most of the prisoners have been trampled to death. The ones who survive are too broken to move. Mostly dead, mostly broken," she added, fingering the bread again. Her stomach twitched and she shook her head. "Enough."

"This happened to Illarion?"

"Yes. And his wife and daughter. The next morning, while Onghwe Khan and his men were sleeping it off, a few black bones came around—"

"Black bones?" Feronantus asked.

"Mongols of lower caste. Tartars, Turks, some Ruthenians. They came to pull up the planks and take ears."

"Ears?" Taran asked sharply.

Raphael explained, "It is how they count the enemy dead."

"Most of us have *two* ears!" Taran protested.

"It is always the right ear," Raphael said gently.

"When they cut off Illarion's right ear, he woke up," Cnán said. "Reached up like a demon out of the muck, snatched the knife from the ear-cutter, twisted it around, and gutted him. A few other black bones bandied their bowlegs his way. He picked up a plank and used it like a quarterstaff. Brained them one by one. Killed them all."

This cheered her a little, and she took another bite. "Collected their horses and rode away. Do you have beer?"

The knights looked at each other and smiled as if at a secret. Raphael poured her a glass of the foaming sour stuff they had been drinking. It tasted like beer but was as strong as mead and made her head swim.

"Since Illarion still lives, I cannot simply dismiss the story," said Feronantus, after thinking about it for as long as he wanted to, "but I suspect it to be half true and half nonsense."

"Plank as quarterstaff," Taran said, tugging mightily at his beard and screwing up his face. "Difficult to get a proper grip."

"Illarion was always good with a staff," Feronantus reminded him.

"I doubt that the ear-taker woke him," Raphael said. "He was probably lying in wait, feigning death."

"His ear is definitely gone," Cnán announced. "His *right* ear."

"We needn't resolve such questions now," said Feronantus, as Taran seemed about to voice a new objection. "You say he is alive, and nearby."

"Barely, and in a manner of speaking," said Cnán. "Two days' ride under normal circumstances."

"I love Illarion," Feronantus admitted freely, "and would do almost anything for him. But there are only a few of us, and we are here for another purpose."

"He said you would say that," said Cnán, "and you should come and get him anyway, and that you would understand when he got here."

Feronantus looked mildly put out. He gave Cnán a searching look. "You would lead us to him?"

"Of course, if you let me finish this bread. And give me more beer."

"Please, eat your fill. Raphael, will you go and tend to Illarion's wound?"

"Of course."

"Take Finn and, in case there's trouble, Haakon."

"We might need Haakon here," Taran warned. Cnán wondered why they needed the boy. He was feckless and clumsy looking. She almost felt sorry for him.

"Raphael will bring him back safe and sound," Feronantus returned, shifting his gaze to the Syrian.

CHAPTER 2:

—

THE KHAN OF KHANS

Ögedei, Khan of Khans, third son of Genghis the Great Conqueror, sat upon his throne. His mighty frame was draped in fine robes—delicate embroidery depicted clouds and dragons in pure-gold thread on a sky-blue background. Around him were the lavishly painted walls of the Great Palace of Karakorum. The lilting music of zithers filled the room, and lithe girls danced about the tall throne, their sheer silk sleeves twirling red spirals in the air. Ögedei divided his attention between listening to the petitions of the bureaucrat prostrated before him and playing with his empty cup. He spun the cup deftly in his broad right hand, tracing the delicate silverwork with his fingertips. The cup was empty. He did not wish it to remain empty.

"O *Khagan*, Master of the World," said the Shanxi provincial sub-administrator, his fat forehead firmly planted against the floor, "I bring myself before you today to humbly request that the grain taxes for Xieliang County be lowered from one in twelve bushels to one in fifteen..." The beaded tassels on the top of his cap dangled back and forth as he talked, and Ögedei found the motion mesmerizing. He was well into the embrace of the wine, and his mind was easily snared.

Weak, he thought, staring at the tassel-topped sub-administrator. *A life hunched over books and papers. Any simple peasant among his subjects could subdue him and choke the breath from his throat, yet he governs them completely.* He studied the man, his ludicrous hat, his soft, fat hands. *One blow,* he reckoned, *I could split his head in two with one stroke, and then he could bother me no more.* Ögedei sighed and looked away. One hand idly stroked his mustache, while he traced the grooves and ridges on the cup with the other. *But another would just take his place, and after him, another. Like swatting at a swarm of flies.*

The Shanxi provincial sub-administrator twisted his neck to look up at the *Khagan,* expecting an answer to a question Ögedei had only half heard. He grew pale, seeing the twisted line of Ögedei's mouth, and he started to stammer, the tassels bobbing up and down.

Ögedei cut him off with a grunt and a wave of his hand. "Let it be thus," he said.

The tassels clattered against the floor as the sub-administrator groveled in gratitude. Praising the magnificent wisdom of the *Khagan,* he shuffled backward until he was far enough away to flee the throne room without causing offense.

The sub-administrator scuttled between a pair of men entering the throne room. One was Yelu Chucai, Ögedei's advisor; the other was a young warrior, wearing dust-covered leather armor. Chucai strode across the room, a floating apparition in his black silk robes. His beard, as dark as his robes, trailed down to his waist, a not-inconsiderable distance of his seven-foot frame. The young warrior looked small next to Chucai, even though the crown of his head was in line with the other man's shoulder. The warrior's eyes were wide, his boyishly smooth face unable to hide his wonderment at the array of treasures arranged in the throne room. Chucai knelt before the *Khagan*, and the young man belatedly scrambled to follow his lead.

"*Khagan*," said Chucai, "this envoy comes from Chagatai Khan."

Ögedei studied the young man kneeling beside Chucai. *Why has my brother sent an emissary?* He tried to recall the last report from the *noyon*, his generals in the field. Batu, Jochi's intemperate son, was still in the West, expanding the edge of the empire with the aid of Subutai, Genghis's brilliant strategist. Kadan and Onghwe were with the great horde as well; conquering lands for their father was a worthy cure for the boredom that had consumed them at Karakorum. Chagatai's holdings—given to him by Genghis—extended from the Altai Mountains to the Amu Darya River. As long as Batu—and, by extension, the rest of Jochi's offspring—kept conquering lands to the west, there should be no conflict between the two branches of the family. *What more could Chagatai want?*

The nagging question gave birth to a wine-spawned idea: the possibility of sending the warrior away, dismissing him outright without giving him a hearing.

"Why has my brother sent you?" Ögedei sighed, putting aside the idle idea.

The emissary started. "I..." he stuttered. "Chagatai Khan has sent me to..." He looked up at Ögedei, and the *Khagan* saw both confusion and something else in the young man's face. "I have been sent to ensure your safety."

"Safety?" Ögedei echoed. A scattering of half-formed thoughts raced through his head, a confusion of trails that looped back on themselves. *Who?* He raised his head and looked around the room. Oil lamps illuminated every inch of the walls; there were no shadows, no places for assassins to hide. There were a handful of men at every door throughout the palace, and hundreds more—thousands—who would die for him at but a word. How much safer could this one man make him? "An assassin?" he sneered, the wine slurring his words.

"No, great *Khagan*," the emissary spoke quickly, attempting to redirect the conversation. "Who would be so foolish to try to assassinate you? Chagatai Khan sends me to…" The emissary glanced at Chucai, and seeing no help in the advisor's hooded gaze, plunged on. "Your brother worries about you, about your drinking. He has sent me to…to watch over you…and…and to make sure you do not drink more than a single cup a day."

Ögedei stared at the emissary for a long time, long enough that even Chucai started to fidget. The young man looked out of place—a warrior more at ease on the steppes than in the halls of Karakorum, a man who did not like the roof over his head—but there was something about the way he held himself, about the way his eyes moved about the room.

From deep in Ögedei's belly a rumbling sound rose, a laugh that shook his shoulders and made his robes tremble. "My drinking? My brother is concerned about how much I drink?" He swiped a hand across his mustache, and noticing his cup on the arm of his throne, he picked it up and threw it at the young emissary. The warrior had the presence of mind to not flinch as it bounced off his leather jerkin, dust rising from the impact. "My brother dotes on me like a brood mare." He stood, looming over the two men, and the last vestige of the laugh became a booming echo in his voice. "I am Ögedei, *Khagan* of the Mongol Empire. I do as I please. My brother's attention should be on the kingdoms he can conquer in my name, like his nephew Batu. Like *my sons*. The rest does not concern him."

The wine was making his legs wobble, and Ögedei put a hand down on the arm of his throne to steady himself.

The emissary's face tightened as he watched the *Khagan.* "It will be as you say, *Khagan.*" He offered a shallow bow and then turned away from the *Khagan,* showing Ögedei his back as he walked out of the throne room.

Ögedei collapsed into his throne, a hot flush rushing up his neck. *How dare he walk away like that?* Gripping the arms of his throne, he pulled himself upright to yell at his guards.

Chucai had not moved, and the stormy expression on his face was enough to quell the shout rising in Ögedei's throat. The wine fought him too, muddling his vision and making it seem as if dark shadows swam behind his advisor. Shadows that could contain...

"I will speak with him," Chucai said. Before Ögedei could argue, Chucai offered a perfunctory bow and went after the emissary, leaving the *Khagan* to brood on his throne.

◆ ◆ ◆

Ögedei leaned back on silk sheets and breathed the aromatic air infusing his private chambers deep into his lungs. Jasmine and magnolia, with a hint of cedar. It wasn't the same as the rarified scent of the open steppes, but it reminded him of them nonetheless. In this room, away from the bowing and scraping sycophants and the watchful eyes of his guard, he could forget about the affairs of the empire for a while. His head throbbed faintly, a pressure against the crown of his skull—a lingering reminder of the wine. Dinner with Governor Mahmud Yalavach was a few hours away, and he hoped the headache would be gone by then.

The bed shifted around him, the light presence of his wives as they undid his robe and removed his fur-lined shoes. Hands ran over his muscular chest, and without opening his eyes, he caught them. He heard a quick gasp, and he knew whom he held. Jachin, the tallest. He had chosen her for her eyes, the brightest green color he had ever seen.

One of his wives put her mouth next to his ear, and he felt her breath. "So tense," she whispered. He released his grip on the pair of fluttering hands and groped for the woman next to him. His hand brushed against her head, touching her thick braids and the thin ribbons she had woven into the strands.

"Toregene," Ögedei murmured, rolling toward her.

She clucked her tongue, and the sound echoed in his ear. He instinctively moved away from her, and her hands slid under his body, pushing him farther. He rolled onto his stomach, still trying to reach back and grab her. She evaded his clumsy grope and tapped him lightly on the bare shoulder. "Lie still," she admonished. "Let us see if we can't work these knots out of your back."

Ögedei grunted and relented, letting his hands fall onto the bed. "If I had my way," he said, "I'd stay like this all evening, in bed, surrounded by my beautiful wives. We'd make love and then eat fried dumplings, then clean off in a cold bath and take a midnight ride. Out, over the steppes."

"As if you'd ever be able to keep up with me," Toregene laughed.

Ögedei opened his eyes and tried to look over his shoulder. "In lovemaking or riding?"

"Both."

Ögedei smiled. "Would you not leave me my pride, woman?"

Toregene snorted. "You would get it back in a morning at court. All those officials crawling on the floor, calling you High Grand Exalted Master of the World. Begging you to notice them."

"It is our job to remind you of more important things," Jachin said as she joined Toregene. She pressed her elbow down hard into Ögedei's shoulder, and he let out a grunt of pleasure. "Tense as a bowstring. What is it that worries you?"

The dust on his shoulders, Ögedei thought. The young emissary from his brother Chagatai. The warrior had ridden countless days across the steppes to reach Karakorum. He had slept outside, nothing but the endless bowl of the heavens over his head. There had been a horse beneath him, and the wind had flowed through him. All he had known was the grass that lay behind him and all he saw was horizon before him.

"Do you know how long it has been since I've been on a horse?" he said. "How long it has been since I've ridden freely across the grasses?"

Neither woman answered. *Nor will they,* he thought bitterly. *They know as well as I.* "Some nights I dream of escaping this cave," he confessed. "I'm sitting in that room, watching an endless parade of bureaucrats and officials. They flow in like a spring river, and every time I blink, there are more of them. A flood that will overwhelm me.

"And in this dream, I escape. I leap from a balcony, and there is a strong pony waiting for me. No one can stop me. I ride out of the gates, and I keep riding forever, until I die in the saddle. But the pony doesn't stop. He keeps going, and my body rots away. My bones are scattered across the empire, and the pony doesn't stop until he reaches the place where the sky bends down and touches the ground. All that is left of me then is my hands, my fingers wound in his mane."

Toregene worked her way down, and Ögedei felt his muscles loosen. He was tight, but it wasn't that half-remembered tightness, that lower-back tension that came from being in the saddle overlong. "Tonight," he sighed, "I have to go to dinner and eat over-spiced foreign food with golden chopsticks. I have to pretend to be interested in talking to overstuffed diplomats. That's all I am now. A man who sits on benches and chairs, who eats and talks. That is all I do."

"Somebody has to be *Khagan*," said Toregene. "You've done a better job of ruling the empire than even your father."

Ögedei scowled. "The empire rules itself. They just need someone to grovel to." After a beat he added, "And no one compares to my father."

He felt Jachin shift to his other side, and her elbow descended into the softer flesh below his shoulder. "Before you were *Khagan* this was all empty grassland," she reminded him. "Because of you, there is a palace now. The grandest palace the world has ever known."

"It would've been better off staying grassland. A palace for the Chinese is a prison for Mongols." He flexed his shoulders, shooing his wives off him, and sat up. Their hands were deft, but their words were not helping him relax. He looked at Jachin and then Toregene, making sure they were paying attention to him. "Would it not be simpler if we rode off together? We could leave all of this to someone else and go live in a *ger* on the edge of a river like we used to. We could live off the land again. Eat what I kill."

His wives said nothing, but they curled up close to him, running their hands through his hair. He clasped his hands on their shoulders, feeling their warm skin. "I think when I die, the empire will die with me," he mused. "I have no worthy heirs. Kadan is too enamored with foreign religions. Khashi is more interested in chasing pretty women than fighting. Onghwe..." He shook his head. "Onghwe is worst of all."

"What about Guyuk?" asked Toregene. "He will be a worthy *Khagan*."

"Guyuk is too quick to anger. Remember what he did in Rus."

"Batu is an arrogant fool," said Toregene. "Guyuk was—"

"Wars aren't won by being cruel to your own men," Ögedei cut her off. "Guyuk is too temperamental. He does not understand how to rule. And his cousins…they would be like wolves in the dead of winter: they would look upon Guyuk as the weakest member of the pack."

"They wouldn't dare!" Toregene's eyes flashed.

"They would," Ögedei sighed. "And perhaps…" His shoulders sagged and his hands pressed down more firmly on his wives' shoulders.

"What is it?" Jachin asked. "It isn't the dream of the steppe that haunts you, is it?"

Ögedei shook his head. "An emissary from Chagatai came today, bearing a message."

"What message?"

"He sent some stripling to keep an eye on my drinking."

The women were quiet for a moment, and when one of them spoke, her voice was almost too quiet to be heard. "There might be some benefit to such a man," Jachin said.

Ögedei whirled on her, and she met his gaze for an instant. She dropped her chin, but the damage was done. Ögedei had seen the sharp glitter of her eyes.

"I am *Khagan*," he roared. The headache pulsed in his head, returning with furious hammering. "I will do as I please. When I please. How I please. No one—not my brother, not you, and certainly not some dust-covered, *boodog*-eating horse archer—will tell me what I may and may not do."

Toregene leaned against him, her weight holding his arm down. *Had he raised it to strike Jachin?* He had no memory of trying. There was nothing in his head but the pounding reminder of how long it had been since he had had a drink, and that sensation only proved Jachin's point. He pulled away from Toregene, dismissing Jachin with a wave of his hand. "You can't expect a man not to drink from time to time. My father drank. His father drank. Drinking is the only freedom I still have."

Toregene put her hands on his shoulders. Her braids brushed against his back as she rested her head against his. "Your brother's not trying to insult you, Ögedei. He just cares about you."

"Does he?" Ögedei stared at the flickering light of the lantern hanging on the wall. "If he really cares about me, then why doesn't he come here himself?"

✦ ✦ ✦

Ögedei could not see the sky for all the dust in the air. Men and horses—and the wind, even—had stirred up the dry ground of the Khalakhaljid Sands. The Kereyid army was endless; every time a break appeared in the clouds of dust, it was only to unleash more riders upon Genghis Khan's beleaguered army.

His mouth filled with the taste of dirt and blood, Ögedei whipped the reins of his horse and drove it on through the sands. All around him, he heard the cacophony of battle: men shouting, the clanging of swords, the shrill screams of horses dying. He could not tell if his father's armies were winning or losing. Ögedei's world was reduced to a red cloud, filled with ghosts.

He beat his heels against the ribs of his horse, trying to keep the animal under control, but it sensed his fear and refused to mind him. Starting at every clang of steel around it, the horse kept shying—first one direction and then another.

He had seen seventeen winters; he did not think he would see another.

The dust swirled in front of him, billowing out from the shape of a charging horse and rider. There was something wrong with his head, and as he emerged from the cloud, Ögedei glimpsed the warrior's helmet more fully and realized the approaching rider was not from Genghis's army. The Kereyid, the long feather on his helm broken and bent, flicked his spear down and drove its point into his horse's flank.

Ögedei felt the shock of the thrust in his legs, and his horse reared, lurching to the right. The reins jerked from Ögedei's grasp, and as he tumbled toward the ground, he caught a glimpse of the sky through the dust. *Blue sky.*

The fall knocked the wind from his lungs and made his ears ring. He tried to spit out the dust in his throat, but nothing came out when he retched. His sword was gone, and he tried to remember when it had fallen from his grip: when his horse had thrown him, or when he had hit the ground? The dust had swallowed it up.

The ground shook. *A horse.* His ears were still echoing with the shock of his fall, and everything was muffled. But he could feel the horse coming at him, and he rolled to the side as the Kereyid thundered past. The tip of the man's sword caught the edge of his helmet, ringing from one of the metal studs in the leather. His head was yanked back and his helmet flew off, eagerly devoured by the dust.

The Kereyid pulled his horse to a stop, wheeling it around again, and as it trotted toward Ögedei, he slipped off its back in a fluid motion. Sword raised, he charged Ögedei.

Scrambling for the dagger in his belt, Ögedei pushed himself off the ground. The wind gusted between them, and the Kereyid's blow came slowly, as if all the particulate in the air was causing resistance against the blade.

Ögedei crouched under the strike and thrust up into the Kereyid's belly. His dagger hit the edge of the warrior's breastplate, skipped down, and then slid into flesh. Ögedei pulled the blade along the edge of the hard breastplate and blood splashed over his hands. The Kereyid howled, and Ögedei shoved him down. He was still holding his sword, and Ögedei kicked it from his hands and then stomped on the man's face. The Kereyid continued to yell, and Ögedei kept kicking until his boots were covered in red mud.

His horse was still alive. It lay on its side, kicking and convulsing around the Kereyid's spear. Ögedei coughed and spat up sand. His legs trembled as he bent and picked up the Kereyid's sword. It was heavier than his, and the cross-guard wider and thicker than he was used to. *It will do.* He squeezed the hilt tightly as he staggered toward his dying horse.

It had been a good steed, sure-footed and responsive to his guidance. It had carried his uncle for several months before Jochi gave it to him. There was blood smeared on the horse's nose and its eyes were wide and frenzied. Incredibly, it was trying to stand as Ögedei approached, but its front right leg failed to hold its weight.

"Run," Ögedei croaked. "Run to the Eternal Blue Sky." His stroke was clumsy, but the blade was sharp enough. The horse's back legs kicked twice as it died, and Ögedei ground the heel of his hand against his face, fighting the sting of sand and salt in his eyes.

An arrow landed in the side of the dead horse, and Ögedei looked at it dumbly. It was a short Mongol arrow, but the fletching was unfamiliar. *A Kereyid arrow.* He was still on the battlefield. He couldn't stay here; he had to find his way out of the sand cloud. He didn't know whether to advance or fall back, wouldn't even know where to advance or fall back *to.* Perhaps he would never see the sky again. He was being buried underground. He wrapped his scarf over his face to keep out the dust, still tasting grit on his tongue.

Something bumped into him, and he fell back against the corpse of his pony. Wildly he looked around, trying to spot a shadow or a shape in the dust. *Who is there?* Horses charged past on his right. Their hooves pounded against the sand, kicking up swirling clouds of dust. He brought up a hand to shield his face, and pain lanced his neck and shoulder. Glancing down, he saw the bloody tip of an arrow protruding from beneath his chin.

His scarf was tangled in the arrow, and he couldn't reach over his shoulder to pull it out. His fingers brushed the shaft, and pain shot through his neck. Screaming, he fell to his knees.

There was blood inside his armor. His scarf was turning red, and what wasn't absorbed by the cloth was running down his chest. His hands were red too, and he realized he was kneeling in the bloody mud of his horse. He shivered, suddenly cold.

The dead Kereyid, though he didn't have much of a face left, seemed to be laughing at him. Ögedei tried to steady himself on his horse. *So warm*, he thought, and the tears started again. He didn't try to hide them this time. He let them run. "I'm sorry," he whispered, though there was no one there to hear him.

The Kereyid kept laughing. Ögedei could hear his voice— a roaring, rippling sound in his head, like a flash flood in the spring as it filled the dry riverbed. It wasn't just the Kereyid; it was the dead on the battlefield. All of the spirits were laughing at him now.

Dark spots swam in his vision. He dug his fingers into the short hair of the horse and tried to remember what it was like to ride.

So much blood, he thought as he toppled over.

◆ ◆ ◆

He was having trouble breathing. His mouth was clogged with sticky mud, and bristly hairs tickled at his nose. *Sit up.* His body seemed so far away. Ögedei tried to move his arms and felt nothing. *I'll try again soon,* he thought. *Maybe when the sun comes out.* Until then he would lie still and listen to the faint rhythm of his heartbeat.

A muffled noise interrupted his reverie, and he realized it was coming from his throat. The sun had come out, and its light was burning a hole in his neck. The pain burned straight through to his throat, and his scream was escaping through the ragged hole.

Above him, there was nothing but blue sky. No dust, no clouds, only the endless expanse of the sunlit heavens. But for the intense pain in his neck, he would have thought he had gone into the next world. *It shouldn't hurt,* he thought, *not anymore.*

It did, though, and the pain kept digging deeper into his belly. He kept trying to spit it out, but nothing came out of his mouth. Everything seemed to be coming out of his neck in crimson gouts.

A shadow passed between him and the sky, a dust-covered cloud. Its surface arranged itself as he focused on it: red-rimmed eyes, a mustache flecked with dirt and blood, lips cracked and dry. The lips were moving far above him, but he could still only hear the sound of his own scream leaking through the hole in his neck. The face dipped down and the smell of sweat and oil from the man's hair filled Ögedei's nostrils. Underneath the stink of battle, he recognized the man's scent. When the face raised itself up again and spat out a mouthful of black blood, a name came to Ögedei.

Boroghul. One of the orphans adopted by his grandmother. The tall one with the face like red stone. Family, yet not-family.

Not-blood, and yet—Ögedei watched Boroghul spit out another mouthful of his blood—a blood-brother.

The sky grew dark, and Ögedei found the strength to move his hands. He grabbed on to the cloth and leather of Boroghul's armor and held on. Stars came out, tiny eyes winking at him like animals hidden in the tall steppe grasses, and eventually he could hear the wind again. *Stay with me, Ögedei,* it said. Or maybe it was Boroghul, whispering in his ear.

It didn't matter. He had been found.

CHAPTER 3:

THE GHOST OF RUS

It was good that she did not have time to make herself comfortable in the chapter house, or else going back out into the Great Khan's empire would have been unendurable.

She rode now, since it was impossible to move stealthily in such a large group. Finn, when he spoke at all, favored a guttural lowland tongue she could barely understand and had poor Latin. Still, he seemed to know the ground better than she, or perhaps he just sensed things more acutely. So she and Finn scouted ahead and signaled Haakon and Raphael when it was safe to move forward, and in that manner, they made good time until twilight and for half of the following day. After that, the forest grew so dense that the horses became more trouble than they were worth. They left them in the care of a local woodcutter whom they found by following the sound of his ax.

The woodcutter claimed to know nothing of Mongols, and cared little more.

Raphael said it was a toss of the coin as to whether the horses would still be there when they got back, but this was better than simply letting them go. They camped in a ravine that night, risking a fire, as the smoke and firelight would be lost in the ever-present fog.

Before midday on the next day, they came in view of the village of Czeszow, and Cnán was then able to use it as a guide star by which to find the hovel where Illarion had been surviving for the last fortnight. Raphael and Haakon caught up with them, and Finn showed with a smile and a gesture that he thought her tracking skills were impressive.

The hovel lay on the edge of a leveled estate. Houses and huts had been burned, livestock slaughtered and butchered where they lay, fields torched. Bones and half-rotted corpses lay in heaps. None of the corpses had two ears.

"Local nobility," Finn opined, pinching his nose. "Dead, not so noble."

Haakon had clearly never seen such devastation. His throat bobbed, and his face turned sickly green. His eyes wandered as if he sought a place to throw up. Cnán wondered that the others put up with him at all—he was so poor in life experience.

"Get used to it. Such is the way of Mongols," she said.

"Of men in general," Raphael said. "In Jerusalem they—"

"These are worse," Cnán said.

A sudden light breeze from the east carried an especially penetrating stench, one so strong that even Raphael gagged and drew up his scarf. He offered perfume to the others for their cloths, but Cnán, who wore none, noted that none other took it—not even Haakon, whose snot rag was a filthy wonder.

"The town?" Finn said softly, turning west, as if that might help.

Cnán nodded.

They pushed through the half-hanging door into the hovel. In the gloom, a man coughed and a knife blade tossed a dismal gleam.

"Who is it?" came a harsh, low voice.

"Friends, brought here by your messenger," Finn said.

"The other girl," the man husked. His skin was bright and slick with sweat. He tried to get up, but the effort was poor, and his legs failed him. Raphael went to his side…carefully. He was feverish and might strike at phantoms.

"We're relieved you're among the living," Raphael said. "Feronantus cherishes you and sends greetings."

"Feronantus," the man said through another racking cough. "Master and monster, where was he, they bound her hands, they bound her feet, she cried and died…a hand's breadth from my face. This far, no farther." He twisted his hand, dark with old blood. Raphael gripped the hand and lowered it. Then he gently took hold of Illarion's jaw and turned his head.

"Let me see that ear," he murmured

"Gone," Illarion said, his tongue heavy. He flinched in pain with each movement of his jaw, but the words forced themselves out. "I'm sure the bastard took it with him. Let's all go to hell and find it, soak it in wine, sew it back on. Illarion of the purple ear. I'll trade that Mongol lackey my ear for his guts. They smear my leggings even now."

Raphael withdrew ointment and simples from his pouch. He looked up as a shadow darkened the single room.

A slight blonde girl in a frayed robe tied with a sash stood in the doorway. She did not flinch or cry out when she saw the big men. Hanging from her sash was a cloth bag filled with leaves. Green juice leaked from one corner of her lips. She had been chewing leaves when she came in the door—no doubt for a poultice.

"Brave lass," Raphael said, rising from his knee. "Where be you from, and who protects you?"

The girl remained mute, eyes distant. She focused with an effort on Illarion and smiled. Her smile was simple, her face untouched by any other emotion.

Cnán was about to explain the arrangement—that the girl was hired to fetch herbs and tend Illarion, for food and jade—when another, an older boy, old as Haakon but as dark as she, appeared in the door and gently pushed the girl aside. He faced into the hut with dagger drawn, saw Cnán, and hesitated.

She took advantage of that moment. "We mean you no harm," she said in Tocharian.

The boy considered her words, and then indicated the others with a thrust of his chin. "Are *they* taking him?" he asked.

She nodded.

"Good. He's mad and makes noises in the night. There are still gleaners and ghouls out there. They will find him eventually. They'll find us all if we stay."

"You shouldn't stay, then," Cnán said.

The boy shrugged. "God protects," he said. "We've survived this long."

The mute girl smiled again. Cnán's heart thudded. She had seen that smile too often around Mongol camps, decking the faces of the mindless and the broken—those kept alive to be used for lust. Men, women, and children...a smile worse than any mad leer.

Had Cnán felt free to speak her mind, she'd have cried out in protest about an arrangement that moved heaven and earth to get Illarion to safety while leaving this girl in a place where the Mongols could get to her again. But matters being as they were, she said no more.

Raphael took a clean cloth from his kit and wrapped it around Illarion's head. "The flesh is mortifying," he said. "But the maggots have trimmed it for you. And the girl's chewed you a good green willow-bark mash. You're a lucky man."

"No," Illarion said. He shut his eyes and crossed his mouth with a fingered X. "Take me. Empty me. I want to die."

The boy touched the girl on the shoulder, and they turned and departed. Cnán went to the door to watch them. The boy ran from the devastated grounds without a backward glance, but the girl lingered, stooping on one knee as if bowing to a lord and looking one last time at the hovel. Then she fled. Watching from beside the door, Cnán tried not to think about where they would go. *God protects,* she thought.

It was difficult to move Illarion over rough territory. The journey back would take almost three days, Cnán estimated, and Raphael agreed. But once they retrieved their horses— for the woodsman proved honest—they made better time. Illarion seemed to improve. He said little now, but what he said made more sense.

He was tall, not especially heavy in build, but strong enough, Cnán sensed, to swing a plank with some abandon. His blond hair contrasted with a darker mustache and beard. His current troubles seemed traceable to the loss of his ear, the stump of which had suppurated, inflaming the side of his head and making it difficult to eat and talk. Sensing that pain was as much a problem as fever, Raphael dosed him with a bitter resinous gum and infusions of more willow bark. This gave the man some comfort and enabled him to stay on a horse for a few hours at a time.

They had hoped to push west quickly and return to the chapter house in the dense woods. However, Cnán spotted steady streams of refugees now moving along that route, harried by Mongol troops, and at her urging, they swung south for some miles before turning west again.

This brought them far too close to the Mongols' encampment. Raphael told Cnán and Illarion that he, Feronantus, and Finn had sallied forth from the woods to reconnoiter, days before, and had seen, from the west, these very mud walls, almost Roman in style, forming a great square. "Ordu built here during the siege," Raphael explained. "When Onghwe showed up, Ordu must have refused him permission to quarter his men, so Onghwe pitched a temporary camp on the field of battle—a terrible place. No love lost between them. When Ordu moved out, Onghwe returned to organize the gleaners and tax collectors, no fit duty for a true Mongol warrior."

The ramparts were patrolled by regulars in pointed helmets, the forward positions occupied by troops of horsemen. They could not see the tents of the soldiers over these ramparts, but a huge hump of a felted pavilion, orange and green and brown, rose high at the center.

Finn drew their attention to a field beyond the ramparts. The area had been cleared, and what he thought might be a castle was under construction—crude gray logs forming a circle, with walkways and tiers of planks visible through the unfinished west-facing side.

"That wasn't here a few days ago," Raphael observed, frowning.

"Mongols don't build castles," Cnán said.

Raphael agreed. "It puts me in mind of one of the great arenas that the Romans built for their gladiators," he said. "That may be where they plan to hold the competitions."

A tall rectangular tower at the south end supported a wide viewing stand overlooking the arena and below that dropped in a sheer face to the straw-littered ground, bare but for a great reddish-purple curtain hung on the lower third.

"Feronantus read us the invitation," Haakon said. "It spoke of a Red Veil through which victors are invited to pass." Cnán cricked her neck and looked back at the young man. His countenance had brightened at the thought of clean battle between champions of honor. Despite all he had seen on this journey, he clung to a vision of battle as a pinnacle to be climbed, with glory or swift death at the summit. Clearly this boy was being groomed to die.

She felt no pity, however. He was a tool, and tools had their uses. When they were gone, you found another one. Getting emotional over one was to develop an attachment to it, and that was not the Binder way. Emotions sapped energy.

Illarion raised his head. "Competitions?" he asked in a voice low and heavy. His ear had stopped bleeding, but his jaw had swollen to grotesque proportions, and his fever had clearly worsened. "You mean a contest of courage between champions, to save the Western lands."

"Yes!" Haakon said.

"It is of this I must speak to Feronantus," Illarion said. But he would not be drawn out, even by curious Raphael, who brought out more bark mash and stuffed it into the man's thickened cheek to ease his pain.

Past the encampment, against both Raphael and Cnán's better judgment, they turned north and west. Both knew this would take them past the ruins of Legnica, but daylight was fading and they needed to reach the woods before nightfall.

At first, blinded by haunted low mists and rain, the rescue party encountered only more burned farmhouses and piles of bones picked clean by dogs, crows, and vultures—or perhaps hungry villagers. Raphael spoke briefly of the habits of besieged populations, but Illarion glared, and the physician stopped.

The remains of the town proper surrounded a low hill on which had been erected a crude fortification of logs and partial stone walls, with square wooden towers capped with wide roofs. The interior buildings were made of stone ramparts, with higher walls of wattle and daub. The log enclosures had been knocked in and burned, the stones pulled down; the inner buildings still smoldered even in the drizzle. The village around the "castle" had also once been protected by several log walls, now breached in so many places they jutted up from the flat land like broken teeth. Few other structures survived.

Deep forest and sanctuary lay just a few miles from the ruins, but bands of Onghwe's Mongols and gleaners roved the broad outlying farms and neighborhoods, having plundered the town over and over again.

Clouds parted and the rain slowed, then stopped. The rescue party was forced this time to merge along the roads with another general, coagulated flow of miserable and ruined people, scattered, stumbling, stalking, staring fixedly forward or heads hung low, wailing or silent—abandoned clumps of human detritus. Haakon stayed near Finn, casting dark looks about him—nothing in his experience had prepared him for such a place. Everywhere lay the bones and rotting bodies of men, women, children, horses. Cattle. The stench was almost unbearable. Dogs and vultures were few by now; they had been hunted, beaten down with sticks, eaten. The rats were more numerous, and some were defiant, fat, and sleek, eyes flashing as they dropped their shoulders and lifted their heads to squeal at the passing horsemen.

The gleaners hunted unarmed survivors for sport, but avoided any who showed resistance, for gleaners were, in fact, the worst of cowards, brave only around the dead and dying. Spying a gleaner stripping a half-dead woman of her upper garments, Finn rode out over the mud and burned straw and slew the wretch with a single downstroke of his sword. Then, swinging his horse about, with a sharp cry and another stroke, he dispatched the woman. Cursing, he returned to the group, his cheeks streaked with tears.

Raphael was about to chide him for this foolishness, but instead clamped his jaw tight and looked away. "Worse to come," he warned.

Cnán knew these gleaners and their types well enough that she could pick them out even in a healthy city. Not always were they the furtive criminals or crazed drunks. Indeed, within her short life, she had seen drunks rise to glorious battle and city fathers turn into ghouls. War did not just level, it plowed the field, raising the muck and sinking the stubble.

The general flow of misery lurched westward. They were forsaking lands that would not be productive for generations, avoiding paths and farm roads patrolled by regular Mongol troops.

Mounted and armed, the rescue party was as kings and princes compared to this rabble and so felt no need to act furtive. Someone might be hungry and desperate enough to attack them, but Raphael felt that it was best to continue to boldly ride straight through and then, once in the woods, proceed directly to the chapter house.

The style of movement that Cnán preferred, which Raphael called "sneaking," made her uneasy with this course. Surprisingly, Finn was also unhappy—unnerved by the monstrous depredation and this endless spectacle of cruelty.

Near the western limits of the town, part of a stone perimeter wall still stood, built to withstand invasions coming out of the setting sun. Moving into the lee of this wall, they slowed as their horses skittishly avoided a rag-ribboned, sinew-strung litter of bones and moldering heads. Even in this carnage, the pitiful remains did not look or feel proper. They were too small...skulls crushed by a single blow...their garb not the undergarments of warriors or townspeople, but light, like nightwear.

Haakon pulled on the reins of his horse, eyes wild, until he fastened his look on Finn, then on Raphael—then on Cnán, who wrinkled her features. "Don't look," she said, "if you can't bear it."

Adam's apple bobbing, Haakon lifted his eyes to the gray, misting clouds. Illarion did the same, touching his huge cheek and missing ear, as if to listen to faraway music.

These were the bones of children, from infants to toddlers to adolescents, and they stretched all along the wall, mounding near the base. Scores of children. An entire town's future, crushed, broken, rotting in the mud.

Cnán knew what had happened here. She had heard stories out of the Far East, at the limits of her ranging. With the hilltop fort broken and the other walls breached, the citizens had brought the infants and youth of Legnica to this final and strongest wall, in the last days. Near the end, as the Mongols swept in from behind and then all around, torturing and killing all in their path, the soldiers and the last of the parents had sacrificed the young that they might not suffer a worse fate. Their crowns had been bashed by hammers or hilts, then their throats cut clean like so many shoats, ten or twenty at a time, the bodies then heaved from the rampart.

Possibly the townspeople had harbored a faint hope of arousing pity within the Mongols or their lackeys, but that was impossible, Cnán knew. The tiger would pity the fawn, the wolf would weep over its lamb before Mongol would cringe at the corpse of a child.

Haakon made small sounds deep in his throat. Surely hell itself lay not far below this stinking ossuary, bubbling up toward the world's incomprehensible evil. None of the rescue party wanted to tarry among these dead. The vengeance of their young, unshaped ghosts might be worse than that of any Mongol.

They rode away from the wall and the bones as quickly as they could—corrupt mud spattering from the hooves of the horses and flecking their faces and armor—to reach the shelter of the thick woods before nightfall.

Cnán wiped a dollop of ooze from her cheek. It was tinted red with blood.

Dusk and more mist stole over them as they crossed the glacis of cleared land. The refugees had flowed south, and the old field of battle seemed deserted of all but the scattered bones of Legnica's defenders. Their path was clear.

Cnán was about to release the breath in her tight chest when, directly ahead of her, pale and vivid in the twilight, Finn's hand flew up like a falcon ready to swoop down on prey. She had learned to respect that gesture; it meant that his ears had picked up a trace of something so faint that he risked losing it by shushing them.

The party drew to a halt to let him listen.

Finn's hand descended and made the prancing gesture that meant *horses*. Then, thumb pinching quick against two raised fingers: *small*. He was hearing ponies. A great many ponies.

Cnán dismounted. She knew better than to try to outride what was coming. Haakon drew his greatsword.

Finn's hands now told them by darts and swoops that the ponies were not in one place, but all around. Cnán could finally hear their hooves, then the low voices of the men who had been quietly riding to surround their party. She bent her knees, dropping to a squat, and then to all fours, pulling her dark cape around her. They had drawn the attention of a scouting party. Perhaps a sentry had sighted them or some scavenger had ratted them out, hoping to purloin some small item of value once the Mongols were finished. Or perhaps someone had reported Finn's attack on the gleaner.

No matter. Cnán could see it clearly. Her companions would end up like hedgehogs, bristling with arrows, but she would hide among their corpses, then scurry to the woods before the sentinels caught her.

Raphael nudged his mount forward and laid his hand on Haakon's forearm. The boy's drawn sword, shining like an icicle in the twilight, would make him the first target of the archers. Haakon lowered the blade, nodding.

A little squadron of Mongols filed into position between the rescue party and the trees. Cnán reckoned she might still be able to steal past them during the confusion of the fight, but some troubled part of her soul was telling her to stay with her comrades.

"The second one, in the armor that looks like fish scales," she said in low tones. "He is rich. Their leader."

"We charge him, then," Haakon proposed.

"And die in a cloud of arrows before we get halfway," Raphael said.

"On *me*," Illarion suddenly commanded, surprising them all. He spurred his horse forward. Unsettled by the corpses and by the tension in the voices, the mount startled, but then, at a soothing word from his gaunt rider, dropped into a slow walk. "Follow. Single file. Slow. Like a funeral procession. Vaetha, walk your horse. All of you, hood yourselves."

They did as Illarion instructed. The Ruthenian rode stiffly, steadily, at a plodding pace, his great hollow eyes staring straight ahead.

A single armored Mongol rode ahead of the band, grinning, striped bow held out in one hand, as if signaling peace, friendship. A chief, no doubt. Cnán counted their opponents. Fifteen horse-mounted bowmen.

Less than a hundred paces now separated the groups.

To bar the Ruthenian's path, the chief crabbed his pony sideways.

Illarion continued straight on, his horse snorting and tossing his head.

She thought she understood Illarion's strategy: by moving so, he projected dogged purpose, hopefully slowing the Mongols from making a pincered feint to scatter their smaller party. If the Ruthenian turned or rode too quickly, the Mongols would instinctively rush in and give chase like dogs coursing a hind.

The chief twitched his bow left, right, then up. He dropped back. The Mongol squadron finally split to the right and left, then began to draw in like a slow snare or a purse string against their flanks and rear, fifty paces, thirty paces... close enough that their first arrows would be certain to strike home, yet not close enough to bring them within range of Haakon's bright sword.

The chief deftly spun his pony, as if daring them to chase after and catch him, *him* personally, with his back turned and everything. Grinning all the while.

Cnán did not understand what Illarion proposed to do when he reached the chief. Perhaps swing on him and die, giving the others some chance of reaching the woods?

Less than five paces now separated Illarion and the chief.

With a sweep of his arm, Illarion drew back the cloak that had swathed him for much of the last two days and hurled it aside, where it spun and flew for an uncanny number of yards, like a bat, then fell—to precisely drape the picked skeleton and conical helm of a Polish knight.

A knight who had almost made it to the forest before taking three arrows in the back.

All heads turned, mesmerized by this.

Bones rattled. The round hump of the skull shifted under the cloak, as if finding new life.

Illarion reined his horse just to the left of the Mongol chief and canted his head with a careless jerk, exposing the swollen, earless right side of his face. Not once did his eyes meet the man's.

Now understanding the Mongol's reaction, Cnán watched him further, seeing first curiosity, then a twist of lip and brow— signaling alarm and confusion. The chief's features went pale and his mouth opened as if to scream. Frantic, heels kicking the pony's flanks, he spun about and dog-yelped to his comrades. His pony bucked and turned but did not know which way to go.

Illarion rode steadily on. His missing ear dripped black blood. His hollow eyes knew death as an intimate comrade; nothing living could stop him...or would wish to.

Leaning over his pony's neck, reining it in, the chief jerked its head left and spurred it even harder, leaving a gap through which Illarion rode without pause and without betraying the slightest awareness that the Mongols were even there. The Ruthenian did not need to act to appear to ride from beyond humanity, beyond life.

The chief gawped in terror. His pony stumbled in the muck.

On the left and right and behind, the Mongols turned and drew back, muttering and shouting.

Behind Illarion, Raphael leaned to one side and cupped his hand to his ear, imitating the gaunt Ruthenian—but with a grim and toothy smile. He swiveled in his saddle to leer at the Mongols.

The entire squadron broke and scattered into the mist.

The rescue party rode on at the same pace. At Finn's gesture, Cnán remounted. She could see that Haakon's shoulders were drawn in, flexing and flinching just like her own.

The trees came up none too soon, and the horses parted to accommodate them. Cold, clean night air swirled from the west, bringing more rain and mist, and water dripped in pattering, rhythmic showers from the leaves and branches, as if to cleanse them of all they had seen.

"You speak Mongol, don't you?" Haakon asked Cnán when they had counted a hundred paces deep into the woods.

"Tartaric, Turkic, some Tungus," she said.

"What did the leader say?"

"You should know," Cnán said, "even if you ken not a word."

Haakon frowned. "You think I'm an oaf."

Cnán grimaced and dropped her chin.

Haakon flicked his damp hair back. "Tell me," he persisted. "I want to hear it anyway."

Cnán touched her right ear. "*We are unclean spirits of the fallen,*" she said, "*returning to the forests of the West from which we came.*"

"Ghosts," Finn said.

"Ghosts," she confirmed.

◆ ◆ ◆

Once in the woods, two hours of picking their way along leaf-littered paths in broken moonlight brought them back to the clearing and the old monastery. By then they had shaken off the clammy dread that had overtaken them during their journey and had begun to converse about topics other than death and how to avoid it. They were received warmly by the *Skjaldbræður*, whose numbers, during their absence, had increased to something like a score. Illarion, of course, was embraced and even wept over. Cnán had expected this. But she was surprised by the hospitality that some of the knights were now showing toward her. In a courtly style that struck her as ridiculous, Feronantus asked whether she would consider gracing their camp with her presence for a while and directed her attention toward a tent that had been pitched, somewhat aloof from the others, and made ready for her. This at first struck Cnán as amusing, since there was no shortage of buildings in the compound, though most lacked roofs.

But when she pulled back the tent's flap and found the interior clean and tidy, with a floor of dry green grass and a raised cot with a fresh straw tick for her to lie on, she better understood the gesture. The buildings of the old monastery were ancient and tumbledown, infested by vermin, stinking in diverse ways.

Peering out the back flap, instinctively checking for an escape route, she saw moonlight reflecting from water about a stone's throw away and knew that she was not far from the monks' old fish pond—the only place around here she could get anything like a bath.

She accepted Feronantus's invitation. The knights retreated to their chapter house, whence she heard the popping of bungs and pouring of ale. She stripped and made a direct line for the pond. Drawing closer to it, she moved faster, since an impressive number of bugs seemed to be landing on her exposed skin. By the time she reached the shore, she was at the core of a humming swarm of mosquitoes and biting flies and had to dive into the water, if only to save her life. But it was worth it to feel the dirt of the road being rinsed from her skin and her hair. She swam for a while, bobbing her head up out of the water just long enough to breathe in air and mosquitoes, then diving before the bugs could do more serious damage.

The way back to the tent was a headlong sprint through an almost tangible mass of aroused insects. Bats swooped as well, making her groan when they squeaked too close. Unable to really see where she was going, she plunged through a group of knights who were on their way to the chapter house.

Being seen naked meant nothing to her, but some of the knights gasped and looked the other way, imagining that she'd be mortified. The tallest of the group—Cnán instantly recognized him as Percival—took stock of the situation, moved adroitly to the entrance of her tent, peeled back the flap, and then stood there as if carved in marble, modestly averting his gaze. She dove through the opening. He let the flap drop.

The knights, now feeling free to speak their minds, issued a few good-natured complaints about her ungenerously having drawn so many insects into their camp. "At least I am clean!" she shouted from her enclosed fastness, "which is more than I can say for any of you." This silenced them. Not, she guessed, because her words had struck home, but because they simply had no conception of what she was talking about.

She spent a few moments rolling around on the grass, slicking the water and the bugs from her skin. It was actually not the worst bath she'd ever had. Then she dressed in a linen tunic and doeskin breeches from her kit—clothes she had been saving against the unlikely possibility that she might have to costume herself as something other than a scurrying wretch.

Some part of her was wondering how she would look in the eyes of Percival. He had, in general, paid her no attention whatsoever. And yet there had been more than simple consideration in his act of holding the tent open. *There had been... nobility? Brotherhood?* She flung her short wet hair briskly at that thought.

She wanted Percival to see her in some better condition than wet and naked and covered with bugs. But another part of her—speaking, curiously, in the voice of her mother—was reminding her just how dangerous it was to feel any such desire. Emotion led to attachment; attachment led to…

While she was dressing, the jovial chitchat in the chapter house ceased. Someone protested he was not ready—voice too drunk and muffled to identify. Moments later, she heard a man howl, then scream long and loud. The murmur of conversation was slow to resume after that. But the aroma of cooking meat drew her to the place anyway. As she approached the door, Raphael came out, shoulders square, flexing his fingers. The fingers were stained green at the tips. He had been crushing more herbs.

His posture spoke of satisfaction, a job well done.

"Was it Illarion who cried out?" she asked.

"Yes. His ear—what's left of it—is fine."

"Fine? One side of his face is twice the size of the other."

"That actually had little to do with the ear," he insisted. "Thank the maggots and that poor girl and her poultice. I finally took the trouble to look in his mouth. The man had an abscessed molar."

The words were unfamiliar.

"A *toothache*," Raphael said. He lifted a sheathed dagger and pulled from one pocket a metal tool with long pincers, still stained with blood. "I yanked it out. The man has a jawbone like that of an ass. He's already feeling better."

She gave him an incredulous look. He tried, but failed, to prevent a grin from splitting his face. "I didn't say he felt *grateful*," he pointed out, raising his hands in mock surrender. Then he used them to shoo her inside. "Get you in. There's hot food and plenty."

Cnán enjoyed the Syrian's company but was happy to take his leave in this case. The pincers evoked a queasy reaction quite unlike her response to swords and daggers.

She entered the chapter house and felt something so unfamiliar that it took her a few moments to identify it: she felt *safe*.

She knew what it was to belong, surrounded by courage and kept from harm by the luck, skill, and daring of the knights of the *Ordo Militum Vindicis Intactae.*

CHAPTER 4:

THE YOUNG PONY

"This is a task for a fool." Gansukh paced back and forth in the long hall outside the throne room. Sunlight streamed through windows covered in intricate latticework, and dust danced in the wake of Gansukh's pacing. "I fought at the siege of Kozelsk. I was handpicked by General Subutai himself, to help infiltrate the city. This...this mission is not—"

"Protecting the *Khagan* is not important?" Chucai interrupted dryly.

Gansukh stopped and peered at the tall minister through the shafts of sunlight. "Of course it is," he said. "My bow and my sword are his to command. I would lay down—"

"It is easy to die for your *Khagan*," Chucai said. He glanced down at the floor, shrugging his shoulders gently. It was a tiny motion, but it quelled Gansukh's outburst as easily as if he had punched the younger man in the chest. "Perhaps that is why Chagatai Khan chose you for this mission. When Great General Subutai picked you to go over the wall of Kozelsk, was it because he needed a wild-blooded fool who would die for him?"

Gansukh shook his head.

"Do you think less of Chagatai Khan, then? Is his vision not as clear and far-seeing as the Great General's?"

"I…I do not know," Gansukh said.

"These Khans are proud men," Chucai said. "Stubborn too. It took me many years to convince Genghis to tax rather than slaughter. This…this is a negotiation, not a battle." A brief smile flickered across Chucai's face. "Warriors fight, Gansukh; that is their purpose in life. But eventually, there is no one left to fight, and they must learn how to think."

"Your words are filled with wisdom, Master Chucai," Gansukh said, bowing his head. "I will reflect on them."

"Do," Chucai said as he began walking down the corridor. "Stay and rest a few days while you reflect, and partake in the pleasures of Karakorum."

"I have my *ger*…" Gansukh eyed the rafters as he followed Chucai down the halls. Surrounded by stone and wood, he felt as if he were inside a tomb. At any moment the high ceilings could collapse and bury him, and he would never see the sky again.

Chucai shook his head. "You will stay in the palace," he said. He eyed the young emissary, and the skin at the corners of his eyes wrinkled, as if he were hiding a laugh. "You cannot hope to understand the *Khagan* if you do not stay close to him." He stopped beside a door panel, his hand resting on the wooden frame. "When you hunt a deer, do you not place yourself in the animal's world? Do you not follow in its footsteps, see what it sees, smell what it smells?" When Gansukh nodded, Chucai slid open the door.

The room was small, not much bigger than the large sleeping platform covered with furs and skins. Sheer yellow silks hung from the ceiling, falling like frozen sunlight around the bed. Behind the bed were screens, painted with red flowers.

On the leftmost one, a heron—its long neck extended—was taking flight.

"Is it to your liking?" Chucai asked.

Gansukh struggled to find some appropriate words, and the only thing he could muster felt totally inadequate. "It is a magnificent chamber, Master Chucai."

Chucai nodded. "It is yours." He held up a hand to forestall Gansukh's objection. "There'll be a dinner in honor of Governor Mahmud Yalavach later this evening. Perhaps you might wish to observe the *Khagan* when he is in a better mood. Have you sat at a formal court dinner before?"

Gansukh shook his head. "Around the fire, we gather each night to make *boodog* or *horhog.*"

"I think you'll find table manners are somewhat different when you're not eating greasy roast goat with your hands. I'll send along some scrolls so you can learn how to behave in civilized society."

"Master Chucai..." Gansukh put his left hand over his closed right fist. The combination formed a double prison, one wrapped around the other. The ceiling and the walls of the palace preventing him from seeing the sky and the horizon. This mission—even with the insight offered by Ögedei's advisor—was another cage. He was trapped. And yet, looking at his hands and imagining what it would be like to be trapped inside—a carrion fly or a moth—he realized that no matter how tightly he squeezed, he could never quite close the narrow gap where his index finger dug into his palm, even if he moved his thumb. "Master Chucai," he said, "on the steppes, the opportunities to read are few, and I..."

Chucai gave him a look of paternal reassurance. "I could send someone to read them to you, if you wish. Perhaps as you take your bath?"

Gansukh opened his hands and stared at his palm. Would the moth be crushed by the pressure of its prison before it could escape? "My gratitude is endless, Master Chucai."

◆ ◆ ◆

Gansukh drifted in a cloud. The walls of the room were obscured by the steam from the pool, and he floated in the hot water. The pool was larger than the interior of a chieftain's *ger*, and initially he had balked at soiling so much water.

His clothes, stiff with dried sweat and dust, had been taken away by pale-robed servants. He had sat naked at the edge of the pool for a few minutes, the steam from the water opening his pores. Eventually he had put his feet in, and the temperature of the water had made his skin tingle. He had then allowed himself the luxury of complete immersion, and it felt good.

He wasn't alone. Gansukh jerked out of his reverie, splashing the water around him as he found his footing on the bottom of the pool. She was kneeling at the pool's edge, the light-blue silk of her robe darkening at the knees from the water. Her long hair was unbound from the twisted coiffure most Chinese women wore, and it fell across half of her face like a sheet of black water. He could only see one of her eyes and half her mouth, but it was enough to tell she was amused.

"Who are you?" he demanded, more strenuously than he intended. He felt exposed in the water, and not just because he was naked. The servants had taken everything, and he hadn't even thought to keep the small knife he usually carried. He slapped the water as if the noise might scare her away, but the woman didn't even flinch. *Fool*, he thought. All it took was the offer of a bath and he had dropped his defenses.

"My name is Lian," the woman said. Judging by the smooth paleness of her skin and the shape of her face, her life prior to Karakorum had been one of indolence and wealth.

"Did Master Chucai send you to attend to my needs?" Gansukh asked. He made the water ripple with his hands. "If so, you should be in the pool." It wasn't that he desired the company of a woman; it was more that he didn't like her sitting there on the edge. There was something on the floor beside her, and Gansukh stood on his tiptoes, trying to see what it was.

"No," she said, the humor leaving her face. "As I tell every other Mongol, I'm a tutor, not a whore." She picked up the bundle beside her, and Gansukh realized it was a thick scroll. She unrolled it and proceeded to read.

Once his confusion had passed, Gansukh listened for a few minutes as Lian read to him about the practices of civilized behavior. Her enunciation and diction were flawless, and her voice was pleasing to his ear. However, the material she was reading was the most tedious recitation Gansukh had ever heard—even more so than the countless reiterations of his ancestry recited in celebration after a victorious battle. "'A son should not occupy the southwest corner of the home, nor sit in the middle of the mat, nor walk in the middle of the road, nor stand in the middle of the doorway. He should be as if he were hearing his parents when there is no voice from them and as if seeing them when they are not actually there.'"

He could hold his tongue no longer. He flicked water, interrupting her. "I am to act as if I were haunted by the ghosts of my ancestors?"

Lian sighed. She pushed her hair back over her shoulder and stared at him. "You have very little imagination, don't you?" she asked. "I suppose I shouldn't be surprised. You are, after all, just an itinerant horseman."

Gansukh growled and chopped his hand into the water, throwing a much larger gout of water at her. She adroitly protected the scroll from the spray of water, but the rest of her wasn't as fortunate. Gansukh admired the shape outlined by the wet cloth and momentarily forgot what he was angry about.

"It is a metaphor," Lian said. She uncurled from her kneeling position and dipped a foot in the pool. "Do they not have metaphors on the steppes?" she asked as she kicked water at him.

Gansukh ducked instinctively, even though the water was harmless rain against his already wet skin. "What does a warrior need with a metaphor?" he grumbled. "Can a metaphor keep me alive? Can it slaughter my enemies?"

Lian danced back from the edge of the pool, avoiding his next splash. "Consider the swallows," she said. "They dart through the air at their prey, then wheel around to retreat and strike again. Now consider how a group of horsemen approach their enemy. Do they not present themselves as one unit: riding in and firing their arrows, and then swooping away? Is that not the Mongol way? If you were a general and you told your men to ride in Swooping Bird Formation, would they not know what you meant? How is that not using a *metaphor* to slaughter your enemies?"

Gansukh let his tongue lie quietly in his mouth, and he acknowledged Lian's point with a gentle inclination of his head.

She appeared to not notice, or perhaps she was feigning ignorance of his gesture. Her attention returned to the scroll and she unrolled it again, searching for the place where she had left off. "Let us continue then," she said. "'A man should not ascend a height, nor approach the verge of a depth; he should not indulge—'"

Gansukh slipped under the surface of the pool, letting his legs collapse until he was sitting down. Lian's image wavered through a layer of water and steam, and her pale skin seemed to glow as if she were a ghost. He closed and opened his eyes a few times, but she didn't vanish. Finally, his lungs burning, he pushed up and emerged from the water.

Lian stood like a statue—one eyebrow raised, one finger poised on the scroll—waiting for him to catch his breath. When he finished wiping the water from his eyes, she continued. "'He should not indulge in reckless reviling or derisive laughing.'"

Gansukh let one of those laughs fly, and he slapped the water. "This is nothing but a book of rules telling me how to live my life!" he complained. "I already know how to live! Are the Chinese so stupid that they need instructions telling them how to do everything?"

"Are the Mongols so stupid they do not recognize the value of moral rectitude?"

Gansukh raised his gaze toward the ceiling. "Put the scroll aside," he said. "This is wearying and useless. Come join me in the water instead."

"Master Chucai instructed me to teach you how to behave in polite society." She lowered the scroll and gave him a dismissive look—the sort an aristocratic lady might have given to an ignorant servant. "Behavior that includes learning how to respect women."

"I respect fighters. I respect those—men and women— who prove their worth to their clan. You Chinese women sit around in gardens all day reading books and eating... I don't know what you eat. Flowers, I suppose. Mongol women ride and hunt and fight until their skin is rough and tanned. What good is 'culture' if it makes you weak?"

"Were I a less cultured woman, I would not have fared so well when I was captured," Lian pointed out. "Master Chucai recognized my value, at least, even if the Mongols never appreciate the things I have to teach."

"And if you were a stronger woman, perhaps you wouldn't have been captured at all."

She looked away, and Gansukh felt a strange thrill in his belly. It wasn't the same sensation he got on the battlefield when he killed a man, but it was similar—close enough that he felt both elation and confusion. *But we aren't fighting.* Glancing down, he realized his body was also reacting to this commingling of emotions, and he pawed the water, disturbing the pool.

Her robe still clung to her body. It was distracting.

"How long have you been in Karakorum?" she asked.

"Not even a day," he admitted, glad to talk about something else.

"You have much to learn," she said, and her tone had none of the brittleness he would have expected from such a statement. "There is more to life than fighting." She swallowed heavily and went to hug the scroll to her body, but demurred at the last second, sparing the scroll contact with her wet clothing. "Yes, I will admit there is value in knowing how to fight, but not all combat is with spear and arrow. The court can be as dangerous as the battlefield, if you don't know how to conduct yourself." She plucked at her robe, pulling it away from her skin.

Gansukh mulled this over, ignoring a twinge of disappointment at her ministrations to her clothing. Master Chucai had said that he had had to teach both Ögedei and his father how to conduct themselves. Did he respect them any less because they knew how to behave at court? Would he not follow them into battle without reservation? "Yes," he said, nodding slightly. He walked backward until the edge of the pool pressed against his back. "So I am naked at court." He raised his arms and rested them on the edge. "I have no armor. I have no weapons. I am like you were, once upon a time. Teach me how to survive. Teach me what I need to know to be strong."

Lian regarded him, her head cocked to one side. She bit her lower lip as she lowered the scroll and let it fall to the ground. She walked forward and, to Gansukh's surprise, didn't stop at the edge of the pool. She disappeared under the water with a small splash, and he watched her slim shape glide through the water toward him. She surfaced not far from him, and he held himself still as she floated closer. She stopped when she was close enough to reach up and put her hand on his forearm. He felt her legs, constricted by the wet drapery of her robe, caressing his. Her breath was on his face, and he found himself staring at her mouth.

"You prefer your women strong, don't you?" she whispered.

"Yes," he muttered, the word getting caught in his throat.

"But you don't think I am strong."

It wasn't a question, but Gansukh felt like he should answer anyway. He shook his head, not trusting that he could form the word.

"Teach me," Lian said. "Teach me to be like your Mongolian women. In return, I can teach you how to survive here at court." She moved closer to him. "A warrior does not learn from reading; a warrior learns from action, from using his hands and his heart. Can you show me that?"

Gansukh stared at her slender neck. Her pulse was visible under her pale skin. She was frail, and he wondered if she'd ever had a violent thought in her life. There was little chance this delicate Chinese flower could become the equal of a Mongolian woman, but it would certainly be amusing to watch her try. She and Master Chucai were right, though: he did not understand the ways of court, and if he had any hope of succeeding at his mission, he needed Lian's help. It was better to submit to the offer of this strange and alluring Chinese woman than run back to Chagatai like a whipped dog.

Gansukh nodded. "I will teach you how to fight."

She nodded curtly and pushed away from him. He grabbed for her, but his hands found nothing in the warm water. She swam to the edge of the pool, and in a smooth motion that suggested she was more fish than woman, she levered herself to the platform. He caught a quick glimpse of her breasts, outlined quite distinctly against her wet robe, and then she swiveled around, curling her legs around her like a flower closing for the night. Her back to him, she picked up the heavy robe that lay on the platform and slipped it over her wet clothing.

She retrieved her discarded scroll. "We will begin our lessons tomorrow," she said with a final appraising glance over her shoulder.

It was only after she left that Gansukh realized she had taken the robe the servants had meant for him.

CHAPTER 5:

THE KINYEN

Despite Raphael's ministrations, two more days passed before Illarion's fever broke and the Ruthenian recovered strength enough to sit up and speak coherently.

Cnán did not begrudge him the time, since she herself spent most of it sleeping and eating. Afternoons she sat in the middle of the clearing, well beyond the graveyard wall, out in the summer sun, mending her travel clothes and watching the Shield-Brethren train. More arrived every day from all over Christendom. As her body regained strength, her mood also improved—and she began to take a more sanguine view of their prowess as fighters.

They fought in pairs over and over, pausing in the middle of the fracas to pick apart each move into smaller elements that they then practiced again and again. She could not fit their halting exercises into any sensible program. How would they ever put the fragments of action together again—learn to face the chaos of a true battle, where nobody pauses, nobody has a second chance? It all seemed like a silly game.

But when they actually sparred, swinging and moving for long minutes at a stretch, strength against strength, they proved capable of feats that astonished Cnán. And studying their determination and their skill, she saw more clearly the weakness in her own training. She had been taught to travel under all manner of cloaks, never to reveal her true self, to bear messages while hiding in plain sight of enemies and friends alike. And always to cross back and forth over the wide, endless, ravaged land, never staying long in one place—like a bird doomed never to nest, never to understand the wisdom of sitting *still.*

Watching these men, these warriors, assemble into a team, under the constant tutelage of Taran and the watchful eye of Feronantus, made her feel a new kind of loneliness and, with it, a sort of bereavement.

After noon of the second day, Feronantus put out word that, tomorrow, the junior Brethren would stand sentry around their encampment while *Kinyen*—the Order's communal mess—was held at the great table of the chapter house. Cnán knew that *Kinyen* was an ancient tradition, one they took most seriously. The camp grew busy with preparations: A wild sow was spitted and splayed over a bed of banked coals to slow cook. The beams were stripped from the monastery and hewn and pegged into makeshift benches so that there would be room for all of the warrior monks—a full two dozen now, even when ten or so initiates were left outside to stand guard—to sit around the edges of the hall.

The Shield-Brethren stayed up late that night drinking and singing and telling long stories of their exploits and adventures in various parts of the West. Cnán mostly stayed outside, in her tent—ignored, she hoped; unwanted, she suspected.

It was during a particularly long tale told by Raphael, about sewing up Crusaders and Moors alike, that she heard a solitary man emerge from the chapter house. An unevenness in his gait told Cnán that he was reeling slightly. The wind came from behind him and she smelled several horns of mead on his shuddering, belching exhale.

"Why alone?" he called. It was Haakon.

"Why so loud?" she countered, in as low a voice as she thought might be heard. The knights, wise though they might be in hand-to-hand, were less than cautious about alerting gleaners to their presence. Perhaps they felt they lived under the charms of their Christian God, or their warrior gods—whichever commanded the daylight of Feronantus's faith. Or perhaps they just believed they now had sufficient numbers to kill anyone short of a Mongol army.

She heard him stumbling over the leaves and the beaten dirt of the fighting field. His moon shadow loomed across the canvas of her tent, leaning one way, then another.

"It isn't natural," he said. "A woman…a man…about to die. You think I'm going to die, don't you?"

Indeed, Haakon seemed the one having the greatest difficulty duplicating Taran's exacting moves. He hesitated, as if thinking everything through twice—and then he swung, or parried, taking sharp, bruising blows as a result. Taran afforded him neither pity nor time to recover.

"You have the best trainer I've seen," Cnán said, surprising herself by this admission. "You'll live if you listen and learn."

"Easy for you to say. You aren't fighting." Haakon dropped to a cross-legged squat beside her tent. He seemed content to talk through the canvas, like a Christian giving his confession through a screen. "I'm brave. I'm good in battle. Steadfast. The greatsword—my weapon. I know it like a friend. Yet whatever I do…whatever I do…" He stopped; slapped a few bugs. "Tell me about yourself."

"I'd rather sleep," she said, truthfully enough.

"I could keep you company. Warm you."

"The nights are warm enough," Cnán said.

She considered it a victory of sorts that she did not actually laugh. She was not above lying with a man now and then, when it pleased her to do so, but she hadn't come here to be wooed—and certainly not by one who was supposed to be a celibate monk!

Suddenly she felt a pang of both sympathy and suspicion. Perhaps the youth wasn't as stupid as she thought. Haakon must have caught her out, seen something in her face that she had been trying to hide from herself and the others...

"Go away," she said.

If she were going to break any man's celibacy, it would be Percival's, but Percival did not look on her that way.

Haakon got up, then bent to brush a few fallen leaves and twigs from her tent—as if conveying some clumsy affection to her shell, her hiding place. "All right," he said. "No harm. A marvelous night. I feel ready...for...for anything. Just thought..."

He left his words hanging and wove his way back to the chapter house, leaving Cnán sadder and lonelier than ever.

What was it a man and a woman were *supposed* to do, when they weren't in constant flight, running on the leading edge of the voracious Mongolian army? Haakon's clumsy words were as close to a kind of courtship as she had ever experienced—and she had bluntly sent him on his way, no thanks, no sympathy.

Haakon was the first that night, but not the last, to approach her refuge and try to make loose conversation. All celibate, all clumsy, all drunk—and not one was Percival. Nor Raphael, of course, who seemed steeped in other, more urbane techniques; the Syrian did not bother her either.

She stayed out of the embrace of any and all drunken monks that night and woke late the following morning, arrayed herself in tunic and doeskin, and when summoned, walked to the chapter house to attend the *Kinyen*.

The knights, after an hour or two of sleep, had recovered enough from their drunken feats of bravado to open another barrel and resume.

In the gloom of the old monastery's refectory, lit by a dusty shaft of daylight through the broken roof and a scatter of short candles, she saw Feronantus sitting at the head of a large table, with Illarion on his right. The shaft of light fell between the two, highlighting their shoulders and hands and brimming cups. The rest of the knights sat in degrees of candlelight and shadow, murmuring to each other and passing bread and slopping flagons. They drank like fish. Most knights drank heavily, now that Cnán thought of it. Likely all that celibacy weighed on them.

The table had originally been rectangular, but they had enlarged it by throwing rough-sawn planks over its top and, in the process, made it somewhat round. The shape surprised her, and she wondered at its significance.

Illarion was almost unrecognizable, so dramatically had the swelling of his face gone down. He had shaved off the dark beard. Food and ale had put color back into his face, and when he spoke, his thoughts were clear and his voice firm. But for the missing ear and the perpetually gloomy mien, one might never guess all that he had gone through in the last few months.

Cnán looked around at the room full of *Ordo Militum Vindicis Intactae* and again felt that disturbingly unfamiliar sense of safety. She shook this off and spited herself as a fool, certain that these knights could not hold out against a storm cloud of Mongols for more than a few minutes. Barring ghostly luck, of course.

Feronantus introduced the *Kinyen* to the one-eared Ruthenian ghost himself and motioned for him to speak.

"What I will say now, I said to Feronantus when I arrived," Illarion began, "but at his request, I now tell you directly: all of you have come to this place on a fool's errand."

Feronantus, a little taken aback, rested an affectionate hand on Illarion's shoulder and explained, "I had hoped you might supply a fuller explanation."

"The arena that the Mongols are building at Legnica, on the outskirts of their tent warren, is but a prefiguring of a thing I have seen before, near the gates of Lodomeria, my own city," Illarion said. "A city that no longer exists. Only I survived. Consider that as you prepare for the competition to which Onghwe Khan has summoned you and the other great warriors of Christendom."

Having got their attention, Illarion whetted his whistle with a long, foaming swallow of ale before going on, in a less plangent tone. For a moment he'd seem to fear his counsel might not be respected. But something in Feronantus's face and in the attentive manner of the assembled monks gave him heart.

"The armies of Onghwe Khan laid siege with cannon and towers, pushed down our sunrise walls, and then captured the eastern quarter and laid it to waste—a story no different from thousands of others ranging from our very doorstep to the eastern ocean. The rest of the city expected to die, and we were ready for it. But then, at the end of the seventh month, as our serfs were starving, as disease coursed through our streets and the barrows went from door to door, something unexpected happened: a magnanimous gesture from Onghwe himself. He summoned me to the south wall, our strongest wall. He knew my name and those of my generals. He had spies in our midst—fur traders, I suspect. Need I say what his offer was?

"He reminded us that our city was at his mercy and that with a wave of his hand he could destroy us like the others.

"He claimed that, contrary to the terrifying rumors that went before him, he was no monster, but a proud warrior of an old and honorable line.

"As such, he was presenting us with a choice. Of course, there is always the choice to surrender or fight. But he could see with his own eyes that we had already chosen the latter, for which he respected us. And rather than defeat us and put us all to the sword, he called us to send forth our greatest warriors to do battle in single combat against his own champions, in an arena that he would build before our city gates. If our champions prevailed, his armies would depart and leave us in peace, with one caveat, which I shall explain. If our champions went down in defeat, we would surrender the city to plunder, but the people would be suffered to live.

"Seeing no alternative, we accepted his offer. I caused a training ground to be cleared in the square before our cathedral. I and the other leading knights of the city spent every day training there—conferring our skills, as best as we were able, on the younger men-at-arms who volunteered to fight in Onghwe Khan's arena.

"During the evenings, we would go to the watchtower above the city's main gate and watch the arena a-building, so close that we could throw stones down into it. A tunnel was dug, leading from our gate directly to the arena's western entrance. On the other side, a similar entrance was prepared, leading in from the camp of the besieging host, and it did not require great shrewdness to see that Onghwe Khan's champions would be entering from that direction. There was, however, a third entrance to—or rather, exit from—the arena. It was on the southern side, below a high platform that was prepared for the Khan to sit upon. As we now understood, these competitions were for him a kind of sport, like bear baiting or falconry, and their entire purpose was to give him pleasure. The exit tunnel beneath the Khan's platform was cloaked by a scarlet veil.

"Messengers came into the city to acquaint us with the rules and traditions of the contest. They explained that, from time to time, after a bout had been decided, the Khan might gesture to the victor, signifying that he should leave the arena, not through the tunnel by which he had entered it, but by passing through this Red Veil, into whatever fate might await him there.

"So the thing took shape, and our chosen champions trained as hard as any men could, knowing that the fate of all who lived in the city rested on their feats of arms. In the end, we chose three and sent them down the tunnel to fight their duels before a howling audience of Mongols and the less honorable scum who follow their camp.

"Our first champion, who I believed to be the best of the lot, was struck down and beheaded in a few moments by a demon with a curved sword. I never heard where that demon came from. I had never seen nor heard of his like before.

"The second was a wrestler, a Mongol, I think—who, to my surprise, was defeated by our champion. I believe that the Mongol was over-proud of his abilities and that my man took him by surprise and got him down and dazed before he could enter into the full spirit of the battle. He had been a favorite, it seemed, and when our champion won, the crowd was not very pleased.

"It then came down to me. For I was the third champion. I fought with a lance against a Kitayan man. I will not pretend to make the story suspenseful, since you can see that I am here. He was good with the point, and his weapon was lithe and fast, being hafted with some species of hollow reed. But his insistence upon using the sharp end gave me the idea he might not be so clever in the use of the butt, and so by closing in, I was able to clear his steel out of my way and bring the blunt end of my weapon around smartly and take him along the side of the head."

The knights nodded and murmured approval. Cnán rolled her eyes.

"He fell and did not rise. I turned to regard Onghwe. This was the closest we ever came. I could have hurled my lance at him with even odds of putting it through his chest. While this would have been satisfying, it would have condemned my city to destruction, and so I did not do it. Never have I seen a more villainous face. He considered me for a few moments, then nodded toward the western tunnel from which I had issued a few minutes earlier.

"I went back into my city. The Mongols tore down the arena, which was cleverly devised so that it could be pitched and struck in a short time, like a tent. They struck their entire camp and went away.

"Three days later they came back and destroyed us."

Illarion took another long draught of ale and allowed that to sink in.

"I could tell stirring tales of our defense and our defeat," Illarion said, "and even more stirring ones of what came after." He reached to his chest and made a fist around a locket that he wore, containing, Cnán knew, a tiny rendering of the wife and child who had been trampled to death next to him, beneath the planks. "But I do not wish to distract you from the main point of the story."

"Which is?" Feronantus asked, though it was clear from his expression that he already knew.

"That I did just what you lot are preparing to do at this very moment...and the place and people I defended were made desolate and slaughtered regardless," Illarion said. "The invitation to which you have responded is a farce. The only difference is in the stakes. For, unless I have been wrongly informed, you are here as the champions, not just of one town in the middle of Ruthenia, but of Christendom in its entirety."

Feronantus spoke: "The offer that Onghwe Khan proclaimed, not just to us, but to every king and bishop and pope of every land not yet fallen to the Horde, was precisely as you have described it. Instead of offering to spare one city, he offers to spare all of Christendom, provided Christendom sends its champions to the arena you saw being erected near Legnica. Because of the great distances involved, he has granted those kings and bishops and popes several months to respond."

"And need I tell you," Illarion asked, "that he has not done so to be fair or merciful? He has done so because this entertainment, the Circus of Swords, is nothing more than a stalling tactic that he and his brother Khans use to divert the attention of their prey, while the Mongol armies are maneuvered and supply lines laid down for the next onslaught."

"Did you truly believe it?" asked a voice.

Cnán and several others turned to find its source: Roger, the Norman who had come up from Sicily with Percival.

"When you were training in the square before your cathedral, did you believe that Onghwe Khan would honor his word?" His voice was skeptical. He was irritated by Illarion's tone.

Illarion bristled at first, but then looked away, conceding the point. "Of course I asked myself that question every day," he said. "But what choice did we have?"

"Exactly," Roger said. "And do you keep in mind that, during those months of delay, it is not only the Mongols who are maneuvering their armies and preparing their supply lines."

"Would that it were true!" Taran barked. "But Christendom has nothing like the Mongol's unity of purpose. Frederick and the Pope are at war over the Italian peninsula. They don't care what happens farther north."

"It is still better to be attacked later than now," Roger said.

"Not if the outcome is foreordained," said Raphael. "It seems that nothing will stop these Khans except the waves of the western ocean lapping against their ponies' hooves."

And here the conversation shattered into at least half a dozen fragments as groups of three or four men fell to disputing one detail or another. But as far as Cnán could make out, all they were doing was finding new ways to agree on the utter hopelessness of the situation.

"How do they do it?" Feronantus demanded, silencing the table. He groped about with his eyes until his gaze found and fastened upon Cnán. "We know so little about them. Only you, Vaetha, have traveled into the eastern lands from which the Mongols issued. At first, there was only the one—the great one—Genghis. Now there are several. His son Ögedei in the center. Ögedei's son Onghwe. His nephew Batu. Others, I suppose, whose names I do not know. How do they coordinate their movements? How can Ögedei control subordinates who are thousands of leagues away?"

Cnán was impressed by how much Feronantus had already learned. Other Binders may have brought him messages before her, but more likely he had bartered information with traders or captives sent to the Roman Emperor Frederick— perhaps the envoys of the Ismaelis, poor pagan bastards that they were. The Ismaelis, broken remnants of the assassins who had plagued Saladin, Caliphs, and Seljuks alike, had also hired Binders to guide them west.

"The answers to your questions could fill days," she pointed out. Perhaps she did have information they needed, after all—information that might suit the purposes of the Bindings, as well as of the *Skjaldbrædur.*

"Is there nothing else in the minds of these Khans," Feronantus asked, "other than to go on conquering until, as Raphael put it, the ocean washes their ponies' hooves?"

"In large part, they have a free hand, as must be obvious to you," Cnán said, "but they obey commands from the center, and they compete against each other."

"What sort of competition worthy of the name can exist between one Khan and another who is on the other side of the world? Their domains seem to be clearly marked out; one never sees two Khans trying to conquer the same place."

"You misunderstand," Cnán said. "When I speak of competition, I do not mean to say that they compete for the same spoils. For a man of such wealth and power, there is only one prize remaining that is worth attending to, and that is to become the next *Khagan*—the Khan of Khans."

A silence fell around the table as this was considered. "The wisdom of this messenger boots us nothing of consequence," someone complained. "What good does it do us to know that several Khans dream of succeeding Ögedei upon his death?"

"I would hear more," Feronantus demurred. "How is this *Khagan* chosen? Does he select his own successor? Or is it determined by a law of succession? And if there is any such fixed procedure, do they respect it? Or ignore its dictates and fight amongst themselves?"

"The *Khagan* makes his successor known, and upon his death, the choice is ratified by the *kuriltai.*"

"And what is that? Some sort of high priest?"

Cnán shook her head. "They do not have priests like you are accustomed to, much less *high* ones. The *kuriltai* is a high council of Khans. They all come together in one place to decide some important issue—in this case, the identity of the next *Khagan*."

"Does the *kuriltai* happen according to some regular schedule?"

"No. It happens when the *Khagan* wills it."

Feronantus looked disappointed. "So we cannot predict when the next one might happen?"

"No."

"I beg your pardon, but I've a question," said a new voice. It was Yasper, the Dutchman whom Cnán had seen drinking with Raphael on the day of her arrival. Not a member of the Shield-Brethren, he was respected nonetheless as some sort of alchemist.

Feronantus nodded assent, and so Yasper went on. "You say that the *kuriltai* ratifies the successor to the *Khag*—this Khan of Khans."

"Yes."

"But you have also said that he is the only one who can summon a *kuriltai*."

"Yes."

"Do you see the contradiction?"

Cnán smiled in spite of herself. "There is another rule I neglected to mention," she admitted, "which is that the death of the *Khagan* causes a *kuriltai* to be called immediately."

Yasper nodded, satisfied by the answer. Which seemed to settle the matter for everyone, save Feronantus. He mulled it over and held up a hand to silence the next person who tried to speak.

"And a *kuriltai* means that all of the Khans must go without delay to the same place?"

"That is what a *kuriltai* is."

"And can it be convened anywhere, or—"

"Unthinkable," Cnán said. "They have a superstitious reverence for certain magic places in their homeland. Only there could a *kuriltai* be convened."

"So you are telling me," Feronantus said, now staring at her intently in a way that made her not altogether comfortable, "that if Ögedei, the Khan of Khans, were to die, then all of the other Khans—Onghwe, here in Legnica, and Batu, down in Hungary, and all of the others wherever they are—they would all have to drop what they were doing immediately and travel back to Mongolia?"

"That is correct," said Cnán, uncertain why Feronantus seemed to be so fascinated by this hypothetical punctilio of Mongol tribal law. "If they wished to become the *Khagan*. And they all do."

Feronantus seemed enormously relieved all of a sudden. A piercing glint came into his eyes, and he clasped his hands in front of his knees. He looked around the room at his smartest tacticians: Raphael, Finn, Rædwulf, Taran. "Well, our path is perfectly obvious, then!" he announced. "We will no longer become one, but *two*. We will split our group, and our efforts, and teach these Devil's horsemen to respect the butt as well as the blade."

The silence in the room, and the expressions of all who stared at him, made it clear that she was not the only one who failed to see his plan. He threw up his hands, exasperated by their inability to see what, to him, was so obvious.

"Some will fight in the circus. That will give us cover and diversion."

Cnán gaped, but turned her gaze immediately to Haakon, who seemed oblivious. She felt ill again, as if looking at Raphael's bloody pincers—or smelling the rot around Legnica.

Feronantus, she knew, had just sealed the young Viking's doom—Haakon would die first, along with his younger and least experienced brethren.

The Order was about to throw their children from the walls.

The *Kinyen* was still silent, waiting for Feronantus to explain the other half of his plan.

"And the rest," Feronantus said, "shall ride into the East, passing over the Land of Skulls and into the sacred heartland of the Mongols, and find the *Khagan*. And kill him."

CHAPTER 6:

IN THE GARDEN

"On the field of battle, who has the power?"

Lian's tone implied she knew the answer to the question. Gansukh found this habit of hers irritating, but knew if he didn't answer, she would only repeat the question. She would phrase it differently or seem to ignore his lack of answer for a short time before suddenly returning to the question. She was like a horsefly: always out of reach, buzzing and biting endlessly, and never landing on the same patch of flesh twice.

"The general," he replied, mentally swatting her away. "He makes the battle plans and gives the order to execute them."

Lian nodded. She was framed by the midmorning sun, and the light tinged her hair red. This was their third time meeting in the eastern gardens. Gansukh liked it much better here, outside, than in his tomb of a room. He could see the sky.

It was only when he couldn't see the endless expanse of blue that he realized how much he missed it. Not like a sword or a horse, or even one of the other tribesmen who had survived the siege at Kozelsk. Those were all parts of a Mongol's life that changed: swords would be broken or lost, horses would fall in battle or grow too old to carry a warrior, friends and comrades would die too. This was all part of the cycle of life under the Endless Blue Heaven, and throughout that cycle, the sky never changed. It was always there.

Until it wasn't.

He hated sleeping in a bed. He was always sore in the morning. Muscles in his lower back and shoulders were knotted in a way that made no sense to him. He had once spent a week in the saddle—riding, sleeping, fighting, pissing, eating—and at the end of the week, he hadn't been as stiff as he felt after a single night in that bed.

"And here, in Karakorum..." Lian paused until she was sure she had his attention. "Who has the power?"

"The *Khagan*, of course," Gansukh muttered.

The east garden had become Gansukh's refuge, and after the way the first few lessons had left him feeling even more confused and frustrated, he had insisted they take place outside. The grounds were nothing like the open steppe, but there was some room to wander, enough that he didn't feel quite as caged.

The garden was huge, extending from the northern wall and the *Khagan*'s private quarters, along the east wall, to the gate. There were several paths, courses of river stone laid in winding paths through an endless procession of groves and bowers of trees. Gansukh had tried to count the different types of trees one afternoon and had given up after several dozen. If the trees were all taken from various places in the *Khagan*'s empire, then it must be far greater than Gansukh could ever imagine. And the flowers: swathes of color on raised beds, tiny blossoms strung like beads on vines that embraced the naked trunks of trees, tall stalks that bore flowers that looked like flaming birds, and long stems that craned overhead to look down on him with their mottled faces.

In the center of the garden was a long pond. Fish as bright as the flowers swam lazily in the clear water. Fat and indolent, they did not fear any predator. Not in the *Khagan*'s garden. Arranged around the pond were a number of stone benches, carved with animals and flowers.

Gansukh rarely sat.

"Yes, of course, the *Khagan* has power." Lian snapped her fingers. His answer was obvious—of little value to their lesson. "Who else?"

Gansukh flushed. He could stand his ground against an approaching enemy without losing his focus, but this tiny woman with her tongue and her dismissive gestures—treating him as if he were an addled child—made him lose his temper so quickly. He kept his mouth shut.

Sometimes it was better to say nothing than to fill a void badly. He had—grudgingly—learned that much.

Lian returned to her initial question, but with one change. "Who *besides* the general has power on the battlefield?"

Gansukh exhaled. This was familiar territory. "The captains. They carry out the general's orders; they are the ones who instruct the soldiers on the battlefield."

Lian nodded. She stared at Gansukh purposefully, and he felt his cheeks flush again. He'd given her a suitable answer, but there was something else he was missing, some subtlety of this game that he could not follow. *What was the connection between the battlefield and the balance of power in the court?*

She had rouged her cheeks and applied some color to the skin around her eyes, a turquoise that matched the pattern of leaves that ran along the edges of her jacket—collar, cuff, and down the front...

"Do the captains execute the general's orders blindly?" Lian asked. "Or do they sometimes offer counsel to their leader?"

Gansukh snapped his attention back to her face. "During battle," he said, "we execute our orders without question." *Yes, familiar territory.* When she nodded, he continued. "But before the battle the general often confers with his captains."

Lian began to smile, and emboldened by this sign of encouragement, he rushed on. "For example, before the siege of Kozelsk, General Batu asked me—"

"Please," Lian's smile vanished, "no more war stories." She crossed her arms and her hands vanished into the wide sleeves of her jacket. The gesture transformed her into a stern matron, an instructor displeased with her student's inattentiveness. "Master Chucai did not ask me to be a doe-eyed companion, one who would listen raptly to your boastful tales of combat."

Growling deep in his throat, Gansukh let go of the tension caused by her interruption. He forced his lungs to move more slowly. This was not the battlefield. This was court, and if he had been raised here, this *education* would be easier, but he hadn't. He had been born in a small camp—a few dozen families wintering on the western slope of a mountain—and his only education had been in how to use his hands and his mind to survive. He knew how to hunt, to fight, and to kill. He wanted to show her. He wanted her to see that he wasn't a helpless child; he commanded respect from other men, and they did his bidding without question.

Why did Chagatai choose me?

Lian was relentless in her focus. "Who else has power in the court?" she asked, reminding him of the point of this... *torturous*...conversation.

Gansukh looked away, letting his gaze roam around the garden. There was no escape. He had to learn these lessons; he had to understand how to survive at court. Otherwise...

A slight wind touched the trees that bordered the path on the eastern side of the pond. They were well groomed—Gansukh had counted more than ten gardeners who kept the gardens immaculately manicured—and as the breeze blew through their branches, they moved as one unit. Almost like soldiers, moving in formation.

In a flash, Gansukh saw the answer. "Those close to the *Khagan*," he said. It was more than physical proximity, though. In battle, a warrior didn't worry about what happened on his left or right, because he knew he was part of a formation. He knew he was protected by those around him. "It's about trust," he said, looking at Lian.

"Yes, good. And who is close to the *Khagan*?"

"His generals."

"And?"

"His military advisors."

"Besides his *military staff*, Gansukh, who can influence the *Khagan*?" Her pleasure at his answer was fading.

Gansukh gave her question serious thought. *Who else is there?* He looked at the trees again. An unbroken line. Interwoven branches. Only as strong as each individual tree. That was how an army was successful. How it survived on the field of battle. Each man knew his place and held it. "Why don't you just tell me what answer you are looking for?" he burst out. "I promise I'll remember it."

She was silent for a minute, and Gansukh stole a glance at her and was taken aback by the expression on her face. She wasn't angry.

"Because," she said, her tone less charged, "if you reach the answer yourself, you'll be more likely to remember it yourself. If I watch you shoot arrows, will I become a better archer?"

Gansukh smiled. "Well said," he laughed. But he pressed once again, instinctively sensing a weak spot in his teacher's armor. "But give me a hint."

Lian removed her hands from her sleeves and lightly toyed with the collar of her jacket. "Does the general have his wife on the battlefield with him?" she wondered.

Gansukh snorted. "Of course not."

Lian remained silent, and realization dawned on Gansukh. "But the *Khagan* has all of his wives here...and they spend more time with him than any general or advisor!"

Lian raised her hand toward her temple and her body trembled as if she were going to collapse. "By the ancestral spirits, I thought we were going to be here all morning!"

Gansukh laughed more readily this time. "I would not mind," he said, which was not entirely true. But the sight of her pretending to faint had dispelled her stony countenance, and under his direct gaze, Lian blushed. The color in her cheeks only made her more comely.

"Gansukh," she said, turning and wandering slowly toward one of the stone benches, "you must learn who has influence on the *Khagan* and, just as importantly, what they do to get that influence."

"What do you mean?" He followed her, well aware that was exactly what he was supposed to do.

"How do captains in the field gain the respect of their general?"

"We execute his orders. Successfully. We win battles and return with the heads of our enemies." Gansukh forcefully planted an imaginary stake in the ground between them.

Lian flinched. "Charming," she said. The blush was gone from her face. "In court, you don't need to bring...*trophies*... in order to gain favor. There are more *subtle* ways."

Gansukh pondered how he had gone astray again for a few seconds, and then he nodded. "Yes, I see. Sex. Food. Drink. Entertainment." He started a count on his fingers.

"Information. Counsel: how to deal with the Chinese, how to respond to the matters of the court…"

He stared at the spread fingers of his hand, and when Lian prompted him to continue, he didn't even hear the elation in her voice. He was already up to seven, more than he had fingers on a hand. He shook his head. "Too many," he said. "It's too complicated. There are too many people with influence." He closed his hand into a fist and nodded grimly at the shape it made. *This I understand.*

She touched his fist, and he jerked slightly. He had thought she was farther away from him, and her sudden proximity startled him. She gripped his hand with both of hers and, with gentle pressure, coaxed his fingers to relax.

"There are different kinds of battlefields," she said softly. A long strand of her hair hung across her face, and Gansukh wanted to brush it back, but his hand wouldn't move. "On some of them, you can't see the enemy as well as he can see you." She raised her head slightly, looking up at him through the strand of dangling hair. "Is that not true?"

Gansukh nodded. She was still holding on to him, her fingers supporting the weight of his hand.

"And do you not use different tactics for these different battles?" She shrugged and let one set of fingers release their hold on him. "For some of them, is brute force the best way to win?" She let go completely, and his hand dropped, suddenly heavy. She smiled as he tensed, grabbing at his right wrist with his left hand.

"Everyone can see a fist coming, Gansukh," she murmured as she retreated a few steps and sat on the bench. "You must learn to hide your intentions better. Use your environment to your advantage. What kind of warrior is the man who rides in plain sight with his sword held in his hand?"

"A dead one," Gansukh said. He let his hands fall at his side. The muscles in his lower back, the ones that were stiffest after a night in the bed, were starting to tighten. He sat down heavily on the bench next to Lian. "Yes," he nodded, "that is a good way to think about it, Lian." His shoulders slouched.

"One last lesson for this morning," said Lian, and Gansukh unconsciously let out a heavy sigh. "Does the general have favorite captains?"

"Favorites?" Gansukh repeated. It was a strange word to use in reference to battlefield command, and he tried to understand why she had chosen it. "He has captains he trusts more than others..."

"And do those favorite captains try to embarrass the other captains in the general's eyes?"

Gansukh looked at Lian. The bench wasn't very wide, and he could smell her fragrance, an aroma muskier than the scent of the flowers surrounding them. She was uncomfortably close.

"We gain our general's respect by winning battles," he said after taking a deep breath. "We do not concern ourselves by trying to embarrass the other captains. We do not have time for such games, and if we engage in them, we are not concentrating on keeping our men alive. If other captains fail in battle, they do so on their own. That is embarrassment enough."

Lian clapped her hands lightly. "Yes. Do you see the difference now?" When Gansukh shook his head, she continued, momentarily forgetting her resistance to providing him the answer. "Your general gives you orders and treats you with respect because he knows that you are a capable man, that you will carry out his orders well and, in doing so, enable him to win the battle. He would not give you those orders otherwise."

She let her hand fall on his forearm. "But here at court, there are no orders to follow, no battle to win for the honor of the *Khagan*. So how does he know whether you are a worthy commander?"

Gansukh sat very still, as if her hand were a bird he didn't want to scare away. He nodded, almost imperceptibly. "I would have to tell him," he said.

"In some ways, the battlefield is more civilized than court," Lian said, somewhat wistfully. "A man's worth is exactly how much glory his actions bring to his general." Her tone hardened. "Here, a man's worth is calculated by what he says and by what others say about him."

Lian removed her hand, placing it in her lap. She directed her attention at the still surface of the pond. "You may have already made enemies, Gansukh," she said softly, a note of caution in her voice.

Gansukh grunted, acknowledging the truth in her statement.

An expression flickered across Lian's face, a tightening of her mouth and eyes. She hid it well, and if he'd been looking at her face, he wouldn't have seen it. "Oh?" she said. "Who?"

She already knows, he thought. "Munokhoi," he said, and he knew he was right when she didn't react to the name. He waited for her to turn her head; he wanted to see what her eyes would tell him. *Like you are hunting a deer,* he thought. *Patience will be rewarded.* He recalled the way she had looked over her shoulder at him that night in the bath. Knowing he was watching her, making eye contact one last time as she left. *She'll look. I can wait her out.*

She did, sooner than he thought she would, and she blinked when she saw the smile on his face. She looked away quickly, but not before he caught a flash of unguarded emotion in her eyes.

"He is threatened by you?" Lian asked, her eyes focused on the pond, as if she were trying to see beneath its placid surface.

Gansukh didn't see any reason to answer the question, not when she already knew the answer. *Not this time.*

Lian pushed back her shoulders, collecting herself. "How are you going to deal with him?" she asked, her challenging tone returning, pushing him.

"I've been avoiding him," said Gansukh. "No reason to provoke the man."

"No." Lian stood and looked down on him disapprovingly. "That is the worst thing to do."

Gansukh reacted as if she had slapped him. "Enough," he barked. "You will not speak to me like that."

It was Lian's turn to react, and she sat down quickly, her shoulder brushing his upper arm. She crossed her arms again, hiding her hands in her sleeves, but the motion was submissive this time instead of domineering. "I…I'm sorry," she said. "I have…I didn't mean to be disrespectful."

"Why were you?" The question came more harshly than he had intended.

"Gansukh, Munokhoi has the *Khagan*'s ear, and not just because he commands a *jaghun* of the *Torguud*. He has become a respected companion. If you avoid the *Khagan* when Munokhoi is with him, you'll be giving Munokhoi too many chances to criticize you when you cannot speak for yourself."

"Why are you telling me this?" Gansukh asked, and he smiled at her confusion. "I thought I could only remember the lessons if I figured it out for myself. Are you afraid for me?"

Lian snorted and shook her head. She plucked at the loose strand of her hair and made to tuck it back into place. "I'm serious," she said. "You should not treat Munokhoi lightly."

"I never said I was."

"You said you were avoiding him."

"I did, but that's not the same as not considering him as an enemy."

"Oh, you are…" Lian stood as if to leave, her shoulder roughly brushing him as she got to her feet. "You will find yourself outside the gates soon enough, *horse rider*, as that seems to be your preference."

"Wait." Gansukh stood and laid a gentle hand on her elbow before she could storm off. "Wait, I'm…I'm sorry. I understand what you are trying to tell me—I do—and I appreciate your concern."

Lian hesitated, though the cant of her body said she was still leaving.

"And your advice." He released her arm and sat down again.

She relented, but didn't rejoin him on the bench. Her attention was directed over his shoulder. "Your initial strategy might work outside the walls of the city," she said, "but you need to formulate a better strategy now. One that keeps you close to your enemies." Her eyes flickered toward him. "Yes?"

He nodded and turned to look behind him.

There was a commotion near the southern border of the garden. Pairs of men were setting up barriers across the paths. Behind them, others were gathering—members of the court, judging by the variety of colorful clothing.

"You need to seek out the situations where Ögedei Khan and Munokhoi are together and make sure you are there."

Gansukh shot to his feet. "Well then, the lesson is over."

"What do you mean? Why?" Lian looked at him quizzically, not understanding his sudden reaction.

"Master Chucai invited me to join a deer hunt with the *Khagan* and Munokhoi this afternoon. I had declined, citing my lesson with you, but…"

Lian glanced once more at the gathering throng, and then grabbed his arm. "A hunt," she said. "Yes, that would be a perfect opportunity to impress the *Khagan*."

"I will need to prepare. I will need my bow," Gansukh said.

She started walking toward the main building, where his tiny room was located. "Good," she said, looking back over her shoulder. "Later, it will be my turn."

"Your turn? For what?" Gansukh asked, hurrying after her.

"We can meet again here before nightfall. You can tell me about the hunt." She let a smile creep across her lips. "If you are successful in your efforts, then…"

Gansukh didn't leap into the void of her words. Letting her lead, watching her walk in front of him, he had a pretty good idea of what she was suggesting.

CHAPTER 7:

THE JOURNEY BEGINS

"*And the rest shall ride into the East, passing over the Land of Skulls and into the sacred heartland of the Mongols, and find the* Khagan. *And kill him.*"

Feronantus's words had been clear enough, voiced in well-framed and unambiguous Latin. Yet during the lengthy silence that filled the room in the moments after he spoke them, Cnán doubted that she had heard correctly. The words described an obvious impossibility. It was a sentence that could only have escaped from the lips of an insane man. And yet as she scanned the faces of the *Skjaldbrœður* assembled for the *Kinyen*, she saw none of the reactions that she would deem appropriate. There was some astonishment, to be sure. But no one was looking at Feronantus as if he were out of his mind.

They were actually thinking about it.

She was in a *room* full of insane men.

She was not in the habit of sitting mute. As Feronantus and the others had been learning since her arrival at the chapter house, she spoke her mind. And yet something about the enormity of this foolishness had rendered her speechless for a time.

"Very well," said the one named Taran—the big gallowglass—as if Feronantus had proposed that they go down to the tavern for a pint of ale. "But do you suppose we ought to wait a few days until some of our other Brothers can arrive? Brother Andreas, for example. His spear would be a fine companion on a Khan-hunting journey. Plus, he knows how to cook and he doesn't snore like Brother Eleázar."

Eleázar was a Spaniard who had only arrived yesterday. After waiting for a murmur of laughter to die down, he said, with great dignity: "Which would do you no good, since I will be with you anyway, snoring as much as I please."

"I shall be the judge of who shall and shall not join the hunting party," Feronantus said gently, and Eleázar responded immediately with a bow, deferring to his authority.

Cnán had finally got her voice back. "Hunting party, you call it? As if you were going out to catch a rabbit for your evening stew?"

All heads turned her way. Many seemed surprised that she found anything about the conversation to be the least bit irregular.

"You are speaking of the most powerful man in the history of the world," she said. "Compared to him, Julius Caesar was a regional governor of modest achievements."

"But if we put two inches of steel into him, he will die," Roger pointed out with stinging quickness. He was idly fussing over one of his daggers.

"But your steel is *here*," she said, slapping the table hard, "and to get it *there*, you must journey across two thousand leagues and kill ten thousand hand-picked bodyguards."

"Hand-picked bodyguards always disappoint," Raphael said.

"Ten thousand of them," Roger said, "means ten thousand opportunities for confusion."

"You do not understand!" she insisted. "You have no conception of what you are speaking of!"

"We did not come here with any expectation of surviving," said Percival. He did not speak scornfully or brashly, but as if explaining a trivial misunderstanding to an elderly relative. "Dying in some righteous quest is far preferable to dying for the entertainment of a dissolute Khan."

"It is not *merely* that it is suicide," Cnán said, "but that it is pointless and immediate suicide. You will not get ten miles." She saw the flaw in her statement immediately.

So did Illarion. "You traveled a great deal more than that to fetch me," he reminded her, "and the same again to return. I can guide you deep into Rus."

"What *used* to be Rus," Cnán snarled. "Now it is the domain of the Great Khan. Four-fifths of which lies beyond your horizon. And how will you find your way across that?"

"That," said Feronantus mildly, "is your job, *Vaetha*. Or whatever your name is."

This silenced her long enough for them to get on with the planning of the expedition. Several names were mentioned of knights who, like Andreas, had not arrived yet but would be good to have along.

Feronantus cut off all such discussion with a pass of the hand. "No," he said, "we leave tonight. The party will be chosen from around this table."

Hands were lifted to lodge polite objections, but Feronantus was firm. "If we wait three days for Andreas, he'll not get here for five, and then he'll mention someone four days behind him who'll be better yet. We will lose the *Vor*."

Cnán had no idea what the *Vor* was, but the argument seemed decisive to everyone else. Some sort of gibberish from their *oplomach*, as they called their arts of fighting.

In the few days she had been a guest of the *Ordo Militum Vindicis Intactae*, she had learned everything she could about this Feronantus—save, apparently, for the most important thing, which was that he was not of sound mind.

She had learned he had been of a high rank within the Order, which meant that if he stayed alive and made no mistakes, he was likely to end up presiding over Petraathen itself one day. As a way of preparing him for that honor, they had sent him out to run Týrshammar, the fortress/temple/monastery they had been maintaining in the North Sea for the last nine hundred years or so—an offshoot of the more ancient Petraathen and, by tradition, a place where future leaders of the Order were groomed.

Whether by accident or design, the Mongols had flanked Petraathen to the north and south. The southern branch, under Batu Khan, had advanced into Hungary and defeated most of Christendom's armies at a place called Mohi. The northern branch, under Onghwe, had come here and defeated the rest of them. Among those who made a study of Khans, it was believed that Batu was the more important, and that the southern prong of the advance was therefore the real one, and that Onghwe's efforts were more in the nature of a diversion. Accordingly, most of the *Ordo Militum Vindicis Intactae* who were actually based at Petraathen had gone south into Hungary, and those who had survived the battle along the Sajó River were there still. When Onghwe had sent out his challenge for the Circus of Swords, the responsibility had consequently fallen to Feronantus, who had come out from Týrshammar with Taran and Rædwulf and a few others who had been on the island at the time.

"I will go into the East, with no expectation of returning," Feronantus said. "The road will be long. We shall travel light. This means we shall have to feed ourselves by hunting for game along the way. I hope that Finn will come along to make up for our shortcomings in the chase."

This was translated to Finn, who beamed and nodded and said something that was translated back into Latin as, "Yes, provided you make up for mine as a warrior."

"Rædwulf complements Finn in the hunt, and we will need the power of his bow to penetrate Mongol armor from a distance," Feronantus continued.

Cnán blushed in spite of herself, recalling how the two had tracked her through the woods. Yes, between Finn and Rædwulf, no deer between here and Mongolia would stand much of a chance.

"Illarion Illarionovitch has already done us the honor of volunteering," Feronantus said, exchanging a nod with the Ruthenian. "Though we have little hope of outriding the Mongol hordes, we shall need the finest horseman at our disposal—the *matamoros*, Eleázar."

The Spaniard looked pleased. Istvan, the Hungarian rider, did not.

"As much as I would like to believe that we could accomplish the journey without illness or injury, we shall require the services of a physician, and so I call upon Raphael, who may also be able to help us with the language of the Saracens.

"Percival has already spoken in a way that tells me of where his heart leads him, and so I summon him on this quest. I would not dare separate him from Roger, and so Roger joins the list, if he can bear our company."

"And if you can bear mine," Roger said.

"Though, like Finn, he is not a member of our Order and is but an honored visitor in our camp, Yasper and his knowledge of alchemical matters might serve us well, and so I invite him to come along with us."

"I thought you would never get around to it!" Yasper said. Though in truth Cnán fancied he looked more nervous than any of the others, which only made her favor the man since it meant he was the least insane of any of them.

"Taran really ought to stay here, to be the *oplo* of the younger men who will have to fight in the stead of those who are going east. But with a broken heart he will be useless, and since it will break his heart to leave him behind, I summon him on the quest. Brother Rutger is more than ready to step into his place here."

The range and intensity of emotion that had flashed across Taran's face during this little speech had been almost frightening to Cnán, but he ended up red-faced and close to weeping, nodding his head vigorously. "Yes," he muttered, "Rutger will serve brilliantly."

"We have ten," Feronantus said. "I hope and pray that the one who calls herself Vaetha will be our twelfth. Which means we need an eleventh. Any man here would serve well. But I am not oblivious to the gaze—perhaps 'glare' is a better word—of Istvan, who I think fancies himself as expert a horseman as Eleázar. Perhaps he is. But there is no doubting that he knows the ways of the Mongols better than any man from farther west, and so I offer to let him share our quest and our fate."

"Accepted," Istvan proclaimed before the sentence was even finished. He had been rocking back and forth on his chair as if it were a horse and he were even now riding it into battle.

All faces now turned again toward Cnán.

In no way did any of this make sense. They would ride hard and live like wild animals for as much as half a year before dying full of arrows on a frozen Mongolian steppe.

But she knew fate when she saw it—or rather, when it closed its grip around her throat.

"My name is Cnán," she said, "and since it appears to be my doom, I shall, as soon as you have finished with all of your pompous words and grand gestures, get up from this chair and turn my back on the setting sun, whose warmth and beauty have been my only solace over many months' striving, and hie to the sacred threshold of the Great Khan's tent, as long as breath remains in my lungs. If you eleven choose to follow me, you shall find your road shorter and safer, and I may even be glad of your company from time to time." She could not prevent her eyes from straying to Percival's as she said this last. He was, finally, paying attention to her.

An hour later they were on the road.

◆ ◆ ◆

Feronantus looked back on the clearing with an expression Cnán could not read. She stayed close to the leader of this group of madmen, hoping to riddle his reasons before he got them all killed.

The clearing, the old monastery, converted into a chapter house—the planks of half-rotten wood laid out to form tables and benches, the Order's standard now flying from a pole mounted to a scalable edge of the ruined roof—the cemetery with its silent dead. Here she had come to be part of this group; here they had taken her in as an equal—mostly. She had guided a few of them across the dead lands to find Illarion, including the wise Raphael, with his Semitic countenance, and the young Haakon, with his awkward searching for whatever sort of manhood might be made available; she had watched them absorb the nastiness of Legnica and fend off Mongols with inspired trickery that, should it have been planned, would have utterly failed.

Here she had watched the beautiful Percival, and she had longed for something else, something other; trying, like the blundering Haakon, to find her way into an unobtainable embrace. A *companionship* she could never have.

She had listened to Illarion's story. She had watched the knights train, and then had watched Feronantus devise a plan sure to fail. Sure to get them all killed.

Still, she would miss this place. And Feronantus? "Sorry to be leaving?" she asked.

He shook his head and smiled. "You wish to know my mind."

"You sent the young ones off to die," Cnán said. "A diversion for a mad journey. I wish to be certain you are not mad."

"That forest is a wild place, happier without us. The chapter house will fall quiet. The dead will sleep more soundly, their bones not shivering ever so slightly at the presence of warriors. The deer will return, not to be hunted by such as us. The air will not ring with steel, nor sing and echo with the high voices of whelps and the gutturals of old hounds, all eager for the scrap and the hunt. The wind will blow, the trees will sough, and we now set out to relieve the burdens of others. But we are *your* burden, Cnán."

She could not follow much of this, but it impressed her nevertheless. "And why is that?" she asked.

"You are a Binder. You connect those who quest, do you not?"

She grimaced. "Your speech may infect the others, but I am not as easily swayed."

"Madness, desperation, vision," Feronantus said. "They define our lives and our time. Would you not say that is true, young leaf?"

"How do you mean, leaf?"

"Yours has not been an easy life," Feronantus said. "You travel like a leaf. A leaf that grew without a tree."

The clearing was behind them now, hidden by trees, and their horses took the long winding paths with patience. She patted the neck of her mount, grateful for once to be riding, because it brought her almost face-to-face with Feronantus. She stared at his face, trying to ascertain what he was implying.

"You never knew your father," the knight said. He glanced beyond her shoulder, suggesting he already knew the truth to that statement.

"Nor did my mother," she blurted.

"That is a surprise," he said after a moment. Her horse whickered at something on the path. She patted its neck again. The rough coat was clean, freshly curried. The horse was reasonably cheerful, having cropped grass for days; its gut was full, so the horse was contented and clean and did not mind her, its burden.

"Many will be born now who know not their fathers," she said, her tone low. "The girl outside Legnica...the one who tended Illarion and brought him willow mash."

"Haakon said you wished to bring her along or stay to defend her. He was impressed by your sympathy."

"Knights are surprised by a wish to save damsels?"

Feronantus frowned. "If wishes were armies..." he murmured. "We are few. The flying lance cannot succor fledglings who fall."

Cnán's heat did not diminish. The topic had been broached. She would not let this *man* off lightly, since he had broached it. "If she survives all the *men* who have their way with her, she will produce children who know not their fathers. They will live in broken villages where such bastards of war are shunned and beaten and perhaps even knifed by bands of young thugs—those who claim purity of breeding—for the bastards' eyes will *slant* and their noses will lie flat on their faces, and their skins will be darker. If she has sense enough left in her to love a child, she will not be able to protect her, for the child will remind all of the enemy, even her mother."

"Hmm…" Clearly the old knight found this conversation unpleasant. "You liked the chapter house," Feronantus said after a while.

Her horse whickered again, though the path was clear, and she patted its neck a little roughly, which it seemed to enjoy.

"I enjoyed the respite," she said. "My mother loved me. She was a *leaf* as well. When we were able to find a place out of the wind, she made a home for me—in old buildings, old towns, places of ghosts and dead history. She swept floors of bones and patched old walls and repaired old furniture. She did not blame me for my father, instead told me that wildness and war made us stronger, that the mix of her blood and *his* seed would live in me all my life, evil up against her love and… the tradition of the Binders. The tradition, she said, would protect me against whatever ghosts trailed me when I moved. For the sins of all fathers, the deaths and monstrosities, make ghosts that trail after the children." She spat. "There is no justice. Your Christian God looks down on all and sees every sparrow, but cares nothing for the children. He is a god of birds."

Feronantus chuckled at this blasphemy. "Birds are more pleasant."

"Only if you don't know them," Cnán said. "They cock their feathers against each other and compete for seeds and grubs. All birds are bastards. But they *are* prettier." She looked up through the trees, where, strangely, there were no birds and no birdsong. "And they can fly swiftly. We will all wish we were birds long before we finish this journey."

"So now I understand you, and you understand me?"

She smirked. "I have not spoken so many words in years. You have said nothing of importance."

"That girl is not like your mother. Nor like you."

"She was born soft and protected. She was the daughter of a noble perhaps, and had been born into silks and furs and gentle words, and always a fire burning against the cold, and porridge and roots and bread and game against hunger. Her father might have loved her. Her father is dead. Her mother is dead. But no ghosts haunt her."

Feronantus looked puzzled. "Why?"

Cnán shook her head. She had taken him far into tale-telling, without intending to. She had no intention of revealing any more of the hidden tales of her kin-sisters.

"Well, we begin in beauty and green, and ride into cold and sere," Feronantus said. "You told me your name. I am proud to know it and proud to know you. I hope to speak more of this with you."

"I am a leaf," she said. "You are a sword."

"True," Feronantus said. "But not so different, for all that."

She snapped out the next few words and regretted them immediately. "What, you are a war-born bastard too?"

Feronantus's face clouded, but only briefly, and his gaze on her flashed wariness before he smiled again. That infuriating, fatherly smile, which so fascinated her, yet made her fists clench.

Then he looked aside and reined his horse back, no longer riding parallel.

Cnán ultimately had this effect on those who were not kin-sisters, and so had her mother before her, the lashing tongue of truth. The value of the Binders lay in the services and information they offered. Otherwise no one would stand for them.

"Your horse whickers because he likes your manner," Feronantus said. "He is coming to trust you. Horses are naive that way. Of all the savagery of war, I regret the disappointment and agony of the horses most of all."

"More than men?" Cnán said over her shoulder.

"Men—knights, at least, and others who ride horses—have some hope of advantage from war. Horses carry burdens and get fed, if they are lucky. Mostly, though, they suffer and die."

"We will take them north of here, away from the Mongol highways," Cnán said, feeling a chill. "Will you say prayers for the team you sent to the circus?"

"I will."

"To a Christian God?"

"Yes. To Him."

"And to others as well?"

Feronantus dropped back farther and motioned her to lead on. Then he wheeled about to confer with Istvan, and what they said she could not hear. Cnán galloped ahead for a while; she told herself to make certain this was the route she had taken before, but also to be alone. To think.

Her contemplative mood continued as the fiery sunset came to pass. The sky filled with the bushy tails of flaming animals. Slowly the fires died, dusk fell, night came on. Stars held steady and aloof against ghostly wisps.

All of this land was turning into mulch. The aftermath of devastation was a renewed garden. Soon the musty stench of Legnica would fade. The winds would blow, snow would fall thick, the land would be softly quieted…then spring would come, the dead would molder into dust, flowers would push up. Mongol-appointed tax collectors, possibly the survivors of old noble families—the black sheep who never found favor in good times—would hire thugs as riders and set up their tables as farmers harvested new crops, woodsmen harvested the forests to rebuild, lime kilns were restacked from old toppled bricks.

Her kind of leaf blew across the land until it too found the anonymity of mulch, but always in the wilderness, never in a field or a garden…never to help push up shoots or flowers.

◆ ◆ ◆

They stayed away from the known routes, and after a few days they entered a dense forest of great oaks, oaks old enough to revive a deep sense of reverence in Cnán and keep the knights more than usually quiet. Cnán remembered these trees had been sacred to the Slavic war god, Perun, now fled (or tempered) by the Greek Christos. The high-arching green branches reduced what little sunlight passed through the thick, eastward-sweeping clouds to a few silvery shafts, and as the summer rains began, water dripped constantly from the leaves, leaving the litter boggy and the horses moody.

Cnán watched the riders, both as they traveled and as they pitched their spare camps in forest and field. She studied the knights' interactions with their leader, Feronantus, and closely observed each member of the party, as her mother had taught her.

"We study all men as we would the beasts. Thus we know them better, and they learn nothing of us," her mother had said. "No one has known our people, nor will they ever."

The eleven travelers in turn paid her little attention. They now seemed to regard her as an irritating little sister, or perhaps a dog, if they thought of her at all. She liked being ignored, even by Percival, who had never shown her much interest anyway.

As they rode between the big oaks, at the prompting of Feronantus, the group spread out thirty or forty paces and assumed a loose double V, such that whatever foes they met could easily be drawn into a fork by simple sweeps one way or another.

Cnán often moved off from the main body, reconnoitering, scouting for war parties or any of the stray, crazed, bloody-minded fragments of dying armies—whatever might have scattered over this broad, flat portion of the Empire of the Great Khan. She also looked for the signals and cryptic marks left by other travelers—and in particular, Binders. Knotted cords and an array of marks had guided her from the East in the first place. When they weren't tying knots, Binders left messages by looping sapling branches around thicker limbs, notching big trees near the base, or draping anonymous, cleverly torn shreds of bog-dyed brown cloth. On occasion, if the skeleton of an animal (or a human) presented itself, messages could be left in the apparent scatter of gnawed ribs. Larger marks scored in the dirt or arranged in rocks could be seen only from high up in trees; still others were obvious only in winter.

Travelers from other societies worked their own signs into the far-stretching earth. Along her paths east and west, traveling with her mother as a child and with other Binders or alone, she had noticed long lines of tight circles cleared with sticks from the litter and grass. Binders could not read them, and the lines couldn't have lasted more than a few seasons, yet they were always there—as if magically renewed.

Together, travelers from all the societies were leaving their itineraries, and their maps, where no roads had yet been laid. Some of those marks had been maintained for thousands of years, not just by guilds and traveling societies, but also by loosely allied foragers and hunters who rarely met in person.

The knight who best understood the secret languages of stones and circles was Istvan, of the dour countenance and immense mustache. Cnán undertook several times to observe him as he too rode away from the party on private forays, despite Feronantus's concern. She kept well away and took care not to fall under his eye, but, on occasion, found means to hide near a path she guessed he would take.

Istvan was moody, his usual expression a scowl of focused attention—or just a scowl. Like many who had survived the advance of the Mongol Horde, he had seen too much that he could not clear from his memory.

On the tenth day of their journey, Istvan caused her a deeper concern—for two reasons. Clearly the refugee knight of Mohi was less interested in traveling east at speed and more interested in old camps, old huts, deserted farms, and what few hamlets could still be found burrowed deep in the forests. Several times he stopped at these rude, threadbare communities, at no pains to conceal his identity or his character, and asked questions about Mongols. He seemed to understand many of the dialects here, occasionally Teutonic, more often variations on Slavic Ruthenian, and sometimes, in the deep woods and tall hills, a tongue very similar to his native Madjar.

Istvan also seemed to have more than a passing acquaintance with the pathways of goods, slaves, and money in conquered territories—and he knew much more about Mongols and their Eastern allies than he let on in camp, where he usually kept silent.

Istvan's interest in old farms was not just a matter of military tactics, Cnán began to realize. He frequently paused to dismount in abandoned pastures choked by ivy and creepers, to part the overgrowth and dig his fingers into the soil beneath.

For Istvan's other quest—and this fascinated Cnán—concerned mushrooms. Sometimes he collected the small mushrooms that grew in those soils, dropping them like gold coins, one by one, into a loose-woven linen bag. Cnán became convinced that Istvan—in contrast to Raphael, who sought out and preserved many herbal simples—was following the nearly invisible petroglyphs and tree arrangements of the ancients: goddess-worshippers, Orphics, Earth and sky mantics—signs of which Cnán, truth be told, knew very little. She had seen none of that sort of activity in her lifetime.

Binders, however, knew something about the mushrooms used by these ecstatics. At times, adept guides collected them on their travels and purveyed them to temples and priests throughout greater Asia, but she was not familiar with their use in these territories and wondered how and why Istvan had acquired his expertise.

He avoided the red-and-white amanitas, and well he might. Their use was often deadly. The smaller wavy-cap and freebuttons and other mushrooms were far more interesting and complex—or so Cnán had heard.

On the fifteenth day, she saw him emerge from a wet, grassy clearing. He paused, opened his bag, and popped a freshly harvested freebutton into his mouth, making a bitter face. He climbed back on his patient horse and sat mounted for a while, not moving, but looking left and right, up and down, before drawing in the slack of the reins and lightly kicking the horse's girth. His path back to the main group did not waver, but he was unusually silent in camp that night, staying awake and looking up at the wet leaves as the others slept.

His scowl eased, his mustache drooped almost to his chest, and he seemed remarkably at peace.

Freebuttons and wavy-faces carried old demons with tricky ways. Swallowing them was not for the uninitiated and never for those suffering the way Istvan suffered. Sometimes the demons in the mushrooms would befriend internal devils and soothe them, but that, she guessed, was not his main reason for gathering them.

In the Far East, freebuttons were sometimes chewed by warriors intent on going into battle in a highly focused, emotionless, killing rage. Some called it putting on the Bear Skin. Feronantus would have called them Berserkers.

On the thirtieth day, on the night of a full moon, under a starry sky, Cnán stumbled over some of Istvan's handiwork.

She had moved north nine verst, planning to head back to the main group that night. The woods and the undergrowth were thick enough that she was obliged to use established trails. Deep down one of these, she had been cut off by a band of Tartars escorting a man dressed in a coat thick with swaying sables. He wore a shining black helmet without a visor, and his features were darker, almost blue-black. He was long-nosed and sharp-chinned, handsome in his way, and she thought he might be from the southeast, the transmontane lands beyond Tufan, warm and humid places that Alexander had long ago thrust into, even now being stormed by the Mongols.

The presence of this sable-hung merchant alarmed her. Cnán had striven to guide the knights away from main-traveled roads, to avoid confrontations, speed them along, and let them keep their strength for their main purpose—crazy as that purpose might be. But now that might be impossible.

She tracked this orderly and quiet band and soon understood their purpose: collecting furs from itinerant trappers. Furs were coin of the realm in these parts, and Mongols had traded them for many centuries. Peoples on the fur routes often used cut-up pieces of sable and mink as earnest of additional reserves—like bills of exchange, only more representative and tangible. The whole, uncured furs were strung on cords like drying fish and hung off the backs of the sumpter horses or piled on top, or, as with this merchant, safely stitched to the owner's coat.

Along the edge of a small lake, where the old oak forests had given way to meadows and young birch, the merchant and his guards approached a thin column of smoke, and there, beside a small, open campfire, they bargained with the eldest of a small band of trappers—a wizened brown man who spoke Georgic and Slav, but no Mongol. He was closely attended by three swart, thick-bodied boys, possibly his sons.

After taking his pick of their finest furs, the sable-coated Southerner ordered that some of his own goods be removed from the pack animals and disbursed to the trappers—dried venison and several ceramic jugs.

There followed a round of toasts, and then the merchant and his guards departed. Soon the trappers were happily drunk, and as dusk settled, they curled up on the lakeshore, letting their fire go out.

Cnán hoped to follow the merchant until the last of the daylight, at which point she would build a lean-to and sleep until dawn. But before that time arrived, from her grassy cover, she heard a single, awful scream. Then shouts, rising to cries, each snuffed out in its turn.

The fur trader and his company heard the commotion as well. As she watched from her cover, they bunched together on the periphery of a grassy meadow, murmuring among themselves. Soon they decided it was best to move along—no doubt making note that bandits were about.

But Cnán suspected this was no bandit. She doubled back to the trappers' camp and found the entire group pieced out along the lakeshore. Two of the younger men sprawled on the ground, a hundred paces or more from the cinders of the campfire, each at the end of a long trail of blood. Both had been shot with arrows that had since been collected, presumably by the assassin who had shot them. Closer to the camp, the third young man had taken an arrow up through his neck, passing into his skull, where it had lodged so deeply that its owner had snapped it in half in a furious effort to worry it loose. Its bloody empennage lay discarded on the ground nearby, and Cnán recognized the fletches of gray goose feathers that Istvan liked to use.

The elder's death had been quick—a single slice across his throat had nearly severed his head—but he had then been hacked and kicked about, limbs and chunks of flesh mixed with the reeking shards of the jugs. The entire camp smelled of old man's blood and thick, sweet Georgian wine.

Abomination, she thought.

She knew the hoof marks of the horse that had wandered down to the lakeshore to drink while her master did his filthy work. It was Istvan's blue roan stallion.

That horse and his rider were now moving northwest, hunting the fur traders.

CHAPTER 8:

THIS IS HOW MY FATHER HUNTED

The buck was mad with fear, its hooves tearing up clumps of earth and grass as it tried to escape. The central pathways had been blocked with makeshift fencing, and most of the narrow channels between the groupings of trees and brushes were protected by a soldier with a spear. Its sandy brown hide was dappled with red; it had tried to crash through the brush a few times already, only to be turned back by the metal point of a spear. None of the cuts were fatal; the privilege of the kill was saved for others.

It clattered to a stop in the center of the path, its hooves sliding on the river rock. Its ears flickered, reacting to the unnatural sound of the hunting party.

They were not quiet.

A spray of crossbow bolts ripped the air around the animal, and one jabbed deep into its right foreleg. It brayed with pain and tried to leap away, but the leg didn't work quite right and the deer stumbled. It shied away from the laughter and shouts that came on quickly in the wake of the crossbow bolts.

Gansukh trailed the main hunting party, bow held at his side. He had an arrow nocked, but he was in no hurry to fire it. The garden had been turned into a fenced arena, and the nobles were hunting captive animals released into the enclosed space. When he had spotted the men setting up the barriers, he had realized how the hunt was going to be held, and at the time, his only concern had been making sure that he would be involved. Now that he was, he found he had no stomach for it. This wasn't hunting. This was slaughter.

He was uncomfortably aware his attitude mirrored his presence at court these past few weeks: he was on the verge of Ögedei's inner circle and, at the same time, a step outside it. Lian's warning kept echoing in his head: it wasn't just his actions that would be judged, but also what the others said about them. He had to hide his disapproval well, before someone noticed and said something to the *Khagan*.

"Missed!" Ögedei shouted at his companion as they jogged toward the quarry. Behind the pair, a retinue of red-faced, panting courtiers struggled to keep pace, lifting the hems of their robes as they ran. The *Khagan* was smiling widely, oblivious to the grass and mud stains on his saffron-gold robes. Clearly he was enjoying the hunt.

"I've got him next shot," Munokhoi said as he slowed to finish loading his weapon. The multi-tiered crossbow—a complicated contraption of springs and levers—seemed to Gansukh to be more trouble than it was worth, but there was no arguing that, once it was loaded, it was a deadly instrument. Munokhoi grunted as he finished cocking the slide and raised it to fire.

Munokhoi kept his hair short to the point of baldness, and combined with the gauntness of his face, this gave Munokhoi a skeletal appearance, despite the youthful length of his facial hair. Thick and muscled, his arms were anything but the thin sticks of a corpse. A pale scar ran from behind his left ear and disappeared into his tunic. There was no shortage of rumors as to how Munokhoi had earned the scar, but Gansukh hadn't cared enough to figure out which one was true. Every warrior had stories about their scars, and most of them were lies.

From behind them, Gansukh watched as Munokhoi focused on the target. Ögedei was still breathing heavily, but the Day Guard stood like a stone, his chest barely moving. The muscles in Munokhoi's neck tightened as he put pressure on the wide trigger of the crossbow, and he leaned into the recoil of the weapon as he released all three bolts.

The buck was turning as the bolts hit it, and two of them slammed into its neck and shoulder. The third caught it in the eye, spraying blood and humor as it drove clean into the animal's skull. Its front legs buckled and it fell into a plot of peonies.

"Just one of a dozen marvelous killing machines the Chinese have invented." Munokhoi grinned and offered the crossbow to Ögedei. "Clever little bastards," he laughed as he strode toward the fallen deer.

The hunting party flocked around Ögedei, making noises of pleasure and encouragement at the sight of the weapon in his hands. Gansukh didn't even bother getting any closer. He could see well enough from where he was.

Beyond the clump of fawning courtiers and nobles, Munokhoi stood over the dead animal and raised his sword. Sunlight caught his blade, turning it into a flash of silver as it came down, and the buck's head was severed with a wet crunch. He knelt and lifted the head by its antlers, blood running down his hands. "For the Lord of All Under the Blue Sky," he said, turning the head toward Ögedei, "I humbly present this trophy."

"Keep it," said Ögedei. "I have far more impressive trophies in my collection." He laughed, gestured for a servant to bring him another wineskin, which he traded the massive crossbow for, and took a huge thirst-slaking swig.

Another deer was already being led into the garden, and as soon as its handler pulled the rope from about its head, it bolted. It bounded toward the eastern wall and eventually realized there was no escape in that direction. It turned right, disappeared for a second behind a clump of trees, and then came into view again, at the crest of a small rise near the southern edge of the garden. It was still frightened, but it was far enough away that the lure of the short grasses at its feet was stronger. It looked about briefly and then dipped its head cautiously toward the grass.

Ögedei belched and seemed to notice Gansukh for the first time. "What do you think of my guard's new toy?" he asked, loudly enough that the attention of the hunting party swung toward Gansukh. "It is an impressive weapon, is it not?"

Gansukh bowed his head, recalling Lian's warnings about reputations and perceptions at court. *Not even the Khan of Khans was immune to the lure of the favorite activity.* "It seems to shoot very well, *Khagan.*"

Ögedei looked at Munokhoi, who had put down the severed deer head. The *Torguud*'s arms were coated with blood. "Yes," he said, "*it* does, doesn't it?"

Gansukh winced internally at the stress Ögedei had put on his words, and judging by Munokhoi's expression, he had heard the same inference.

Before Gansukh could figure out a way to turn the conversation, Ögedei waved the wineskin at the servant holding the crossbow. "Show me how it works," he said, and when the servant froze, Ögedei shook his head. "Not you," he snarled. "Gansukh."

The servant almost fainted with relief and rushed toward Gansukh, all but throwing the complicated crossbow at him. He would need both hands empty to hold the thing, and suddenly he couldn't remember the sequence of knobs and levers Munokhoi had had to operate to wind it. The servant thrust the weapon at him, entreating him with his eyes to take it, but Gansukh made no move to do so. "With all respect, *Khagan*," he said, forming each word carefully and slowly, "I believe we should leave some of these Chinese contraptions to the Chinese. I hunt best in the way my father taught me—with a simple bow."

His bow had belonged to his father's father, a simple recurve of wood and horn and sinew, worn and repaired over the generations. *Like the sky*, he thought as he took several steps forward to put him a little bit in front of the cluster of bodies around the *Khagan*. *It would never change*. It felt right in his hands. There was no complicated machinery that drove it. It was just an extension of his own arm.

Munokhoi snorted. "That old stick? Good for hunting sickly oxen, I'm sure."

Gansukh allowed himself a slight grin as he gauged the distance to his quarry. The buck was still grazing on the hillock, keeping a wary eye on the hunting party. *Yes*, he thought as he lifted his bow and took aim, *let him do all the talking. He is better at it than you*. A difficult shot, but not an impossible one. Gansukh inhaled slowly until his chest was full, and then he held his breath until he was sure his frame had settled. His arms were like stone. The point didn't waver. Waiting...

"Too far," Munokhoi said, too loudly. A slur of noise went through the hunting party, assent voiced but not as pointedly—as publicly—as Munokhoi's dismissal.

The buck reacted to the sound, sensing danger, and it raised its head. The muscles in its legs quivered, but it was too late. Gansukh's arrow, released on the heels of the noise from the gathered crowd, struck the deer in the breast. The buck staggered once, blood trickling down its white fur, and then it collapsed.

There was no sound coming from the group now, and Gansukh steeled himself to not turn and look at them. "And that," he murmured, almost to himself, "is how my father hunted."

Ögedei's mighty laugh broke the silence. "I see your father was as good a marksman as mine."

Gansukh turned to face Ögedei, bowing his head respectfully at the suggested compliment. When he raised his head, he realized Ögedei was still looking at him with that penetrating gaze he had seen before, when he had first arrived. It was as if a cloud had cleared from the *Khagan*'s sight, and he was seeing something that had been hidden from him for a long time.

Out of the corner of his eye, Gansukh watched the servant put Munokhoi's Chinese contraption down on the grass. No one else seemed to notice, or care.

◆ ◆ ◆

The early autumn sunrise spilled into the valley too slowly for young Ögedei. He lay prone on the frozen ground at the edge of a marshy clearing. Cold seeped into his bones and the dim light played tricks on his eyes. The hunting conditions were less than ideal, and he had been lying there too long.

Before the sun had threatened to peek over the ridge, Ögedei had been watching two shapes in the grass near the river's edge, alternately sure they were animals or his older brothers in their hide jackets. His muscles were starting to cramp. Even if he could be sure of the identity of his quarry, he might not be able to pull his bow well enough to shoot it.

He pushed himself up on his hands and knees and inched forward. The brittle grass stalks scraped against his shoulders.

The sound was like tree branches thrashing in his ears, and he was sure his quarry could hear him.

Ögedei pressed his belly and chest to the ground and breathed out slowly. He was nearly within shooting distance. If he nocked his arrow, stood and shot in one motion, he'd have a reasonable chance of bringing down a deer.

But if the shapes were his brothers, there would be no end of ridicule around the fire that night, and more than ridicule if he actually hit one of them.

Ögedei cursed under his breath and slowly got up on his knees. He had to be sure. Suddenly the quiet of the valley was broken by loud laughter, and Ögedei felt all the air rush out of his lungs. He remained still for another few seconds, listening for the ridicule that was sure to be coming, and when it didn't, the fact his brothers weren't laughing at him did little to lessen the sting of what might have happened. He waited for another burst of laughter, and then he stood and strode forward as if he had just entered the clearing, unconcerned now with the loud rustle his body made against the brush. Jochi, his eldest brother, had turned toward the sound, and he waved in recognition.

"Third Brother! Come over here. Chagatai is telling of his great exploits last night," he laughed.

Ögedei smiled as he jogged toward his older brothers. He felt no shame at the nickname, for it was the simple truth: of Genghis Khan's four sons, only Tolui was younger.

Of the siblings, it was generally agreed that Chagatai was the fairest, and his ability to spin a tale as well as any court entertainer certainly contributed to his ability to charm the women in the camp. Jochi relied more on his position as the eldest son, and Tolui managed to parlay his ever-present maladies into a constant flock of attentive and doting women who followed him everywhere. While Ögedei thought the image he saw in the water pail was somewhat comely, most said he was much like his father—both in physical appearance and mannerisms.

"She had such natural bounty," Chagatai exclaimed to Ögedei as the younger brother approached. He held his hands out in front of his chest, as though this gesture was enough for Ögedei to understand all he needed to know about the story he had been telling Jochi.

"Have you ever been with a woman with small breasts?" Ögedei asked.

Chagatai screwed up his face with an expression of mock outrage, and Ögedei laughed, forgetting his disappointment.

"Indeed, Chagatai, it seems every girl you bed has fully ripened," Jochi teased. It wasn't just his height that made it clear he was the oldest of the three. There were already lines around his eyes, and his gaze was much more direct and piercing. He stood with his shoulders thrown back as if he were ready to accept the weight of leadership. He raised his hands and began to massage the air in front of him. "Ooo! Firm!"

Chagatai backhanded him across the shoulder. "Those are my melons!"

Their laughter was cut short by a new voice booming across the clearing: "I'm impressed!"

From the line of trees behind where Ögedei had been lying, an imposing figure and four other men strode into the morning sunlight. Light glinted off the gold around Genghis Khan's neck, and that same light seemed to vanish into their black cloaks.

"Truly, what great hunters are my three sons," Genghis said. "You've killed your deer and skinned them already, because here you are, telling stories. Come, show me what you have taken."

Ögedei looked at Chagatai first, and seeing nothing but panic in Second Brother's face, he turned his gaze toward the river. His cheeks burned with shame, and all the bitterness of the failed hunt churned his stomach. Genghis and his four men surrounded them easily, as they stood rooted to the ground. *Like frightened deer*, the thought flashed through Ögedei's mind. If Genghis had been alone, if there were no witnesses to the Great Khan's discovery of his sons' failed hunt, they might have escaped with only the sting of their father's tongue. As it was, they were liable to receive a real lashing.

"Father—" Jochi started.

"We have more than seventeen hundred mouths to feed." Genghis spoke without rancor or anger, but they knew better. "The farmers of this territory cannot supply us with enough food—even if we were to eat them as well."

Ögedei shivered uncontrollably, not just at the thought of cannibalism, but the calm and effortless way his father suggested the possibility.

"I know you are not skilled hunters, but I sent you out to *learn* how to hunt," Genghis said, responding to the statement Jochi would not be allowed to finish. "We need provisions. Every member of the tribe must be able to—"

Ögedei silenced his father with an upraised hand, and out of the corner of his eye, he could see a pair of the Great Khan's guards react as if Ögedei had slapped his father. He ignored them, raising a finger to his lips. He turned his head slightly, enough to see his father's face.

"Deer," he mouthed, and pointed. Downstream, on the opposite bank, stood two good-sized does and a huge buck.

Genghis's eyes followed his son's finger, and with a nod, he motioned for the guards nearest the river to kneel. The familial discipline was forgotten as the group instinctively focused on their prey. The guards slowly lowered themselves to the ground; their swords were of no use in this hunt, and they were only in the way of the hunters. Jochi and Chagatai began to creep along the riverbank, their boots crunching softly on the river rock. Genghis unslung his bow and stepped toward the river, his eyes locked on the deer. Ögedei was at his side, bow ready as well, and as one they moved into the shallows, their boots submerging in the icy water.

The deer heard Jochi and Chagatai and looked up, presenting perfect broadside targets for Genghis and Ögedei. The two men were ready, and their bowstrings hummed at nearly the same instant.

Two arrows buried deep into the neck of the buck, the soft slap of the impacts nearly inaudible across the river. The does started, though, much closer to the sound, and bounded off, disappearing into the woods. The buck struggled to keep its footing and then pitched forward, falling into the river where it thrashed helplessly.

Ögedei whooped loudly and, raising his knees high with every step, splashed downstream as quickly as he could to stop the downed buck from floating away.

"Good shot," shouted Chagatai. The guards whistled their appreciation, and Jochi even clapped as Ögedei splashed past.

The deer had stopped kicking, and the river was starting to tug at its body as Ögedei reached it. He stopped with a splash, made sure he wasn't standing on loose rocks, and grabbed at the deer's rack of antlers. "Help me," he shouted.

"No!" Genghis's voice cut across the water.

Bracing his feet, Ögedei looked back over his shoulder. Jochi and Chagatai were halfway across the river, and they too had stopped at the sound of their father's voice.

"You two," Genghis said, "go back to camp with the women; this is not your kill."

Chagatai looked crestfallen immediately, and his shoulders slumped. Jochi hesitated.

"Go back!" Genghis roared, and Ögedei's older brothers reacted quickly to their father's tone and reversed their course. They stood, dripping, on the bank, unwilling to fully depart from the scene, and Genghis's personal guard came down to stand with them as Genghis drew a great bone-handled skinning knife from his sash and strode into the river.

Ögedei felt his balance slipping, and he had to turn back to the dead deer. The buck was bigger than he had thought, and his grip wasn't very good. He couldn't pull it out of the river by its antlers. He needed to get in a better position, and as he was trying to get behind the animal's hindquarters, his father appeared at his side and slung his left arm around the shoulders of the dead animal.

"Ready?" Genghis asked, his face close to Ögedei's.

He could smell his father's breath—meat, garlic, the slightly sour aroma of *airag*. For an instant, he was a baby again, being held close by his father—this strange man he had never seen before, but who looked at him with fierce eyes. He had felt—without knowing these concepts—safe...protected...

"Lift!" shouted Genghis, and Ögedei stumbled back, the buck's body lurching toward the bank. He stumbled over his own feet and slammed hard to the ground, the buck's antlers jabbing him painfully in the thighs. The deer's head lay in his lap, its body mostly out of the river.

Genghis stepped up onto the bank and looked down at Ögedei, a peculiar expression on his face.

"What?" Ögedei asked. Then, taking his father's expression as disapproval, he contended, "If we'd kept talking, the deer would have heard—"

Genghis shook his head. "That was the right decision," he said. "I am not angry that you interrupted me."

Ögedei tried to reason what his father was thinking.

"Why did you choose the buck?" Genghis asked.

Ögedei glanced at his brothers and the guards, and made a snap decision. *Tell him the truth.* "Father, it was the best choice. It never crossed my mind to shoot one of the females. I should have. I'm sorry—"

Genghis waved off the apology. He sank down to the ground beside Ögedei. He pushed the skinning knife into the ground between them, and then he looked back across the bank at the other men. "Do you know what your brothers would have done?"

Ögedei wasn't sure of the right answer, but sensed Genghis was going to tell him the answer anyway, and so he stayed silent.

"They would have known I would take the buck and they would have chosen a doe."

Ögedei's stomach knotted again, and suddenly he was the foolish stripling again. The one who had nearly shot one of his brothers, mistaking him for a deer. "We would have had more meat," he said, the words burning in his throat.

"Yes, that's right, Ögedei. We would have had more meat."

Ögedei stared at the animal in his lap. He wanted to shove it away. The thrill of the kill was fleeing, and all that remained was the sickening shame of his own inability to think beyond his own desires.

"You took the buck because you wanted it," Genghis said. "You wanted the prize it offered. You didn't defer to me or ask my permission, and you didn't hesitate."

Ögedei looked at his father, but the Great Khan was still looking over the river, his eyes unfocused.

"You did," his father said slowly, "exactly as I would have done." He looked at Ögedei finally.

Ögedei stared at his father, searching his face for some explanation of the sadness he heard in his father's voice. He sensed everything around him—the hardness of the buck's antlers in his hands; the water of the river flowing beside them; his breath, in the cold morning air, mingling with his father's; the deep lines around his father's eyes that had been drawn there by the sun and the weight of his position; the sudden emptiness in his stomach as his fear and panic vanished—and he knew there was more to his father's words than a simple compliment. For a moment, it was just the two of them on the riverbank, and the rest of the world didn't exist.

Father and son. More alike than not.

Genghis nodded, and the moment passed. He pushed himself up from the grass and undid the leather tethers at his belt for the skinning knife's sheath.

"What are you doing?" Ögedei asked.

"It's not my kill," said Genghis. He looked down at Ögedei once more, and then turned on his heel and walked into the river.

Ögedei looked at the knife in the ground. He recognized it as his grandfather's. An object that predated him, predated even his father. He pulled the blade free of the wet earth. The metal glinted dully in the bright morning sunlight. It was a long blade, but weighted well, and it moved easily in his hand.

He pushed himself out from beneath the corpse of the deer and considered the animal's bulk. Perhaps half the weight of a pony. It would take more than one trip to carry it back to camp, even after it had been parted. It would take the better part of the day to haul all the meat back to camp.

Ögedei looked across the river. Genghis had reached the far side, and one of the guards had given the Great Khan his cloak. "Hey," he shouted. "One of you. Stay with me and help carry back this meat."

A long moment followed where the only sound was the river gurgling between them, and then Genghis threw back his head and laughed. He shooed Jochi and Chagatai off, sending them back toward the camp, and two of the guards followed. Genghis spoke to the remaining pair, and the one who had given the Great Khan his cloak nodded. The Great Khan looked back at Ögedei one last time and then left, a guard following him.

By the time the remaining guard made it across the water, Ögedei had gutted the deer and was peeling the skin back from its haunches, revealing the lean meat beneath.

CHAPTER 9:

THE MADNESS OF THE MUSHROOMS

At the morning camp, Feronantus took the news of Istvan's nocturnal malfeasance with irritated resignation. He thanked Cnán, then walked off to the edge of a river, where Eleázar and Percival were idly trying to fish with a weir made of stripped and woven branches. They spoke for a few minutes, then gathered the rest of the group. Cnán watched the leader with no less interest than she had Istvan. She'd had trouble making sense of his name—which sounded vaguely Latin but wasn't—until she had heard Taran addressing him as *Ferhonanths*. Then she had come to understand it as an old barbarian name—probably Gothic—that had been Latinized for use in polite company.

Feronantus motioned for the young Binder to join them. "Cnán has been scouting," he said.

"Gone much of the time," Roger said brusquely.

Feronantus took exception to his tone. "She returns often enough to keep us on course, and she sees to it we don't cross paths with anyone who might distract us. But she brings us a problem I've been dreading since we gathered at the chapter house."

He described what Cnán had seen on the lakeshore.

"Surely we can't criticize a man for his grief," Roger said.

Percival saw it otherwise. "We are on a quest," he said. "We work as brothers. Istvan has never truly joined us, and now... It's not grief. It's pure, mad vengeance. Why would he kill a family of trappers?"

"He's after the Mongol guards," Feronantus said. "He's tracking tax collectors and studying hamlets that cooperate with the Mongols. Cnán has seen the results of one night's work. I doubt that this was the first. He has done it before and plans to do it again. This will attract attention—probably has done so already. The countryside is in shock. War parties wander everywhere—Mongol and otherwise. No doubt there will be teams of horsemen riding guard wherever there are goods and money to gather and carry off."

"We tend away from the main paths," Cnán said, "but fur traders go everywhere there are woods and fields and water."

"What you saw," said Illarion, "was but one small contingent of a larger group. You may be assured that there are other parties just like it, ranging over the country, venturing into every forest and valley where furs are to be had. By this point in the season, they will already have harvested a small fortune in trade goods. Which means..."

"They'll have protection," Taran said.

Roger stared at Cnán resentfully. She glared back. A wry grimace came over his face. He looked away for a moment, then glanced back and nodded by way of apology. "It's not good news," he explained. "Istvan was one of our bravest and most loyal."

"Mohi broke him," Finn said, in rough Latin.

"Illarion saw his family killed and did not break," Feronantus reminded them. "We can ill afford to lose anyone. I will send a party of three with Cnán—Eleázar, Percival, and Raphael. She will track Istvan, and the three of you will persuade him to rejoin us."

"With respect, the girl is no rider," Eleázar said. "Should we get into trouble—"

"For that reason," Feronantus said, "she will do her utmost to keep you out of trouble. Which is how I prefer it."

And that was final. All the knights looked on Cnán, some with hooded eyes.

Cnán had not expected to be hobbled by a trio of knights. She stated clearly, in a piping voice, that she could not range wide enough to find clear paths and also accompany Istvan's search party. "He might return on his own," she added.

Feronantus waved this aside. "You've done a fair amount of ranging already, have you not? He's a big man, on a big horse, with a distinctive hoof and gait. You will find him quicker than we could, and Percival, Raphael, and Eleázar will jess and hood him, if necessary, before he attracts more attention. We shall tarry in this place for one day, mending our britches."

Cnán suppressed a smile. This was Feronantus's all-purpose phrase covering not just britches-mending but sock-darning, meat-drying, herb-gathering, and all the other chores that, if they did them today, would enable them to ride hard tomorrow.

"Then," Feronantus said, "we shall head east on our present course. Kiev is—at most—a fortnight's ride. If you don't find him in three days, return to our track. Our trail will be embarrassingly obvious to one of your talents. We need you, Cnán, to show us a safe route through the outskirts of Kiev. All there is likely misery and confusion."

"We should not go to that accursed place at all," Roger remarked.

"Ah, but we must," Percival said. "It is a matter of honor." But Feronantus, weary of this argument between friends, held up both hands to silence them.

◆ ◆ ◆

This region as a whole was inclined to marshiness, and of late the band of would-be Khan killers had been skirting the southern borders of a broad wetland—a *mariscus*, in Feronantus's favored tongue—that covered more ground than some European kingdoms. Cnán knew as much because she had recently spent the better part of two months working her way across it from east to west. For the most part, they had been good months, since edible plants were as common in the bogs as Mongols were scarce. With no assistance from humans, plant life sorted itself out from low to high, according to its preferences regarding drainage.

In the bottoms, reeds grew thick and green in rain-swollen waterways; low, shrubby willows populated a patchwork of sandy islands; and other water-hardy stuff grew in such profusion that only the most wretched fugitives were to be found there. Merely to dwell in such a place was to confess oneself an outlaw or a witch. The valleys and ravines that drained into it were choked with trees, generally too small and mean to be of interest to any, save charcoal burners.

The rolling lands above, while hardly high and dry, were at least suitable for cultivation, striped with fields where people still lived, otherwise open grassland that was perfect for conveyance of Mongols.

Cnán favored none of these fens and banks as routes for the party's expedition. But she soon discovered that, through these wetlands, there was often a buffer—sometimes miles across, sometimes only a few paces wide—between the impassable woods of the damp ravines and the open farm country where trees grew thick enough to provide cover but not so dense as to impede progress.

She had schooled these knights in the way of traveling along the edges of the less brambly forests, slicing briskly over open land when she provided a favorable report but rarely straying more than a few moments' gallop from the cover of the trees.

The country along Istvan's likeliest course of travel alternated between stands of oaks and meadows, broken by the odd low rolling hill and a mottle of bogs and small, clean lakes. Rarely, mounds and crowds of rounded boulders poked up through forest and field, as if dropped from the pouches of giants. Cnán knew some of these as hideaways for robbers; on her long trek west, venturing up from the great marsh to filch apples or raid farmers' root cellars, she had found their leavings on several occasions at the entrances to the tumbled boulders.

The hideaways were empty now. That was not a good sign. Robbers knew when the pickings were too dangerous.

Raphael kept mostly silent as they rode, moving steadily beside her. Eleázar, with his heavily inflected Latin, was more voluble and quick with plaints—to her irritation at first. But as the day wore on she came to understand that it was simply his way, and the way of his people, to say what was on his mind.

Eleázar had been the last of the group to arrive at the chapter house outside of Legnica, and she knew the least about him. During the first day or two of the journey, she had rarely been able to suppress her amusement over the preposterous size of his weapon—a two-handed sword that was slightly taller than he was. It took him forever simply to draw the thing, hand over hand, out of the long sheath slung along his back, and the other knights had much fun at his expense, discussing how, in the event of an attack, they would set up a defensive perimeter around Eleázar so that he would have time to draw and poise his sword, hopefully before the rest of them were dead.

Percival also kept his thoughts to himself, and dark thoughts they might have been; he rarely smiled.

The first run of tracks they encountered was perhaps two days old. Cnán dismounted from her mare—the only mare in the group, as the knights preferred stallions—and knelt in the sun-dappled mud and grass of a narrow meadow. Raphael and Percival joined her, kneeling on the other side of the run, two steps back. Mongols at this late stage of their campaign often rode horses other than steppe ponies; war, as Feronantus had observed, was hard on horses, and armies continually replenished their stock. When Mongols rode larger and more complaisant Western horses, the combination made for unique tracks. Unhappy mounts tended to sidle when given unfamiliar prods or spoken to in strange tongues.

Cnán pointed out the disarray of tracks to Raphael, who nodded. Percival bent to observe splattered remnants of the stale, less than a day old. He lifted mud to his nose and curled his lip. "Could be a farm beast or sumpter. Lowly black bones are left with the least spirited mounts."

Cnán knew that gelded animals could serve well in battle, but these knights, by long tradition, preferred stallions and were tough to convince. Mongols, on the other hand, rode mares into battle—sometimes mares in heat, perfectly capable of distracting stallions.

Two of the riders in this group, however, had been mounted on destriers that met the knights' full approval, likely stallions from the stock of a local voivode. Their stale cut deep into the mud and smelled pungent. The tracks showed that the horses were frisky but contented enough and their riders adept.

She thought that a fair sign that a pair of dukes or their minions were being protected by the Mongols, much as the fur trader had his cohort. Betrayers of their people—opportunists. Survivors.

No wonder Istvan was on a rampage.

Percival walked away twenty paces and followed the verge. Their horses watched with ears cocked, then shook their heads and bent to pick at the weeds and grass. Eleázar, quite rightly, pushed them away from a growth of white-flowering creepers. No need for sick or drunken mounts.

Cnán summed up the facts to Raphael as they watched Percival. "Twelve riders," she concluded. "Mongols or Tartars. Of middling discipline, bored by their duties. But they are accompanied by two voivode—or at least local officials riding noble horses. Possibly tax collectors or surveyors. Not prisoners."

"Good," Raphael said. He smiled at her skill.

"Surveyors?" Eleázar asked sharply. But the look on his face was baffled rather than skeptical.

"The invaders measure their lands and count their wealth," Raphael said. "They plan to stay."

Percival rejoined them. "Istvan watched them from the woods," he said. "Then he rode after. He's turned wolf."

No more needed to be said. Cnán also went to the verge to study the tracks of Istvan's roan, and when she returned, they mounted. The woods here were thick with berries and nettles, the ground boggy, which discouraged passage by riders and possibly all but the local bears. Earlier, Cnán had caught the spoor of several of those. One, interestingly enough, appeared to have briefly tracked Istvan.

"A regular caravan," Raphael observed. "Whom shall we greet first?"

Eleázar and Percival suggested they follow Istvan and not the tax collectors.

"We will meet with both soon enough," Cnán said.

Raphael and Percival saw her meaning. The dense woods would soon bring quarry and prey together. Did Istvan truly believe he could outfight such a group?

Eleázar took this news glumly.

Percival nodded. "Istvan is our quarry. It matters not whom he hunts—for now."

"He rides quickly," Eleázar observed.

"And so will we, now that we've found his trail."

◆ ◆ ◆

Cnán had thought she knew the general lay of this country, but she was taken by surprise when the forest spread wide around a shallow oxbow. The greater width of riverbed was a long swale interrupted by mounds of boulders. The swale ran generally west to east, and their little party had fetched up along its southern verge. It did not have a bank as such, for the floodplain was broad, interrupted by a complicated plait of rain-fed streams and willow marsh.

The forest kept well back from this intermittent course, but several farmers had lately taken advantage of the rich soil, and of not having to clear trees, to lay out fields of green oats. They had plowed around the cromlech-like rocks and between the low, damp runnels thick with reeds.

It was late in the day. A warm breeze sprang up from the southwest, spreading waves across the reeds. A low habitation was visible on the opposite side of the river, about a verst away. There was no sign of human activity. Perhaps the locals had planted, then hid—from both tax collectors and war parties.

"There must be a ford we can use," Raphael said, scanning up and down the bank.

"Let's not linger," Percival said. "No high vantage, lots of opportunities for sudden attack."

Before them the riverbed was overgrown with tall, winding stands of reed and willows through which riders moving east or west, following sandy or shingled shallows, could pass unseen. Warriors, even mounted ones, could rely on scrub-hidden pickets and spring out with complete surprise. Higher banks and even low mounds complicated an already confused landscape—the worst place imaginable for tracking, finding, and avoiding surprises.

Cnán surveyed the skies above this tangle and spotted the greatest concentration of crows and other birds—starlings, blackbirds, even robins—wheeling to the east. No buzzards—yet. She sniffed the air, but the westerly breeze was unhelpful. "Horses and cows that way," she said. "Another bigger farm, maybe. Birds pick the dung."

Eleázar gave a low whistle. "Can you tell whether it's cattle or horses from here?" he joked.

Cnán pursed her lips.

Percival rode between them, wheeled, and looked south into the trees from which they had only just emerged. "Devil's own woods," he said. "The fur traders must have crossed—and Istvan behind them. Let us go and find whatever ford they used."

They arranged their tack and gear for a crossing.

"Istvan won't fight us, will he?" Eleázar asked.

"Those hellish mushrooms—" Raphael began but didn't finish his thought. Percival looked downriver, then spun his horse about and suddenly plunged ahead toward the sun-warmed side of a boulder pile.

The rest followed.

"There's a war party on that hill," he explained. "Thirty or forty of them. Sun's in their eyes. Don't see us yet, I hope. We're the prey now."

They skirted into the long shadow of the outcropping and gazed east through the sheltering fronds of tall reeds. Percival was right. The war party consisted mostly of Mongols, riding an assortment of horses.

"The main body, as Illarion predicted," Eleázar said.

"Maybe. They're going the same way we are—maybe even tracking us. We can't go back."

"Following Istvan too," Raphael said, and it was difficult to tell whether this was meant as question or assertion.

Percival shook his head. "We can use these rocks to our own advantage—unless they track as well as Cnán. But we must warn Feronantus." He struggled with a difficult decision: whom to send, whom to keep here to protect their guide and their doctor—whom to sacrifice. He stroked his horse's neck, his brows drawn tightly together. "The last bloody thing we need is a pitched battle," he said.

"Not much choice. The forest walls us in on both sides. We can't escape into the woods unless we dismount," Raphael observed.

"We can't walk all the way east!" Eleázar said.

"You have another idea?"

"Outride them!" Eleázar said.

For the first time in quite a while, a trace of a smile stole across Percival's lips. "Outride a company of Mongols?"

"We can do it," Eleázar insisted, "if we gather some spares."

"Spares," Percival repeated.

Raphael, to this point, had been silent. He cleared his throat and glanced significantly at Cnán.

She was ready for it. Some part of her was already saying good riddance to these heedless adventurers. What was an adventure, anyway? To any normal person, a problem. A disaster. Only the rich and the foolish would actually seek one out. "I'm faster without you," she said, as if agreeing. She dismounted and handed the reins to Eleázar. "A spare," she explained.

"But, my lady—" said Percival.

She sneered at being called that. "I'll cut through the woods on foot and reach Feronantus by morning. The rest of you, do as you will. If you lie low, they'll probably pass you by. If they don't kill Istvan, you can do it."

"Kill one of our Order? Are you in command now?" Eleázar cried.

She ignored him—as did Percival. "It would be best if they learn nothing of Feronantus," Percival said. "Killing Istvan may not be enough. Perhaps we here need to make a stand and die to save the rest."

Cnán squinted up at the knight. Truly, he seemed happy to make it easy for his death to find him. Perhaps he was as crazy as Istvan. "If the Mongols pass," Cnán said primly, "and there's no fight, we can join up at the end of this tangle, beyond the farms. I'm pretty sure there's a route directly east from there."

"Hold up," Raphael said, rising in his saddle. He pointed north. "More riders coming out of nowhere. Those damned reeds. They're surrounding the farmstead on the other side of the swale. Nine, ten...and...another formation, rising up like the spawn of dragon's teeth. A patrol. Breaking off and coming this way."

A moment passed while they all absorbed that news.

"No," Raphael said, "I'm wrong. They too are looking for a ford. Going to rejoin the big group on the hill."

The others watched in silence as their doom closed in from two, perhaps three, sides.

Percival leaned over Cnán. "Go," he said. "Go now. This will not get better."

CHAPTER 10:

THE ARCHERY LESSON

Lian waited for Gansukh within the enveloping embrace of the willow. The tiny leaves didn't hide her completely, but the drape of its boughs was enough to give her some semblance of security. Plus the shadows were getting longer… She sighed as she flicked tiny fallen leaves from her hair, regretting she had opted to wear it down. She'd told him to meet her again before the sun set, and now it was getting perilously close to slipping behind the bulk of the palace.

She wasn't supposed to be here, not without an escort.

The garden still stank of blood. The gardeners were still working on a flowerbed when she had first arrived, and she had hurried past them, barely sparing them an imperious glance that would—hopefully—suggest they turn their eyes elsewhere. Also, she hadn't wanted to look too closely at what they were doing.

Something had died in that flowerbed. She'd heard from one of the Chinese servants that the main course for the banquet had been shot just a few hours earlier. In this garden. It had died *right here.*

A momentary shudder ran through her frame. *No better place to learn how to fight,* she mused.

Lian had pressed the servant woman for details, and she had given a very satisfactory account. Everyone was talking about the young warrior and his bow. She hadn't dared to ask the servant woman about Munokhoi's reaction; while there would be satisfaction in hearing this tale, Lian knew what to expect: Munokhoi would be even more on his guard against this *intruder* from the Great Khan's older brother. Her task would be even trickier now. Gansukh had been right this morning: she was afraid for him.

Lian sighed with relief as she spotted him, and she rustled the willow boughs to get his attention.

Gansukh approached and parted the boughs carefully. "Why are you hiding in there?" He cocked an eyebrow. "If you're trying to look like a beautiful painting, don't bother. I'm not that sophisticated." He seemed more at ease, pleased with the day's events.

"I don't have free rein to walk the compound at night like you," she snapped.

"Ah." He looked over his shoulder and then stepped closer, letting the boughs cover him as well. "I suppose I should offer to protect you then…"

She put her hand against his chest and stopped him. "You should," she said. "By teaching me." She smiled at his expression. Clearly he had been thinking something else had been planned for tonight. "Remember? We made a deal. I help you; you teach me to fight."

Gansukh frowned at her hand on his chest. "Yes," he said. "We did."

Lian was pleased that he didn't try to deny making the deal. She hadn't brought it up since that first day in the bath. It had been a dangerous proposition, one that could have gotten her killed had Gansukh been more inflexible in his ways. But Master Chucai had said the young man had promise, that he seemed to be able to think for himself and had confidence in the decisions he made. As long as he trusted her, she could trust him; while she had that trust, there were some skills she could stand to learn.

She wasn't going to stay here forever.

"But you weren't planning on training like that, were you?" Gansukh gestured at her green silk robes—much finer than the one she wore earlier in the day. "Tie your hair back, at least."

She gathered it up—slowly, knowing he was watching her—and wound it into a bun.

"What?" he asked, some irritation creeping into his voice.

"I need something to hold it in place," she pointed out.

Exasperated, he grabbed a willow branch and snapped off a long piece. With a jerk, he stripped the leaves from it and held out the thin stick. "Will this do?"

She smiled and took the offered twig. She slid it into place without a word.

Gansukh admired her. "You're too small," he noted, and as she drew breath to object, he continued. "Until you get a little more muscle, I don't think you're going to beat anybody in hand-to-hand combat. If it comes to that, you don't have a chance. We need to try something else." He stepped out of the confines of the tree and scanned the garden grounds. "Yes," he said when he spotted a pair of guards. "Wait here."

Before she could object, he hurried off. He called to the guards, getting their attention, and they came together, their heads bent toward Gansukh as he launched into some complicated story. Somewhat curious, she stepped forward so as to better see what the three men were talking about, and when Gansukh paused and the two men looked in her direction, she realized she was standing out in the open.

The guards laughed, and one of them handed Gansukh his bow and quiver before slapping the young man on the back. Saluting them with the weapon, Gansukh trotted back to Lian. "Come," he said, handing her the quiver to carry. "Let's go over by the wall. There will be less distractions." He looked back over his shoulder and waved at the guards as they walked off the path.

"What did you tell them?" Lian wanted to know.

"They're *Khevtuul*," Gansukh said.

"Yes, I know that." The *Khevtuul* were the imperial Night Guard, the ones who watched over the *Khagan* while he slept. "What did you tell them?"

"Munokhoi is *Torguud*. Day Guard." He grinned at her. "You said it yourself. People like to talk at court. Word has gotten around already."

She stared at him, amazed at what she was hearing. He shrugged, misinterpreting her look. "I told them I wanted to show you my bow, but as I had left it in my chamber, I was in danger of losing face to a pretty woman. I asked if they could lend me one." He hefted the weapon. "They were happy to be of assistance."

He slowed, glancing around at the open space they had wandered into. "Plus," he noted, "they'll leave us alone, thinking that we're…"

Lian nodded, trying her best not to smile. "Engaged in an *archery lesson*," she finished for him, arching an eyebrow. *Yes,* she thought, *Master Chucai was right. He does have promise.*

Gansukh blushed. He took the quiver from her and gave her the bow instead. "Try it," he said gruffly, embarrassed now.

She lifted the weapon and put her left hand on the grip. She drew the string back and let it go with a faint twang.

"Not like that." Gansukh moved behind her and touched her shoulders lightly—pulling them back, adjusting her stance. "Arm all the way out. Point your knuckle at the target. Now draw back across your body." He brought her elbow back slowly, guiding her arm. "Same thing with this hand, knuckle at the target." Her body turned slightly under his guidance until she was pointed toward a stand of aspen trees, their pale trunks glowing in the late-afternoon light.

He stepped back and she let go of the string, feeling a difference in the motion. "I feel it," she said.

"Okay," Gansukh said. "Try it a few more times, but without letting go. Just work on making the motion of pulling back smooth."

Lian shifted her footing and shook her shoulders loose. She took a deep breath and raised the bow as Gansukh had shown her. Wrapping her first two fingers around the bowstring, she used her back and shoulders to pull the string back—farther this time. She wished she could see Gansukh's expression, but couldn't spare a glance in his direction; she'd lose her grip if she let her concentration lapse that much. Satisfied that she could draw the bow, she relaxed and then repeated the exercise two more times before letting her arms collapse. Her biceps were burning.

"Well done," Gansukh said. "You took to that very naturally."

Lian said nothing as she reached for one of the arrows in the quiver Gansukh held.

Gansukh caught her hand before she could pull it out. "Careful, that's sharp."

"I'm not a child." Her tone was petulant enough that she might as well have stomped her foot and threatened to throw a fit.

"Just try not to cut those soft hands," Gansukh said, not averse to needling her more. "Place the arrow here." He put the quiver down and approached, intending to show her more directly. "Grip the end tightly like this. See?" He drew the bowstring back in one smooth motion. It was testament to their difference in size that Gansukh could reach around her and pull the bow back nearly without touching her. Nearly.

After a moment, when they both silently acknowledged their proximity to one another, he let out the tension in the bowstring and moved away. "Your turn," he said.

Lian firmly grasped the bow and tried to draw the arrow back, but the taut bowstring barely moved. The combination of gripping the arrow and pulling back the string was thwarting her efforts. Gansukh was right. She had drawn a bow before, but this one was much stiffer than others she'd used. Gansukh had made it look so effortless. Determined, she pulled her shoulders back and, firmly wrapping two fingers around bowstring and arrow, managed to stretch the bow half as far as Gansukh had.

"Good," he noted. "Now shoot that tree." He pointed at the one they had been aiming at earlier.

She grunted as she released the arrow. It flew wide, to the right, and vanished, with a whisper of sound, into a thick bush. Her fingertips burned from the rough string. She looked at them, expecting to see blood, and was surprised when there was none.

"I should've told you to hold your breath when you aim," said Gansukh.

"You're not a very good teacher," she said, embarrassed to have missed the tree completely.

"Weren't you prattling on about patience a few days ago," he said, "in one of those scrolls you've been reading to me?"

She smiled as she bent over and pulled another arrow from the quiver on the ground. "I didn't say I was giving up." She nocked it and drew the string back, trying to remember everything she was supposed to do. Gansukh tried to guide her with his hands on her arms, and she shrugged him off. "I'd prefer to try without your help."

She tried not to think about him watching her. *Hold your breath!* she thought at the last second. Her right hand opened and the arrow sprang from the bow, sailing across the garden to land square in an aspen's trunk.

"There," she said. "Perfect shot."

Gansukh shrugged. "Not bad. Can you do that again?"

She glared at him and then bent to retrieve another arrow. "How went the hunt?" She tried to keep her tone nonchalant.

"Fine."

She looked at him. "Fine?"

He remained oblivious to her tone. "Yes, it was fine." When she stood in front of him—eyebrow cocked, hand placed on hip—a bewildered expression crossed his face. "Oh," he realized. "Thank you for your encouragement. You were very helpful." He nodded toward the bow and arrow in her hands. "Now nock that arrow and see if that last shot was just luck."

"Luck?" she said, not moving. *Is that all you're going to tell me?* she suggested with the tilt of her head, and when he didn't respond, she turned her back to him with a sweep of her skirts. "I'll show you luck."

Lian braced her shoulders and pulled the bowstring back as she had before. It was still very hard to pull it back far, but the motion felt a little easier, a little more natural. She even remembered to hold her breath this time. The bowstring gave a soft twang and the arrow stuck into the tree three hands below the first.

"Not luck," Gansukh acknowledged. "Let's try something a little more advanced then, shall we?"

"Wouldn't you say that was a good shot?" she asked.

Gansukh gave the matter some thought. "I'd say it was a good shot," he said, "for someone shooting a non-moving target at close range in near-perfect conditions." He glanced around the quiet garden. "But I've never been given a shot like this in hunting…much less in battle."

He was going to be impossible.

She sighed. "What would you have me do then?" she asked.

"You mean, in terms of archery?" He smiled.

Lian gave him a cold stare.

His grin faded and he cleared his throat. "I'd have you take the same shot while walking." He picked up the quiver and held it out to her. There were only three arrows left.

"While walking?" Lian asked.

Gansukh nodded.

Lian took the arrow and nocked it without looking. She started to her right, but quickly realized she'd lose sight of the target in a few steps as she passed behind a row of manicured hedges. She switched directly and raised the bow, front knuckle pointed at the tree. Even at a slow walk, her front knuckle refused to stay on target—bouncing not only up and down, but also side to side. She tried to predict when she would be on target and let the arrow loose. It hit the ground barely a horse-length in front of her and skipped across the grass.

Gansukh offered her another arrow. "Don't look at your knuckle this time; look at the target."

Lian grabbed the arrow from him and nocked it quickly in the bow. He knew what he was talking about and she should listen to him, but his calm was getting under her skin. She pulled the bowstring back, and as she walked to her right, she released the arrow almost immediately. She had been shooting blindly, just trying to use up the arrows so that this lesson could be over. The arrow flipped end over end and rattled into the tree's lower branches.

"Not bad!" Gansukh said, much to her surprise.

"You are laughing at me," she said.

He shook his head. "You stopped thinking about what you were doing. That is a large part of shooting well. It's also the hardest thing to teach." Gansukh grinned again. Lian couldn't decide if this near-constant grin of his was getting annoying or endearing. Perhaps both.

"You lied to me," she said, holding the bow in both hands.

"When?" he asked.

"When I said you weren't a very good teacher."

Gansukh shrugged. "I didn't correct you," he said. "But you didn't tell me you'd handled a bow before either." He took the last arrow out of the quiver and held out his other hand for the bow. The grin was gone and his face had become unreadable.

Lian handed him the bow. "Not that tree," she said, swallowing hard. She couldn't tell what his intention was and thought it best to try to redirect him. Had she gone too far? Trust had to be mutual. "That's too easy for you."

"Pick a tree, then," he said and swept his left hand wide to indicate she had the entire courtyard to choose from.

Lian looked about and spied a sapling some ten horse lengths away. "The young birch, by the wall there," she pointed.

Gansukh turned abruptly and walked away from her at a brisk pace. For several moments, she was sure she had made a terrible mistake, and when he turned and began sprinting toward her, she was certain she had. As he closed the distance between them, he showed no sign of stopping; in fact, he was increasing his pace.

"Gansukh!" She threw herself to the grass. He jumped over her, bow raised and arrow drawn back. She heard the bowstring twang. Where she had fallen clumsily, breaking her fall with her hip, he tucked his head and rolled in the grass three paces in front of her.

"Are you okay?" He walked over to her as if nothing had happened.

Wanting to get off the grass as quickly as possible, she accepted his hand. His grip was firm, and she flew off the ground as he pulled her up. Their bodies pressed together, their faces but a few fingers' width apart.

"Did you hit your target?" she asked in an attempt to make him turn around and look. Even though she didn't want him to move.

He didn't. "I don't know, did I?"

Lian rolled her eyes and failed to stifle a laugh. His grin came back, larger than before. She pushed him roughly away.

"The tree, Gansukh. Did you hit the birch?"

Gansukh feigned surprise. "I was supposed to shoot a tree?"

She looked. The sun had gone beyond the palace now, and the entire wall was covered with shadows. She could still see the thin sapling, but she couldn't tell if his arrow had found its mark. She started walking toward it, and Gansukh fell in beside her.

"Nice fall," he said. "But you'll need more practice."

Lian shot him a look.

"I'm serious!" he protested. "Falling is an important skill in hand-to-hand combat. You'll see."

"I can't wait," Lian replied sarcastically, but couldn't help but notice how her body thrilled at the thought of being so engaged with this man.

Preoccupied, she came to a full stop in front of the birch before focusing on the arrow buried a quarter of the way up its shaft. Without comment, Gansukh began gradually working the arrow loose.

"Gansukh, you should have…" she faltered.

Gansukh continued to loosen the arrow from the tree but looked at her.

She met his gaze and started again. "Why didn't you shoot the crossbow as Ögedei Khan requested?"

His face darkened and he chose to focus on the task of retrieving the arrow for a little while longer before answering. "There's a difference between hunting," he said as the arrow popped out of the tree, "and slaughter."

"You killed your deer with a bow," she said.

"Yes," he said. "With my father's bow. And Ögedei appreciated the significance of my choice." He dropped the arrow in the quiver. "After the *hunting* was done, we walked in the garden together for a little while. He told me a story about hunting with his father, the Great Khan, when they were on campaign together."

She was surprised. The serving woman had failed to mention that the two men had had a private moment together. "Excellent, Gansukh. That was beyond my expectations. You are proving to be a good study."

They retraced their steps to the aspen grove.

"I need to be," Gansukh said as they walked. "I may have impressed the *Khagan*, but I fear I made Munokhoi even more my enemy."

"Any time spent trying to curry Munokhoi's favor is not only futile but dangerous," Lian pointed out. "It is wiser to focus your energy on the *Khagan*."

Gansukh nodded thoughtfully. "I think you're right." They reached the tree with Lian's arrows in it, and he plucked them out with a sharp twist of his left wrist. "Enough archery for tonight," he said, changing the subject. "How about some basics in hand-to-hand…"

Lian raised an eyebrow. "I think all this archery has worn me out."

Gansukh laughed. She liked his laugh, low in timbre and from the belly. His eyes nearly disappeared when he laughed, much like her father's.

"Next time, then," he said. He slung the bow across his back and indicated the path toward the servants' quarters. "Let me walk you back to your chamber, at least."

She accepted his offer and kept the notional pleasure of more physical contact with him to herself.

✦ ✦ ✦

The sun had departed, and the palace was transitioning to its nighttime activities. Voices could be heard from the main palace, and servants carrying dirty dishes and piles of clean linen scurried around Gansukh as he ambled toward his own chamber. He stepped aside for a group of concubines. They glided past with effortlessly small steps, their elegantly coiffured heads bowed down in polite deference, leaving a scent of flowers in their wake. Groups of dark-cloaked *Khevtuul* were out there in the gloom, patrolling the grounds.

Near the garden gate, Gansukh encountered a familiar imposing figure. Gansukh bowed respectfully. "Master Chucai. Good evening."

Ögedei's chief advisor responded with a slight nod. "I trust the evening finds you well." His robe and beard were dark spots in the gloom, making the man seem like an apparition, a floating head come to haunt him.

"It does," Gansukh replied. "I was just getting some fresh air. This first hour of nightfall has a splendid quality to it."

"You have been keeping up on your reading?" Chucai smiled. "Or I should say, has Lian been reading you up?"

"Yes. She's a talented young woman, as far as the Chinese go," Gansukh said. "The scrolls are boring, but she certainly gives me something to look at."

Chucai looked at him shrewdly. "I heard about the hunt today," he said.

Gansukh nodded and waited for him to continue.

"Karakorum is different from anywhere else in the empire. We are transformed by it, would you not say?" Chucai pursed his lips. "No, that's not correct. We are *revealed* by it."

Gansukh shrugged, mainly to hide the shiver that ran up his spine at Master Chucai's words. He was spared from replying by a crashing sound behind him. He turned, and for a second, he couldn't place the source of the sound, but then he spotted the broken tile on the ground. His pulse racing, he immediately looked up at the roof of the palace, and a flash of movement caught his eye.

"Intruder!" Chucai shouted behind him.

An assassin, Gansukh thought. *Here to kill the Khagan.*

"Guards!" Chucai continued to raise the alarm.

The figure had disappeared already, and Gansukh glanced around wildly for any sign of the *Khevtuul.*

Too late, he thought. He started to run toward the back of the palace—in the direction it seemed the figure had been moving. *By the time the guards arrive, he'll be gone.*

It was up to him to catch the assassin.

CHAPTER 11:

THE BANKHAR

The reeds were tall enough to hide Cnán, as long as she skittered through them in a crouch. She could not see more than an arm's length in any direction, and so she paused every so often to check the direction of the sun and make sure she had not strayed from her line: straight along the slowest, shallowest flow of the main channel, close enough to the bank that the reeds remained high, not so close that the ground beneath her feet turned into sucking mud. This path would cut between the Mongols who were surrounding the huts on the opposite side of the swale and the main force on the near side. The only thing the least bit chancy about it was that it might bring her nearer to the patrol Raphael had noticed crossing between the Mongol groups, but all she need do was keep her wits about her and squat low if she heard hoofbeats. Gazing into the sun, they would never see her. Her movements might shake the tops of the reeds. But here fortune was with her again, for the southwest breeze was shaking all of the reeds, and as long as she didn't do anything stupid, like move in a perfectly straight line or trample the stalks into the mud, she would be hard to detect.

Those men were distracted anyway; she could tell as much from their shouts, trying to deliver some urgent news to the main group, but unable to make themselves heard over the wind whispering through a million stalks.

This was hardly a way for Cnán to make good time, but before long she would be past them and into a section where she could make her way down disused channels or dart from one stone outcropping to the next, favoring the long shadows of the late evening.

The more she could collect from sounds, the less she needed to risk looking. Splashing hooves told her that the patrol had found a ford. Light clashing at first as the horses— she guessed four of them—trotted through ankle-deep water. Then deeper sloshing as they went in up to their knees, followed by near silence as they passed through the gut of the channel, the horses' bellies, she imagined, carving wakes in the stream like boats' hulls. Then relieved and satisfied words from the riders as they felt the ground angle upward again, sporadic liquid bursts as knees broke the surface, and then the same series of noises, reversed in order, until hooves were once again thumping on solid ground—this side of the river, perhaps an arrow shot ahead of her.

She was about to risk movement again when her ears picked up something else—another creature emerging from the river, following in the wake of the horses. Not a man, for it went on four feet, but too small for a horse.

Then a shuddering, flopping noise, enveloped in a hiss of spray.

She crouched and froze. It was a dog. It had entered the ford at the same time as the four riders, but had fallen behind as its paws floated free of the river bottom, forcing it to paddle across the main stream, fighting the current the whole way. Finally it had trotted up onto the shore and shaken itself. It let out a suggestion of a whine, seeing how far behind it had fallen, then sprang forward, running to make up for lost time. Then, just before entering the tunnel that the horses had trampled through the reeds, the dog stopped.

Stopped and sniffed the air.

It happened to be straight downwind of her.

Dogs had poor eyesight. She rose just high enough to see it. She did not recognize it at first because she had been imagining something in the way of a hound, small and lithe. But what she saw, casting about for her scent, looked more like a bear. She'd seen them before. She'd even been chased by them. And she had watched others, not as skillful at evading pursuit or climbing trees, being torn apart by them. This was a bankhar—one of the heavy-boned mastiffs that the Mongols kept roped outside their tents as watchdogs.

They must have been using it to track Istvan.

And it knew she was here. That was obvious from its posture: it stood on its stout, corded legs as still as she was. Other than a slight quiver of its flanks, the only thing it moved was its nostrils. It would hold this stillness for as long as it took to catch a definite scent or hear some movement. Then every muscle in its body would go into action. If it was like the others she had seen, it had twice her weight and could run at double her speed.

Again a faint whine. The great head lifted and turned. The massive jaws opened in a slow pant. The bankhar was trying to make sense of the new spoor. Watching it, she found herself wondering what it could guess about her. The scent it had found was human, but not the one it had been tracking for the last couple of days. Her scent would betray her sex, obviously, but could it tell if she was frightened? She wasn't. Not yet. But she would be soon.

She couldn't run. To trigger the chase instinct of a bankhar was death—about the worst kind of death imaginable. Better to stand and face it.

It gave out a low, gruff bark, declining to a suspicious growl, and began trotting toward her, lowering its head and casting its heavy muzzle back and forth.

Cnán backtracked along the trail of parted reeds she had made in her own wake. Putting more distance between herself and the dog couldn't hurt, as long as she did it quietly—and she could move very quietly. There were no trees to climb. She couldn't outrun a bankhar on open ground. She could probably outswim it, though. But first she would have to get to water that was deep enough for swimming and too deep for the dog's paws to get purchase on the bottom. She remembered a backwater, about a stone's throw behind her, where she had suddenly slipped knee-deep into a stagnant pool. A lateral sprint out of the reeds, across the intervening sandbar and straight for the water might work. But it was her last resort; it would betray her position, not only to the bankhar, which would come right at her, but to the four Mongol riders now picking their path up a rocky stretch of riverbank, still oblivious to the fact that their dog was on the trail of new and unexpected prey.

He—for she could see now that it was a non-gelded male—let out a little woof and broke into a trot, confident now that she was worth chasing. She began retreating with greater speed and more noise, fighting what the Shield-Brothers referred to as the *fobo*, the irrational fear that would, if you let it rise out of its hole, seize control of your body and make you do things that would assuredly lead to your death. In this case, the *fobo* was telling her to turn on her heel and run for it.

The ground grew muckier under her feet. She risked a quick look, saw the dark backwater growing closer and closer, but it was shallow enough that the bankhar could wade it, and it was separated from the main channel by a sandbar, which she would have to cross before the creature plunged its fangs into her leg.

She prepared to slip off her tunic. She could trail it behind herself as she ran. The dog would snap at it, rip it out of her grasp, waste a few moments shaking it like a squirrel while she dove naked into the water and swam away...

Or was that the *fobo* trying to bubble up?

A whine from the bankhar quickly rose to a shrill bark. It was very close now.

Her feet felt the backwater's slimy edge. This was foolish.

She stood tall and faced the dog. Startled, it plowed to a stop. Then it barked loudly and steadily, alerting its masters. She glanced over its head and saw the four Mongols. One had reached the top of the bank and was looking in her direction. The other three abandoned their climb, turned, and began picking their way down the bank to see what was happening. They first spotted the bankhar, then her, and pointed, exclaimed, stood high in their stirrups to get a clearer view—and reached for their bows.

Keeping the bankhar in sight but not staring it in the eye, Cnán slowly sidestepped, going knee-deep into the stagnant water, a loop of current only a couple of arm spans across. The bankhar started after her, stopped, growled, barked again. A bluff charge, trying to make her panic and break for it.

She did not like dogs, but she understood them in the same way as she understood men: they needed a leader. A boss. And if you weren't the boss, the dog would appoint himself to the position. It had nothing to do with size. She had seen a rat chaser dominate a lumbering wolfhound with the sheer force of its personality.

She locked her eyes on the bankhar and willed it to submit.

A rumbling growl emerged from its huge chest.

She backed up out of the water and onto the sandbar.

One of the Mongols was riding straight for her. She could feel the terror rising in her chest, her heart hammering at the underside of her breastbone, booming in her ears.

The Mongol called out a word of command. The bankhar looked back at him, remembered who was boss, bounded into the water, and came up on the sandbar, close enough that he could have reached Cnán's throat with a single lunge. Only some cautious instinct, a concern that Cnán was more than she seemed, prevented him from killing her then and there.

Her fear took charge. She knew she was about to die— if not ripped apart by the bankhar, then shot through and through by the Mongol following after or the two behind him. Her heart slammed with such force that she could feel it in the soles of her feet.

Her feet?

The dog looked beyond her suddenly, then crouched and quailed. A word of astonishment escaped from the Mongol's lips.

Cnán swiveled in the water and mud just in time to see a colossus thundering up out of the river's channel, over the crest of the little sandbar, then springing nearly over her head, hooves plowing the air. She fell to the ground more from vertigo than anything else and lost sight of it for a moment. Twisting about again, she saw the bankhar somersault backward, a red missile hurtling from its shoulders to tumble along the sandbar.

Stumbling in reeds and muck, catching herself and straightening, she identified the colossus: a man on a horse. The setting sun was on his back, and his armor shined in her eyes. His left hand held the steed's reins; his right gripped a short staff whose head was lazily orbited by a fist-size lump of black iron studded with spikes. The spikes threw off a thick spray of the dog's blood.

The bankhar had skidded to a halt and lay on its back, one hind leg jerking. Half its head was missing.

The interval between the bankhar and the lead Mongol was a long stone's throw. Percival, in full gallop, took it in a few thundering hoof strikes. The iron ball, tracing an unhurried and inexorable path at the end of its taut chain, accelerated suddenly and passed without apparent loss of speed into the side of the Mongol's face—for he was attempting to turn away—and out the back of his skull.

Percival studied the reeds. "A spare!" he remarked casually.

Dumbfounded, she realized he was addressing her.

"Should I..." she fumbled.

"No. Reach the other side of the river," he said, and ignoring the two Mongols who were down at the river's level, spurred his destrier forward hard and steered it directly toward what looked like a low place in the bank. The steed faltered, then understood, drove itself at the notch in the skyline, and attempted the leap. Its front hooves came up on the top. Its hind legs had to scrabble at the bank for a few anxious moments, peeling off shovelfuls of dusty earth. But then its massive hindquarters bucked up into the air, and it was on the lip of the scarp. With a cry of triumph or encouragement, Percival drove it hard to the left, headed, apparently, straight for the lone Mongol who had made it to the top earlier.

And then Cnán lost sight of him.

The two Mongols remaining on the sandbar were finally unlimbering their bows. She doubted that they could hit her from this distance if she kept moving and made use of cover, but one could never tell when a lucky shot might strike home, and so she was disinclined to wait around and see what happened. She completed the move she had been trying to make while fleeing the bankhar, sidestepping across the bar to the main channel of the river. She had to take her eyes away from the Mongols for a few moments as she picked her way over a slimy fallen log.

When she looked back, one of the Mongols was settling awkwardly to his knees, reaching up as if to make some adjustment in his helmet. Then she noticed a shaft going in one side of his neck, angled downward, and she concluded that an arrow fired from the other side of the river had struck him.

She turned, dove, and swam for a dozen strokes. The current was sweeping her downstream toward the concealed archer, but she reckoned that was not a bad thing, and so she did not fight it, putting all of her energy instead into crossing the channel.

When she felt the bank rising beneath her feet again, she turned to look, letting only the top few inches of her head jut out of the stream. Now came the same thunder in the earth that had preceded the demise of the bankhar, and sure enough, Percival's head—and that of his warhorse—rose majestically above the edge of the bank. He had holstered the flail he'd used to such effect against the dog and the first Mongol, and now held a bloody lance in one hand and a teardrop-shaped shield in the other. Two arrows jutted from the shield, suggesting that the second Mongol had put up more of a fight. Thus encumbered, he let the horse find its own way down to the riverbank. Percival kept a sharp eye on the one surviving Mongol, who had sought cover in the reeds and was raising his bow. Percival was plainly visible from the bank's top. With an easy plunge of his shield, the armored knight collected a third arrow that would have pierced his mount's shoulder.

A shaft flew directly over Cnán's head and arced downward into the reeds; a bowman on her side of the bank—she guessed it was Raphael—was hoping for a lucky shot.

The destrier crashed down into the reed bed, Percival leaning so far back that he was nearly supine on its hindquarters. After a few moments of staggering about and realigning, horse and rider were once again united, and Percival now did something that—hard as it was to believe—made Cnán feel sorry for the Mongol: he wheeled on the firmer, sandy bed and charged, lance fixed at a low angle.

The Mongol understood perfectly well what was about to happen. He leapt up and ran, zig-zagging along the bank, feet sending up silver spray. Like a million terrified victims who had been caught out in the open by the riders of the *Khagan*'s hordes, he was now presented with a nasty choice: be trampled into the muck, spine and ribs crushed like so many crusts of bread, or have an eight-foot-long lance skewer his guts.

The Mongol spun about at the last instant, screaming his rage, and chose the lance. Percival gave it to him, hefted until the man's feet dangled, then rode on, torquing the corpse through the reeds until it slid off like a knotted rag. Glittering tails of spray from the horse's hooves almost hid the gore.

Cnán turned away with a sick sensation in her stomach, then climbed into a cleft on the northern bank, where she suspected that Raphael was hiding in some gnarly scrub. And that was where she found him, though he had already turned his back to her and was clambering through loose soil toward the crest. As he neared the top, he slowed, crouched, and held out a cautioning hand, warning her not to pop her head up. Then he seemed to change his mind. He'd seen something from the crest that let him know they were all right. He vaulted onto flat ground, resumed his squat, and gave Cnán a hand up. From any of the others—with, as always, the exception of Percival—she would not have taken kindly to this gesture. She was perfectly capable...but something in Raphael's manner always let her know that—between her and him—things were simple and fine, and so she slapped her hand into his and kicked against the bank with both feet until he'd hauled her over the top.

Below and behind them, Percival was collecting the Mongols' horses, stringing them out on a line so that they could be led.

"Spares," Cnán said.

"Good," Raphael answered and nodded across the river: not along the main channel, but to the south bank, which Cnán, trapped in the low reeds, had not been able to see until now. The first thing she noticed was the reed-hung corpse of the Mongol whom Percival had run down and slain during his foray over the bank's top. But then her eyes were drawn by movement farther off.

The hilltop where the main body of the Mongol force had gathered a while ago was now bare, but something like an avalanche or mudslide seemed to be flowing down its near side, throwing up a dusty plume that glowed like fire in the light of the setting sun.

They had been seen. The Mongols were coming for them.

"Gorgeous, in its way," Raphael remarked dryly, "but I don't recommend we marvel much longer. You, at any rate, are unlikely to take in any new or useful impressions."

"What the hell are you doing then?" she snapped.

"I believe I shall tarry, in case Percival needs assistance. I may be able to help him manage the spares or slow the Mongols when they reach the bank's edge."

"Did you have anything in mind for me?"

"Look in on Eleázar."

"And where is Eleázar?"

"Likely visiting whoever is surrounded in that farm," Raphael said, and he swiveled on deft toes, keeping as low as possible, to gaze in the opposite direction. "Judging from the number of dead and screaming Mongols in its vicinity, I wager it's Istvan."

To Cnán, this did not sound like a plan, or even the beginnings of one, but she knew better than to expect something fully thought out, and she approved of anything that would take her away from the forty or so horsemen coming for them across the floodplain.

Not far away, Raphael had tied his horse to a lance thrust into the ground. Trailing behind it on a lead, head down, pushing its nose through grass, was the pony Cnán had been riding. She unwound the taut lead from Raphael's saddle and sprang onto the pony's back with a confidence that surprised her. She was not above hoping that one of her companions might have witnessed her dexterity.

She pulled hard on the right rein and dug in her heels, then shouted in the way that the men did when they really wanted their mounts to sit up and take notice, and indeed, the pony reacted with a neck-arching start and broke into a gallop.

She was now riding hell-for-leather into the battle unfolding in the little farm. This was about half a verst away, on a weak rise that kept it above seasonal floods. From their former vantage point, they'd been able to make out very little of the stead, but now, closer, Cnán could see that it was an untidy warren of lean-tos, outbuildings, sheds, sties, smokehouses, coops, and stables. Not satisfied with that, the residents had added a haphazard assortment of peat ricks, haystacks, trellises, hutches, and beehives.

Cnán, in the last couple of years, had become a connoisseur of hiding places, shunning the open and gravitating toward the hidden, the complex, the knotted and gnarled— anyplace confusing and nasty for warriors and hunters. Had she been chased across the floodplain by Mongols—as, come to think of it, was now the case—she'd have gone straight to this farm. She'd have kindled a fire in the hearth, done all she could to make them think she was lodged in the main house, and then she'd have crept to its outskirts, buried herself in dung or straw, and peered out at them.

Waited them out. Watched and learned.

Istvan had likely done something similar. Cnán could not know this for certain—she had not yet reached the farm—but Raphael seemed to think Istvan was still alive, and it was simply not possible that he could have survived any other way.

Drawing closer, she saw evidence of a fray: Mongol bodies draped over split-rail fences, then what might have been a Russian noble in a black cape, sprawled and muddy in a hog wallow. More Mongols lay curled like fetuses around moldy bits of tossed haystack—along with one dead cow, its flank covered with arrows. Someone had cut the animal's throat and taken shelter behind the dead bulk.

Istvan had done more than just hide and watch. Some of the dead lay where they had fallen, but others had been arranged in grotesque postures. At some point—and recently, since only a little while ago they had seen ten live Mongols surrounding this place—Istvan had crept from concealment and gone to work with fast, eager blades, at close quarters. For the Mongols, keen on killing their prey, had committed the error of dismounting and entering that filthy and tumbledown maze. Not understanding that the one they'd been hunting was no terrified fugitive. Not just another gleaner, run to ground, praying that he could find some way to slip out of the noose.

Istvan had been waiting for them, chewing his mushrooms, timing it, perhaps, so that the ecstasy would come over him at just the right moment.

It had been a long day of odd and unforgettable sights, and now another presented itself: a Mongol backing away from the corner of a poultry hutch, slashing and thrusting with a short curved blade. He cared nothing for what lay behind his stumbling feet, but stared in horror and grunted like a whipped donkey—for the last second of his life.

From around the hutch, striking from on high like a silver bolt, a six-foot sword caught the Mongol where neck joins the shoulder, sliced down through his torso, and emerged from his opposite side, just above the hipbone. The two halves of him fell in opposite directions, intestines boiling out, as if they'd waited twenty years for an opportunity to leap free.

Not Istvan's work—that huge sword.

Eleázar stepped into view, making no effort to break the sword's momentum but letting it follow through, raising his hands above his head to keep its tip from plunging into the ground. He gracefully stepped around, with the sword's point as the center of his arc, checking behind to make sure that no one else was creeping up.

Getting caught in this melee was not going to help Cnán, and might complicate matters for Eleázar and (assuming he was in there somewhere) Istvan, and so she drew back and spoke calmly to her mount, peeling off from her course and convincing the horse to adopt a judicious trotting gait.

Not a horse person, she'd been slow to understand the others' fascination with spares. It made sense abstractly, of course. But it had taken the sight of the onrushing horde to really fix it in her mind. Several Mongol ponies were now wandering aimlessly about the perimeter of the farmstead, nosing about for forage. Thanks to Istvan, who had apparently shot some of their owners from cover—she recognized his shafts projecting from the Mongols' bodies—they were now spares, and she reckoned she could do something useful by rounding them up. To her, they paid little heed, but they were social animals and not above joining a herd. So she devoted a little while to gathering up the ponies and leading them in a slow whorl around the farmstead while she counted dead Mongols and waited for the final few to be hunted down by Istvan and Eleázar. The ponies became used to her, and she began speaking to them in Turkic, with which they seemed familiar.

The two knights finally emerged from the warren, and at the same moment, Raphael and Percival came galloping in from the riverbank. Istvan, red with gore, led a few more spares, and Percival, nearly pristine, tugged at a balky string of four. They now had three or four mounts for each of their group.

Cnán joined them. An interesting conversation might now have passed between Istvan and the others, but of course, there was no time. Indeed, the first and most impetuous of the Mongol outriders was already cresting the bank, though this had to be guessed by sound rather than sight, as the sun was well down and the scene lit only by gray twilight.

"The woods?" Percival suggested, raising his clutch of reins. "It's either brambles or arrows. I prefer brambles."

"Follow," said Istvan.

So they followed. And the Mongols followed them.

◆ ◆ ◆

Cnán found a partly open path through a stand of older trees. Almost immediately after they entered the shelter of the woods, cursing as they plunged in and out of the dense, prickly shrubbery, it became obvious that the knights had no idea what they were doing. Nor did Cnán.

All were inclined to view Istvan's actions with the utmost skepticism and argued among themselves whether their noisy movement was a mere feint; Eleázar reached the conclusion they were trying to draw the pursuing Mongols into a killing ground.

Percival said nothing. His plan was far from clear to the others—if he actually had a plan—and so the group spent several dangerous minutes reeling about, losing sight of each other, then regaining it, never knowing if the horseman approaching through the heavy brush was a lost member of their band or a Mongol scout.

"Nobody can fight in here," Istvan muttered, his words slow and slurred. His head passed through a slanting moonbeam, and he looked up and gaped with half-lidded eyes. A finger swipe of blood marked his face. He was still half-possessed by his mushrooms.

Cnán asked Percival if this was the moment he had spoken of earlier, when they would sacrifice themselves so that Feronantus's team might go on its way unmolested. If that were the case, she planned to disappear. At last, Raphael prevailed on Percival to explain his thinking and to please stop assuming that any of his companions had the faintest idea of what was in his mind.

Percival sidled away from brambles, then halted, only dimly visible. Cnán saw resolution in his posture. "We shall rejoin Feronantus," he announced, as if this had always been obvious.

"If we can find him, which I doubt," Eleázar said. "We shall be leading the Mongols directly to the others."

"Yes," Percival said, "and by the same token, we shall then have sufficient numbers to destroy them utterly."

"It would be…polite, at the very least, to give Feronantus a bit of warning before leading a company of furious Mongols into his camp," Raphael pointed out.

"I will ride ahead," Istvan began, spinning about on his roan, crashing through the brush—but faltered, as even he saw the fallacy.

"Not in these woods," Eleázar said dryly.

"Cnán shall go before us, swift and quiet as always," Percival said, "and we shall trail behind, slowly and noisily. Go now!"

This was the moment at which she would have gladly abandoned them all to the fates they deserved had it not been for the startling detail of Percival staring straight and steady into her eyes as he gave her the order. And so, grumbling, she led her pony between the trees. She could no longer see where she was going, but her feet could tell which way was downhill. At some point, she would have to recross the river—in the dark. She reckoned the best time for that was now. The Mongol company had only just made it over to this side. All of their energies, for the last little while, had been directed to that goal. They had braved risks and worked hard to achieve it. It was a simple fact of human nature that they would be strongly disinclined now to turn around and cross back, particularly if the evidence of their senses told them that the enemy, or at least the slowest and noisiest part of it, was right here.

◆ ◆ ◆

Once she had crossed the river, she traveled at a pace that she'd have been proud of on any other evening, but every time she paused to make water or to leave an exhausted pony behind came the rumble of hooves not far to her rear.

The Mongols were driving Percival and his company, or being dragged along in their wake; either way, both groups were moving at desperate speed, and since Cnán's only responsibility was to arrive in advance of them, she had to do likewise.

In the hours before dawn, as the sky brightened, she found that she was able to ride at a quicker pace. Cnán's remaining horses were fresher than the knights', which had been embroiled in this running skirmish ever since nightfall. The hoofbeats behind fell away, caught up again, swung to the east, then back to the west. She half believed they would circle around her and reach Feronantus, all of them, in a furious, fighting mob.

But she galloped into the Shield-Brethren's camp before the sound of the approaching combatants had grown loud enough to alert them. Rædwulf was on watch while the others slept. He recognized her from a distance and so greeted her with smiles and gestures rather than singing arrows.

"I hope you have finished darning your socks," she said.

"We're done with all that," Taran said evenly, from a relaxed squat. Rædwulf came around from the opposite end of the camp, bow in hand. "Why are you alone?"

"Percival sends his fond regards," Cnán said. "He's leading a small army of Mongols directly toward you and hopes that this will prove no special inconvenience."

Taran rose to his feet.

Rædwulf asked, "How far back?"

"You might have time for a good piss," Cnán said.

CHAPTER 12:

CHASING SHADOWS

O f the *tumen* who guarded the *Khagan* while he was in
Karakorum, a *minghan* (one thousand men) was desig-
nated *Khevtuul* (the Night Guard). They patrolled the palace
and the grounds after nightfall, and Gansukh knew there was
a distinct difference between nocturnal patrols and hunting
during the day. As the *Khevtuul* began to respond to Master
Chucai's alarm, Gansukh turned his attention to the buildings
surrounding the palace. The Night Guard would surround
the central building, and men with bows would be ready to
fill the dark sky with arrows. Some of them might even start
to search the surrounding area when they failed to find the
assassin on the roof, but by then it would be too late.

The tile had given away the assassin's location. Whatever
his mission had been, it was no longer foremost in his mind.
He was thinking about escape. Much like a deer once it is
spooked—it forgets everything in its headlong rush to flee.

The square around the palace was filling with leather-clad
figures brandishing bows and torches. Courtiers and concubines panicked, lifting up the hems of their robes and scattering like geese, the tassels on their hats and hairpins swinging
wildly. Gansukh silently cursed the men with torches—the

flicking light was spoiling everyone's night vision. Already it was almost impossible to see where the roof of the palace stopped and the sky began. Too many shadows now. Too many places for a man to hide.

The first moments of the chase were critical. Prey, once spooked, would bolt—either for a hiding place or to put the most distance between itself and its hunter. A hunter had only a few seconds to judge his quarry; he had to either anticipate its flight and get in front of it somehow, or if the prey was faster, he had to have more stamina. And know how to track.

The Imperial Guard wasn't comprised of hunters. Those who did go hunting with the *Khagan* simply spread out in a great circle, driving all the game before them. They weren't hunting one animal; their tactic was to round up every living thing possible—useful for the *Khagan's* sport, but a tactic that couldn't catch a solitary quarry.

Some of the Night Guard was pointing now, and Gansukh looked up. A pair of guards had found the assassin's route onto the roof and was giving chase. One slipped on the slanted tiles and fell, screaming. He clattered off the roof in a cascade of broken tiles and landed heavily on the courtyard stones. They were stupid to follow the assassin that way, Gansukh noted, but they were easy to spot, and they gave him a valuable hint as to the direction the assassin had gone.

The second guard trotted with more care, and when he raised his bow, he stopped. Before he could shoot, something hit him in the face and his arrow went wild. He slipped, but managed to catch the cap tiles and hang on. His bow slid partway down the roof.

The assassin had to go to ground somewhere, and Gansukh tried to recall the location of all the buildings surrounding the palace. To his recollection, they were all too far away. But jumping was the only way—the only *quick* way—off the roof.

The assassin had made a mistake, obviously, and had been spotted. Fleeing to the roof had been a desperate gamble, one that might have been successful had he not been betrayed by a loose tile.

Gansukh reached the southeastern corner of the palace and came to a halt. The southern courtyard was even more open, and the only structure that could possibly be a spot for a man to jump to was the enormous statue—the silver tree crowned by the four serpentine spouts that each spewed a different liquid. But the tree was barren other than its spouts and offered no place to hide, and the open ground surrounding it was rapidly filling up with a mob of agitated *Khevtuul.*

Men shouted to the west, and a clump of Night Guards raced toward the far side of the palace, drawn by a cacophonous crash of more tiles. Gansukh started to follow and then stopped. Behind him lay the garden. Its walls weren't very tall; he could, if he stood on his toes, reach the top of the wall, but the trees were much taller.

Something flickered across the sky, and a tall ash tree inside the wall of the garden swayed violently as if buffeted by the wind. The trees on either side barely moved.

Marveling at the assassin's agility and daring—such a leap was clearly the sign of a desperate man—Gansukh reversed his course and raced for the garden. With a grunt, he hauled himself up and over the wall. He landed easily and pushed his way through the hedges toward the vibrating ash tree.

Stones rattled on the path beyond the cluster of trees, and Gansukh tried to remember the route the path took through the manicured maze of trees and bushes. As he remembered it, the track wound haphazardly through the long rectangular space of the garden—clearly not a tactical route. More often than not, he had been distracted when he had been in the garden during the day. Gansukh dashed beneath a willow, its long branches whipping his face and shoulders, and found himself at one end of the long central clearing.

Not far, in fact, from where the deer he had shot earlier that day had been standing.

Ahead—*to the north,* he thought as he oriented himself— he spotted movement. A figure in dark clothes, nearly invisible in the shadows of the garden, but betrayed by spears of moonlight. Gansukh sprinted after him, trying to close the gap.

There was a gate in the northern wall of the garden and a guardhouse as well. Perhaps the assassin was running blindly and didn't know what lay ahead of him, but Gansukh couldn't rely on that chance. The man had gotten all the way into the palace. Surely he knew enough of the buildings and the *Khevtuul's* routines to plan both his assault and his escape. And if he didn't...

At Kozelsk, their plan had gone awry almost immediately, and he had to improvise a solution. He could still remember that feeling, that panic that gave way to a singular focus. Choices became easier. Survival became all-important. Nothing else mattered.

The assassin veered right, disappearing from the path, and Gansukh waited until he was past a large clump of cedar trees before dodging right as well. *The eastern wall.* While taller than the wall between the garden and the main compound, the outer wall of the palace wasn't intended to repel intruders so much as it was meant to separate the *Khagan* and his court from the sprawl of Karakorum. It wasn't wide enough to post guards on, but it was higher than a man could jump—even from horseback.

Behind him, Gansukh heard voices shouting, and when he spared a glance over his shoulder, he saw some of the trees outlined with orange light. *Torches.* The *Khevtuul* had figured out the assassin's ploy too, and were now charging into the garden. He thought he could make out the word "two," and then an arrow rushed by, nearly clipping his head.

In the confusion, they had mistaken him for another intruder.

◆ ◆ ◆

Lian had finished brushing her long hair when she heard the faint cry of alarm. Within moments the corridor outside her room was filled with the sound of running feet. She threw a long jacket over her light silk robe and went to investigate the commotion. As she left the narrow confines of her room, she was immediately swept up in the flood of similarly half-clad bodies. She tried to piece together a coherent story from the snatches of conversation she heard in the tumultuous rush toward the building's exit. A fire in the storehouses, an attack by the *Khagan*'s enemies, an assassin sent by the Chinese to kill the *Khagan* as he sat for his evening meal, a dozen assassins, each trained in a different manner of swift and silent execution—there was no coherence in the stories, she realized; they were all equally true and false. Panic was the only constant.

Outside was no less chaotic, and the concubines and courtly ladies huddled together like clusters of clucking chickens while the *Khevtuul* swarmed like an outraged hive of bees. Their attention was directed toward the palace, and Lian drifted like a ghost through the confusion until she reached the edge of the wide avenue around the central building. Ahead, on the western side of the palace, a flurry of *Khevtuul* boiled around a pair of lumps on the ground, and as Lian wandered closer, she realized the bodies were wearing the same garb as the guards around them.

She let out the breath she had been holding as she realized she had been worried that one of the bodies might have been Gansukh. Chiding herself for her reaction—as well as acting like a simple country girl where the young warrior was concerned—she turned to return to her quarters, but she paused when she heard Master Chucai's voice.

He was striding toward her, a black cloud that eclipsed the play of torchlight behind him. "What are you doing?" he demanded.

She clutched her jacket closed and dropped her gaze toward the ground. "There was a great deal of excitement amongst the ladies of the court," she said. "Like them, I was concerned for my safety."

Chucai growled in his chest, a noise not unlike distant thunder. "Go back to your room," he snapped. "Gather up the—" He flapped a long sleeve at the cluster of women. "Take them with you. It isn't safe. You should be inside."

Lian bowed. "Yes, Master Chucai." She brushed past him, hurrying to be out of his presence.

He caught her arm as she passed and brought her up short. His stare was indomitable, and she looked away, trying to hide from his gaze. "I'm sure young Gansukh is in no danger," he said, and when she blushed at having her heart read so plainly, he released her.

She fled back to her room, neglecting to bring any of the other ladies with her. All she wanted was to hide from the fact that he might be right: that Gansukh was safe and that she cared at all.

✦ ✦ ✦

There was no time to stop and explain. Gansukh slowed as he came to the outer wall of the palace, and he tried to quiet his breathing and listen for some sign of where the assassin had gone. The effort seemed futile, as the shouting and thrashing of the *Khevtuul* in the garden made it nearly impossible to hear any subtle sound, but he was rewarded with a scraping noise, followed by a grunt.

He had missed it at first, looking for the wrong thing. Not far ahead, wriggling against the wall like a black snake, was a knotted rope. He ran over and pulled it taut. There was some weight near the other end, and when he looked up, he could see the dark shape of the assassin as the man neared the top of the wall.

He chided himself for not bringing his sword and bow with him. But he hadn't realized the meeting with Lian was meant to be a martial one. He had thought...

Gansukh pushed those thoughts aside as he started up the rope. However the assassin had anchored it to the top of the wall, Gansukh hoped his weight would be enough to make the man not tarry and release the rope. The fall wouldn't kill him, but following the assassin up the rope was the only way he could hope to keep up. It would take too much time to race around through the north gate—longer if the guards continued to confuse him for another intruder.

The assassin didn't stop, and by the time Gansukh reached the top of the wall, the dark-robed figure was gone.

Arrows bounced off the wall around him, and Gansukh didn't wait for the archers to correct their aim. He leaped off the wall, landing and tumbling in a clumsy roll. He banged his left shoulder against the ground and ignored the flare of pain as he scrambled to his feet.

Which way? He was in a back alley behind one of the long buildings the *Khagan* used to store his possessions, and there were no doors or windows on this side. *North or south?* To the south lay the front gates of the palace and the large staging grounds at the head of the paved road that stretched through the main part of Karakorum. If the assassin were trying to disappear into the teeming chaos of the city, that would certainly be the route to take.

Gansukh hesitated. Going to ground didn't seem like the right choice. In that case, the prey counted on the hunter losing interest. But for an assassin who had just killed the *Khagan*? The hunt would never stop, and the only hope the man had for survival was to run as far as he could—as fast as he could. Trying to escape through a city of tents would take too long.

To the west and north of the palace were a number of gates out of the city. Most of them were crowded during the day with shepherds and goat herders trying to sell their animals, but at night the markets should be empty.

A woman screamed somewhere beyond the storehouse, and Gansukh's decision was made for him. He sprinted to his left, and when he reached the corner of the building, he spotted a small Chinese courtesan dressed in blue silk sprawled on her back in the middle of the street beyond. She was hurling curses at a swiftly moving figure.

"Stop! Intruder!" The northern guardhouse was behind him, and Gansukh ducked around the corner of the building as the guards on the elevated platform started shooting arrows.

It probably would have been wiser for him to wait for the *Khevtuul* to catch up, identify himself, and join with them in their pursuit of the assassin instead of being mistaken for the assassin's accomplice. Gansukh stared at the receding figure of the assassin as he raced down the empty street toward the market gate. *It would be wiser...*

Muttering a half plea/half curse to the Blue Wolf, Gansukh sprinted after his quarry.

CHAPTER 13:

WEST MEETS EAST

"**I** don't mean to distract you from what is most important..." said Brother Rutger as he poised the helm above Haakon's head.

"You mean, not dying under the blade of whatever comes out of yonder tunnel?"

"Indeed. But we need information about the Khan. His special pavilion sits above the south end of the arena, positioned so that the sun will never shine in his eyes. There must be wooden walls behind all that canvas, behind all those hanging drapes that obscure its interior. We know so little about the layout inside. How many sit with the Khan? Does the pavilion have gates or doors that we would need to break down should the javelin throw fail? A railing over which we would need to vault? Guards who would need to be put out of the way? What is the Khan's escape route should our first and second attempts miscarry?"

Haakon wanted to roar with anger, but it came out as a strangled laugh. "I am about to do battle with a demon," he complained, "and you want me to—"

"It's no demon," Brother Rutger said and spat on the loose ocher ground that had been tracked down the tunnel on the boots of surviving combatants. "It's a man dressed as one." He rammed the helm down onto Haakon's head and slapped him on the ass. Even through surcoat, chain mail, gambeson, and drawers, the impact came through solidly. "And the Red Veil," he added. "We still wish to know what lies on the other side."

Haakon grunted as he adjusted the helmet to suit him. The mysterious veil. It hung from the outer edge of the Khan's box, obscuring the southern gate from the arena. Victorious fighters were allowed to pass beyond the veil, but they had to be able to walk out of the arena without assistance. So far, no fighter had won his bout so decisively as to be without injury. Three other Brothers had fought in the arena before him. Two had won their fights, but their wounds had been severe enough that they had not survived the night.

Rutger put his hand on Haakon's shoulder. They regarded each other silently. Saying good-bye would be worse than useless, since Rutger and the others would see it as a premature admission of defeat. Like his brothers who had fought before him, Haakon knew he was supposed to be full of martial bluster. If anything, he should scoff at Rutger's unspoken concern and say something to the effect that he would return from this fight in less time than it took to run out to the gutter and take a shit.

But that wouldn't be true, and to speak so falsely—especially when Rutger would know he was lying—seemed to be behavior ill-suited to the role he was supposed to be playing.

I am a Knight of the Virgin Defender.

Haakon slapped his hand over Rutger's briefly and then tromped up the tunnel, adjusting his mail. With each step, the loose red earth became deeper and softer under his feet.

As he walked through the narrow tunnel, he reflected on Taran's final words to the young members of the

Shield-Brethren who would be fighting in the arena. As their *oplo*, Taran had never been one for grandiose speeches. His instruction had always been brusque, and his directive to his student had been equally to the point: *This is not a sparring tournament like the ones offered at Týrshammar. Here, given the chance, your opponent will kill you. Your field of battle will be constricted, and the ranks of spectators will confuse and disorient you. Ignore all of that. Remember the one rule: do not die. Keep your focus. Know thy way, warrior; know thy balance and strength.* Sophrosyne. *That is how you will prevail.*

Haakon had never understood the meaning of that Greek word, one of Feronantus's favorites. Raphael had once chided Feronantus that, in Alexandria, it meant *virginity*. Their leader had not demurred. Still, Haakon *was* a virgin...

At the end of the tunnel, two men—Mongols both, armored in the layered scale and lamellar of the steppes—stepped out to bar his way. Haakon paused as one spoke a single guttural word and held out his hand: *hold.*

Even though he was ready for the fight to begin, Haakon slowed. There was no reason to hurry. The sun was shining out there. As soon as it struck his helmet, he would begin to overheat. The rag-stuffed cap that protected his freshly close-cropped head would become saturated, and then the sweat would begin trickling into his eyes, ruining the view through the helmet slits. Not long after that, he would begin to lose focus and strength.

Sophrosyne. He could wait.

A third Mongol appeared and said something to the two barring Haakon's path, a flow of words both harsh and lyrically smooth, but babble to Haakon's ears. The two guards stood aside, and the third gave him a nod whose meaning could not be mistaken: Haakon was now to enter.

As he stepped out of the shadows, sunlight greeted him in a flash, blinding him. Blinking—waiting for his eyes to adjust—he tried to orient himself. The Khan's box, supposing it even existed, should be up there somewhere to his right, above the thick swath of red fabric that hung down to the sandy floor of the arena.

Haakon's view, from the western entrance, was obscured by ranks of spectators. Not Onghwe's Mongols—a snooty lot who didn't like to mix with inferiors—but a rabble of Saracens, Slavs, Germans, and Franks. All of them had betrayed their races to curry favor with the rulers of the world—or, depending on how you looked at it, made necessary deals to prevent their people from being destroyed.

In spite of these obstructions, he could see the bulbous shape of a pavilion draped with heavy fabric, shielding not only the Khan from view, but also protecting the pale necks of the Khan's concubines from the browning radiance of the sun. Satisfied that he knew where the Khan would be, he looked to his left, scanning the recently raked sand. The circle was large, maybe as much as twenty *faðmr* from where he stood to the opposite gate, more than enough space for two men to fight.

Haakon's brain quailed at the idea that this arena would host more than a pair of combatants. Surely they wouldn't send more than one against him at a time, not even for the perverse pleasure of the dissolute Khan...

Focus. Taran, again. *Fight as you were trained. The rest does not matter.*

Haakon scanned the circle again. He was the only fighter in the arena. He glanced over his shoulder at the Mongols behind him. Why had they blocked him? Why was he alone? Were they going to loose animals on him? Why...

Center, he chided himself. *Your mind will betray your hands. Stop thinking.*

Haakon adjusted his grip on his Great Sword of War and decided he would walk cautiously to the center of the arena. He kept his eyes on the dark opening of the eastern portal— the place where his opponent would emerge—and let the rest of his body relax.

The spectators became a blur of color and motion. Their raucous noise became nothing more than a rhythmic pulse, like the sound of the waves against the rocky foundation of Týrshammar's citadel. His heart slowed too, seeking to be in concert with those waves, and his breathing followed.

Zzzu! Zzzu! Zzzu!

He listened more closely. The crowd was shouting a single word in unison. Blurred together, their cries washed across the arena in a buzzing sweep:

"Zug! Zug! Zug!"

The spectators roared now, a thrashing storm of sound. Haakon slowly realized they were calling out a name, working themselves into a howling, ravenous mob. They craved blood, demanded death, and worst of all, they wanted *Zug!*

Haakon felt like puking.

In the darkness of the eastern gate something moved—a shadow of black and red with broad, square shoulders and a large white mouth. Slowly, emerging into the bright sunlight with all the panache of a royal concubine making an entrance into a court somehow filled with rude bumpkins, the outlandish figure emerged into the open.

◆ ◆ ◆

They were making that familiar noise—that buzzing sound as if a hundred bees were trapped inside his skull. His mouth was filled with the taste of metal and his jaw ached. He had vomited once already—a bilious stream of acidic *arkhi* that had spattered his *suneate*—and his stomach was so knotted he couldn't puke again.

His *suneate*, strips of armor bound in parallel and tied to his legs, had been spattered many times over the last few years— mostly with blood. More recently, throwing up before the fight had become a common occurrence. It had become part of the ritual of preparation. Just before he put on the mask, his stomach would rebel. The one part of him that had any feeling left, only his stomach could still muster any outrage at what he had become. The rest was numb, too pickled by the *arkhi* to care.

He was dead. A ghost, held in this world by the iron of his cage, by the blood debt he had incurred. They summoned him, screaming and shouting the name he had given them— the name he had *earned*. Their cries—that insistent buzzing of honeybees—woke him from his stupor; he would animate the bag of flesh, would wrap it in the carapace of his shame, and would send it stumbling toward the light.

Only then would he be given the skull-maker.

The noise would stop when he collected a head. The skull-maker, so bright in the light, would go round and round until it wasn't bright anymore. They would scream and shout for a while after he was done, but the pain in his head would start to lessen. They would let him go back into the darkness; they would let him crawl away, sloughing off his mask and his shell as he went. Until there was nothing left of the monster. Until there was only the dead man who would plunge into the bottomless pit offered by the *arkhi*. The ghost who would return to the void of senselessness.

He tottered, bumping into the wall of the tunnel. The skull-maker scraped along the ceiling, whining that it was cutting wood instead of bone. It was thirsty too.

He tried to swallow, but his mouth had gone dry. His tongue was a slab of rock, and he ground his teeth against it, trying to feel something. Anything.

Place the foot before lifting the other, he instructed the bag of flesh. *Control the skull-maker. It has to wait.*

His instructions, always delivered along with the skull-maker as if he were a child and couldn't remember, were simple: *don't kill him too quickly*. The audience wanted a show, as did the shadow in the pavilion. His duty was to entertain. It wasn't to kill a man; it was to make them howl and laugh. It was to make them believe they controlled the monster. They could make it perform for them. Make it dance. Make it sing. Make it kill. He was their toy.

Soon, he whispered to the skull-maker as he stepped out of the tunnel.

◆ ◆ ◆

Haakon's opponent stalked slowly out of the gate's shadow. Its armor was the gaudiest and most complex that Haakon had ever seen. Layers of plates overlapped, much like the lamellar of the Mongols, but constructed by the hand of a true artisan. Mongol armor was a patchwork assembly of jagged scrap in comparison to the perfectly shaped pieces of the demon's equipage. A polished black helmet lay low over its brow, topped by a spreading crest that reminded Haakon of the wings that some of his ancestors sported on their helms. A mane of white hair thrust from beneath the helmet's slanting cowl, and a cunningly wrought mask—mouth drawn back in a sneering roar, long tendrils of white horsehair spilling off the upper lip, eyes rimmed with spires of painted fire—obscured his opponent's face.

It was the face of a demon.

Haakon had heard stories of Onghwe Khan's grand champion, of course; gossip and local legends returned with every group of Shield-Brethren that ventured into the shantytown surrounding the arena for supplies. As soon as the Mongolian engineers had begun to construct the arena, the surrounding plain had begun to sprout makeshift markets of trinket-sellers, soothsayers, gilded-tongued minstrels, footpads, mercurial physicians, and sharp-eyed traders, all drawn by the promise of bloodsport and commerce, all filled with an endless supply of lies, legends, and horror stories about the sorts of monsters the dissolute Khan had at his disposal.

Haakon was familiar with similar stories from his own childhood—tales of the *jötnar* and their role at *Ragnarök*, for example—but he hadn't given them much thought. Not until today.

It is the nature of fear, Feronantus's voice reminded him, offering an alternate viewpoint to Taran's precise lessons. *Your own mind betrays you with bogles from your childhood. Images that would not disturb you at any other time become huge, magnified by energies you do not control. You are not open to the flow; every muscle in your body is tight, and there is no path. Every tiny spark is getting caught, and a fire is building around you.*

Haakon gasped.

Breathe, you idiot. It's just a man in a suit of armor. Taran's instruction was like his sword work—simple and direct.

Breathe. Focus. Use your eyes.

The noise from the stands remained an unceasing, overwhelming flood. The buzzing voices seemed to snarl up inside his helmet. Echoes battered his ears. The sun beat down on him now as well, mercilessly heating his mail and armor. Already his corded browband was soaked, and salt sting slithered toward the corners of his eyes. His armpits itched, and the weight on his shoulders seemed impossible to bear.

Breathe. Let energy in; push it out again. You are not a rock.

The demon—*nay, it must be a man*—halted near the center of the arena. In its—*his*—right hand was a pole, half again as long as the demon was tall, tipped with a single-edged blade.

The noise lessened. Haakon thought he had gone deaf, that he had passed into that void of combat that came before death, where one's self vanished into a broad ocean of awareness. *Fate-sight*, Feronantus called it, an excruciating sense of mortality tempered by unwavering sensitivity, a revolving awareness of field and enemy, surrounded by darkness.

But that wasn't the case. He could still hear his labored breathing, could still feel his heart pumping blood fiercely through his body. He was still very much in his own skin; it was the rest of the world that had fallen silent.

The demon had not moved, but the audience had abruptly cut off their collective buzzing roar. From far away, Haakon heard a cry like a baby's wail, and part of him wondered how a baby could still be alive after what he had seen before the walls of Legnica. More likely it was the cry of some bird.

But as if that cry were his signal, the demon moved—but not into a combat stance.

Instead he bowed, a short inclination of his upper body, and from there, with one graceful motion, he shifted his left foot back and lifted the pole. Couched across his body, the glaive now pointed straight at Haakon, sunlight reflecting from its bright blade.

The demon's brief bow was so incongruous, so against the threat of his frightening raiment, that Haakon took a half step back. *Of a certes, a man, disguised as a demon.* Several realizations followed in a clumsy rush: first, his opponent came from a cultured place where people had manners; second, they hewed to their manners even before fighting, suggesting that ritual combat was an established practice.

Third, this was not a good sign.

He's waiting, Haakon realized, wondering if his opponent thought him such a fool that he would initiate an attack against that pole sword. *I am not*, he thought. With a fluid motion, he responded with a proper bow, planting a leg well in front of him so that the weight of his coat of mail would not simply jerk him face-first into the ground.

When he heaved himself back up again, he noted the opponent looking at him with what he guessed was curiosity. And why not? While he wasn't as gaudily dressed, Haakon's armor was more complex than that of your average infantryman. He had left off several of the extra pieces that were meant to keep a knight alive in the chaotic melee of the battlefield.

The demon knows, Haakon realized. *He's seen armor like this before.* His eye went naturally to the blade attached to the end of the pole; it had an edge on only one side, tapering from a thickened spine that doubtless gave it strength and stiffness. The blade's curve suggested it would be most effective when accompanied by a drawing or pushing movement, just as a butcher uses when slicing meat. Such attacks worked best against unarmored targets, but the pole's extra reach and heft made the blade dangerous to armored men as well.

Most of the techniques that Haakon knew were useless against such a weapon. Haakon's greatsword was symmetrical and double-edged. Brother Rutger had recommended the tried-and-true method: a short sword in the right hand and a shield on the left arm. *If it was good enough for the Romans and good enough for your Viking forefathers—*

The demon let out a bloodcurdling shriek. Even though his mask muffled his voice, the cry was so sudden, so shocking, that Haakon felt like he had been struck by lightning. His muscles jumped, and instinctively he fell back a step as the demon lunged forward. The long blade of the glaive snapped past him, and with a flick of his wrists, the demon whirled the pole in a tight circle. The blade seemed to jump sideways, coming right for his face even though his passing step back had turned his body sideways.

Haakon threw up his sword, and he heard rather than felt the impact, a grating clang of steel against steel. The demon had struck him with the flat of the blade—a slap more than a slice—and before Haakon could react, the blade was gone.

A *test*, Haakon realized as the demon stepped carefully across the sand, whirling his pole in short, deadly circles. Each pass of the blade was in a different place—first high, then low, then high, then in the middle. Haakon wasn't about to stand his ground against one of them. The slapping attack hadn't been that focused. Had it been, it would have smashed through his frantic parry. These strikes, while not as fast as the demon's initial attack, all carried the demon's full strength. His sword wasn't strong enough to bear the brunt of a hard swing.

◆ ◆ ◆

Zugaikotsu no Yama waited. Not for the Western knight to ready himself after his perfunctory—and somewhat stiff—bow. Not because he was concerned about the man's armor. Head, shoulders, chest, legs, feet—the Western knight was covered from the crown of his head to the soles of his boots in metal. Zug waited for the sound, the horrible, tearing noise that would spring from somewhere deep within his bag of flesh. That exhalation of grief and rage that never seemed to die.

The *kiai*.

The shout flew violently out of his mouth, rattling his mask. It signified an awakening within him, a sudden birthing of desire and anger. The shout brought life to his limbs, and in the wake of the cry came the muscle memory, the knowledge of what to do, how to fight, how to kill.

He thrust the skull-maker, and when the knight turned away from his attack, he almost laughed at his opponent's naïveté. His hands twitched, flicking the flat of his long blade toward the knight's armored face.

It would be easy to kill him now, but it was too soon. He circled the frightened knight, letting the skull-maker play for a little while with a complex series of strikes and feints.

His opponent was cautious, staying out of his blade's reach, and Zug found himself breathing a little quicker, a little harder.

Perhaps he was not as clumsy as he first appeared...

◆ ◆ ◆

The demon's blade arced past Haakon, another swing that came up short. *He knows his range, so why is he pulling back?* The next swing was low, but still short. Haakon only had to slide his left foot back a span to be out of range. *He wants me to close the distance.* The feints were meant to lull Haakon into thinking he no longer needed to flee the flashing blade.

Haakon slid his left foot forward as he raised his sword—point high, edge toward the incoming pole-arm. His stomach tightened, a warm ball of force coalescing in his body. He kept his eyes locked on the demon's wild mask; he didn't need to watch the blade coming. The sunlight shining off it would blind him anyway. He knew where it was going to be.

If his opponent was wielding a sword, he was in position for a good crossing of the blades, but against the glaive, such a position was a mistake. He couldn't stop a full swing with that guard. If he was a full step closer, he wouldn't even be able to deflect it; the blow would come right through his defense and bite deep into his head or neck.

But he wasn't that close. As the blades struck each other, he relaxed his grip, yielding to the demon's attack. The momentum imparted to his sword allowed him to twist his wrists and flick his blade forward toward the demon's head.

Haakon's sword point fell short of its target, and the demon, having read the measure correctly, did nothing to stop Haakon's strike. He pulled his blade back and, with a twist of his body, brought it around again in another sweep.

The demon's motion brought him incrementally closer to Haakon. As the pole-arm flashed toward him, Haakon took one more step, jerking his sword up so that the blade smacked against the palm of his left hand.

You never withdraw when you've broken the bind. Taran had drilled them relentlessly. *A warrior doesn't flee from a fight. He closes to finish it.* Had Haakon been fighting one of his fellow Brethren, they would not have withdrawn their blade from the first contact. They would not have given him the opportunity to go to half sword.

He braced his sword in both hands and took the demon's swing. The shock of the blow traveled down his arms, but Haakon let it go. The energy ran through his chest and legs until it left his body through his right heel.

He felt the difference—wood against metal. His blade against the shaft of the pole-arm. *Inside his range.*

Haakon brought the pommel of his sword down. Much like running his hand along a flat wall, he could feel the demon's weapon plainly against his sword blade. Using the wooden shaft of the pole-arm as an axis, he performed a complicated finishing technique: levering his weapon so that the hilt could hook around his opponent's hands, tangling the other's weapon, and snapping the point of his sword forward with his left hand.

The demon pulled his head back, avoiding Haakon's sword point, but all that accomplished was to give Haakon enough room to line up perfectly for a short thrust.

The demon fled from the unexpected thrust with an almost dainty back step and twirl. He had to let go of his pole with one hand in order to extricate himself from Haakon's hilt, and as he retreated, the pole-arm dragged behind him, a long tail flapping against the dirt.

For a second, the demon's back was turned to Haakon. Desperately, he shifted his hands to a two-handed grip and let loose with the sort of flailing strike one expected from a boy when he first picked up a sword. If it connected, he told himself, pride wouldn't matter.

Remember the first rule: do not die.

The swing missed, and as Haakon recovered for another attack, the demon pivoted and snapped his pole-arm back up.

Sword and blade connected. They stared at one another: Haakon, with his sword half extended toward his opponent; the demon, crouching as if he were making ready to spring. The pole-arm was pointed up, its blade scraping against the crossguard of Haakon's sword.

In the moment where they sized each other up, Haakon became aware of the shouts coming from the audience. By now, he realized, the rabble who lined the arena had seen enough to handicap the opponents, choose up sides, and lay wagers. They were cheering accordingly, and some were calling out, "Che-val-ier! Che-val-ier!" Had he not been so distracted, he'd have enjoyed a laugh over the idea that he, a monk descended from Nordic fishermen, had been mistaken for a knight of the Crusades.

The remainder screamed out, "Zug! Zug! Zug!"

◆ ◆ ◆

The skull-maker wanted blood, wanted to feel bones and flesh separating before its shiny blade. It pulled at Zug, and he had to follow its desire.

But he knew a mistake had been made.

As the pole-arm—the *naginata*—whirled around for should have been the final stroke against the armored knight, Zug felt like a stone falling from a great height. When the knight's sword connected with the wooden shaft of the pole-arm, a shock went through his body. He gasped, suddenly conscious of the constricting weight of his armor, of how difficult it was to breathe in his mask. Sweat ran down his back, and it felt like claws raking his flesh. His bowels trembled, and he nearly lost control of his bladder.

Suddenly *aware*, like being jerked out of a deep sleep.

Sunlight shivered off the knight's helm, and Zug squinted against the glare, pulling his head back as his opponent moved closer. Distantly, like the sensation of wind-blown rain sluicing across the felt roof of a *ger*, he felt the knight's blade slide along the pole in his hands.

The knight's hands came down, metal fingers wrapped around a plain pommel, and a point of metal danced in front of his face.

Zug hissed. His body responded slowly—the way a boat turns on a placid lake when its occupant has no oars. He had been gone too long, lost in his mind, and the flesh had become a slave to other masters: the crowd, the skull-maker, the *arkhi*. He had become nothing more than a ghost.

Not yet, he thought. The *naginata*'s blade dragged on the ground as he retreated from the knight's thrust. *I am not a ghost.*

His hands tightened on the shaft of the pole-arm, and he knew where his feet were. The skull-maker sang as he snapped it up. The knight was close behind him...

✦ ✦ ✦

Haakon spotted a tiny movement of the demon's—*Zug's*—forward leg as the other man shifted his center of gravity. The motion gave away Zug's intent; he had settled too far into his guard, and now he had to shift his weight before he could execute his next attack.

Even before Zug started to move the pole-arm, Haakon was already moving. He lunged forward, keeping his blade in contact with the pole-arm. As his blade slide down onto the wooden shaft, he lifted his elbows and locked the shaft between his blade and crossguard. Zug couldn't extricate his weapon, and as Haakon took another step forward—*flee toward danger!*—he forced the pole-arm up. With a flick of his wrists, he rotated his sword around the pole-arm and clasped the blade with his left hand again.

He wasn't close enough for the half-sword thrust to be deadly, but the move was a replay of a few moments ago. Haakon hoped the repetition would break Zug's concentration for a second or two as the other man tried to second-guess Haakon's intention. Would Zug think he was foolish enough to try for the hilt snare again?

Haakon closed, rolling his sword around the pole-arm so that his arms reversed their position. His point was no longer in Zug's face, but he was still inside the reach of the pole-arm's blade.

With a sharp motion, he snapped his hilt toward the triangular opening behind Zug's left forearm. It was a similar lock to the snare he had just used, but his target was different.

Brother Rutger liked this technique: tangling the other warrior's arm with the hilt of his own blade before he stepped in and stripped the weapon free. Haakon doubted he could get the pole-arm from Zug—the technique worked best with shorter weapons—but at this range, the pole-arm was about as dangerous as a willow switch.

Zug was not to be entangled a second time, and his hand darted out, seizing Haakon's hilt before the lock could be completed. His response wasn't unexpected; Haakon would have been surprised if the other man's martial arts didn't include close-quarters fighting techniques. As Zug pulled at his sword, he let go of his blade with his off hand, grabbing at the shaft of the pole-arm. Zug was caught in a tug-of-war, trying to retain his pole with one hand, jerking the heavy sword from Haakon with the other.

This divided his energy. Haakon could feel his focus smearing, two flows going in different directions. And right there, in the middle, was a swirling mass of confused energy. Without thinking, Haakon did something Brother Rutger never would have done, something that, if he took the time to fully consider the implications, he never would have done either.

Haakon let go of his sword, grabbed Zug's pole-arm, and heaved upward.

Zug grunted as the lower length of the pole sword slammed into his groin. His stance had been too deep, and during their tussle, the pole had drifted between his legs.

Haakon was much taller, and he put all the strength of his legs into the dead lift. He had no idea what sort of armor Zug kept down there, but if it was anything like his own, it wasn't much. Hardly a killing blow, but no man liked getting hit between the legs.

He lifted hard, twice.

Zug was either armored down below or Haakon had missed, as the demon-faced man barely shivered and then recovered quickly. He cast Haakon's sword aside and went for his own blade, the short one in the scabbard at his waist.

Haakon swept his left leg back, pivoting around his right hip. He twisted his wrists out, trying to throw Zug to the ground, with the pole high and hard between his legs. Zug was still hanging on to the pole as well, his hand firmly in place below Haakon's.

Zug jabbed at him with the short sword, quick stabs that slid ineffectively off the metal of his bracers. Eventually, though, Zug would get the point behind Haakon's breastplate.

He needed to break this impasse, but what could he do? He had given up his sword. He had his opponent's weapon, but it was still tangled up by Zug's legs and hand. What else could he use? His dagger was at the small of his back, and he didn't dare let go of the pole-arm to reach for it.

Zug tried to twist around the pole, bending like a snake, and Haakon felt something tear in his side. Zug had found his mail.

Keep your head, Taran admonished him. *Focus.*

Haakon stared at Zug's frozen mask; this close he could see that it wasn't metal. Zug exhaled noisily as he ground his point against the chain of Haakon's mail, and even with the mask obscuring his face, Haakon could smell the foul odor of his breath.

Arkhi. An alcoholic drink the Mongolians favored.

Zug had been drunk recently. He might even *still* be drunk, which meant his reflexes were impaired and his balance was off.

Keep it simple, Taran suggested.

Haakon snapped his head and helm forward, tucking his chin so that the brunt of the blow came from the hard metal ridge that protected his forehead. The blow landed true; Zug's head jerked back violently, a grunt of pain escaping from beneath the helmet and crest. But the blow did not knock him senseless. It shoved him off balance. As Zug tried to recover, Haakon shoved him firmly. Zug staggered back, and Haakon kept his grip firm on the pole-arm.

As he found his balance and sank into a stance, he twirled the weapon around until the blade pointed at his enemy.

The spectators laughed and shrieked with merriment over this sensational turn of events. Haakon remembered that there *was* a crowd. And suddenly, just like that, he was out of the fight, aware that he had forgotten to breathe, that his heart was going so fast it felt more like a shivering in the chest than a beat, that sweat was gushing out of him. He realized he was closer to the wall than he wanted to be, and he sidestepped toward the center of the arena.

Zug put his hands to his helmet, repositioning it on his face. The top edge of his mask had been crushed, and one of the tall spires drooped. Sun fell through a gap between the demon helm and a neck frill of shining black.

Haakon caught sight of smooth brown skin at the corner of his jaw, where a man would have stubble or real hair.

He has no beard. A boy. A mere boy.

Zug's hands snapped down. He had been holding on to his short sword as he adjusted his mask, and with the sudden flick of his wrist, he threw the weapon. The sword wasn't a very good projectile, but his aim was true and he threw with considerable force. Haakon twisted the pole sword and managed to deflect the missile just enough that it clattered off his metal shoulder—but the maneuver took him off guard long enough that Zug was able to dart across the sand and scoop up the other unclaimed weapon.

Haakon's greatsword.

Now the crowd went mad with frenzied glee. Their roar became a kind of devilish, porcine squeal, sharp and painful.

They squared off again, getting the other's measure. Haakon kept his hands loose on the pole-arm as he stalked Zug, moving him around the arena floor.

Zug crab-walked at a right angle to Haakon's blade, framing himself before the long column of red silk that obscured the southern tunnel—directly beneath where the Khan sat ensconced in his private pavilion. Sunlight reflecting off the silk made it shift and move as if it were a column of fire.

The Red Veil.

What lies on the other side?

Haakon had the longer weapon; his armor was stronger. He was up against a beardless boy, or perhaps a eunuch—but not a demon.

For the first time since the fight started, he began to like the odds.

CHAPTER 14:

———

THE WAY OF THE LAPWING

O nce Feronantus was awake, Cnán reported on the events of the previous day and what was coming. She finished the story with a suggestion: "If you were to strike your camp and disappear into the forest—which I could arrange, by the way—none would think the less of you."

Feronantus screwed up his face. "How many Mongol riders did you say there were?"

"Perhaps four *arban*." Seeing how this word meant nothing to him, she explained. "They ride in groups of ten," she said. "Ten *arbans*—ten of ten—is called a *jaghun*."

His face relaxed. "Then I don't see any difficulty."

Cnán barely restrained a snort—and then thought of Istvan's handiwork. "You have very little time to get ready," she warned.

"*Getting ready* is something best done *before* one's camp has been overrun by horse archers. We have been *getting ready* ever since we arrived," Feronantus pointed out. "Now...young Binder. Are you acquainted with the way of the lapwing?"

Cnán was.

"Then might I ask that you go back a ways and be flushed from cover, then flee in panic toward our camp...? Men on horses like to chase things, and Mongols are no exception."

Cnán sniffed. "These last few years, I have become rather good at not being seen, much less *flushed*."

"I understand," Feronantus said. "Today we shall all be doing the unexpected."

When Feronantus put it that way, Cnán found it difficult to refuse. She had been riding hard all night, fording rivers in the dark and taking risks that she never would have considered had she not been caught up with these Brethren and their insane quest.

Meanwhile, Feronantus had been taking his leisure in camp with the six others who had stayed behind: Taran, the big Irish *oplo*; Rædwulf, the English archer; Illarion, the Ruthenian nobleman; Roger, the Norman who carried too many sharp things; and two who were not actual members of the *Ordo Militum Vindicis Intactae*, Finn the hunter and Yasper the alchemist. Both were men of northwestern Europe and speakers of languages that troubled Cnán's ear. Most in the camp had been asleep when Cnán had galloped in on her last surviving horse, but now they were awake, armed and armored with an alacrity that suggested they slept in steel.

Which Cnán would too, were she fool enough to pitch a camp and light a fire in this country.

She felt woolly headed. The light of the morning was flat and bleak in her tired eyes. Every instinct told her to get out, get rid of the noisy, smelly beast she had been riding, and use her formidable skills to simply disappear. Instead Feronantus wanted her to become, for a few moments, like a mother bird leading predators away from her nest—as conspicuous and vulnerable to enemies as she could possibly be. Had he made the request in the wrong tone of voice or with the wrong look in his eye, she would by now already be so thoroughly *gone* that only Finn, with luck, would have been able to find her again.

But Feronantus—damn him—had asked politely and in a way that made it clear he well knew what he was asking: for her to humiliate herself in front of foes and friends alike.

She pushed past Feronantus with an attempt at a swagger, made more ridiculous by her exhaustion. "Then *get ready* to greet my pursuers," she said and mounted, with less grace than before. She wheeled her pony and rode in the direction whence she had just come.

Her brief pass through the camp enabled her to view the Shield-Brethren's preparations, some of which (stringing ropes between trees at the level of a rider's neck, planting sharpened poles in the ground) were obvious, others (Yasper lighting torches in broad daylight) baffling.

All through the hours of darkness, Cnán had been riding across open territory, substituting speed for wit and relying on the four behind her—Percival, Raphael, Eleázar, and Istvan—to draw the attention of the pursuing Mongols. The route she had taken into the camp only a few moments ago was still marked out by a gash of trampled grass crossing over a pasture that was perhaps a verst in breadth and notching the skyline of a grassy rise.

The pasture was bordered on its lower slope by a tumble-down stone wall. Purple-flowering thistles and pea vines had thrust their roots between the rocks and turned the old wall into a wild hedge that was far too high to be jumped. A gap in the wall—an old gate or stile—had been narrowed by the lush greenery to a sort of mouse hole through which only one rider could pass at a time. Beyond the wall spread an abandoned field of rye, now feral and losing a war against more potent weeds. Like most arable fields, it was much longer than it was wide so that the farmer would not need to turn his team around frequently while plowing. The hedge wall ran along one of its long sides. The opposite side, perhaps a hundred paces away, was not fenced, unless one counted a stubble of old stumps where the farmer had cut away some trees. Dense black alder and ash came up to that side of the field and extended down a gentle slope for perhaps half a verst before falling decisively into the endless marsh.

So much for the field's long sides. The short ends were defined, at one end, by more forest. Pines lunged out into the grassland, forming a salient where the land's former occupants had erected their hovels—deserted for a year or more—and, at the other, by a line of rubble trailing across the ground, scarcely knee-high. Perhaps the remnants of another stone wall that had been pulled apart by scavengers in need of building materials.

The knights had pitched their shelters a few days ago back in the pines behind the hovels. The place was not quite a clearing, for a few ash trees of some size were salted through it, but the undergrowth was sparse—a consequence, obviously to Cnán, of a fire that had hurried through earlier and destroyed the young trees, while not burning long or hot enough to kill the big ones. Farmers often set such fires, but this one had probably started from a lightning strike in dry weather.

As she passed from the rye field through the mouse hole and out into the big pasture beyond, her eye picked out a blasted snag, lonely and stark along the skyline over which the Mongols would soon be coming. Echoes of many unwelcome sights witnessed during her long trek across the Mongols' empire.

She nudged her pony to a canter and rode up the trail she had trampled in the grass earlier, retracing her path until she drew near the crest. But before exposing her head, she dismounted and led the pony across the slope until she reached the snag—a moribund ash.

She threw the pony's reins over a low side branch, which she then used to get a leg up and ascend to a higher bough. The ash was not as big as it looked from a distance, and its branches were dry, burnt, and brittle. They would not have supported any of the men in the party; they barely supported Cnán. With some care, however, she was able to climb about twice a man's height to where the trunk forked into two roughly equal parts, a secure cradle from which she could look out over the other side of the rise and see what was coming.

Her fear, strangely, had been that she would see nothing at all, since this would mean that Percival and the others were dead. Further evidence that being around Percival had destroyed her wits, since their deaths would have been the best possible result if her only purpose were to save herself.

But a rooster tail of dust, catching the low light of the morning sun, was growing visible in the west—much more dust than could have been made by four men. A sizable host was on its way, pursuing one or more fugitives.

Since the ground's gentle swell was blocking the near view, she climbed higher and, after some anxious waiting, noticed four glinting Vs, like the formations of wild geese, cutting across a wide stretch of river she had forded at dawn.

She was looking at the wakes made by four horses as they waded across the shallows.

Turning her head around, grabbing the trunk as a branch crunched under her, then rebalancing her weight, she picked out Rædwulf, perched behind the hedge with his bow slung across his shoulder, gazing at her. She tucked her thumb into her palm and held up four fingers. Rædwulf nodded and dropped out of view. She felt that she should inform them too about the size of the pursuing host, but then reflected that Finn would soon know this by listening to the ground.

The points of the Vs plunged into the near bank of the ford. Cnán began softly singing a little song, a tune of the Binders that moved to the steady and compulsive beat of a dance. It sounded best with a *shawm* playing the melody and a *daf* pounding out the beat, but she could conjure the memory of hearing it played with such instruments around a fire in happier times and better places. Reaching the end of the chorus, she stuck out her thumb and began the song again.

Finishing for a second time, she stuck out her index finger.

Her ring finger was up when the first Vs appeared at the far side of the ford. Their vertices struck the bank at about the time she raised her pinky; when she had progressed to her other thumb, the host had become so congested that it was no longer possible to make out individual wakes. And yet she did not think it was any larger than the group she had seen at yesterday's twilight.

They had not, in other words, been joined by more *arban* during the chase. But just to make sure, she tore her gaze away from the group thronging the riverbank and stared across the greater distance for other plumes of dust. She saw none.

It was all as she had described to Feronantus. No need to fly back to camp with a correction.

The wait that followed was long and gave her time to consider how she might best carry out her duty. It was an ugly word, *duty*, from which part of her recoiled as she might have jumped back from a snake. But she had grown accustomed to ignoring that voice, and she ignored it now.

She was still up in the tree, still repeating her song, when Percival led his group of four up the hill, their mounts foaming and sweating, half dead. She made sure that the men saw her, which was not difficult since they were using the snag as a landmark. Once she had their attention, she waved them vigorously toward the mouse hole through the hedge wall.

Istvan, riding a couple of lengths out ahead of the others, took her meaning immediately and veered toward the opening. Raphael and Eleázar, who came along next, hesitated.

"Clog it up, why don't you!" Cnán shouted down to them. "Like drunks rolling out of a burning tavern."

They responded by showing her their teeth and followed Istvan. As they went, Raphael and Eleázar jostled each other playfully, acting the role of the panicky drunks, just to amuse her. In their relief at still being alive, they acted like little boys. She was pleased that they appreciated her wit.

Percival pulled up suddenly and stopped near the tree. "Go on," Cnán called to him, "do as the others." Looking away, she resumed singing, beating time with her fist.

"My lady," Percival began. He had called her that yesterday, and she had guessed it was some kind of elaborate sarcasm. But this didn't seem like the time for unpleasant jibes. Maybe it was just the way he'd been raised. Cnán wished she could meet Percival's mother. "I cannot recommend that you remain in that position," he said, "considering that hostile archers, in large numbers, are about to surround you."

She did not respond. She was nearing the end of the chorus and did not want to lose her place.

"And if you do remain," he continued, "you might leave off singing. Your tune is beautiful, but it will soon draw many arrows."

She stuck out her thumb and said, "It's part of a plan— Feronantus's plan, if that impresses you—which you are currently fouling up. Go and fight for a place in that hedge hole." With a quick scowl in Percival's direction, Cnán took up singing again and stuck out her index finger.

"Ah, you are to be the lapwing," Percival guessed. He turned and looked toward Raphael and Eleázar, who were about halfway to the gap. "You will run toward yonder gap and find it blocked by those selfish clods. You will then divert round the other way in—the low rubble wall at the end of the field. Which happens to be much better suited for Mongols anyway."

Next came her long finger. She badly wanted to climb down out of the tree, but it was important that the Mongols catch sight of her first.

Percival looked up at her and said, "The performance will lack verisimilitude if I fail to give way to a lady in distress. For it is my duty as a knight to see you safe to your destination—as difficult as you sometimes make that."

Cnán thrust the current finger at him and interrupted the song long enough to shout, "You're fucking it up! Go!" Then she noticed movement along the rise—the tips of Mongol lances bobbing up and down.

"I shall follow you in," Percival said thoughtfully. "The ruse shall work just as well."

"Suit yourself," Cnán snarled. She could clearly see the broad faces of Mongols beneath their helmets, and one of them pointed directly at her, calling excitedly to his brothers.

Cnán began to descend the tree. This went slower than she'd hoped, since a branch broke under her foot and forced her to dangle for a few beats of the song while she flailed for a handhold.

Percival, adroitly maneuvering his mount underneath her, took her ankle and guided her down over her patiently waiting pony, then saw to it that her ass slammed directly into the saddle. Even as she reached for the reins, he smacked the pony on the buttocks. It bolted. Percival cut behind, getting between Cnán and the Mongols.

Cnán, finally securing a grip on the reins, rushed along the same path that Istvan, Raphael, and Eleázar had followed. Trying to ignore whatever Percival might be doing behind her, she rode hard in the direction of the mouse hole, a ride long enough, she hoped, to let the Mongols get some sense of what she was trying for.

Raphael and Eleázar were overplaying their roles, berating and shoving each other in front of the narrow opening.

She could hear the Mongols shouting as they turned to follow her. Cnán veered the pony into a sharp turn. The pony veered onto a course roughly parallel to the hedge and maybe ten paces distant. She would have to cover about one bowshot, then execute a full reversal and jump the low barrier of rubble in order to gain entry to the field. Concerned about the pony's ability to make such a tight turn at full gallop, she guided it away from the hedge wall.

The disaster came so quickly that she was tumbling ass-over-ears through the rye before she was fully aware that something had gone wrong. She used the last of her momentum to roll back on her feet. A loud snapping noise was fresh in her ears. She looked back. The pony lay in a motionless heap. Perhaps it had stepped into an animal's burrow, broken a leg, tossed her...landed on its neck.

Dazed, she stood tall in the weeds and stalks—not the best strategy when archers were taking aim.

Two noises sounded at once: the hiss of an arrow by her left ear and thunder rising through the soles of her feet. She turned to see more arrows arc across the sky—and Percival riding for her at a high gallop.

Again, if it had been anyone else, she'd have hesitated, thinking it through, not knowing what was on his mind, what his intentions might be. But because it was Percival, she knew instantly. He would save her or die trying. She didn't want him dead. So she stuck her hand up in the air.

Percival's steel-clad arm came swooping from the sky like a bright-winged falcon, whirling in an underhand movement; his gauntlet slammed Cnán's upraised arm between elbow and shoulder and clenched it in an excruciating grip. A sharp bolt of pain—her arm was being jerked out of its socket—compelled her to grab for a fistful of bunched mail, swing her other hand up, and hook her fingertips over the edge of the steel cop that covered his elbow. For a time, she held on with all the strength she had left, seeing in bumping, spinning glimpses Percival's thigh, the saddle, the horse's pumping flank, the sky above, and the reeling ground beneath. Clods and grass flew up to strike her in the face.

She pulled her knees in just before Percival heaved her up like a bag of grain and slung her sideways across the front of his saddle. Had she been expecting a longer ride, she'd have slung her leg over and struggled upright, but this position felt more secure even though she was being punched in the stomach and ribs by the saddle. So she held on to whatever bits of tack her flailing hands could discover and tried as best she could to review their situation.

The horse was definitely turning—making that wheeling maneuver into the open mouth of the long field.

Something streaked past the horse's left flank and embedded itself in the ground ahead. Even more impressive thunking noises startled her—arrows hitting Percival in his back, which was at least partly protected by his slung shield. But his mount had no such protection.

The horse gave out an awful scream and lost its gait, staggered for a couple of paces, tried to return to the gallop, but staggered again and fell into an off-rhythm, off-balance diagonal stride that felt like a slow descent. The saddle stopped pounding her belly. Rubble flashed beneath her, a plunging hoof cracked down on a big rock, and then the ground came up fast.

Sky and rubble and rye vied for her attention as she and Percival skidded and tumbled over each other. Ending up on top, she rolled to unsteady feet, sucked back the wind that had been knocked out of her, and turned to face the enemy, wondering how many more times she would fall off a dying horse today.

Four Mongols abreast rode toward them, with many more negotiating the turn behind. One archer had drawn his bow and nocked an arrow. He pushed the bow forward, loosed the arrow. Another was in the act. Both arrows found their target.

With the apparent strength of a Hercules, Percival hefted body, mail, and armor from a crouch and swung his shield off his shoulder. Three arrows stuck out of it. Another shaft flew his way—no, for Cnán—and he extended the shield just in time to catch that one as well. Another *whanged* off his steel helmet.

The knight staggered sideways, turned, crouched, and hurled the bristling shield into the pounding legs of the nearest Mongol horse. It fell in a heap, its shriek cut off as its muzzle plowed into green grass and dirt. The rider somersaulted out of control and slid across the grass like a child on a sled. Percival abruptly halted the Mongol's glide with a downward, double-handed thrust of his sword, pinning him to the ground.

The other three Mongols hurtled past. Cnán knew that their next move would be to pivot in their saddles and loose Parthian shots. So she turned to face them just in time to see them go down—one, two, three—as arrows from sides and front pierced their leather armor.

Istvan was the only archer she could actually see; the other shots had come out of concealment. The Hungarian now galloped to the fore, leaning in his saddle, and shot a second arrow through the neck guard of a wounded Mongol lurching to his feet. The Mongol dropped again to his knees, hands reaching, unable to cry out—the arrow had pierced his windpipe and come out the other side, almost clean through.

"Run, my lady," said Percival as calmly as if he were inviting her to dance—and Cnán ran. He was right behind her. Naked, he might have outpaced her; in full armor, even he lagged.

They were being chased up into the field, and as Cnán's lightly shod feet pounded through rye and weeds, from the corners of her eyes, she became aware of men lying flat in shallow trenches under piles of uprooted grass. She also saw more long cords beneath her feet—cords run out over the ground and left there, straight, but slack.

Istvan rode past going the other way. She turned to watch as the Hungarian shot an arrow into the foremost of the next wave of riders. He wheeled his destrier and returned the other way, twisting in his saddle to shoot his own Parthian shot. As he passed, the cords jerked off the ground—three ranks of them, pulled taut by knights working in pairs, one at each end, levering them around hefty sticks jammed into the earth.

Percival burst forward and in a few strides caught up with Cnán, grabbed her already aching arm, steered her toward the hedge, and tossed her into it. Vines and thistles welcomed her. Rocks bruised her face and shoulder—light wounds and a fair trade. More arrows buried themselves in the ground just a couple of yards away.

Cnán nestled into the hedge, delicately plucking thistles and draping tendrils to hide herself. But curiosity won out over caution. Parting the vines, she saw that disaster was about to fall upon the Mongol horsemen. Two *arban*—twenty riders—were galloping at speed—right into the rope traps.

All but two of the riders and their ponies tripped over the stretched cords and tumbled headlong, kicking and squealing, in a cloud of dust. The two that made it through were brought down by arrows from Rædwulf and another reverse shot from Istvan. The Hungarian grinned like a demon, his huge bristling mustache still caked with black blood from the massacre at the farmstead.

In a patter of heavy, thumping footsteps, a man ran right by her hiding place in the hedge, panting with exertion and trailing a long, stretched-out cloud of smoke. It was the alchemist, Yasper—and he seemed to be on fire. Every couple of paces, he stopped to hurl a smoking object plucked from a satchel slung over his shoulder. He tossed them in the direction of the entrance to the abandoned field, where the two squadrons of Mongols were staggering to their feet, drawing swords, or still trying to drag themselves from under thrashing horses.

The burning objects tumbled along the ground and jetted smoke—not the translucent white smoke that came from fires, but a yellow-brown vapor, thick as river mud. And it kept coming. One fell from Yasper's bag and lay on the ground not far from Cnán. It was a gourd, about the size of a fist, with a vent hole cut into one side. She was fascinated by the sheer volume of smoke hissing and belching from the tiny object; it was like watching a hundred men leap out of a single wine barrel.

In a few moments, the jets and clouds of smoke combined to form a dense wall around the fallen riders, like a low storm cloud. The day was calm, the field was sheltered by woods, and the pungent yellow vapor was in no hurry to blow away.

From the shallow trenches sprang Taran and Feronantus, then Roger and Illarion, drawing swords with a strange, ululating, hooting cry:

"*Alalazu! Alalazu!*"

The war cry, she guessed, of the *Ordo Militum Vindicis Intactae.*

Running straight down the center of the field came Eleázar, drawing and poising the colossal sword that he had used to such effect yesterday evening. Trotting after him came Raphael, bow out, arrow nocked, scanning for more distant foes.

But the blinding power of Yasper's smoke cloud was absolute, and so the remainder of the Mongol force, still finding its way around and through the hedge, dared not use their bows for fear of striking comrades.

The cloud expanded. Terrible sounds came out of it now. A Mongol hopped through the billowing yellow wall on one leg, coughing and waving his free hand, smoke trailing from his hair and clothes. A hatchet whirled out of the cloud and split the back of his skull. Eyes suddenly red and bulging, he threw out his arms and sprawled flat on his face.

Roger, arms covered in blood, backed out of the cloud, reached down, and pulled the hatchet loose. Another Mongol charged out after him. Roger backhanded the weapon with a casual flick, making it skim whirling across the ground at knee level. It did not cut the Mongol but destroyed his gait and staggered him. He raised a short sword, not so much to deliver a blow now as to protect himself from what might come next; Roger ran forward, caught the man's elbow, and with all his might, shoved it back so that it grazed the Mongol's ear, spinning him round and leaving his neck an easy target for the dagger in Roger's other hand. The dagger found its mark.

Streaked and dripping all over now with fresh blood, Roger wrenched away the dying Mongol's sword and stalked back into the cloud, his face contorted with battle rage, crying, "*Alalazu!*"

Raphael turned toward the hedge to look directly at Cnán—no, just above her—and loosed an arrow. There were loud rustling noises and a Mongol fell from the top of the hedge, striking a heavy blow on her shoulder. He and she— and a great deal of torn vegetation—all fell in a heap. Cnán scrabbled out from under and tried to leap back, a groan of fear and disgust rumbling from deep in her gut. The Mongol had an arrow in his right lung. Still he lashed out and grabbed Cnán's ankle. With his other hand, he pawed at his belt, trying to reach the hilt of a dagger that had been knocked askew in the fall.

Cnán dropped to her knee, making sure that knee came down hard on the Mongol's nose. She then grabbed the wayward dagger and buried it in his stomach. Leaves rattled from above and she jumped off the loudly dying man just in time to avoid being bowled over by another Mongol, this one sporting *two* deep-shot arrows.

She'd had the bad luck to hide at a banked spot on the hedge wall, easily scaled from the other side. Probably it was a good thing to be disabused of the foolish notion that there was any safe place in this melee, and so she ran to the middle of the field.

The smoke cloud slowly drifted her way, or perhaps it was just growing—and the battle came with it.

She glimpsed Illarion whirling a ten-foot spear, stopping only to jab one end or the other into a foe. Feronantus cruised with grim ease round the fight's perimeter, wielding short sword and shield, striking down those who tried to escape.

Smoke peeled back to show Taran engaged in single combat with an impressive Mongol wearing good, thick armor, clearly a commander of an *arban*, if not the whole group. The two matched each other stroke for stroke, but the Mongol looked exhausted and unsure, while Taran was calm, implacable, and—for lack of a better word—curious. Taran used the opportunity of a raised sword to step off line and drive his own blade up the commander's unprotected armpit.

Yasper seemed to have used up all of his alchemical supplies and was now walking about alertly, sword in hand, but showing no interest in going into the battle cloud. This struck Cnán as exceedingly prudent—an eye on the periphery of the battlefield meant they would not be surprised—and in fact, as she watched, Yasper pointed his sword up at the other end of the field. He shouted to the others, sharp words that Cnán did not quite catch but were clearly an alarm.

Raphael and Rædwulf and Istvan, preoccupied with picking off stray Mongols trying to climb the hedge, had been paying no attention to the end of the field by the forest salient and the old farm hovels. Another squadron of Mongols had found their way through by that route. They were slicing furiously at the neck-high ropes that had been strung from tree to tree. Four riders had passed through and gathered at the head of the field, waiting for several more comrades to join them.

But when they heard Yasper's shout and saw the archers turn and aim their way, they mounted a direct charge rather than wait to be picked off.

Istvan loosed a single shaft and then spurred his stallion right at them, slinging his bow over his shoulder and drawing his curved sword; he and the foremost of the charging Mongols clashed in the center of the field, blade on blade. The Mongol rode away, upright, but with a dismayed, fading look, missing half of his sword arm.

Two others went down with arrows in neck and chest, but the fourth somehow managed to thread his way through Istvan, the archers, Yasper, and Cnán. He galloped straight for Taran, who had his back turned. In the Mongol's wake followed half a dozen more who had found their way over the same path as the first four.

The fighters in the smoke cloud had heard the commotion and become aware of the danger. Illarion and Feronantus came running, leaving Percival and Roger to guard what had now become the battle's rear.

Cnán was captivated for some moments by the sight of Feronantus, on foot, entering into single combat with a charging Mongol knight on a horse. Feronantus tossed his sword into the air as if playing with it, letting it spin lazily end over end, and caught it by the flat of its blade, which he pinched between the balls of his fingers and the heel of his hand. Stepping aside so that the Mongol's blow whistled past his chin, close enough to sever whiskers, he brought his sword's hilt up, swinging it like a pickax so that the sharp end of the crossguard jammed upward into the rider's armpit and caught there, jerking him backward off his horse.

Pinning the downed man with a foot on his neck, Feronantus reversed the sword again and drove it up beneath his helmet.

That was the last of the Mongols to die. But it was not the last of the Mongols.

One remained at the head of the field, near the old hovel. He half squatted on his saddle, bent over, one foot out of its stirrup and raised behind the pommel, elbow on that knee, fist supporting his chin—defiantly casual, confident. Watching. A stocky man, even by Mongol standards, attired in armor that was good but not flashy. He rode an excellent horse but wore no helmet, and his gray hair hung loose beneath the shaved tonsure that all of the Mongol warriors affected.

When Cnán first noticed him, Rædwulf was in the act of shooting an arrow at him, but the gray-haired Mongol leaned back, deftly raised his shield, and caught the shaft just short of his face. He peered over the shield, eyes glinting, and see-ing there was not another arrow coming, he held his curved sword high and shook it in what might have been anger, or a salute. Communicating with his horse with guttural shouts and knee-and-heel work, he spun it around and galloped into the woods.

Istvan wheeled as if to give chase, but Feronantus, stand-ing nearby, reached over and grabbed the horse's rein. "Stop," he said. "You will never catch him. Your mount is half dead. And besides, for now your rage has accomplished more than enough."

Istvan seemed proud to have received this compliment, until, noting a grim look on Feronantus's face, he followed the older man's gaze to a place about ten strides away, where Taran lay on the ground, facedown, motionless.

CHAPTER 15:

A NOCTURNAL PURSUIT

Gansukh dozed, the rhythmic motion of his horse and the distant sound of the Orkhun River lulling him into a somnambulant state. His lower back and left shoulder still ached—the former having been bruised when he had leaped from the wall and used a *ger* to break his fall. The structure had collapsed under his weight, preventing him from serious injury, but he had sprawled into a bulky object inside the *ger* as everything had come tumbling down.

The jump had been the last in a litany of foolish actions undertaken in the last few hours, a list he had had ample time to relive in his mind as he tracked the assassin.

The assassin had fled Karakorum, as Gansukh had suspected he would, via the western gate, though he had opted for a much less traveled route—over the wall instead of through the market gate. A pile of timber and stone—building materials awaiting a location in which to be assembled—had afforded the assassin and Gansukh a shortcut to the outer wall. The assassin had—much more deftly—leaped from the pile of timbers to the crenellations of the wall, clambered up, and leaped again over the far side. When Gansukh—slamming himself against the battlement as if he were a boulder from a catapult—had managed to climb atop the wall, he had seen that the assassin had used a *ger* to break his fall.

There were many *ger* to choose from; the population of Karakorum always swelled to a density greater than the walls could hold when the *Khagan* was in residence. Many a clan pitched their tents in tiny villages along the outside of the walls. What had given Gansukh pause was the *height*.

He had stared down from a bird's-eye view as tribespeople began to stir from their tents at the disturbance caused by the assassin landing on—and collapsing—a *ger*. His muscles had refused to move beyond the wall's edge, his brain telling him it would be insane to follow, that the chase had to end here.

But he had forced his body to jump, and the rushing air had been exhilarating, so much so that he hadn't noticed the ache in his back for several hours. Not until the excitement of the chase had given way to the endless drudgery of night tracking. And then his body had threatened to collapse from exhaustion.

The terrain around Karakorum was flat, mostly scrub and pasture; to the west lay the Orkhun River, a broad ribbon of water that bisected the valley. Typically the *Khagan* stayed at Karakorum for a few weeks during his transition from his summer to his winter residence, and during that time, the population of the city increased a hundredfold. Dozens and dozens of small clans made pilgrimages to the city to pay tribute to the *Khagan*; long caravans, weighted down with all manner of exotic goods, spilled into the trade district; priests, representing more religious sects than a man could reasonably count, erected shrines—some grandiose, some very austere—as physical manifestations of their spiritual inclinations; princes, courtiers, and displaced nobility sought to curry favor from the *Khagan*. They all arrived at Karakorum on hooved animals—horses, asses, oxen—and the ground around the city was trampled again and again.

But it had rained a few days ago, driving away the dust and softening the ground, and Gansukh had been able to find a few hoofprints—sharp indentations in the ground pointing away from the city. The river was a natural barrier; the assassin wouldn't try to ford it at night unless he knew exactly where to cross, and Gansukh doubted the man had that information. The tracks indicated the assassin's intent: keep the river on his left, the city behind him. Hanging low in the night sky directly ahead were the Seven Gods. *A simple route.* Gansukh could track the man all night.

He kept his stolen horse pointed at the brightest of the Seven Gods and let it pick its own pace. Even though the ground was very flat, there was no reason to push the animal. It might step in a hole and injure itself, and an exhausted horse would be of no use to him. When he caught up with the assassin, a fresher horse might make all the difference in the final chase.

He would have to answer for taking the mount when he returned. There hadn't been time to negotiate a loan—not that any true steppe warrior would *loan* his horse to a complete stranger who had just come running up to him. In some clans, horse thievery was punishable by death. He could only hope that catching the assassin might provide some extenuating circumstances by which the *Khagan* might grant him amnesty.

Gansukh sat up a little straighter as his horse's gait changed. He peered ahead, straining to see anything in the near darkness. The sky was clear, and the moon was still in the sky, but he couldn't see anything distinct on the plain around him. The river called to him and he tried to block out its noise; then the smell hit him and he realized what had spooked his horse.

Tightening his legs, he forced the horse closer until he was sure the large shape on the ground was just a horse and not a horse and rider, and then he let his horse shy away from the dead animal—its blood still wet and fresh on the ground. He kept his horse's head canted to the left as he made a large circle around the corpse, trying to ascertain which direction the assassin had fled after killing his downed mount.

The assassin had been riding too fast, and the horse had stepped in a divot, breaking its leg. The assassin had killed it quickly to prevent its screams from giving away his position, but Gansukh had been tracking him closely enough that the smell of blood had been enough to betray him.

Wolves howled in the distance as Gansukh pulled his horse's head around. There hadn't been any clear indication on the ground of which direction the assassin had gone, and so Gansukh continued north. Behind him, he could make out the distant glow of Karakorum. The Seven Gods, the dead horse, and the city—that was a line easily followed, and there was no reason to think the assassin had changed his course.

He leaned forward as he rode, listening intently to the world around him. Overhead, thousands of stars stared down at him, a multitude of silent observers watching tiny shapes crawl across a wide plain. The hairs on his neck bristled as he was momentarily filled with an awareness of the immensity of the world and the heavens. *No matter how big the empire,* he thought, *there is always a greater world beyond.* Ordinarily such a thought comforted him. He loved to be alone on the plains, loved to surround himself in the vast majesty of nature. Tonight, though, that vastness unsettled him. There were things out there in the darkness, things he couldn't see or hear or feel, and they were ghosts of a world he could never completely understand. Ögedei Khan—and the Khans after him—would spread throughout the world, but the world would spread through them too, and it would change them.

He looked back over his shoulder at the faint bubble of light that was Karakorum—a tiny flicker of fire in a vast emptiness. Gansukh had heard stories of other empires riding out from the steppes, riding out to conquer the world, and he couldn't help but wonder what happened to them. What happened when their light went out and the darkness rushed in again? He had seen the weathered foundations of their ruined forts. Would Karakorum share the same fate in a thousand years' time? *If the Khagan is dead,* Gansukh thought, *what will happen to that light?* Was the plain already starting to nibble away at Karakorum while he rode through the night? Were the wolves already calling to one another? *Fresh meat, brothers. Fresh meat for all of us.*

Gansukh shivered slightly, trying to drive away the darkness that had invaded his brain. *Which is better?* his brain asked, undeterred in its course. *To be the bright fire that tried to dispel the darkness, thereby attracting all manner of scavenger and hunter, or to die like that horse back there, lost and forgotten, picked clean by the weather until the very ground itself grew over his bones...*

On his right, something bolted, a sudden explosion of pounding feet. *Two legs,* Gansukh realized in a flash, and he jerked his horse toward the sound, kicking it into a gallop. He leaned low, his head nearly level with the horse's, straining with all of his senses to pinpoint the runner.

He had found the assassin.

Out in the gloom, he spotted a running figure. The assassin was both larger and smaller than he had expected: bigger because he was now so close to the man, who was smaller than Gansukh had expected him to be. He kicked his horse in the ribs, and the animal lunged forward. The assassin, still dressed in black, twisted like a shadow slipping away from an approaching torch, and Gansukh's horse bumped him heavily as it passed, sending him sprawling.

Gansukh tried to jerk his horse to a stop, and when it started to buck against his pressure, he threw his leg over its back and jumped off, landing lightly on the hard ground. The assassin was getting up and tried to draw his sword, but Gansukh slammed into him. He got his hand over the assassin's, and they wrestled for control of the half-drawn sword as they went down on the ground. A knee glanced off Gansukh's thigh, and as his left arm was pinned beneath the squirming figure, he slammed his head forward and bashed the assassin with the peak of his forehead.

The assassin went limp, and Gansukh extricated his arm as he disentangled himself from the other man. Something sharp slit his right thumb, and he jerked his hand up and back, his fingers finding the hilt of the assassin's weapon. He scuttled backward on his ass, pulling the sword with him, and the blade rasped noisily against the metal rim of the scabbard. But it came free, and he had control of it.

When the assassin lowered his hands from his bloody face, he found himself staring at the tip of his own sword.

"Don't move." Gansukh tried to hide his ragged breathing. The blade trembled in his tight grasp.

The assassin froze, his hands held out in a supplicating position. His chest was moving as rapidly as Gansukh's, big heavy breaths, and with a sudden shock, Gansukh realized why the assassin was smaller than he had expected, why he had been able to physically dominate the other person. He flicked the tip of the sword toward the wrapped scarf that obscured most of the assassin's face. "Take it off," he growled.

Moving very slowly, the assassin complied, and her long hair spilled out of the tight embrace of the scarf.

She reminded him of Lian, and not just because they shared the same elongated face and long black hair. There was a spark in her eyes, a fiery refusal to be tamed, and Gansukh felt both his stomach and groin tighten—a momentary flash of panic and elation—even though he knew that the similarities between Lian and the assassin were merely racial and not familial.

"Who sent you?" Gansukh demanded.

The woman grinned, a mouth full of white, bloodstained teeth. She said something in a dialect he didn't know, and when he didn't react, she spat at him.

He flicked the blade, slapping her on the cheek, reminding her of her situation. "Do you speak Mongolian?" he snarled. "If you don't, then you are no use to me. I'll just kill you like you did your horse. Let the wolves have you." He put the tip of the blade against her throat. "Who sent you to kill the *Khagan*?"

She stared at him for a long moment, daring him to follow through with his threat, and when he didn't flinch or look away, she swallowed heavily and spoke. Her grasp of the language was rough, her accent clipped, and her words enunciated too clearly as if she had never spoken any of these words more than once or twice before. "You make mistakes. I am not a killer. Your *Khagan* is alive."

"I don't believe you."

She pursed her lips, defiant, but she didn't try to convince him. As if it didn't matter what he thought. The truth would be the same either way.

Gansukh shifted his weight, lowering the tip of the sword so that it rested against her breastbone. Just enough that she didn't think he was a fool. He didn't believe her—not entirely—but there were a number of details that were starting to clamor for his attention. If she was an assassin, what had been her tool of choice? Not this sword. It was plain and functional—a horse rider's sword—and to be used effectively, one had to be bigger and stronger than she appeared to be. Poison? If so, had she discarded the poisoned weapon? There were no visible pockets or pouches on her plain black garments.

"Roll over," Gansukh said. When she didn't move, he elaborated. "I want to search you. There must be a knife…"

She shook her head, but complied when that refusal made no impression on Gansukh. Keeping her hands raised, she shifted onto her hips and rolled toward Gansukh, forcing him to pull the blade back or cut her. Silently cursing at himself for not being more explicit, he shuffled a half step in reverse to keep his measure the same. As he moved, he rocked back onto his toes so that he was no longer on his knees. Anticipating her.

She tried to bolt when she got her hands on the ground. Half running/half crawling, she scuttled away from him and nearly got upright before he body-slammed her again and took her to the ground. She gasped as she felt his full weight, and she squirmed until he punched her twice in the lower back with the hilt of the sword. She lay still after that, head turned, cheek pressed against the dirt, glaring at him.

He ran his hands roughly over her body, feeling through the fabric of her clothes. She was thin and angular, more like a bird than a woman, but he felt nothing hard enough to be a knife. And nothing soft enough to be a pouch. He grabbed at her jacket, meaning to pull her over and search her front, but he stopped as his hand encountered something hard. He tried to tug her jacket around without having to roll her over, and she reacted, violently bucking under him. He slammed his elbow against her spine and put the sword blade against the side of her head.

"Lie still," he hissed when she quieted down.

He continued to yank at her jacket so that he could get his hand inside it, but the angle was all wrong. As he struggled to get the jacket open, he heard the rumbling sound of hooves.

Glancing over his shoulder, he spotted a quartet of lights bouncing across the plain. Torches, held by a search party. His prisoner started to squirm again and he leaned against her body, hissing at her again. Gansukh felt her relax, and together they lay as flat as possible on the open ground, hoping the riders wouldn't notice them—he, because he wasn't ready to give up his prize; she, because while she might still escape one captor, more only reduced her chance of success.

There were five of them, riding fast with torches, and they passed on their right, seemingly intent only on what lay directly in their path. Gansukh was about to congratulate himself on remaining undiscovered when one of them suddenly reined in his horse and shouted at the others. Gansukh's heart sank when he heard the rider's voice.

Munokhoi.

CHAPTER 16:

THE MAN FROM ROME

Dietrich von Grüningen had officiated at a number of tournaments since becoming *Heermeister*—the military master of the *Fratres Militiae Christi Livoniae*, the Livonian Brothers of the Sword. He was no stranger to the tedium that surrounded such proceedings. But this gladiatorial spectacle, sponsored by one of the Khans of the invading Mongolian army, was not like the others. It was similar in the sense that crowds did gather to witness feats of arms between single combatants, but unlike other tournaments, which were typically over in one or two days, the duration of this one depended on its host's willingness to continue watching.

The invitation, which he and the masters of other martial orders had responded to, spoke of a tournament to decide the fate of Europe. Representatives would meet in single combat, but it hadn't been clear what would be the spoils of victory. The Khan—Onghwe, a son of the Khan of Khans, Ögedei—had suggested he would spare Europe if he lost. But he was only one of several generals—and not even the most powerful—who was threatening the West. What was the real purpose of these games?

Sport, His Most Holy Father had said when Dietrich had asked that question two months earlier, during his audience with the Pope in Rome. *It is a distraction they can afford to entertain themselves with. It speaks of how little regard they have for us. After the devastation they visited upon good Christian soldiers at Legnica and Mohi, they do not fear our martial strength.*

What is the purpose, then, of participating in this mockery at all? Dietrich had asked.

The Great Khan wishes to extend his dominion, Pope Gregory IX had finally replied. *Like all conquerors before him—men of small vision who thought land and tribute were what defined an empire. These are matters that do not concern us.*

What does? he had asked.

His answer was not to come from the pontiff himself, who had fallen senseless. His eyes remained open, and his chest still rose and fell, though the motion was difficult to discern beneath the voluminous robes and blankets that covered him. The room faced west, and the windows were wide and tall enough that the sun looked in on the room for most of the day. He had been standing there for but a few minutes, and his back was already warm. The Pope had been there much longer, and still his body shivered slightly.

Dietrich had not been able to shake a sense of foreboding at how frail the Bishop of Rome had become. The weight of the Church was immense, and it slowly crushed every man who took the office, but in the year since his last audience, Gregory IX looked as if the life were being wrung out of him like juice from a grape.

The persistence of the Church, Cardinal Fieschi had said as he led Dietrich back to the main hall of the Lateran Palace. *To answer your question, we are concerned with the persistence of the Church, for it is the soul of the people. We are the rock to which they cling when everything around them is swept away.*

What am I to do? Dietrich had asked, seeking the answer to why he had been summoned to Rome, an answer the frail Pope had failed to offer during the brief audience.

Make certain of our survival. It would be best if the Mongolian rabble does not encroach any farther into Christendom. Should that be impossible to avoid—and we realize such indolence on the part of this horde is, indeed, most unlikely—how do you reduce an army's strength before it arrives at your gates?

By making the journey costly, Dietrich had replied. *Every league they march is a league farther from their homes, a league farther into territory that they do not control. Ground they must earn.*

Redirecting an unstoppable army and whittling away at its host of fighting men until the cost of conquest was too high was a seemingly impossible puzzle, one he pondered daily— nay, *hourly*—until his arrival at Legnica. The circus itself seemed like nothing more than a passing fancy, an idler's summertime indolence. In the fall, the Mongol hosts would have finished resupplying and would be looking south for warmer climates to conquer. How was he to turn their attention away from Rome?

And then a solution presented itself. North of the killing fields and the recently erected arena—as well as the ramshackle sprawl of the new city growing around it—was an old monastery. Abandoned by its previous residents, it housed new penitents now, more martial than spiritual in their inclinations. Their standard, raised above the old hall, was a red rose laid over a yellow thirteen-pointed star.

The *Ordo Militum Vindicis Intactae.*

Gladiatorial fights were the sort of peasant entertainment that used to be the mainstay of the Colosseum in Rome; clearly the Mongolian Khan knew the best way to keep his troops from becoming disenchanted with the lack of opportunities for rapine and pillage. Mortal combat was held once a week. The other days were filled with nonlethal bouts, a slip-shod tourney through which combatants earned the right to fight before the dissolute Khan. As long as the venerable Shield-Brethren could provide ready fodder for the arena, Dietrich suspected that this *circus* could last a very long time.

Long enough that the impetus to march before winter might be lost.

It wasn't much of a respite, but it was a start. Every season that passed without the Mongols encroaching any farther into Christendom was time his masters in Rome could use to negotiate a peace treaty. It wouldn't last. The Mongols, much like the Arabs in the Levant, were heathens, and Rome knew they couldn't be trusted. But a peace treaty might be enough to make them turn their attention elsewhere...

The crowd was on its feet, shrieking and howling at the spectacle in the arena. The Mongolian fighter, a man dressed in a garish costume, complete with a lurid mask with white whiskers, had lost his weapon; the Shield-Brethren knight had managed to take it, but clearly had no idea how to use it properly. The Mongolian fighter—someone named *Zug*, if he understood the audience's chant correctly—had at least traded his pig sticker for something longer. Throwing his short sword at the knight was an ineffectual move at best—a blade like that had no chance of penetrating the knight's armor— but it gave him the opportunity to seize the knight's sword. Whether he knew how to wield it effectively was another question; Dietrich doubted the man had any experience with the Great Sword of War.

Some of his knights used such a weapon, but it was much too big and clumsy for his liking. It was a weapon for a man who liked to wear armor, who preferred to be in the thick of battle. In Dietrich's experience, being that close to one's enemies meant a mistake in tactics had been made, and such mistakes were invariably costly.

He had heard reports about the Mongolian general, Subutai, from the survivors of the battle at the Sajó River. He used horse archers, incredibly fast and mobile fighters who remained out of reach of the sword and spear. By the time you could get close to them, they could empty an entire quiver of arrows into your ranks.

Costly mistakes.

Burchard, one of his two bodyguards, nudged Dietrich, drawing his attention toward a rippling movement in the crowd. Dietrich came away from his reverie and looked for what had caught his fellow Livonian's eye.

"A heckler," Burchard pointed. "He threw something." The tall German had been a scout for years before he became one of Dietrich's bodyguards, and his eyesight was well known among the Livonian Sword Brothers.

Dietrich squinted at the tiny object rolling around on the sand and then gave up trying to ascertain what it was. The reaction in the stands was much more interesting anyway.

Some sort of thrill was running through the crowd like a gust of wind across a field of rye, a rippling of bodies as heads were turned toward the enormous pavilion that housed the Khan and his retinue. Some signal passed from within the shade of the tent, and the motion through the throng reversed itself, splitting the audience apart. The crowd drew away from a single man as if he had burst into flames. A Saracen, judging from his clothes. His terror was abject, and he scuttled toward the rim of the growing circle as if to escape notice, but half a dozen hands lashed out and shoved him back. He slid across the floor, and as he passed through the center of the open space, he jerked to a stop, suddenly transfixed by three arrows that sprouted from his body.

Dietrich noticed the fletchings pointed outward in very different directions. Reflexively he glanced around the arena in an effort to note the locations of the snipers. He spotted two readily enough—positioned on fixed platforms around the periphery of the arena. Burchard indicated the third, a Mongol standing just under the edge of the Khan's pavilion. A fourth stood on the opposite side, though he had not shot his bow.

The Saracen writhed and screamed, and the crowd remained at a distance until two burly Mongols pushed their way through the cordon of bodies. One whipped a round-headed mace down on the dying man until he stopped screaming, and then they roughly dragged his corpse away.

"A costly mistake," Dietrich murmured. Burchard raised an eyebrow, and Dietrich waved the Sword Brother's unspoken question away.

The mood was starting to turn. The audience was getting restless. The Khan was showing signs of boredom. This did not bode well for a continuance of the tournament. Dietrich glared down at the two men on the sand as if to invoke a change in their behavior through the force of his gaze. *This game of switching weapons and grappling like drunk peasants is not going to keep the Khan's interest.*

The Shield-Brethren should be more adept than what was currently on display. It had been a number of years since he had actually seen them fight, but he found it hard to believe they had fallen so far from the paragons of martial expertise he knew. Even though the Order had withdrawn from nearly all of their existing commissions, they still held a few citadels of their own, and he had not heard any rumors that their ranks had been decimated in battle. Even at Mohi.

Keeping this competition alive was critical, and he couldn't risk the safety of his own Order by putting his men into the tournament. Whenever the tournament did finally end, the Mongolian army would return its attention to Europe, and it would serve his Order and his masters in Rome little if the Livonian Brothers of the Sword had earned a reputation as fierce fighters. He needed the Mongols to feel threatened by someone else, but if all that remained of the *Ordo Militum Vindicis Intactae* was old men and children, then it would be very difficult to focus the dissolute Khan's attention on the Shield-Brethren.

✦ ✦ ✦

Haakon's first instinct upon gripping Zug's pole-arm had been to adopt what Taran referred to as the Scared Little Boy Pose, which was to say an extended position, aiming the tip of the blade straight out before him. To the extent that his mind was working at all, this was probably an attempt—which any scared little boy would certainly understand—to keep the bogeyman as far away as possible. He began to come to his senses, though, during the pause for hilarity that ran through the arena in the moments after Zug had picked up Haakon's longsword and thereby effected a complete weapons swap.

Haakon felt instinctively uneasy whenever he stood with his blade held straight out for more than a few moments. Was this experienced fighter going to rush forward and impale himself on its tip? Unlikely. Besides which, he'd seen enough to understand that this blade was made for long, sweeping attacks, and from this position, he couldn't deliver one.

So he lowered his right arm, dropping the glaive's tip until it was only a hand's breadth above the ground. By moving it to one side or the other, he could now block a blow, or deflect a thrust from the longsword at any height. From here, he could swing it to either side as needed to shut out the enemy's onslaught. And yet, by making a push-pull motion with his hands, he could snap the cutting edge upward, to send it carving into whatever part of Zug's anatomy might present itself. At the moment, the obvious target was the right leg, which was planted out in front of the left and not especially well armored.

In the moment when they stared at each other, an object had come hurtling into the arena. It had bounced off Zug's helmet with a clang, and while it hadn't caused any injury, they were both momentarily surprised.

Haakon had been trained relentlessly in the importance of seizing the initiative. According to Feronantus, fate bestowed blessings upon him who had the courage to act first. Taran's voice cut through the mysticism: *Make him react to you, damn it!*

Haakon stepped forward, feinting a low cut (an obvious strike, given the starting position of the blade), then drew back and whirled the glaive end-for-end, bringing its edge all the way back and around and up over his head and finally striking downward.

Zug had been holding the longsword out in front of him, a pose not dissimilar to his own stance. As a guard, however, it was only useful against quick strikes to the hand or forearm. Further evidence that the man was drunk and not thinking clearly. Haakon's only opportunity lay in taking advantage of Zug's sluggish reactions.

Zug didn't fall for Haakon's feint, and he quickly raised his sword, catching the glaive on the crossguard. The guard—nothing more than a steel bar—stopped Haakon's blow, but the force of his strike collapsed Zug's arms, and the blade of the glaive glanced off the side of Zug's helmet.

Haakon had been trained to expect that his first attack would invariably not succeed, and so he took advantage of the rebuff of his weapon by sweeping it back and around again, coming up from his lower left. No feint this time. A hard strike, aiming for Zug's right leg.

Zug, making a much smaller movement, was able to snap the tip of his sword downward and get it in the way of the strike. Again he could not hope to withstand the glaive's momentum, but this time he had the ground to act as a brace. When their blades crashed together, the tip of the greatsword was driven into the sand, where it came to a dead stop. As did the glaive.

But the tip of the glaive was now pointed directly at Zug's thigh. Haakon shoved it forward. Zug, sensing such a thrust, flexed his knee, allowing the blade to pass between his legs. The best Haakon could do was to give the weapon's handle a sharp right push, levering over the longsword's planted blade, to buckle Zug's leg and send him toppling to the ground.

Which, to judge from the crowd's reaction, was the most sensational thing that had ever happened in this arena.

✦ ✦ ✦

A pair of drunk Slavs were jumping up and down in front of him, and in their excitement, they were not handling well the skin of fermented horse milk they were sharing. The third time they slopped *arkhi* over their shoulders, spattering Dietrich's gambeson, he intercepted the skin as it passed between them, and when one of the two men tried to follow where his liquor had gone, Dietrich backhanded him in the face.

The second Slav, his face screwed up in confusion, gave a muffled cry as Burchard slammed a meaty fist into one of his kidneys and shoved him forward, where he slammed into the bodies below them. The crowd parted, swallowing the lurching and moaning drunk like a lake swallows a stone.

The first man—clutching his broken and bleeding nose—stared dumbly at the wall of bodies below him, trying to understand what had just happened. Dietrich raised his hand again, but his motion was stayed by his other bodyguard, Sigeberht.

"My lord," the tall Frank said. "We are only three."

Dietrich grunted, acknowledging his bodyguard's words, and hurled the *arkhi* skin into the crowd after the man Burchard had forcibly moved. The bloody-faced man fled too, more to retrieve his liquor than to aid his companion.

We are only three. He had twenty-one more in their camp. Fully equipped Livonian Brothers of the Sword. There were more than a thousand Mongols scattered across the countryside around the ruins of Legnica, and God only knew the population of the sprawling tent city that had sprung up around the arena. Most of them would flee at the first sign of battle, but of those who remained, how many would side with him in any useful way?

This was nothing compared to the main Mongolian army that, having won at the battle of Mohi, was gradually spreading farther into Hungary.

How am I supposed to stop them?

It was easy for the Cardinals to tell him to put his trust in God. They were safe in Rome. Here, surrounded by a shrieking horde of bloodthirsty savages, he found a wide gulf between belief and action. Even though he often prayed to God for counsel and succor, Dietrich preferred to rely on the steel and skill of his men.

But they were too few for this present task. He needed an army.

It was all well and good that the current competitors were thrilling the audience with their shenanigans, but he knew this wouldn't last. Even the most experienced court jester eventually ran out of means to entertain his increasingly jaded audience.

Dietrich fumed silently, his hands clenching and unclenching at his sides, as he watched the Shield-Brethren knight try to spear the Mongolian champion to the red sand with the pole-arm.

CHAPTER 17:

THE MYSTERY OF THE ASSASSIN

As Munokhoi and the other riders approached, Gansukh got to his feet, the tip of the sword reminding his captive to remain still.

Munokhoi reached the pair first. He looked like a hungry wolf, relishing the moment before he sank his teeth in the throat of a mortally wounded deer. "Caught in the act," he said, though he didn't clarify what *act* he was referring to.

"She's my prisoner," Gansukh said.

The other riders formed a semicircle around Munokhoi, dust from their horses' hooves rolling across Gansukh and the woman. By the white fur trim on their *deel*, they weren't Night Guard, but *Torguud*, Day Guard. Members of Munokhoi's *jaghun*.

Munokhoi leaned against his saddle. The torchlight made shadows scurry across his face. "*She?*" he said. His tongue touched his lips as if he were savoring the word, and Gansukh regretted having spoken. Munokhoi slipped out of his saddle and approached the pair. "*She* is a prisoner of the Imperial Guard, pup."

Gansukh bristled at the derogatory word, more so because he knew Munokhoi said it to engender precisely the reaction he was having. He wasn't much younger than the other man, but "pup" implied a vast difference between them. Gansukh swallowed the angry words in his throat, realizing they would do nothing but give Munokhoi the excuse he clearly wanted.

Munokhoi pulled a long blade from his belt and looked down at the captive. He toyed with the tip of the knife with an unconscious familiarity. "Step back, pup," he said to Gansukh, his attention fully on the woman.

The woman was staring up at Gansukh, blinking heavily—whether from fear or from the dust that had settled on her, Gansukh couldn't tell. Her mouth was open, and she was breathing rapidly. He knew what she was going to do as soon as he moved the point of the sword away from her back.

"Very well," he said, and he lifted the sword.

She sprang up, like a deer bolting from brush, and sprinted away, trying to disappear in the darkness beyond the torchlight. One of the men on horseback dropped his torch as he scrambled for his bow, and sparks scattered on the ground, startling the horses. They moved, jostling each other, and the men started shouting at the one who had dropped his torch.

Munokhoi threw his knife, almost lazily, and from the darkness, Gansukh heard a squeal of pain and then the sound of a body falling. "Hai!" Munokhoi shouted at his men. "Control your horses."

The riders brought their mounts under control, moving them away from the guttering torch on the ground, where a tiny grass fire was starting to spread. As the animals calmed down, Gansukh heard a guttural moaning from beyond the circle of torchlight.

Munokhoi glanced at him, his face suffused with the feral grin again.

"Now she has your knife," Gansukh said, enjoying the change in Munokhoi's expression that his words caused.

Munokhoi stalked over to the fallen torch. He stamped out the grass fire and scooped up the torch. "Careful, pup," he snarled. "When I get it back, I might use it on you." Munokhoi walked quickly in the direction he had thrown his knife, and after a moment, his torch swept down as if he were sweeping a stone floor clear of debris. The woman screamed, a long wail that collapsed into a sob.

Who is she? Gansukh hadn't had a chance to consider the woman's claim that she wasn't an assassin. If what she said was true, then what had she been doing in the palace? Was she a thief? What had she stolen?

They needed answers, and the discovery of the woman and subsequent chase had been fraught with confusion, including, Gansukh realized, some of the guards mistaking him for the woman's companion.

He glanced at Munokhoi's men, his throat suddenly tight. Even though the men were *Torguud*, sworn to protect the *Khagan*, they were Munokhoi's handpicked warriors. *We're far from court*, he thought, *away from the eyes of the Khagan. It would be easy for there to be an* accident. *No one would claim otherwise.*

"She's not an assassin," Gansukh shouted. "How can we *protect* the *Khagan* if we don't learn what she was doing at the palace?"

Two of the riders stiffened in their saddles, their body language changing with Gansukh's reminder of the *Torguud*'s primary purpose. He had just bought himself a little breathing room. As long as he kept their focus on the woman, the rivalry between him and Munokhoi would be an awkward distraction to the issue at hand. His men wouldn't tolerate Munokhoi indulging in petty revenge.

Exhaling, Gansukh turned away from the riders and strode toward Munokhoi's now dancing torch.

Munokhoi was struggling to control her. Hampered by both torch and knife, he couldn't hold her still. There was blood on her shoulder, a wet darkness made slick by the torchlight, and the aroma of burnt hair filled Gansukh's nostrils as he got close. She spotted Gansukh approaching, and her movements became even wilder, clawing and scratching at Munokhoi. She hit his left arm—the one holding the torch—and the fire danced dangerously close to his face; when he jerked his head back, she pulled herself free of his grip.

She ran—not into the darkness, but straight at Gansukh. Surprised, he lowered his sword so she couldn't impale herself on the blade (if that was, indeed, what she was trying to do), and she didn't slow down. She collided heavily with him, and he staggered, trying to keep her from attacking his face or grabbing at his sword. She did neither, and for an instant her hands were pressed hard against his chest, and then Munokhoi was on them.

He grabbed her hair, yanked her head back, and slipped his knife under her neck. Gansukh flinched at the approach of the blade, but he couldn't get free of the woman. Her hands pulled at the cloth of his *deel* as if she could rip it open and hide inside the voluminous garment, and it was only after Munokhoi applied a little pressure to his blade—drawing a thin bead of blood on her exposed neck—that she relented.

Munokhoi glared at Gansukh from behind the woman as he wound his hand more firmly in her hair. "She'll talk," he laughed. "I'm very good at *not* killing people."

She shivered uncontrollably, and the wild look in her eyes reminded Gansukh of an animal that saw its death approaching.

"She's my captive," Gansukh said, not giving any ground.

Munokhoi snorted. "I command a *jaghun* of the *Khagan*'s *Torguud*," he said. "You are nothing but a lapdog of the Great Khan's brother. Your word means little in Karakorum."

But it means something, Gansukh thought, *which is why you have only threatened me out here, far away from the ears of men whom you don't command.* Gansukh stared at Munokhoi for another second or two, and then he looked away. He stepped back and to the side, relinquishing his claim on the woman. *For now.*

Munokhoi grunted, assured of his superiority in this situation, and he marched the captive—*his* captive now—past Gansukh. "Tie her up," he called to his men. "Let's take her back to the city." He shot Gansukh one more contemptuous glance.

Gansukh watched the men tie the woman's hands together and then lash her across the saddle of Munokhoi's horse. In a few minutes they rode off, quickly dwindling to fireflies before disappearing entirely.

Gansukh retrieved the torch Munokhoi had dropped, and as he was stomping out the fire it had started, he realized the woman had slipped something into his *deel.*

◆ ◆ ◆

Gansukh returned to Karakorum as quickly as he could, but it took some time to find his horse, even with the assistance of the weak torchlight. As a result, he reached the palace after dawn—dusty, aching, worn out, and irritable. Even the respite of a morning breeze licking his face as he dismounted in front of the palace did nothing for his mood.

The large doors of the palace were shut, the imposing motifs of carved dragons thrust out at the world. A quartet of guards stood in front of them, dressed in the ornate bronze armor and pristine white lamb furs of the Day Guard. They were stoically formal as Gansukh approached, unmoved by his approach or his mood.

"I have important information for the *Khagan*," said Gansukh, "about the intruder last night."

"The intruder has already been interrogated," one of them said.

Gansukh thought about the tiny box the woman had given him. Nestled against his undershirt, it was rectangular, lacquered black, just big enough to fit into his palm, and without a visible seam. When he had shaken it, he had heard something rattle.

"I was the one who captured her," he said. "The *Khagan* will want to hear my report."

"*Torguud* commander Munokhoi captured her," countered the guard.

Gansukh stepped closer to the man, and behind him, two of the other guards dropped their pikes to form a barrier. "Are you calling me a liar?" he said, putting his face very close to the other man. "I am the envoy of Chagatai Khan, and I have been sent to personally report to the *Khagan*. If you do not step aside and let me in the palace, I will…"

The guard tried to call his bluff. "You will what?"

"I will bury my knife in your guts." Gansukh pulled his lips back from his teeth. "Your companions will probably kill me, but then they will have to tell the *Khagan* who they have killed, and why. Do you think they are willing to do that for you? Perhaps the *Khagan* will even let them live long enough to tell Chagatai Khan himself what they have done."

Behind the guard, the pikes rattled as they were withdrawn. The guard heard the noise and blinked heavily.

Gansukh shoved past the nervous guard and hauled open one of the heavy doors. He stalked through the narrow opening, hiding the sudden sweat on his palms and forehead beneath a battlefield swagger. But he was bolstered by the affirmation of what he had realized on the plain: his word did have weight. Munokhoi certainly did outrank him within the palace hierarchy, but he was under direct orders that came from the *Khagan*'s brother, orders that even the *Khagan* himself couldn't completely ignore.

He swept into the throne room, his pace and bearing made strong by this realization, and pulled up short.

The long chamber was nearly empty. There were no ceremonial guards, no throng of obsequious courtiers and provincial administrators. A number of servants labored on the floor, scrubbing the tile clean with wet cloth and pumice stones. The only other individual in the room was Master Chucai, who stood near the *Khagan*'s enormous throne, lost in thought.

"What...?" Gansukh started, and then he realized what the servants were attempting to scour away. His throat closed spastically, and his bluster deflated. There was no mistaking that smell—still so fresh in his head after having smelled it on the plain—even under the masking aroma of the scented water and the incense that had been burned earlier. "What happened?" he asked, even though the answer was obvious.

"An interrogation," Master Chucai said. He approached Gansukh, his face drawn tight by exhaustion—both physical and mental. He hadn't slept either. "The *jaghun* commander, Munokhoi, has a certain facility to old techniques, ones the empire wished it could forget." He shrugged. "But sometimes, it is best—"

"She was my prisoner, Master Chucai," Gansukh said, interrupting the *Khagan*'s advisor. "I could have made her talk with less"—he stabbed a stiff finger at the scrubbing servants—"with less cruelty."

"Cruelty is sometimes necessary to running an empire," Chucai explained. He showed no reaction to the younger man's interruption. He spoke in calm, measured tones. "Regrettable as it may be, an application of intense force can be used to reveal threats to the *Khagan* and to the stability of his rule."

"Was she a threat?" Gansukh demanded.

Chucai's gaze focused on Gansukh, his eyes narrowing. "An enemy is an enemy," he said, his voice even more flat than before.

"That isn't what I asked you," Gansukh replied. "On the steppe, my clan always treated our enemies with respect, even those who came at us with swords and bows. She was unarmed. This...this was butchery."

"She had no weapon," Chucai agreed. "But you are being naive to think that she could not wield one."

"Was that what she was doing here?" Gansukh asked. "Did she tell you she sought to assassinate the *Khagan*?"

Chucai looked at him quizzically. "Is that what she told you?"

"She didn't tell me anything," Gansukh replied quickly.

"You are a bad liar, Gansukh," Chucai said, his gaze intensifying. "Has Lian taught you so little?"

"This isn't about..." Gansukh started, a flush rising in his cheeks.

"What were your instructions from Chagatai Khan?" Chucai asked. "Were you supposed to go chasing after thieves? To interrogate foreign spies? Or were you just supposed to keep an eye on the *Khagan*'s drinking habits?"

Gansukh kept his mouth shut, biting back the torrent of words in his throat. He knew Chucai wasn't interested in hearing them.

"What this woman wanted—what she sought to accomplish—is none of your concern," Chucai said, dismissing
Gansukh with a wave of his hand. "I have placed Lian at your
disposal so that you may learn the ways of court—simply so
that you may more readily accomplish your mission. Chasing
after an intruder like you did last night is the hotheaded
behavior of an *uncivilized* nomad from the steppes."

"Uncivilized?" Gansukh snorted. "I wouldn't have tortured her." And he spun away from Master Chucai, leaving
the *Khagan*'s throne room and its blood-tainted floor behind.

He didn't like running away, but he *had* learned something from Lian: to know when he had lost the advantage.
Master Chucai had twisted their conversation around to focus
more on Gansukh than on what the woman had wanted. He
didn't dare push back. Chucai would see that he did know
more than he was letting on.

Though did he know more?

He slipped a hand inside his *deel* and touched the lacquered box.

CHAPTER 18:

THE PARTING OF THE VEIL

Later, after he had killed this giant steel cockroach, Zug would worry about the humiliation of being down on the ground. Of having been sent there with his own weapon! But he had not fought hundreds of combats in this and other such arenas without having acquired certain skills. One of which being that he could draw power from the energy of the crowd when it suited him, but ignore them altogether when they were only honking like excited geese.

Chevalier—as the crowd appeared to name this big Frank—had some experience with pole-arms, and while he wasn't exceptionally proficient with the *naginata*, he was good enough. Zug knew he had been lucky—*twice!*—and such fortune was more than a dead man could hope to receive. He would not be afforded any more such chances.

Lying on the ground, he could not use his legs or his body to put force behind his blocks. He had to get in close, like the Frank had done.

Though unlike the Frank, he was flat on his back.

Zug curled like a prawn, contracting his chest and knees toward each other. As he arched his back to move across the ground, he flicked the blade of the Frank's sword toward the closest target—the Frank's right ankle.

Unlike the rest of his body, the Frank's ankle wasn't armored. The strike would either take his foot clean off or break bones and cripple him.

The Frank lifted his foot adroitly, just high enough to let the blade hurtle through underneath. But he was off balance and would have to plant the foot again before he could formulate his own attack. He had lost the initiative.

Zug kept the enormous sword moving. He whirled it all the way around as he shrimped across the ground again and brought it back for a second pass—the same strike, but with even greater power.

The point of the *naginata* drove into the ground in front of him and brought the sword's movement to an abrupt stop. It was almost an exact mirror of how Zug had stopped the Frank's second *naginata* strike a moment ago.

Levering himself up on his right elbow, Zug reached up with his left and grabbed the *naginata*'s wooden shaft, his hand only about a foot away from the Frank's. The weapon was neutralized, and Zug had something to lean on.

The Frank's left knee was exposed, at about the altitude of Zug's head, in a perfect position to be kicked. Zug pulled his knees up almost to his chin and then lashed out at his opponent's knee. The Frank, seeing an opportunity of his own to kick Zug in the head, had started to pivot on his left leg, but Zug was faster and drove the other's knee sideways at the precise moment when all of his weight—and that of his massive coating of armor—was firmly supported by that leg.

The Frank collapsed to the ground, nearly landing on top of Zug. His right elbow was now on top of Zug's left, immobilizing that arm, and his stinking armpit was almost in Zug's face. Zug's right arm, however, was shielded by his body and free to move.

Zug discarded the Frank's sword, and in a well-practiced motion, he reached to the small of his back and drew out the *tanto* sheathed there. He brought it around the front of his body in a small, quick movement that the Frank could not even see and jammed it with all his strength upward into the Frank's armpit. As he did so, he had to control an instinct to flinch away, since he expected a fountain of blood to erupt from the big artery that was pumping life into the Frank's arm.

But nothing happened.

✦ ✦ ✦

Haakon had been struck in some painful ways during his training, and Taran had made a point of teaching them to poke each other in certain spots, such as behind the point of the jaw, where it was especially unpleasant. But he had never felt anything quite as bad as what Zug did to his armpit.

He was no longer holding the shaft of the glaive; the impact of the thing in his armpit had made his hand go slack. He raised his arm, more to see whether it still worked than as a martial tactic, and was horrified to see a silver steel blade projecting from Zug's right fist, going straight up to where it hurt.

Haakon's mail had stopped a perfectly aimed thrust.

Then, much later than it should have, Haakon's training came back to him; he grabbed Zug's wrist with his left hand, palmed the blade with his right, and pushed in different directions. The hilt peeled up out of Zug's fingers, pinky first, followed by the rest, and then the dagger was in his hand. Forearm-to-forearm pressure kept Zug's right arm buckled and pinned against his chest. With no real planning or effort,

Haakon found that he had brought the dagger into a position where its tip was only inches away from his opponent's throat. A small movement of his hand and it would be over.

But he could not bring himself to kill this man. From a distance, swinging the huge glaive—that was one thing. But he was so close now that he could see, through the narrow eye slits of the demon mask, the bloodshot veins in the whites of Zug's eyes.

By almost any fair accounting, Zug had won the duel. Haakon had been standing over him wielding an immensely superior weapon. But this man had taken him down and delivered a perfectly aimed strike that ought to have left him helpless and bleeding to death on the ground.

Sometimes, when he was intensely focused on a fight, he stopped hearing things. Later, when it was over, hearing returned. He thought he was in one of those instances now, but he could hear Zug breathing, the faint jingle of his mail as he shifted his position.

It wasn't that he had gone deaf. It was that the arena had gone absolutely silent.

He pushed away from Zug, heaving himself up to his feet. He heel-kicked the *naginata* backward, out of reach, and backed clear of his sprawling opponent.

Zug's mask was askew, and it no longer seemed to be the face of a ferocious demon. The white whiskers were matted and dirty, and the mouth was stretched sideways, more of a drunken leer than a howling maw.

In a rush, the audience started screaming. A flood of noise that staggered Haakon with its force. Zug flinched as well, and his mask tilted upward as he looked at something over Haakon's shoulder.

Haakon turned, taking in the blur of a rapturously ecstatic crowd—the entire arena was on its feet, shouting and cheering—until his gaze settled on the Khan's pavilion. Onghwe Khan, his large frame covered in robes of crimson and gold, stood at the edge of the pavilion, his hands upraised. He brought them together, sunlight sparkling off the multitude of rings on his fingers, and he saluted Haakon.

Haakon had the presence of mind to do the same. He touched the hilt of Zug's dagger to the forehead of his helmet, and for a second he heard Taran's voice in his head. *Do it!* his *oplo* shouted. *You can make this throw.* His hand tightened around the hilt of the dagger.

Onghwe Khan brought his hands apart, palms out, as if he were parting a curtain, and Haakon realized with a start that he was doing exactly that. Below him, the Red Veil moved. It was drawn back by invisible hands, and Haakon got his first glimpse at what lay beyond.

The audience, already making enough noise to be heard for leagues, became louder still. Haakon's chest seized. He couldn't draw a breath, and all thought of trying to assassinate the Khan fled from his brain. The world seemed to slow down. The shrieking noise of the crowds became a muted roar that buffeted his ears like the slow pound of military drums, and above the thunder of the audience there rose a single chattering voice.

Zug had risen to his feet. His face had changed, and Haakon dimly realized he had removed his mask. His face, while mostly smooth, was not that of a boy. Apoplectic, his eyes bulging, his cheeks red, his mouth spitting out words Haakon did not understand—this was the face of a grown man. Haakon stared at him for a frozen moment, marking all the rage and despair he could read plainly on Zug's visage; it was a face he would not soon forget.

He bowed to Zug and then turned his back on his defeated opponent and walked toward the opening beneath the Khan's pavilion.

He had won. The Red Veil had parted.

◆ ◆ ◆

Dietrich watched as the Shield-Brethren knight disappeared from view. From his position on the western side of the arena, the veil and a section of the tunnel beyond it were visible, though as soon as the knight stepped past the veil, it dropped once again, obscuring everyone's vision of what was happening on the other side.

The audience was still celebrating, and the stadium was starting to shiver with the rhythmic vibration of stomping feet. The exultation of voices was dying out, enough that Dietrich could make himself heard to one of his companions without having to shout; he had turned to Burchard to speak when a piercing scream rose above the ambient chatter.

Down on the arena floor, the losing competitor was howling. His mask was off, and his outrage was directed at the Khan's pavilion. Instead of tapering off, his scream ended abruptly as he spun on his heel and lunged for the pole-arm lying in the sand.

The eastern gate was opening, disgorging a quartet of Mongolian soldiers with long poles of their own—tipped with sand-filled bags that would bruise and coerce. The dispersal team, deployed to separate combatants and to shuffle the survivor off to his proper destination, was a well-known sight in the arena, and Dietrich had seen their heavy poles in action on more than one occasion, though usually they were facing a fighter armed with just a sword.

Zug's weapon was as long as theirs, and sharp.

The first Mongol discovered how sharp the pole-arm's blade was when it took his head cleanly from his shoulders.

The second Mongol tried to get his pole-arm up to block Zug's spinning blade, but all he managed to do was deflect the blade up so that it sheared through his skull instead of his neck.

The remaining pair stumbled back, trying to keep out of Zug's reach.

Dietrich glanced up at the walls surrounding the arena, looking for the Mongolian archers. They were tracking the crazed fighter down below, and one loosed an arrow. Zug lifted his arms, spinning his weapon in a circle between himself and the archer, and the arrow deflected off the ash of the pole-arm shaft.

Burchard grunted in admiration. "Look," he said, pointing at the pavilion. The pair of archers stationed there had arrows nocked in their bows, but they weren't drawing them. "The Khan is not ready to lose his champion."

The pair of archers stationed farther away finally heard the shouted command to hold. The crowd was turning into a clashing sea of opinions: some were chanting Zug's name; some were raising a cry for clemency; others were chanting for blood, anyone's blood; and a small part of the crowd was starting to get angry. Down below the Livonians, near the wall, a fight broke out, and from this grunting mass, a body was ejected over the rail.

The body—a Northerner, judging by the pale color of his hair—collapsed bonelessly on the sand. There was blood on his face. His limbs twitched; he was still alive, but knocked senseless by the blow that had catapulted him into the arena. What happened next was not his fault, but he was the one who opened the floodgate.

Two Mongols dropped to the sand, and while one hunched over the supine Northerner to finish him off, the other scrambled across the arena floor, heading for the knight's discarded sword.

Having scared the two remaining pole-wielding guards back as far as the eastern gate (which had been summarily closed behind them as soon as Zug had attacked the first of the four and which wasn't being opened no matter the pleas they made to the men on the other side of it), Zug charged back toward the center of the arena, and his pole-arm caught the running Mongol in the back, nearly severing his legs from his trunk.

More bodies dropped into the arena from several locations, and Dietrich realized they weren't all Mongolian. The archers began shooting. The audience—no longer giving vent to a cry of "Zug! Zug!"—were now responding with fear and anger. They started hurling their own missiles—rocks, mostly—and some were directed down at the men in the arena, but a larger number were directed at the archers and the occupants of the pavilion. The archers responded, turning their attention toward the surging masses around them, shooting into the mob.

Sigeberht pulled at Dietrich's arm, a clear signal that it was time to leave. Somewhat reluctantly, Dietrich allowed himself to be pulled away from the chaos of the rioting audience. "Fascinating," he murmured as Sigeberht shoved his way through the crowd, clearing a path toward the stairs at the back of the stands. An idea was beginning to suggest itself, an answer to his nightly prayers to God for insight.

For all their bluster and military superiority, the Mongols were still men. Men who were far from their homes, occupying a foreign land. These men—the fighters who would be doing the bloody work of the Khan—were starting to lose their edge. The army was getting tired, and a tired army was more readily frightened.

Yes, he thought, *and frightened men lash out at the things they fear.* Dietrich saw the standard of the *Ordo Militum Vindicis Intactae* in his mind's eye, snapping in the wind above the ruined monastery, and he smiled.

CHAPTER 19:

MY FATHER'S LEGACY

Lian found Gansukh in the garden, stripped to his light pants, practicing his swordplay against a hapless tree. Such practice was technically not allowed in the *Khagan*'s garden, but Lian had sensed the young man's fury as soon as she heard the sound of metal against bark. The gardeners were equally sensitive, and they were scarce from this corner of the garden. Cut leaves and branches were strewn all over the ground, and with each flashing stroke of the blade, another flew off. He stopped when he saw her coming, planted the tip of his sword against the short grass, and leaned on it, panting and sweaty.

"I have heard...*stories*...from some of the servants," she said.

He grunted wordlessly and turned back to the tree, intending his brusque attitude to be read as a dismissal.

"I heard it was a woman," she said.

He stood still, sword in hand. "Did they tell you what happened to her?" he asked.

She shook her head and took a few steps closer. She could almost touch his naked back. "No," she said, which wasn't entirely true. The servants had been reluctant to speak clearly about what had happened in the throne room, which spoke quite plainly about what *had* happened.

With sudden rage, he jabbed his sword into the heart of the tree. His fury startled Lian, made her jump back like a frightened animal. "What am I doing here?" he said, whirling on her. His face was distorted by his anger and confusion.

Lian chose her words with care. "You were sent by the *Khagan*'s brother, to help the empire."

"How?" Gansukh demanded. "By becoming a lapdog of the *Khagan*'s court? Am I supposed to be more like...like *him*?"

"Munokhoi?" Lian shook her head. "No. You are nothing like him."

Gansukh yanked his sword free of the tree and, somewhat ruefully, ran his fingers along the edge, checking for nicks. "What am I, then?" he mused quietly. "Chucai admonishes me for being a hunter. Am I supposed to set aside everything that I have done, that I have learned, so that I may be more *likable* to the *Khagan*? How does that help the empire?"

Lian approached him and placed a hand on his bare shoulder. He almost shuddered at the touch, as if he had been expecting her to attack him. His muscles were tense, his bare skin hot beneath her hand.

He completed his examination of his sword. "If the *Khagan* is all-seeing and wise, then why does he not see Munokhoi for the sheep-killing dog he is?" he wondered. "And Master Chucai. He taught the *Khagan*'s father so much, and the *Khagan* does not..." Gansukh abruptly stopped, and when he glanced back at Lian, he couldn't hold her gaze. She sensed he was holding something back.

"What?" She tried to draw him out.

He shook his head, and she didn't press it further. The trust between them was still too tenuous. She couldn't afford to lose it. Not now...

"It's all wrong." He made a sweeping gesture, indicating the palace. "I was sent here to help the *Khagan* find his strength, but no one here thinks it is missing. Instead of being a strong warrior, I am being taught how to bow and crawl on my belly for his amusement. When a threat against him is exposed, it is simply silenced as if it never existed. This whole place is an illusion, and I am the only one who can see it for what it truly is. What can I do?"

She slid her hand down his arm, stood beside him, and grasped his hand tightly. When he looked at her, when he squeezed her hand, she fought hard to keep her face expressionless, to keep the flush from rising in her cheeks. *So lost,* she thought. *So earnest, but without knowing which way to go.*

"What you know is right," she heard herself say, and she was quietly surprised to realize she meant every word.

◆ ◆ ◆

The sun had crossed the sky and begun to slip behind the mountains by the time Gansukh managed to talk his way into the *Khagan*'s private quarters. He had spent the day tracking down all the *Khagan*'s personal advisors—other than Master Chucai, whom he carefully avoided—and he had even gone to several *Torguud noyon* before, finally, one of his wives— Mukha—agreed to speak to the *Khagan* on his behalf. She had confided to him that his humor was "most black," which Gansukh took to be her euphemism for "drinking heavily." As he approached the portal to the *Khagan*'s sitting room, he noticed the lanterns in this corridor smelled like oranges rather than the musty smell of beef tallow so prevalent in the rest of the palace.

The touch of a woman, he thought, reflecting again on the feel of Lian's hands on his body earlier that day.

The black-cloaked guards at the *Khagan*'s door nodded with tight-lipped smiles, signaling that they had been warned of his arrival, while simultaneously giving him a look that said, *Better you than us.* They shut the door quickly behind Gansukh, just in case he tried to change his mind.

The room was long and dim, lit by only a few lanterns. Most of the light came from the balcony, where Ögedei Khan stood, a broad-shouldered silhouette against the darkening sky. The night wind—the last breath of a vanishing sun—slithered through the room, rustling silk curtains and making the candles in the lanterns dance. Bands of flaming red clouds streaked the indigo sky, and as Gansukh approached, he could see the stark line of the mountains along the horizon, their tips outlined in orange fire. Soon that light would die too, and the world would plunge into darkness again.

Gansukh tried not to think about what course of events had begun at this time only a day before. He lowered himself to one knee and cleared his throat. "Oh Khan of Khans, master of the world, long have I...I have..." This flowery language did not come naturally to him, but he thought it best to pay proper respect to the *Khagan* before even embarking on the bulk of the questions he had. *A most black humor,* he thought, and faltered.

Ögedei turned from the balcony. There was a cup in his hand, and his gait was unsteady as he came into the room. "Ah, young pony," he rumbled. "You have been looking for me."

Gansukh nodded. "I am in need of some...guidance."

"Get up and come over here, then." The *Khagan* sipped from his cup. "I do not need a statue." He waved a hand toward the open balcony. "I have one down there already. Have you seen it?"

Gansukh had. It was hard to miss it. Especially when there was wine and honeyed drink and Blue Wolf knew what else pouring from the spouts. He rose, one hand straying to his sash, where he had tucked the tiny lacquered box. "The woman who tried to enter the palace last night," he started. "Do you know what she was after?" *Did you watch her being tortured?* was the question he couldn't bring himself to ask.

The *Khagan*'s face remained expressionless, giving Gansukh no sign he understood the subtext of what the young man was asking. "Secrets," he slurred. "Chucai said she was a spy, gathering information. She ran off before she could learn anything useful."

Gansukh swallowed heavily, forcing his stomach to hold still. "Did she tell you this or did Master Chucai?" he asked, still unable to speak plainly.

Ögedei drank from his cup as he wandered closer to Gansukh, staring intently at the young man's face. "Master Chucai did," he said.

Gansukh felt his knees tremble—a sudden terror colliding with an unwarranted joy in his guts. "You weren't there," he whispered.

Ögedei leaned toward Gansukh and put his finger to his slack lips. His breath stank of sour wine. "Shhh," he whispered back. "I am rarely where I am supposed to be, and that's a secret." He laughed suddenly, spraying spittle on Gansukh's face. "I know many secrets, young pony." He clapped Gansukh on the shoulder. "Is that what you need to know? Is Chagatai concerned that I will become such a drunk that my lips cannot remain shut? That one of my enemies will send someone in to steal them while I sleep?"

"No," Gansukh countered, flustered by the sudden change in Ögedei's mood. "It's Master Chucai—"

"Chucai." Ögedei spit out the name like it was something caught in his throat. "He's an old goat herder who thinks the hills are full of wolves." He drew himself up to his full height and thrust out his chest. Some of the liquid in his cup slopped out, darkening his already stained sleeve. "I am not a goat."

"No," Gansukh replied. "Of course not."

Something caught Ögedei's attention and he beckoned Gansukh to follow him. He staggered out onto the balcony and pointed at the great war banner mounted at the edge of the balcony. It was a gigantic spear, much too long to be wielded easily from a horse; beneath the iron blade hung thick strands of black horsehair, the tails of an entire herd, and they streamed and twisted in the embrace of the night air.

"The Great Spirit Banner of Genghis Khan," Ögedei said. "Do you know the story, young pony? My father's spirit is still alive, inside that pole, making sure his empire expands until it covers all the lands."

Gansukh nodded. "I've heard the story."

"It's just a story," Ögedei slurred. He leaned against Gansukh, who staggered, trying to support the *Khagan*'s sudden weight. "It's superstition," Ögedei hissed. "There's a secret…" He became entranced with his cup. When he drank, some of the wine spilled down his chin. "It's older than my father," Ögedei continued, oblivious to the wine dripping off his face. "He did not make it. It was given to him, long before he became *Khagan*. He never told me where…" Ögedei stared at the banner for a while before continuing.

"He told me how to listen to it, though. He told me how to see things in the way the hair moves. It's more than a banner…I can look at it, and it tells me of battles I have never seen, battles that have not happened, and even some that I know never will. I can put my hands in the hair of a thousand horses and feel the rhythm of their movement. How to attack, how to feint, how to retreat—I can feel how every battle can be won."

Gansukh gazed at the banner, trying to see what the *Khagan* saw, but all he saw was black horsehair vanishing into the approaching night. "My Khan, with all due respect, you are drunk."

Ögedei's attention snapped to Gansukh's face and then to the cup in his hands. He drank greedily from it, as if there were answers to be found in its dregs. His eyes were even more glazed when he lowered the cup, and he stared out at the horizon, not seeing anything, not even the fact that the sun was gone and night had fallen. "You don't understand, pony," he said. "I am *Khagan*, and I do as I like. And the empire depends on that. My father's empire. It must continue on. For the memory of all those who sacrificed themselves. For the memory of Tolui." Tears started to form in the corners of Ögedei's eyes.

"You don't understand," the *Khagan* shrieked suddenly, pushing Gansukh away. He threw his cup too, and Gansukh ducked, letting it sail past him and into the room. "None of you do. Not Chucai. Not Chagatai. Not any of my generals. None of you understand what is truly important. You all want to tell me what to do, but you don't know. You don't know what to do!"

Gansukh backed away, his hands held in front of him. "My Khan, I'm—" he started, but he was cut short by a tremendous wail that came howling out of Ögedei. He watched, startled, as the *Khagan* tore an ornamental cap off the balcony railing and hurled it into the night. When the *Khagan* whirled on him, Gansukh retreated quickly, but the *Khagan*'s interest only lay in the furniture and vases in the sitting room.

Gansukh continued to retreat toward the door, stunned by the transformation that had come over Ögedei Khan.

He was no longer the leader of the Mongol Empire; he had become a gigantic infant, throwing a horrific temper tantrum. He threw vases across the room. He picked up furniture and dashed it against the floor, and when he couldn't pick it up easily, he kicked and hit it. All the while, his body shook with great wracking sobs.

The door opened, and Gansukh, filled with both shame and revulsion, slipped out of the room. The guards closed the door and stood in front of it, their eyes forward, their postures saying quite plainly that they would never acknowledge any of the sounds coming through the portal. What happened behind them was a secret they would never reveal.

Gansukh's hand slipped inside his *deel*, touching the tiny lacquered secret held therein. Ögedei's voice chased him as he walked away from the *Khagan*'s private room, an echo that grew louder and louder in his head as the real sounds grew fainter: *None of you understand what is truly important.*

CHAPTER 20:

THE DEATH OF A FRIEND

A messenger does not kill; a Binder does not take life. But there was blood on her hands and on the knife.

"Do you need help?"

Cnán heard Raphael's voice distantly, and for a moment she thought he was asking the question of her, but when she raised her head to reply, she saw he was speaking to Percival.

"I raised him from a foal," Percival said. His face was a mask; his lips barely moved as he spoke. "I will do it alone. Help the others see to Taran." The solemn knight turned and walked into the woods, following a trail of blood and crushed grass.

The silence of the field and forest closed around Cnán. Her knife still dripped blood into the hoof-trodden dirt and grass. She stared, seeing but not seeing the trees at the edge of the woods in their strangely placid beauty. Yasper's lingering smoke rendered the sight eerie and ghostlike. The dagger in her hands felt light as air, and that seemed wrong. She wanted to be rid of it, but at the same time couldn't make herself throw it away.

They had wrapped Taran in a cloak and taken him back to camp, where a grave would be dug. The Dutchman wandered the field, dousing the flames, and about him the remaining smoke wreathed and whirled. She stepped over the corpse of a Mongol, facedown in the dirt, the body positioned just as Taran's had been. She suppressed a shudder and moved on, feeling as though she would be violently ill.

How far had she fallen, to permit herself to arrive here and to use this tool, a killing tool, as it was meant to be used? She wiped the blade clean with a clutch of dried leaves, shock wearing away slowly, like feeling coming back into a sleeping limb and, with it, the first prickles of returning conscience.

Not what she wanted to feel.

She took another step, planning to get away from the company and be by herself. Her feet took over. As she walked, she heard arguments behind her: Roger's raised voice, Feronantus's reply. The words were empty and distant, intrusions into an awful dream. Was this the penance for what she had done?

A strange, sad sound reached her, seeped into her mind, and pulled her along the direction in which she walked. Tall weeds brushed against her legs. She stopped at the edge of the wide open stretch through which Mongols had rushed only a short time ago, and her focus returned with a sickening lurch as she realized that she had not been wandering aimlessly, but following another's footsteps across the field and back toward the woods.

Cnán stood still, watching as Percival knelt by his mount. Obeying some instinct that had told it to seek refuge, the horse had staggered into the shelter of the trees and then collapsed.

The knight's frame caught the rays of sun falling through the canopy of high trees, mail over muscle moving with a deliberate, gentle softness so utterly at odds with his violent motion before. Cnán heard again the husking, ragged sound that had pulled her from her malaise—deep whimpers from Percival's mortally wounded destrier.

His own breath seemed to blend with the slow panting of the large horse where it lay amidst the ferns.

Her stomach clenched, and a lump formed in her throat as he removed a mailed glove and ran a callused hand over the animal's thick neck. A shaft jutted from the animal's flank. The horse gave a louder moan, and its chest heaved. Percival stood back a few steps as it thrashed and then twisted in agony.

So often in her short life, she had witnessed horses and men fall, had absorbed the horror of the image and moved along—as was required of her. Yet this was different. Here and now, the sight stopped her, stilled her; she was suddenly unable or unwilling to move from where she crouched half concealed among the ferns that grew along the forest's edge.

As Percival tried to soothe the beast that had borne him across the miles, it seemed as if she were watching an essential part of the great, noble man suffer and die.

What sort of world was this, she thought, *that made such a man? A person for whom violence could be summoned like an obedient hound, then put away with the sheathing of a sword.*

How immediate the violence had been for her, how utterly sudden and desperate. Was it the same for Percival every time he drew his sword? Did he feel the same shock as she did? If not, how easily a person might be pulled into a life where the hound of violence became a mad wolf, pulling at its chains, ready to come out whether its master wished it or not!

But now he knelt on one leg as if in prayer, and she saw in this stance that it was not just the destrier that drew forth his silent grief.

Her throat constricted. Her eyes grew wet. She was shaking. This aftermath, this horror and shock, was what Percival endured, what they all endured, every time they were called to fight.

Abruptly Percival's voice broke through her gray misery, speaking to his horse. "I have asked so much of you, *Tonnerre*. You have crossed miles and endured hardships, many of them meant for me. Always, you have been loyal, patient, and kind. A man could not reasonably ask for a tiny share of what you gave."

The horse's tail twitched, as though in answer. Cnán saw its head rise, and she caught a look of sorrowful intelligence in its dark eyes. There was pain, but also a remnant of questioning innocence that brought Feronantus's words back to her heart. The lot of their faithful mounts: food and burdens, suffering and death, for the sake of the men who raised and trained and rode them.

"You have traveled far and served us wonderfully well," Percival said, his voice almost too low to hear. He moved beside the great head and leaned over, gently taking one ear and angling it toward his lips. "I cannot take away the pain, nor ask you to run again. And so I will not keep you here to suffer, *Tonnerre*."

As Cnán watched, the knight drew his dagger with the reticence of a man who would sooner cut off his own hand than do what he was about to do.

Her view of him blurred, and she felt hot tears roll down her cheek.

Her knife, in desperation; Percival's, in mercy.

"We are lessened by your departure," Percival said, his voice breaking. Two companions lost, one at the hands of the enemy, one he must now release himself. Again, she had seen this last rite many times across the years and across the miles. Animals so grievously hurt that it was a mercy to put them down rather than leave them to suffer and die slowly.

But never before had it been like this. The truth of that was etched in the way he held the blade and in the quaver of his eternally calm voice. Cnán turned away and tightly closed her eyes. She couldn't bear to look.

There came a spasmodic pounding of hooves, a brief, rustling flurry of violent shuddering, and then stillness.

The trembling and heaving of the Mongol she had killed flashed before Cnán's closed eyes. She clenched her teeth. When she forced herself to look again, she found Percival standing alongside the unmoving animal. He turned toward her slowly.

In the shadows of the woods beyond, she also saw Raphael, arms crossed, watching with that analytical expression she sometimes found so irritating. How could the physician not be moved?

Percival, however, saw only Cnán. He opened his mouth to speak. His cheeks were slick with tears. But he said nothing. He faltered. Slowly his body turned sideways to her, and his eyes rose up in his head until only the whites showed. He sagged to both knees and dropped his chin to his chest. He might have been sleeping, but his head moved slowly from side to side, as if he were listening to secret music. Then, impossibly, he smiled, as if at the sight of a long-absent friend. He raised his eyes to the branches and sky overhead and stretched out both arms, palms upward, as if catching a warm rain. From the former rigidity of grief, she saw the knight's body loosen, and then he jerked once, twice, at some inner paroxysm.

He began to murmur in Latin, and she strained to hear his words. "*Ego audio Domine. Animus humilis igitur sub ptoenti manu Dei est. Mundus sum ego, et absque delicto immaculatus. Verbum vester in me caro et ferrum erit.*"

The glow upon his face—impossible in the morning light, in the woods! He looked around, seeing nothing earthly, but beaming like a small child, and the light of his expression seemed to flash through the forest.

Light without shadows.

Stifling a cry, Cnán fled. Her feet carried her out of the ferns and into the open field, wonder, guilt, and memory hot on her heels. At twenty paces, she paused, stood with shoulders stiff as stone, then—she could not help herself—she turned and looked back.

Percival had not moved. Raphael, who had witnessed this moment as well, was walking away—not *toward* Percival, she noted—a bemused look on his sun-browned face.

Cnán ran once more, slipping through the mouse hole in the hedge wall, getting out into the large field beyond, where she could have some privacy. The old snag that she had climbed earlier was a short distance away. She ran to it, circled around to the other side where no one could see her, and sank shuddering to the tangle of roots at its base. Pressing her fingers against the ancient bark, she wept until her entire body ached, for the pain, the grief, and in the middle of grief, the unexpected, impossible beauty of Percival's illumination.

✦ ✦ ✦

Sometime later, chest still full and cheeks tight with dried tears, she made her way back to the camp. The voices of the Shield-Brethren, less ghostly now, seemed to be handed from tree to tree across the field before Cnán caught sight of them. Yasper's smoke had long since faded, and the air was clear. In the aftermath of the battle, silence had given way to anger. The Shield-Brethren were at odds now, and the former battleground resounded with the din.

"Roger, stop!" The shout rose over all as the camp came back in view. Raphael had interposed himself between the

Norman and Istvan. The former held a drawn hatchet and arming sword.

"Stand aside," Roger said. "He'll be the death of us all, one by one. He doesn't deserve your protection, much less your faith."

"We are *not* barbarians," Raphael said sternly, "to cut down one of our own when the enemy is yet near. Lower your weapons. For God's and all our sakes, be reasonable."

"Reasonable?" Roger snarled. "Taran is *dead*, and that man"—he leveled his sword in the direction of the Hungarian—"as good as drew down upon us all the Mongols who killed him. It is madness to keep him—and his insanity—in the company; reason demands he be put down before he gets us all killed. It would be a mercy to him—and to us all!"

"Enough," Feronantus said, rising from where Taran lay. Illarion still sat on the opposite side of the body, and the two had been speaking in low voices. As she drew closer, she saw that the Brethren's leader wore an expression between grief and grim determination. There was a calm hardness there that would brook no argument. "His foolishness has cost one life; let it not cost us more. Break camp and round up the spares we have found; we set out as soon as we have properly seen Taran to his rest."

Roger, his weapons poised, did not move. Istvan's hand rested on the hilt of his curved blade, his eyes set on the Norman's with a hard glare bespeaking a ready willingness to do more violence, even to take joy in it.

The blood and dust in the Hungarian's beard had caked to muddy black. He looked more demon than man.

Raphael remained between the two, eyes leveled steadily on Roger's. The others waited, hardly daring to draw breath, none wishing to make the move that would provoke their brother into retaliation.

Roger broke his stance first. "So be it, then," he said as both sword and hatchet dropped. He half bowed and stepped back, moving his attention toward Feronantus. "On your head be this, Ferhonanths. God and the Virgin save us all if this…if this…"—he cast his eyes once more on Istvan—"*mad dog* cannot be kept to leash. He is nothing to me—no companion, no warrior. He is a demon-ridden butcher, and I am done with him. He should be staked to a tree and left for the Mongols."

Istvan received this imprecation with a courtly nod, his assurance unbroken, his arrogance galling to all around him—with the exception of Feronantus.

Disgusted, Roger turned on his heel and stalked away. The group slowly dropped their shoulders, shrugged them out, and then set to breaking camp.

Only Istvan seemed to notice Cnán's arrival, though she raised her shoulder to avert his look. A demon-beleaguered man, cursed by his comrades, yet still defiant and proud. She understood nothing, clearly, about Feronantus and his intentions.

When Percival returned, they set about the finality of laying their comrade deep under foreign soil. Together, two on each side, they grasped Taran's cloak, carried him a few steps, and lowered him into the fresh-dug grave, then wrapped him against the coming fall of dirt.

Slowly and in silence, the *oplo*'s comrades, eyes downcast, gathered around the grave. Feronantus spoke a quiet eulogy. Cnán understood the old Latin words well enough. She had some passing familiarity with the ways Christians buried and blessed their dead. She knew that they laid the bodies in the earth intact, in the belief that, upon the final Day of Judgment, their God would raise them up again and that any whose body was destroyed would have no vessel in which to return. It was a strange practice to her, no less so having now seen it, so unlike the burials she had witnessed in the East. Though in truth, one way of disputing the finality of death was as odd and pointless to her as the next.

Feronantus's speech was short, but imbued with an ardent affection and sense of loss in every word. "God keep you, Taran, *oplo* to many, and best amongst us. The world may not remember, but we will never forget."

Now he began to speak in a different language, one she had seldom heard before and only sparingly. Low-voiced, yet strong, he chanted rhythmically in the tongue of the Northmen who had given the fortress on the rock its name. She knew nothing of what was being chanted, but soon the others joined their leader. Something in the rhythm and the hard guttural words of the chant told Cnán that this was also an old, old ritual, perhaps older than Christianity itself—a ritual of which the Church they supposedly served would never approve.

When the chant was finished, all had tears in their eyes, and one by one they knelt, and each dropped a handful of earth into the grave.

It struck her then, the true meaning of the word they used to refer to him: *oplo*. Taran had been their friend, but for some of them, he had been more: their teacher, their confidante, their calm and patient tutor. In the way they lingered at the grave, and in the way they let their loss wash over them, she saw the first hints of uncertainty. One of the best warriors amongst them had fallen. No amount of confidence would remove the hard truth that they all faced this same fate—if not on this journey, then on another. Miles of hardship and toil, with nothing at the end but a ragged hole in the ground. What dirges would be sung would be voiced by fewer and fewer still.

Cnán watched as Feronantus quietly took Taran's battle-scarred sword, removing the scabbard from the fallen man's horse and affixing it to his own saddle, clasping the hilt with closed eyes and whispering a prayer.

The others finished filling the grave and built a cairn of stones over it, then pounded a cut shaft of wood, tall enough to serve as a staff, at its center. The shaft rose from the ground, already ancient looking, their pronouncement of ageless grief.

Cnán remembered Percival's whispered words to *Tonnerre*. Only now was it sinking in to all of the group that, on this journey, they were all expendable—no different from horses.

◆ ◆ ◆

"I need a drink," Yasper said as he brought his horse in line with Raphael's. They had been riding for several hours, traveling more south than east by Raphael's reckoning, and the company had been lost in their own thoughts. Raphael had been reflecting on the siege of Córdoba, remembering those—both Moorish and Castilian—whom he counted as friends, and he was glad to be interrupted by the Dutchman. The litany of loss that always came on the heels of battle was the perpetual wound sustained by the survivors.

"A drink, you say," he replied, glancing shrewdly at Yasper. "I suspect that you are not seeking permission to drink so much as to inquire if I would like to join you."

Yasper nodded, his eyes twinkling. His hair was still stained by the smoke from his alchemical smoke pots, and Raphael smelled the acrid aroma of his chemical reagents. If it was not evident from the proliferation of pouches and pots as well as the curling spouts and narrow mouths of other arcane containers that peeked from his bulging saddlebags, then the pervasive smell that surrounded the smiling Dutchman was ample clue enough as to his profession. "Of course, Raphael.

You and I have traveled together long enough that my preferences are well known to you." He thrust a round object at Raphael.

It was a leather skin, and Raphael noted that, among the panoply of equipment burdening Yasper's mount, there were several others just like it, each hanging from a cleverly tied loop, identical to the strap on the one in his hand. The skin—horsehide from the feel of it—was oblong, narrow at the top, much like their own water skins, and when Raphael lifted it to his lips, his nose was assaulted by the smell of the liquid within.

"This is putrid," he said.

"That is the point, I believe," Yasper chuckled. He motioned with his hands, indicating that Raphael should drink.

Dubiously, Raphael tried again, expecting the taste to be as foul as the smell. The liquid was thicker than he expected, though not unpleasant, and it tasted like... "Almonds," he noted. "Where did you get it?"

"The Mongols. Each of them had a skin, as well as..." Yasper shuddered.

"What?"

"Under their saddles." Yasper made a face and indicated Raphael should either drink again or give back the skin. "Meat, wrapped in oiled rags."

"Raw?"

Yasper took a huge pull from the skin and nodded as he wiped his mouth. "It was," he said, and Raphael noted there was a note of admiration mixed in with the revulsion in his voice, "the most tender meat I have ever seen. But..." He handed the skin back to Raphael.

"We are not that hungry," Raphael said. He tried the drink again, noting that the back of his throat tingled as he swallowed.

"Not yet," Yasper agreed. He leaned toward Raphael, lowering his voice. "But this"—he indicated the skin—"this is pretty good. Not strong enough, in my opinion."

"Can you make it stronger?" Raphael asked.

"Probably. But I will need assistance. And some supplies."

Raphael glanced over at Istvan, who was riding ahead and to the right of the main party. Far enough away to be out of range of simple conversation but close enough that they were aware of his presence. "We already have one member of our company who wanders off, looking for *supplies*. I do not think another will be tolerated."

Yasper snorted. "Nothing as illicit as what *he* seeks. I can find what I need in any good-sized settlement. Provided we travel near one."

"I hesitate to offer any hope in that matter, my friend. We are far from any settlement I would call friendly."

Yasper took the offered skin. "I agree, and in reflecting on the matter, I have begun to wonder about this journey of ours."

"Begun?" Raphael responded.

Yasper quirked his lips. "If, as you say, we are far from friendly lands, and as I judge, we are but a fraction of the way to our destination, what is our plan for the supplies and aid that we might require?" He drank from the skin of Mongolian liquor. "We are accustomed to long marches and sleeping under the stars, but after this morning's…loss, a man's mood darkens. It becomes more difficult with each passing hour to sustain his…*enthusiasm*. A man begins to think of a warm fire and a bed—a roof overhead, even. If only for one night."

"Every soldier dreams of the night when he can put aside his armor and sleep without care," Raphael said. "It is a familiar part of our burden to be denied such comforts—or any comforts." He returned the skin bag. His words were slurring.

"As you say, we have all marched to war before; these hopes and disappointments are not new."

"True," Yasper said. "But in the past, I have always found solace with hope of our destination, of knowing that we will—someday—reach a shining goal. If my destination is a place I have never visited, there is usually someone in my party who has, and I can persuade them to tell me tales of that place so that it becomes more real to me."

"None of us has visited this destination," Raphael pointed out. "We knew that when we accepted Feronantus's call to join the company."

Yasper laughed. "I'm not a member of your Order, remember. I volunteered." He took one more swig from the skin and offered it back to Raphael, who held up his hand in denial, then relented and accepted another swallow. "But," he said, all levity gone from his voice, "it has occurred to me since we buried Taran that you and the others are good soldiers. You will follow Feronantus wherever he may lead you, and that is all you need to know. But me? I fear not the repercussions of curiosity, nor of insubordination, and so I do wonder if that man knows where he is going. Where he is taking us all."

Raphael recalled the look on Percival's face in the woods, the serenity of *knowing*, and he mentally noted how cleverly Yasper had maneuvered their conversation. He knew the alchemist to be an intelligent and inquisitive man. The strange and esoteric matters that he strove to comprehend and master with his experiments were much more arcane and mystic than simply crafting smoke pots and figuring out how to distill this Mongolian liquor into something stronger. Of all the company, the Dutchman was probably as fluent in as many languages as he was himself, and he didn't doubt the man could read and write all of them as well—even, very possibly, Arabic. If he knew the Greek physical sciences, then it followed he knew their rhetoric and philosophy as well. The man was no fool, as much as his countenance and his jangling pots and potions suggested otherwise.

Raphael nodded. "'It is an ill plan that cannot be changed.'"

"I raise my drink to the wisdom of Publilius Syrus," Yasper said.

Raphael lightly kicked his horse. "And I will go inquire after our leader's mood." He rode ahead, leaving the Dutchman to his depleted skin of fermented drink.

Feronantus was in conversation with Cnán, the dark-skinned Binder who had proved to be an interesting addition to their company. She was not the first Binder Raphael had met. She carried herself with the same distance and arrogance that most Binders did, but over the course of the last month, he had had time to observe her. She conversed mainly with Feronantus when she was with the main party, and Raphael knew the bulk of their conversation dealt with her reports of the surrounding terrain and the route they were taking. Once or twice, she had found some excuse to talk with Percival, whose deferential responses were so off-putting to the young woman that she never stayed long in the conversation.

He knew she had seen him in the woods, watching Percival. He did not know if she understood what she had seen, but she had seen enough.

He rode up to the pair and caught Feronantus's eye. "A moment, if you please," he said, and then nudged his horse farther on. He kept the pace for a little while, until Feronantus joined him.

"Raphael," the old veteran of Týrshammar said, "what is on your mind?"

"A topic on Yasper's mind, actually," Raphael said. "I did not have a suitable answer for him."

Feronantus twisted in his saddle and looked back at the column of riders. "What is it that Dutchman seeks to know?"

"Our route to Karakorum."

"I do not know that route. That is why we have brought the Binder, why we have Illarion. He knew that before we left, and nothing has changed. Our route will be revealed to us as we travel, by—"

"When?" Raphael interrupted.

Feronantus's face darkened. "By what our scouts discover, and by the information they glean from local sources," he said. "You know this, Raphael."

"Of course. Nor do I doubt it. But, as you have just said, our route will be *revealed*. My question remains. When?"

Feronantus pursed his lips and considered Raphael's question for some time. His hand fell to the hilt of Taran's sword, not in a threatening way, but unconsciously, the way a man might put his hand against a wall or a rock to steady himself on uneven ground. "I would ask that you speak plainly, Raphael," he said. "So that there is no confusion."

"Have you had a vision?" Raphael asked bluntly. "Has our path been *revealed* to you?"

Feronantus's hand tightened on Taran's sword.

When it was clear that Feronantus wasn't going to answer, Raphael continued. "I saw Percival in the forest, when he went to put down his horse. I was there when the Virgin came over him."

Feronantus shook his head. "That cannot be."

Raphael glared at him. "I saw it. Cnán did as well, though I doubt she understands it. We have been given a sign, Feronantus. We would be foolhardy not to recognize it."

Feronantus did not relent, nor did his hand leave off from clenching the hilt of the dead *oplo*'s sword. "You presume much, Raphael, to speak to me of prophecy and visions, as if I were a slow-witted shepherd who seeks council and guidance from phantoms—"

"I was at Damietta," Raphael interrupted, "when one of the Brethren was granted a Visitation. The legate, Pelagius of Albano, did not care for our Brother's vision, and so he had one of his own fabricated. They even approached me to translate it into Arabic for them so that it would seem more authentic. When I refused, they wanted to drive us out of the city, and were it not for Saint Francis, we would have been cast out. We stayed behind while the army marched up the Nile." His voice grew bitter, choked by the memory. "We stayed, while our friends and fellow Christians were led to their death by the pride and arrogance of the bishop."

Feronantus released his grip on the sword, and the ferocity of his gaze softened, transforming his face into the visage of an old and tired man. "I am sorry, Raphael," he said. "Too many, over the years, have been lost for similar reasons. Too many..."

Surprised by his own outburst, Raphael found he had no more words, and he nodded, his throat tight with emotion. *Too many...* His arms ached suddenly, as if his body had finally decided to accept the strain from this morning's combat, and all he wanted to do was to let go of the reins of his horse and let it find its own way. Part of him hoped it would turn west on its own accord...

"Ride with me a little while longer, would you?" Feronantus asked. "I would appreciate your company while I give some thought to what you have said."

Raphael flicked the reins of his horse, and the animal shook his head, as if to deny that it had been thinking of turning back. "Of course," he said to Feronantus, and he sat up a little straighter in his saddle when he saw the comfort his presence gave to the old veteran.

CHAPTER 21:

⟶

A PLEASANT STROLL

When Kim had first met him, the man who now fought as Zugaikotsu no Yama had been hanging around the docks of Byeokrando, scraping barnacles and unloading ships for whatever coins the skippers would throw at him. Local opinion had been divided as to whether he was insane or merely an imbecile, but he was definitely Nipponese. In those days, he gave a different answer whenever asked his name, and Kim—who had picked up a few words of Nihongo by talking to traders and fishermen—had figured out that he would merely glance around and say the words for whatever object first presented itself. So on successive days he might be known as "Barnacle," "Stray Cat," "Cresting Wave," or "Bucket of Fish."

Kim—who had been chased down to Byeokrando after the Last Stand of the Flower Knights—had found employment as a sort of constable, maintaining order along the waterfront. Even at that age, he had been tall, broad of face and shoulder, heavily bearded, and serious looking. These qualities, which intimidated most of the rough characters who hung around the docks, had only provoked the many-named Nipponese vagrant. They had had many fights. Some of these Kim had won. Kim considered this to be the normal and expected outcome, given that he was, as far as he knew, the last living embodiment of a martial tradition reaching back for over a thousand years. But it always seemed to astonish the man who would later be known as "Zug." When Kim did lose, which was extremely remarkable as far as Kim was concerned, this outcome seemed to confirm to Zug that all was as it should be.

It would be too much to say that Kim and the Nipponese man had become friends, but they had established a relationship of wary respect. Enough so that Kim had once insisted that the other tell him his real name. He had responded, "Shisha," which Kim suspected, and later confirmed, meant "Dead Man" in Nihongo.

Exasperated, Kim had looked out the window of the tavern in which they were having the conversation, saw a pair of dogs copulating in the street, and dubbed the man "Two Dogs Fucking," later shortened to "Two Dogs."

In due time the Mongols had extended their control over the entire Korean peninsula. The royal court had taken ship at the docks of Byeokrando and sailed to exile on the nearby island of Ganghwa, visible only a short distance offshore, from which they meant to organize a military resistance. The Mongols had been hot on their heels, and so it had been deemed necessary to fight a delaying action to prevent the docks from being overwhelmed before the king and his court could get away. In this manner, Kim and Two Dogs had found employment in the capacity for which they were best suited: dying in a hopeless, valiant struggle against vastly superior numbers.

Fighting back-to-back, they had killed an inordinate number of Mongols and thereby drew the attention of the young Onghwe Khan, who had ordered his men to down their arms. Through an interpreter, he had called out to the two exhausted fighters, asking them their names. "Kim Alcheon, last of the Flower Knights," Kim had answered, which was the truth. Two Dogs, who had been quite busy with his *naginata,* had taken a quick look around and answered, "Zugaikotsu no Yama," which meant "Mountain of Skulls." The name stuck.

Rather than having them killed on the spot, Onghwe had inducted them into his Circus of Swords, to fight in what had been their occupation ever since.

All of which helped to explain why when Kim was made aware that Zug was going through histrionic death throes in a locked iron cage, he only rolled his eyes. It served the idiot right for having gone crazy and beheading all of those Mongols after his defeat at the hands of the Frankish knight.

When the "death throes" extended into their third day, Kim went to visit the cage and insisted to the horrified guards that the door be unlocked and that he be allowed to venture inside.

The situation there was really quite disgraceful. Given the nature of the circus's operations, it was naturally equipped with a number of cages suitable for confining human beings. This was not the first time that Two Dogs had been confined in one. Normally he had the presence of mind to make use of the bucket provided. But whatever demon had taken him now had caused him to lose control of his bowels, and so there was diarrhea all over the place. Two Dogs was lying in the middle of it, trembling all over, pawing and scratching frantically at his skin. Quite understandable when one was covered in his own shit, but Kim suspected the frantic clawing was something else. He had heard stories of drunkards who, deprived of drink, had come to believe that insects or small rodents were crawling all over them.

When questioned, the guards, somewhat gleefully, confirmed that, by express order of Onghwe Khan, Zug had been

deprived of alcohol. It was clear that had they been given freedom of action, they would have inflicted far greater injury on
Zug than simply taking away his liquor. So Zug's current state
pleased them, and they were in no rush to ease the Japanese
man's torment.

Kim patiently explained to them that if Onghwe had
wanted one of his favorite gladiators dead, he would have
simply killed him. As that was not the order he had given, it
followed that the loss of alcohol was a mere *punishment*. To
deny Zug medical treatment might be the same as a death sentence. One of the more quick-witted guards leaped at Kim's
suggestion and saw to it that a Chinese doctor was brought in
to treat the ailing patient with an extract of poppies.

Once the drug had calmed Zug to the point where entering the cage was no longer considered to be instantly and
invariably lethal, slaves were sent in to clean the place up a bit
and wash the shit off of him. Thanks to these ministrations, his
condition improved. Over the next few days, he was weaned
from the poppies, and eventually he grew lucid enough that
talking to him was not a complete waste of time.

"We have been reduced to the condition of slaves and are
no longer fit to live," he answered to Kim's general question
about his state of health. He was speaking in the language of
Korea, which he and Kim used when they did not wish to be
understood by the Mongols.

"You are only just realizing this now?" Kim asked. "Because
in that case your dementia is even worse than I had supposed.
Either that or you have begun to believe the stories that the
Khan tells of you."

Two Dogs waved him off with a trembling hand. "I have
known it for years," he said, "as have you, O Flower Knight."

Kim had been trained to endure great pain—and had
been for years—but the casual declaration of Zug's words cut

deep, and he struggled to not react visibly to what the other had just said. "The world is full of slaves," he said carelessly, "most of whom are in a much more degraded condition than we."

"Some would say that they are less degraded, in that, being shackled and whipped, they are unable to delude themselves as to their true condition," Two Dogs returned. "The events of the last few days, thrashing around in my own shit and begging on my knees to be given a swallow of wine, have left me with a very clear understanding of how things really are. And I do not care to continue living in these conditions."

"This is not the first time you have expressed such dismay at the state of your existence," Kim reminded him. "Three times? Or is it four? I cannot remember. But what would you do to change things?"

"Kill the Khan and get away from these people."

"Get away to where? You are an infinity of miles from your home."

"I don't want to return to my home." He struggled to sit upright and leaned toward Kim. "But I no longer want to die *here*. Do you?"

Kim regarded Zug carefully. *Why not?* he shrugged. *He's right. My cage, while cleaner than his, is still a cage.* "No," he replied. "I do not. But how do you propose to accomplish this...this *mission*, though? There are only two of us, and you're half dead and locked up in a cage."

"We must form an alliance with the Monks of the Red Plum Blossom."

Kim shrugged. "Who are these monks? Some martial order in your native country...?" Suddenly he wondered if Zug's dementia might be subtler than he had first thought. An imaginary order of assassins...?

"No, they are here. I have seen them. The Frank I fought in the arena. The man who—"

"Who defeated you?"

"He did not defeat me," Two Dogs insisted. "I had my *tanto* in his fucking armpit. He had better armor, is all."

Kim did not think it was fitting to belabor a sick man, and so he allowed this to pass without comment.

The floor of the cage was dirt. Two Dogs arose from his litter with some difficulty and then used the tip of a stick he had scavenged to scratch out a design—a five-lobed flower resting upon a sunburst design with many sharp-pointed rays. "The warrior monks who use this as their *mon* are different from the other Franks. I think that they are like us."

"Like we used to be," Kim corrected him.

Two Dogs waved his hand as if the distinction were trivial. "They will become like us, or be destroyed, if the Mongols are not stopped. We need to get them a message to that effect."

"How do you suppose this is possible, given that we have no language in common with them?"

Two Dogs raised a quivering index finger, drawing attention to the following important point: "In the village of scum and rabble that surrounds this circus, there is a Frankish priest who has spent years among the Mongols and speaks their language nearly as well as his own."

"Yes," Kim interrupted, "I know the one."

Zug nodded. "Go and find him and ask him to write out a message in one of the languages of Christendom and deliver it to the Monks of the Red Plum Blossom."

"I might not be able to trust him."

"Of course not. But is there someone you could trust more?"

Kim stalked out of the cage in a state of considerable irritation. No one could make the anger rise up in his face the way

Two Dogs could. He did not like being sent out on errands, but he could not defeat the riddle Two Dogs had posed to him, nor could he argue against the simple truth of all that Two Dogs had said.

◆ ◆ ◆

He had been told never to stray from the immediate vicinity of the Mongol compound and the arena. But Kim knew that this rule would never be enforced so long as he remained in the Khan's good graces. He had tended to remain close to home anyway. He had been provided with a private *ger* that was of adequate size, clean, and comfortably furnished. Its situation in the heart of the Mongol encampment meant that it was well guarded at night so that he could sleep soundly. Food, drink, women, and massages were available to him. He did not avail himself of these quite so lavishly as Zug. Yet the mere fact that he could get them gave him little reason to wander past the camp's defensive lines and out into the slum that had sprung up, like toadstools on a stump, around the arena during the months that the circus had been in operation.

He now disguised himself by casting a hooded cloak over his shoulders and went out into it.

The disguise, of course, would not fool the Mongols guarding the camp's exit. They knew perfectly well who he was. His reasons for donning it were twofold: one, to show a decent respect for the Khan's order that he not go out, and two, to prevent himself from being recognized immediately by the young aspirant fighters who had flocked to the arena from all over the known world when Onghwe Khan had sent out his call for combatants. This slum was in large part the monument that such men built to themselves when they tried to settle in one place. Compared to any other city it was oversupplied with adventuresome and cocksure young males, prostitutes, bladesmiths, armorers, and drinking houses. It was lacking in sanitation, cultural refinement, officers of the peace, and decent women. Those who arrived soonest and defended their turf with greatest ferocity ended up in possession of the permanent structures, which, here, were the old stone and wattle-and-daub buildings of a tiny village, burned out and gutted some months ago, now supplied with improvised roofs and doors. The slow and the weak had ended up living in shanties and lean-tos constructed from rubble that had been hauled in from the nearby ruins of Legnica, or mere tents. These had been piled up willy-nilly.

There were no real streets, just wandering and forking paths paved with the shit of humans and beasts. Every time Kim ventured into it, it was bigger and dirtier. Every time he was reminded why he had no inclination to leave the comfort of the camp and his *ger*. The squalor he could tolerate; what made it truly insufferable was the young fighters who wanted to challenge him. They came to this place because they believed they knew something about fighting and imagined they would find opportunities to prove as much. What they found was an arena to which they had no hope of gaining admission, save as spectators, once a fortnight, when the Khan held his great competitions. At other times there might be preliminary bouts, used by the organizers of the circus to choose the fighters deemed worthy to appear in the next great competition. But these were by invitation only. The way to get invited was to know someone, to bribe someone, to have been noticed in battle, or to distinguish oneself in the informal fights that were staged in a few makeshift dens that had been constructed in the slum by extremely unsavory characters who knew how the system worked and how they could profit from it. It was these places more than anything else that drew in the rootless and damaged young men who believed that they had a future in the Circus of Swords.

The last time Kim had ventured out here, there had been a few yards of open space remaining between the edge of the slum and the old temple of the Christians, which had fared surprisingly well during the initial Mongolian advance. But now the warren of tents and lean-tos was washing around the building's foundations, with only a small clear space around its entrance so that people could go in and come out.

When Kim went into the temple, a priest was standing at the front of its largest room with his back turned, holding a cup above his head and chanting some sort of mystic incantation. Arrayed round him in a semicircle were three other priests, all raising their empty hands as if in sympathy. Scattered around the main floor were perhaps a dozen Christians all down on their knees. Kim, of course, could make no sense whatsoever of the rite, but this suited his purposes since the man he sought, Father Pius, was one of the three lesser priests standing at the front. He was tempted to go tug on Pius's sleeve and draw him aside, but something about the way the people in the temple were behaving gave him the idea that this would be considered impolite, and so he stood there quietly and waited until the head priest stopped chanting and began handing out food and drink to the assortment of wretches who had been kneeling and waiting. The amount of food given out seemed extremely small and scarcely worth the trouble. Moreover, the priest laid it directly onto the congregants' tongues, apparently to make sure they didn't grab too much of it. Kim thought that if they were a bit more generous, they would not have to husband the stuff so carefully.

But that was neither here nor there. When the serving of the food was finished, Kim approached the one named Pius and made it known that he wished to talk to him. All of the priests gave him dirty looks, and Kim belatedly understood that the ceremony was not actually finished yet. Nevertheless, Pius—once he had seen Kim's face in the light of a candle and recognized him—assented to break away from the rite and led Kim out a side exit into a little room in the back of the temple that was illuminated by slats of daylight shining in between charred roof planks.

"I require your help in writing a letter to the Monks of the Red Plum Blossom," Kim began, speaking in Mongol, "and in delivering it to the master of their order. In exchange for your assistance, I offer to give you money, or to make myself useful to you in some other way."

Father Pius seemed too dumbfounded by all of this to say anything in return. While waiting for the priest to collect his wits, Kim supplied a description of the sigil, or *mon*, that Two Dogs had earlier scratched on the floor of his cage.

Eventually the priest began to nod. "It is not a plum blossom," he said, "but a red rose."

"Very well. The Monks of the Red Rose, then," Kim said, shrugging to indicate that he did not really care what sort of flower it was or what this order called itself.

But Pius would not let go of the topic. "The rose is a symbol, in the heraldry of the Franks, for the Virgin."

"Fine. They are celibate monks. We have them too. Or at least we have ones who claim to be celibate."

"All monks are celibate," Pius said. "That is not what the rose symbolizes. It means, rather, the Virgin Mary, Mother of God."

A number of questions came immediately to Kim's mind, but he forced himself not to utter them, since the conversation had already dwelled on this topic much longer than he had any use for.

Pius was unstoppable, though. "They are the *Ordo Militum Vindicis Intactae*," he said, switching briefly into some other language that made no sense at all to Kim, "which means, the Order of Knights of the Virgin Defender."

"They are defenders of virgins?"

"No. Well, yes. Of course they defend virgins. But that's not what it means. The Virgin Defender is a sort of manifestation of the Virgin Mary that once appeared above a battlefield, holding a shield and a lance, inspiring the founders of this order to extraordinary feats of arms."

"Can you get a message to them or not?"

"Yes. By all means." Father Pius had begun rummaging in a chest socked away in the corner of the little room. All of its furniture had been burned or looted; this chest had been put in place after the battle. As Kim now saw, it contained the stuff that Franks used to write: dried animal skin, quills, and small clay jars that, judging from the stains around their necks, contained ink. A bit of time was lost now to fussing about with this gear, trimming quills and mixing mysterious fluids into the jars to get the ink to the proper consistency. Kim could see clearly enough that this was a little show that Father Pius was putting on to remind Kim of all the trouble and expense he was going to—trouble and expense for which he would expect to be compensated later. But in due time he got himself situated on the flat lid of the chest with all in readiness: candle, ink, quill, parchment, and Father Pius himself.

Kim cleared his throat. "*Kim Alcheon, Last of the Flower Knights, to...*" He paused. "What is the name of the master of the order?"

"They guard their secrets closely," said Father Pius, "but it is rumored that one of their masters—a man named Feronantus—has been spied in their camp. And if he is really there, then he is unquestionably the man in charge."

"...*to Feronantus*, then," Kim concluded. "*Greetings. I and my brother-in-arms, Mountain of Skulls, have taken note of your prowess and—*"

"Would you like me to translate that literally?" Pius asked.

"What?"

"Mountain of Skulls? It seems a trifle...undignified."

"You may write *Zugaikotsu no Yama*, then, or whatever other name pleases you," Kim answered, "as long as this Feronantus understands that the man being referred to is the one who fought their champion in the Circus of Swords most recently."

"Very well, I shall make that clear," said Father Pius, and he spent a good long time scratching out a series of odd-looking glyphs. Kim had difficulty telling one apart from the next. They all looked approximately the same in his eyes.

Pius was looking up at him expectantly.

"*We would discourse with you respectfully and honorably, warrior to warrior. If it would please you to accept, send word with the bearer of this note or make yourselves known to us within the encampment of the Khan, which is where we dwell. Yours in respect and honor...*and so on and so forth."

"That is all? You would not like to say anything more specific?" Pius asked, seeming a little crestfallen. Clearly he had been hoping to glean something of personal interest or value by eavesdropping on the exchange of letters and was disappointed by the lack of detail in what Kim had said. Kim gave him a sharp look. Pius cringed, understanding that he had revealed too much of his own desires and motives. Without any further editorial remarks, he finished scratching it all down, dusted the parchment with sand to blot the ink, and then blew it off and rolled it up into a tube. He dripped candle wax along the edge to seal it, and Kim used his own personal chop to mark the wax.

"When will you deliver it?" Kim asked.

"I was about to go out anyway," said Father Pius, "to run some errands. I shall do it now." He paused. "Their chapter house is some distance away, and I will not be back for some time…"

Kim ignored the priest's hesitation. "When it has been done, I shall come back and talk to you about how you shall be compensated," Kim said, forestalling any complaint from the priest with a stern look, and then took his leave.

Pius had not been the only one to recognize him, and word had already gotten round that he was inside the church. When he emerged from the back room, he found several young warriors waiting for him. Fortunately they were all boys seeking instruction, not men who wanted to fight. Feeling no interest whatsoever in giving instruction to these unwashed and unruly novices, he was about to tell them gruffly to go away. Then, though, he recalled the words of Two Dogs Fucking: *Is there someone you could trust more?*

Some of the boys were half Mongol, and others seemed to have learned a few words of the language during the months that the Mongols had been running the place. After a few minutes of verbally sparring with them—seeming to show interest in them one moment, brushing them off like flies the next—he settled on one of the older and more fluent boys. His name was Hans, which stuck in Kim's memory because, unlike many other Frankish names, it was easy for him to remember and pronounce.

"Stealth and guile are fine qualities in a warrior," Kim said to Hans as he drew him aside. "See if you can follow Father Pius without being detected, and bring me a report of his actions. If I am pleased by the results, I shall teach you something."

Hans's blue eyes flicked to one side, then the other, counting the number of other lads in earshot.

"You may translate what I have said to these others, or not," Kim said, guessing his thoughts. "The choice is yours."

"What will you teach me?"

Kim looked him up and down. "Since you do not have a sword, I shall teach you how to defeat an armed man with your bare hands."

Hans spun and took off as if Kim had just threatened to kill him. He was pursued by several other lads who wanted to know what Kim had just said.

Kim smiled and, leaving the ruined church, enjoyed a pleasant—and unmolested—stroll to the shop of a certain woodworker, a carver who had been making Kim a staff out of a certain type of local hardwood. It was difficult, in this part of the world, to obtain woods as dark and heavy as the ones that were used for such weapons in more civilized parts of the world, and so the project was proceeding slowly.

The artisan spoke no Mongol and Kim spoke none of whatever language was common in these parts, and so the conversation was slow as well. They were only a few minutes into it when they were interrupted by Hans, who barreled into the workshop with the news that Father Pius had gone straightaway to talk to the Master of the Something-or-other Knights.

This was just what Kim had hoped to hear, and so he told Hans to wait for him to conclude his business with the turner.

A few more hard-won sentences passed between them, but Kim noted, after a certain point, that he had not heard a word of what the artisan had said to him. Something was troubling his mind. He held up his hand to still the woodworker's tongue and devoted a few moments to thinking about what Hans had said.

"Did you say that Pius is meeting with this man now?"

"Yes, I saw them talking to each other at the knights' compound."

"That is odd," Kim said, "since I was led to believe that the knights were staying at a place some distance away from here."

"Oh no," Hans said, "it is no more than a bowshot from where we are standing."

"What is the name of this master who Pius is talking to?"

"Dietrich."

"Not Feronantus?"

Hans looked confused. "Feronantus is the master of the *Shield-Brethren*. Father Pius is at the compound of the *Livonian Knights*."

"Take me to him," Kim said. He snatched a staff from the woodworker's supply—not the one he had commissioned, but a stout piece of oak that would do, in a pinch—and hustled after Hans. There was no time to explain to the woodworker that he was only borrowing and not stealing.

But by the time Hans had led him through the maze to the place in question, Father Pius had already finished his conversation with Dietrich and set out northeastward, in the direction of the camp of the Shield-Brethren. This news was given to Hans by a younger boy who was apparently acting as Hans's deputy. Kim noted with interest and approval that Hans, even at his young age, was already capable of delegating responsibilities to followers. As Hans conversed in the local tongue with the younger boy, Kim scanned the stone building that the Livonian Knights had seized and made into their local headquarters—a building somewhat smaller than the standing church, but like it, in fairly good condition—and observed their sigil on a banner. The symbols were red—that much was correct, at least—but neither was a rose. This was not the standard of the *Ordo*—what had Hans called them?

A simpler name than the impossible one that Pius had used. The *Shield-Brethren.*

Had Pius betrayed him to Dietrich? Or merely stopped by this building on some unrelated errand before proceeding to the meeting with Feronantus? *I might not be able to trust him.* Kim could already imagine the conversation with Zug.

There was only one way to be sure: check the seal on the letter.

CHAPTER 22:

━━

TO SAVE THE EMPIRE

Gansukh kept his left hand on the pommel of his saddle and stretched his right hand out in front of him. He looked at his hand against the green of the vast grasslands of the Orkhun River Valley. The width of a man's hand was called an *aid*, and it was used to measure everything a man could lay his hands on. Out here, he could measure the height of the grass, the depth of his stride, the length of his horse's shadow, but all of these things were insignificant against the endlessness of the steppe.

The late-summer pasture grasses undulated like water, revealing the capricious pathways of the wind. The sighing sound of the stalks was a song the Blue Wolf had taught him to hear. He could anticipate the gusts and brace himself against the sudden blows that tried to rock him and his horse.

He closed his eyes and stretched both arms out to embrace the wind; bracing against a strong blast, he squeezed his thighs to stay in the saddle. His horse lowered its head and laid back its ears, groaning deep in its chest. The wind carried the scents of men—smoke, meat cooking for an evening meal, the musky scent of sheep, camels, and cattle—olfactory markers of the pervasive spread of the *Khagan*'s empire. Along with that came an underlying stink of shit from both beast and man, and abattoir offal, that no city could ever hide—and many didn't try as hard as Karakorum to hide it.

There are no secrets here.

His nose flared again, and he leaned his head back to draw in more of the cool air—finding other wilder and more promising smells. The scent of rain was faint, the tiniest whiff of the oncoming change in the seasons, that time of year when the clans turned south and east.

Ögedei would be leaving Karakorum soon, heading for his winter palace, and while Chagatai Khan had laid no fixed deadline on Gansukh's task to curb the *Khagan*'s drinking, he could not escape the feeling that time was running out. Time for what, though? Gansukh had tried to flee that thought since he had visited the *Khagan*'s chambers, but now, out where no one could see the expression on his face or hear any word that might slip from his lips, he could face it.

What was he supposed to save? The *Khagan* was a drunk, and the entire court was caught in an inward turning spiral of sycophancy. Was this the pinnacle of the Mongol Empire? Like an arrow fired at the sun, eventually it flies as high as it can and then begins its calamitous plunge back to the ground.

Gansukh's horse lifted its head and nickered, shifting beneath him, as if to offer an answer to his question. He looked out across the grasslands again. The sun hung like a coal over his left shoulder; he was facing west and north, the same direction he had ridden a few nights ago when he had pursued the thief. Momentarily he indulged in the fantasy of escaping all this decline and misery—by simply kicking his horse into a trot. He would ride west to the Orkhun, and then beyond, across the endless plain to the edge of the empire.

Leaving it all behind before it destroyed him too.

Lian.

What would happen to her? Why did he care? He frowned. She had nothing to do with his duty—other than the pledge that she was going to help him. She was a slave—and a rather demanding one at that. Most of the time, he was sure she was laughing at him, and while he thought of punishing her for her insolence—both imagined and real—he knew it would only prove her point. He would gain nothing by such physical domination, and he was starting to realize he would actually lose something valuable by indulging in such brutish behavior.

An image of the thief's terrified expression flashed through his head, that last instant before Munokhoi dragged her away. The look in her eyes. Despair, and a glint of anger, directed at him. He had failed her somehow, and he couldn't shake that sensation. He couldn't shake the impression that he had seen something similar in Ögedei's expression as he had raged about his chamber. *Failure.*

If he rode away—if he *fled*—it would be his failure that he was running from, not the empire's.

The wind shifted again, carrying now the rhythmic thump and hissing stalk rustle of an approaching rider. Gansukh looked back at Karakorum. He squinted, trying to guess the identity of the rider. *Not Munokhoi. Too short. Too slender.* He felt like a fool as his breath caught in his chest. *A woman?*

He curled his lips at the sour taste in the back of his mouth—his stomach's reaction to the elation he felt at the possibility that the approaching rider might be Lian. *What is she doing?* he thought. *How had she managed to get out of the city without an escort?* The horse and rider were unhurried in their approach, signaling there was no urgency, which made the possibility that it was Lian both more real and stranger.

The mounted figure slowly dropped out of sight behind a gentle hill, and when it reappeared, there was no doubt as to the rider's identity. Lian lowered her head to hide her smile, but not before Gansukh saw a flash of white teeth.

He turned away, shoulders twitching, to face the honesty and honor of the endless steppe, and to hide from her the grin stretching across his lips. By the time she brought her horse alongside, he had his face under control, burying his delight under the stern expression he tried to maintain in anyone's presence.

The wind died back, and the grasses rose to their full height. The riders sat quietly for a minute, watching the verdant plain settle into stillness, and finally Lian broke the silence.

"Your world," she said.

"Yes," he nodded. "Simpler. Safer."

"For you," she said. "I would have thought I would feel safe too, but all this emptiness frightens me. I don't know what is out there."

"True, but the rules are less complicated. It is easier to know what to do."

Lian smiled. "The rules at court are simple too, Gansukh. You have shown a ready ability to learn them. It is just that they are...foreign to you. Still. It is a matter of comfort. You look across the land of grass and you see... What? Freedom?"

"The falcon soars," he said, pursing his lips. "The rabbit knows to hide."

"Freedom for you," Lian said. "Not for me. And why is that? Because I am a woman? Because I am Chinese?"

"Are those truths any smaller inside the walls of Karakorum?"

"No," she said, "but there is less wind." She braced as the grasses bent again. "A moment ago, I would have felt confident in being able to aim an arrow, but now...the wind plays tricks. How can people from the land of grass ever hit their mark?" As if taunting her, the wind rushed in and flung Lian's hair about her face. She used her left hand to push aside the black strands—pulling one moist from between her lips, he noticed—while her right gripped the reins. "You know that secret, don't you?"

Gansukh nodded. Above all the things he'd grown to appreciate about Lian—her beauty, her intelligence, and her knowledge about the ways of the court—it was her confounding way of speaking about two things at the same time that continued to surprise him. He wondered if Master Chucai knew this about her, or if he simply saw her as a useful tutor for an ill-attired steppe barbarian.

Gansukh tried to think of a clever response, and failing to come up with anything that seemed remotely daring or insightful, he opted for cautious response and a simple question. "We'll return to the secret of shooting through and between the wind," he said. "For now, tell me why you risk leaving the city walls alone."

"I'm not alone." She again stroked hair out her eyes and looked for his reaction.

Gansukh twisted in his saddle and peered back toward Karakorum, in time to see a second rider disappear behind the hill. Gansukh recognized the peaked hat. *Master Chucai.*

"He invited me to ride with him." Lian folded both hands across the pommel of her saddle, giving up on trying to keep her hair in place. He studied the freedom of her hair, then the sweep of the grass. *The secret is studying the flow of the wind between your arrow and the target, measuring the battle between gusts, and finally—watching your target's hair. The arrow must be nudged a cat's whisker against the direction of that hair.*

With a sinking feeling, Gansukh acknowledged that Chucai arranging a meeting was far more believable than Lian risking leaving Karakorum alone. Although he was pleased she had sought him out, he should have known she would have done so at her master's request.

Gansukh had not sought out the *Khagan*'s advisor since the day they had last spoken—that day when everything had changed—nor had he felt any urge to. He should have reported Ögedei's behavior that night, as well as confronted Chucai about their unfinished conversation from the throne room—not to mention the issue with the lacquered box (which he had not been able to open)—but he couldn't bring himself to do so. It was much simpler—like a rabbit hiding—to simply avoid Master Chucai until he could decide what to do.

Which had also meant staying away from Lian, and that had been harder to do.

Still… Seemingly by accident, he nudged his horse closer to hers. Taking advantage of their proximity, as well as the privacy the open plain offered—inside the *Khagan*'s compound, it was impossible to have any real privacy—he reached out and laid his hand over hers where they gripped the saddle.

Lian bowed her head but didn't pull her hands away. The wind-whipped hair made it impossible to read her expression—another way for a rabbit to hide—and then, just as Chucai's hat again rose into view, Lian raised the little finger of her left hand and wrapped it around Gansukh's thumb. Before he could react, she slipped free and tugged at the reins. Her horse exhaled noisily and took several prancing steps sideways, moving Lian out of reach. Only a few *aid* away.

"Young Gansukh!" Chucai called as his horse topped the rise. "Lian told me she had seen you ride out earlier. I am most pleased we have found you." His face was bright with windburn and exertion, and his voice was brisk and cheerful, as if the events of the past few days did not weigh in the slightest. As if he had not presided over the torture and execution of a defenseless woman.

"Master Chucai," Gansukh returned. "Indeed, it is a surprise that we must meet so far from where we pass our days."
He was trying for the same sort of cheer, even levity, but judging by the flat response in Chucai's eyes, his tone did not
convince.

Chucai brought his horse around in front of Gansukh and
Lian, blocking their view. Making sure he could keep an eye
on both of them. "Had I been able to find you, we could have
spoken this in the city."

"I have been—" Gansukh started.

"It doesn't matter," Chucai cut him off. "It is what you
haven't been doing that concerns me."

Gansukh flushed. *Was this all that Chucai worried about?* "Do
you mean, learning how to simper and preen at court? To
what end? Ögedei is blind to everything and everyone around
him."

Chucai's face was impassive and his eyes still flat, but he
nodded. "You are plain spoken, Gansukh. It is, as Lian has
mentioned to me on more than one occasion, one of your
best traits, and most dangerous. I had hoped that she could
teach you how to wriggle your tongue like a snake's rather
than shoot it out like an arrow. A devious tongue would allow
you to more readily gain the *Khagan*'s ear. But that skill is still
beyond you, and you do not yet rise above his lobes…and *penetrate*…with soft words, do you?"

Gansukh glanced at Lian, who was looking down at her
horse's flank, not embarrassed by this metaphor, but not
affording it the dignity of a response.

"Does the fault lie with your tutor?" Chucai said, noticing
Gansukh's glance. "Is she incapable of teaching you the ways
of the court?"

"She teaches well enough," Gansukh growled.

"Is he not an able student?" Chucai asked Lian.

"Able enough," Lian replied.

Chucai peered at Gansukh. "Then what is distracting you from your education?"

Neither answered, and Gansukh dared not glance at her this time. His heart beat quickly, and he wiped his hands on his pants. *Is she thinking the same thing?*

"I see," said Chucai, leaning back and tugging at the few long hairs on his cheek. "Perhaps you need to refocus your efforts. Both of you."

Gansukh controlled his breathing. As stung as he was by Master Chucai's words—as well as by the implication therein—he couldn't so easily forget what he had witnessed in the throne room.

"Master Chucai—" Lian began, but Gansukh cut her off.

"What goals are those?" he demanded. "Yours? The empire's? Ögedei's? Chagatai Khan sent me to help the *Khagan,* and I thought my mission was simply to stop his drinking, but now I am confused. Now I wonder if the assistance the *Khagan* needs is far greater than taking away his drink..." His words stumbled to a stop. He found himself unwilling to say more, fearing he had already said too much. *Arrow for a tongue...*

A tiny muscle twitched in Master Chucai's cheek, making the corner of his mouth lift, as if he might smile. Or he might have been trying to suppress a roar of outrage. Gansukh wasn't sure which, but like a standoff with a wounded predator, he knew it was best to show no fear. To give no ground until his adversary made the next move.

Master Chucai almost seemed to deflate a little in his saddle. "Plain speech," he sighed, allowing his gaze to rove out across the land of grass. "In the court, the more *refined* refer to this as the 'country eye,' and they whisper of it as if they fear its coming. The horrible day when the horsemen would follow this longing gaze back to the plains of grass, back to chasing the endlessly migrating herds. Back to...oblivion." A thin smile creased his lips. "The court, however, would be vastly improved if there were more men like you, young Gansukh, and fewer of the two-faced creatures that surround Ögedei now."

This caught Gansukh off guard. Lian was surprised by Chucai's candor as well.

"I need to speak plainly with you, Gansukh—that is why I followed you out here." Master Chucai sounded tired. "It is possible that even if you succeed in reducing the *Khagan's* drinking, *we* will still have accomplished nothing."

"I do not..." Gansukh met Chucai's gaze, and in the older man's small, dark eyes Gansukh saw conflicting emotions: hope and resignation, elation and exhaustion. *He said "we."* Chucai *did* understand his confusion. Gansukh had witnessed Ögedei's frustrated outburst, the *Khagan's* desperate cry for someone to share his view of the world, to understand his *country eye*, and while he hadn't confided that information to Chucai, it was apparent such information would not be news to Chucai.

Gansukh was startled. *If we accomplish nothing, then what has been saved?* Was Chucai suggesting the very thought he had been turning over in his head before they arrived? The idea felt like a betrayal, not just of the *Khagan*, but of the whole of the Mongolian Empire, and he immediately wished he could undo it, that he could wipe his mind clean and go back to the innocent naïveté he had been full of on the first day he had rode into Karakorum.

Was Ögedei Khan worthy of leading the empire?

"The *Khagan* is great," he muttered, trying to muster some enthusiasm for what those words meant, but he felt off balance, his mind and spirit fractured by the revelation he had seen—reflected—in Chucai's expression.

Chucai was still looking at him. "The empire must be great, Gansukh. Not just the *Khagan*. You have seen what lies beneath the mask, haven't you? Not just the *Khagan*, but everything—and everyone—around him. It is our duty to help him. It is our duty to help the empire. *Your* duty."

"Why me?" Gansukh asked.

Chucai laughed. "Why not?"

"But it is...too great..."

"Of course it is," Chucai snorted. "No one person can change the course of the empire, and yet one man created this very empire." He swept an arm out to indicate the open steppe. "Before Temujin brought the clans together, this was just grasslands. Before Ögedei inherited the empire, Karakorum was nothing more than a few tents clustered around the river. Look at it now. All change happens because *one man* wants something different. Ögedei has forgotten this; most of the men who cluster around him and dog his steps don't want the world to change—as much as they claim otherwise.

"You are not special, Gansukh," Chucai continued. "When you came to Karakorum, you were nothing more than a bumbling warrior from the steppe, regardless of all the glory heaped on your shoulders from your exploits on the edge of the empire. You were *nothing* to the court; you still may account for *nothing*. But..." Chucai stopped with a shrug.

"But what? Is your speech supposed to inspire me?" Gansukh asked.

"The anniversary of Tolui's death approaches." Chucai pointed toward Karakorum, ignoring Gansukh's question. "A grand festival is planned, to distract the *Khagan* from the depression that always falls upon him at this time. Caravans arrive each day bearing gifts from every corner of the empire. Games will be conducted—wrestling, riding, shooting, fighting. There will be minstrels, acrobats, dancers, poets—every sort of entertainment possible. The festival grows every year, but Ögedei attends to less and less of it, as he drowns himself in drink."

Tolui. The younger brother of both Ögedei and Chagatai. Chagatai had spoken briefly of his younger brother's death, and Gansukh tried to recall the details: Ögedei had fallen ill during a campaign in Northern China—a disease caused by angry spirits. The dead had demanded blood, payment for what had been taken from them.

Gansukh shivered. "You didn't answer my question," he said, pushing aside the thoughts of ghosts.

"I didn't think I needed to," Chucai said with a grim smile. "What we taught you about court protocol and practice was meant to open your eyes—and it has, has it not? I'll ask you a question in return: what is worth saving?"

Gansukh rubbed his arms, feeling chilled even under the gaze of the sun. *A sacrifice*, he thought, *to save the empire.*

"You don't need inspiration, Gansukh," Chucai said. "You simply need *permission*, and not from me or the *Khagan*."

CHAPTER 23:

A CHANGE OF PLANS

For several days, they traveled east through a seemingly endless landscape of broken marsh and straggling forest. Even with Yasper's discovery of Mongolian *arkhi*—a drink Cnán knew well enough to avoid—the pall of Taran's absence refused to lift. The nights when they made a fire were oppressively dark, and the awareness of higher, greater things—the soughing of the wind, the haze of cold, sharp stars—brought no comfort, even to her, though she loved the wilderness.

When the quiet of an evening was broken, it was more often than not by Istvan, who rambled on at length of Mongol myths he'd once heard, or perhaps dreamed up in the magic haze of his freebuttons—barely coherent stories of endless seas of horses and of a banner, tall and terrible, from whence the Khans drew their power. The Brethren paid him little heed; most turned away, rolled over, tried to ignore the Hungarian. None were inclined to speak with him while the sting of Taran's death was still so fresh.

Never had Cnán seen a man so alone and so blissfully unaware of his isolation.

In the aftermath of the departure, Roger's anger at Istvan did not waver or lessen and was echoed, Cnán saw, in the eyes of the others, though none of them were so bloodthirsty. She later heard Feronantus and Roger privately arguing the matter. Given what chaos had been caused by Istvan's insanity and bloodlust, Cnán was inclined to sympathize with the Norman's point of view.

"We need him," Feronantus had said with gentle firmness. "He is mad, he is dangerous, yes. But he is also a fine horseman and, next to Rædwulf, the best archer we have. Furthermore, he is a veteran of Mohi. Few know better how the Mongols fight."

"Are you certain," Roger responded testily, "that you're not remembering a debt to his teacher? The younger boy may have had potential. The man is deranged, and he is *not* one of us."

After that, they spoke more often in the Frankish tongue, of which Cnán had less knowledge, but she did not forget what she'd heard. Though Istvan had never been a member of the Order, he'd been trained by a member, or one at least known to them, a man important to Feronantus. The arguments of the Brethren's leader seemed sound, if overly forgiving, but Roger's words made her uneasy, and now she wondered, was it wisdom that kept Istvan alive or sentimentality?

The matter of where their road took them next was not broached for several days, until Feronantus spoke, addressing Illarion.

"You must guide us through Kiev," he said.

"Are you mad?" Roger said from where he sat. The Norman was sharpening one of his axes with a whetstone, the rhythmic scraping sound coming to an abrupt halt as he spoke. "Don't let me be the one to affront our prowess, but it was as much fortune as skill that left only one of us dead just days ago." At this, he cast a dark glance at Istvan.

"We have a duty," Percival calmly asserted. His words, however, lacked conviction. The loss of Taran and his horse had shaken the Frank and left him uncertain in a way Cnán had never thought to see him. It was unsettling to witness, and there again was the memory of the sound of his voice in the woods, alone but for her—and Raphael—unknowingly bearing witness.

When he looked her way, she could not meet his eyes.

"We have been seen," Feronantus said, not ignoring Percival's statement, but not standing by it either, Cnán noted. "And not by some stripling fool of a Mongol scout, who alone would have been enough to raise alarm. Enough well-blooded warriors have crossed my path to make knowing a wise one easy when I see him. Word of us will travel back to the greater horde, and they will watch us. We need an excuse to be traveling east, so arrayed, one that does not alarm our enemy."

He leveled world-weary eyes at Percival and for a moment seemed unable to continue. "Percival has spoken to me, of a role required of us in that city, and while I am unable to fully explain the task"—he glanced at Raphael, who nodded slightly, and then looked over at Cnán as if to dare her to speak—"there is another purpose that visiting Kiev may serve; for there, we may learn something of what has been going on in the world as we kept to the wilderness."

"What task?" Roger asked of Percival.

The knight shook his head. "I do not know," he said softly, "but I have been given a sign of what it is that I seek."

"In Kiev?" Roger pressed.

Percival smiled at him, and Cnán's breath caught in her throat. *How could the Norman not see the light shining from his face?*

"I still say it's a mistake," Roger murmured, still too caught up in his own disillusionment and anger. "If we've been spotted, better to put as many miles as we can between them and us. Mongols and their lackeys run thick here, like flies on a corpse."

"And that will not change from here to the heart of the Khan's empire," Eleázar replied in his accented Latin. He had spoken very little since their journey had begun, and Cnán had not gotten used to the quiet way in which he spoke. It was so unlike everything else about him. "I am with Feronantus and Percival—eleven visiting Kiev will be less strange to their eyes than eleven riding east with no reason. Whether or not they guess our errand means nothing. If they follow us closely—and likely they will—we will be slowed regardless of our motives. We must attempt to shake undue suspicion."

"I can take you there, though I do not know how much we will find," Illarion said in his low, sad voice. "I have heard only rumors about the fate of Prince Alexander's city. If they are to be believed, then the city will be little more than a ruin filled with ghosts." Suddenly a light came to the Slav's face, and he actually smiled, then nodded toward Feronantus. "I can think of no better place to shake off pursuit."

They changed their course the next morning. The fresh horses acquired from the fight made travel a little easier, though heat and the humidity evened their score of misery. As day by day they drew imperceptibly nearer to the city, they passed many tributaries and branches of the great Dnieper as it wound along its southern track, toward the *Axeinos*, as the people of Rus called it. The Unlit Sea.

The heat bore down during the days and only sometimes relented at night. Cnán found herself more than once thankful that she was unburdened by the armor the Brethren wore, weighing down their bodies and damping both energy and patience as they rode. Watching them, she thought of men traveling in their own ovens, slowly steaming to death, all unawares, like the legendary frog in a witch's cauldron.

At times, the heavens would show mercy, and the skies would darken with rain clouds that poured down some relief. The armor actually steamed afterward, as did the horses, and the riders trailed a thin haze of mist. The water certainly brought welcome coolness, but then they had to deal with the frustrating tendency of steel to rust and with bedrolls soaked completely through. Despite their best efforts, the armor was slowly tarnishing, and rusty streaks even marred Feronantus's greaves and mail.

Gradually farmsteads, hamlets, and finally villages became more numerous. Many had been burned, however, and most lay abandoned. The absence of people from even the larger villages gave the landscape a ghostly feel, like riding through a place left behind by all who cared, to be observed again only by those foolish enough to pass through forsaken lands.

Eventually they began to see people, stragglers moving along the goat paths and game trails Finn had found. Small families dispossessed by conflict, some with little more than the rags on their backs, and others with an animal or two, packs of possessions, and downcast eyes hollowed by what they had seen. Most fled at the sight of the armored company, abandoning their animals with an alacrity born of desperate practice.

Here and there, as signs of civilization increased so did signs of atrocity. Hundreds of victims of Mongol plank-crushing lay in shallow, dug-out ditches, the planks long since retrieved for structures or firewood, the corpses left naked, worm-eaten, and shriveled under the sun, their jaws and sunken eyes lost in half-amused, unending screams. Once, they passed an astonishing pyramid of skulls, stacked carefully atop a *kurgan*—a burial mound of the ancients—to give testament to the power of the conquerors.

The Khans were the masters of Rus, and the Shield-Brethren were riding headlong into its greatest city. Yet Illarion seemed to think, for all the foreboding that hung about him, that they stood a chance therein. Cnán could not help but remember the way Illarion had frightened off a group of Mongols when they had first found him by pretending to be a ghost, back from the dead.

There was a grim determination about the Ruthenian, a grinding set to his jaw, as they drew near the city that Cnán had seen in many a warrior returning home to a place that was no longer home, but knew it could not be avoided. Perhaps more than any of the others, save Istvan, Illarion understood the toll the Mongols would reap upon the conquered.

The bare space on the side of his head offered mute testament to a mortal awareness not all that different from the gaping smiles on the crushed corpses in their ditches. Cnán tried to take what comfort she could from the knowledge that at least the man who was guiding them knew the path well.

And what of this path? Feronantus had refused to tell them any more of what he had learned from Percival, and while the Brethren—after the initial discussion—were stoic in their acceptance of their leader's decision, she was not held to the same traditions. She hadn't spoken to any of them about what she had seen in the woods, nor had she seen or heard Percival speak of the *vision*.

In the lands of the Great Khan, the Mongolians had shamans to whom they went for aid and advice, and she had seen more than one of these mystics perform their strange animistic ceremonies where they were afforded glimpses of other realms and deities, or so they professed. She herself would profess to having seen too much of the cruelty and barbarity of men—and how much they enjoyed it—to believe the claims of divine guidance or inspiration in their actions, but at the same time, she did believe in the presence of a greater spirit. It was what lay at the core of being a Binder, and so she could not completely disregard what she had seen.

The Shield-Brethren had no trouble adopting the mantle of Christian piety, for it was not unlike the true faith they held in their hearts, but she was beginning to see how deep the roots of their belief went. She thought of the orange lilies that would flood the hillsides in the spring. The roots thrived belowground, and every year, for a brief time, they grew new stalks and flowers.

Was Percival's vision a stalk that was soon to flower? Did it flow from his sense of honor—held dearer to him than life itself? The first few times he had spoken of this honor, she had snorted and rolled her eyes, but since then, she had seen him act under its power—several times at mortal peril.

The memory of him pulling her from the path of the Mongols and slinging her across his saddle, defending her even when his horse fell, weighed on her. She stole a glance at him as he rode, some yards away, on a steed taken from their enemies. For all Percival's skill in the saddle, the animal would never be as responsive or as swift and powerful as his lost *Tonnerre*.

Was it honor or grief that drove him? Should she feel pity or sympathy? She looked away, unable to resolve the confusion in her head and heart. In many ways, the unforgiving and savaged terrain of Rus was easier to understand.

When she had come west across the Great Khan's empire, Cnán had taken care to avoid cities, except where absolutely necessary. She had seen, on more than one occasion, what was left behind by the Mongolian Horde as it swept across the plains. Like Illarion, she was prepared for there to be nothing left but the shattered remains of the crown jewel of Rus. Still, she was taken aback by the vista laid out before them when they crested a rise that brought them within view of the city's southern walls.

The only sign a city had once occupied the plain was the ragged outline inscribed by the remnants of the city's defenses. Amidst the rubble and devastation, there were paths—avenues between houses that had not been entirely filled in with heaps of rubble and the charred timbers from houses—but there was little sense in the chaos that a great many people had once lived here. Some buildings still stood, edifices of stone and brick that had refused to succumb to fire and the Mongol pillage, but all that remained of their former glory was a sad struggle to remain upright, like old soldiers who, on their deathbeds, try to wear their armor and lift their swords one last time.

Illarion pulled up his horse. "There is the south gate," he murmured as the group paused beside him. "We called it the 'Golden Gate,' and in the morning light, it would be so bright. But now…" The bitterness in his voice, and the ache, was unmistakable.

Cnán turned her eyes to where he and the Brethren stared and there caught sight of the ruined majesty of Kiev's fabled Golden Gate. They were tall, wrought of reddish stone that caught the light of the summer sun like dull fire. The wrath of the Mongols had badly damaged the keep about the gate-house, and much of the carved stone had been savaged by the siege, but even from this distance, and through those scars, she could appreciate the beauty the craftsmen had wrought.

They lingered for a long moment, Feronantus watching Illarion closely, but not intruding on his reverie. Cnán took the opportunity to study the city more closely as the others began to talk.

"My wife had family here," Illarion said. "I had thought... if they had survived, somehow, they might have been of assistance, but..." He didn't finish.

"On the hill," Percival said, idly patting and stroking the neck of his mount, as if from long habit. "A church still stands, does it not?"

Illarion pulled himself out of his reverie. "Yes, *Sobor Svyatoi Sofii*," he said, and then translated the name for them. "The Cathedral of St. Sophia."

Roger grunted at the name, but he did not push the matter further, instead looking to Feronantus, waiting to see what he would say.

The old leader of the Shield-Brethren sat on his horse like a judge, scrutinizing the walls, towers, and gates with the eye of a man attempting to discern the safest route across a territory he did not wish to enter to begin with.

Caution, and concern, narrowed his eyes. After a long while, he spoke. "Illarion, what lies beneath the church?"

The Ruthenian glanced at him and then at Percival before answering. "A monastery. *Pechersk Lavra*."

"This is your land," Feronantus said, ignoring both Roger and Cnán's gazes. "And though the city is a ruin, that church still stands, and its stones must have some power." He smiled grimly. "The sort of power that would draw pilgrims, penitents who seek solace in the wake of the armies of the Great Khan. It is the sort of place a man such as yourself might go, having survived the ordeal you have been through."

Illarion nodded. "Yes, that is a role I can play."

"Take Raphael, Percival, and Roger. They are your escort," Feronantus said, the plan decided. "We will follow at pace, after we ascertain the intelligence of our pursuer."

CHAPTER 24:

THE BRAWL AT THE BRIDGE

Hans's deputy told them the priest was not going to visit the Shield-Brethren alone, but in the company of two Livonian Knights. Their destination lay across the river and past the battlefields where the armies of Christendom had been defeated by the Mongols—a route that, even after a few months, was not safe for a solitary priest. As they were making the trip on horseback, they would have to travel to the west—to reach the bridge that had been built over the river—before they could swing north.

If they wanted to intercept the priest, they would do well to do so before he reached the bridge. Hans, with a smile, informed Kim that he knew a shortcut.

Hans led Kim on an utterly confusing footrace through the seediest of the seedy places that filled the bulk of the makeshift slum: past impromptu drink houses (so denoted by patchwork roofs of canvas strung haphazardly between the remnants of ruined walls), slipping and dodging the pools of filth and waste strewn in the back; through fields of ragged tents, laid nearly atop one another; across blackened fields that were still nothing more than mud and ash, filled with piles of detritus and scrap that were the refuse of the refuse diggers.

Kim was not surprised such routes existed through the city; all *natives* quickly learned the most expedient way to travel from one location to another. He knew many similar routes through Byeokrando, in fact, and had surprised a number of rough characters on several occasions by suddenly appearing in front of them when they thought they had left him behind. He followed Hans closely, trying to step where the youth stepped, matching the handholds as they clambered over piles of trash and rubble.

Before long, Kim began to get glimpses of Pius and the two knights through the clutter of tents and lean-tos. The escorts' mounts were less bowlegged than the mule Pius was riding. Beneath their surcoats—emblazoned with the red cross and sword they had seen on the standard—the knights wore mail shirts that extended past their waists. Their gauntlets were stiffened leather, and their helms were short cones of metal with crosspieces running across the front and extending down over their noses. They wore swords on their belts and each carried a long spear—a pole longer than his staff and topped with a pointed blade several inches long.

Kim nudged Hans as the young man slowed down, pointing ahead of them toward where the slum thinned out. The bridge, exhibiting all the hallmarks of Mongolian engineering, was a choke point controlled by the Khan. Kim would not be surprised if there was a levy collected on all travelers who used it; Onghwe Khan knew that most travelers would submit to parting with a few coins versus fording the narrow river on their own. Such methods of taxation had become an integral part of the Great Khan's empire. And anywhere money was collected, there would be security—at least an *arban* of

Mongolian troops who would be much more rigorous in their duties than the lazy soldiers guarding the camp.

If he was going to catch up with Pius, he had to do it before the priest reached the bridge.

Hans nodded, understanding the need, and altered his route accordingly. After leaping over a foul-smelling trench of shit and piss, they skirted a copse of scraggly pine trees that ran close to the road. The road kinked slightly at the trees, and there was a small stretch of ground where the view from the bridge was partially blocked.

Useful, just in case the conversation wasn't entirely peaceful. Hans hung back, hiding among the trees, while Kim stepped into the path of the oncoming riders and planted his staff on the ground. "Pius," he called. "A word, if you please."

The three riders were startled, and Kim noticed that the knight on his right had trouble controlling his horse. The animals were skittish, not bred for combat.

"Ki...Kim," Father Pius said. "I have not completed my errands." His eyes tracked back and forth between the two knights flanking him.

"Yes, Pius, I know," Kim said. "When we met, I asked you to deliver my note to the men who wore the red rose." He took a few steps closer to the trio as he used his staff to point to the knight on his left. "While that *mon* is red, it is not a rose. It looks not unlike that cross you wear about your own neck."

"They...ah..." Father Pius nervously played with the reins of his mule. "They are my escort. Not every road is safe for a man of God."

"I see," Kim said. He was even closer now. If he stayed too far from the knights, they could charge him, and while the ground was open enough that he might be able to evade the thrusts of their spears, a running fight against a man on horseback was a foolish battle for a man on foot. It was much better to be in close, where the benefit of being on a horse was lessened. Especially a horse that was not trained for combat. "And when you went to these men, did you only ask for their aid, or did you discuss another matter?"

From the way Father Pius blanched, Kim had his answer, but he gave no outward indication other than to relax his grip on his staff. *The one on the left,* he thought.

Pius flapped his reins. "Out of my way," he snorted, trying to goad his mule into motion, but the animal showed no sign of budging.

The knight closest to Kim leaned forward and jabbed his spear at Kim, lending a martial imperative to the priest's command. Kim whipped up his staff as he took a deep step forward, batting the tip of the spear to the outside. The knight's arm was above Kim's head, an unnatural and exposed position to be in during a spear fight, and Kim jabbed the tip of his staff deep into the mounted man's exposed armpit.

The knight recoiled, his spear flopping in his suddenly weak grip. He tried to bring the point back to bear on Kim. Kim whipped his staff to his left, smacking the knight's arm hard, and then flipped the tip to the right—left hand forward and down, right hand drawing back—connecting solidly with the side of the knight's head.

The whole exchange happened so quickly that it seemed to be one fluid reaction to the knight's thrust with his spear. Pius's mule, still being reluctant to respond to its rider's commands, started in surprise as the knight fell off his horse with a chingling thud. The other knight swore and kicked his own horse in the ribs, trying to get into a better position. He charged Kim, thrusting with his spear, but Kim was already moving to put the riderless horse between them.

The knight charged off into the fallow pasture beside the road, getting enough distance from Kim that he could turn his animal safely. Far enough to generate some speed on his return, making his mount an effective weapon as well. Not a bad tactic.

Kim picked up the fallen knight's spear and took a moment to turn and poke Pius's mule with the tip. Not enough to wound the animal, but enough to make it react. The mule reared, dumping Pius on the ground, and Kim turned his attention to the remaining knight.

The knight's horse was still skittish, and when he didn't charge immediately, Kim glanced over at the knight he had unseated, and seeing he was conscious, he stepped over and smacked the man in the head with the butt of his spear. *Stay down.*

The knight abandoned his horse. The animal was too uncontrollable, and Kim was surrounded by supine bodies and other animals. There was no advantage to charging into that mix. On the ground, at least, they would be more equally classed. He approached Kim cautiously, his spear held in a grip that positioned the weapon across his body—butt near his head, point directed at the ground. It didn't seem that aggressive of a stance, and so Kim remained still, the tip of his spear pointed at his approaching adversary. Waiting for him to make a move.

As the knight came closer, he raised his tip slightly, and then he came on in a rush, beating Kim's point aside to clear the line for a thrust. Kim, moving more quickly, stepped into the man's attack—past the lazy point that would have struck him had he remained still. He brought the butt end of his spear around in a quick smash to the man's head. The knight pulled up short, yanking his head back, and only caught part of Kim's butt against his helmet. His eyes widened as he realized where his face was, and he tried to pull back even farther as Kim drove the end of the spear into his nose.

Cartilage crunched and blood spewed out of the man's broken nose. Kim stepped back with his left leg, putting some distance between them now, and he brought the tip of his spear up and around, smacking the other man's spear down so that the point buried itself in the ground. The man tried to hang on to his weapon. His face was a mass of blood and snot, and his teeth were bared as if he could scare Kim off with his monstrous expression.

Kim—centered, coiled, calm—looked him in the eye and then snapped his hips forward, driving all his energy up his trunk, into his arms, and into the arc of the moving spear. The impact—high on the knight's chest, above the red cross on his surcoat—lifted him off his feet.

He landed in a heap and made no move to rise. Kim tossed both spears toward the cluster of trees, far enough away that no one would think of them as readily accessible, and returned to the fallen priest.

Pius was senseless, more from nerves and shock than any obvious blow to the head, but he was still breathing. Kim didn't waste any time trying to revive him; he had had enough of the priest's scurrilous behavior. He rummaged through the man's satchel and found what he was looking for. In fact, he found more than one.

Hans was at his elbow suddenly, pulling at his sleeve. "The guards," the young man said, pointing. A handful of Mongolians, astride their short ponies, were coming in their direction from the bridge. "We need to go."

Kim fumbled with the pair of small scrolls. Neither was sealed, though it looked like one had been at one time—there were still bits of wax stuck to the edge. They both seemed to start with the same letters. *Kim Alcheon, Last of the Flower Knights, to Feronantus…* he imagined the words read. The unsealed one appeared to have been written more hurriedly, though what it said he could not divine.

"There is no time," Hans said, trying to get his attention.

Kim grabbed the young man's shirt and thrust both scrolls at him. "The Shield-Brethren," he said, holding Hans's attention. *Is there someone you could trust more?* "Are they honorable?"

Hans squirmed in his grip, clearly more concerned about the approaching Mongols than a conversation about honor.

Kim held him tight. "Will they protect you?"

Hans stopped and met Kim's gaze. "Yes," he said. "Yes, they will."

"Go, then," Kim said, taking a quick glance at the approaching riders. "Take them these messages. One of them is true. One is not. Both may have value to them. They will understand." *They have to; my time has run out.* He shoved Hans toward the trees. "Run, Hans. Run all the way."

One last glance over his shoulder was all Hans needed as encouragement, and he grabbed the scrolls from Kim and darted away, running like a rabbit for the security of the slum's maze.

Kim watched him go and then let out a long breath, letting all the tension flow from his body. He bent to pick up his staff, and as he stood, he pushed back his hood. The sun felt good against his face, and he waited until the leader of the Mongol group shouted at him before he turned around.

◆ ◆ ◆

When they heard the signal—the distinct *weeka weeka weeka* of the black-tailed godwit—Andreas and his students stopped their sparring. After the last unannounced visitor, they were more sensitive to the appearance of strangers in the wood surrounding their Brethren chapter house. Weapons in hand, they moved toward the front of the ruined monastery—not aggressively, but with a clear *unfriendly* disposition.

A hooded figure emerged from the tree line, guiding a small figure. The sentry's name was Eilif, a blond-haired phantom of the woods, and his captive was a scrawny lad, yet lithe and active—this boy wasn't like the typical urchins who seemed to spring out of the ruins like weeds growing in an unplowed field. "Said he has a message for Feronantus," Eilif said as the group of Shield-Brethren gathered around.

"Does he now?" Andreas said, appraising the boy. It was not lost on him that the boy seemed to know a little Latin; he tried to seem bored and without a care, but his eyes tracked them too well. He was listening intently to their words. "Was he alone?" he asked Eilif.

"Been following him since the river."

Andreas nodded. Eilif took that as a dismissal and faded back into the trees, vanishing once again to his phantasmal role as the chapter house's watchful eye.

"Boy," Andreas said, catching the youth's attention, "what message do you bring?"

"For the leader of the Red Rose," the boy said, haltingly. He pointed to the standard flying over the ruined monastery.

"I'm their leader," Andreas said. "You can give it to me."

The boy screwed up his face and shook his head. "Feronantus," he said, holding steady to his demand.

Andreas squatted and looked the boy squarely in the face, intrigued by the youth's persistence. The youth didn't know Feronantus wasn't here, but he knew enough of the Shield-Brethren master to know that Andreas wasn't the man he was looking for. "Who sent you?" he asked, wondering whom the boy had been talking to. *Haakon?* The Mongol camp continued to rebuff their inquiries about the fate of their missing

Brother. It had been more than two weeks since the young
fighter had gone through the Red Veil, and no one had been
able to discover what had happened. The mood among the
Shield-Brethren was turning more and more murderous, and
Rutger had his hands full with their tempers in check.

"Flower Knight," the boy said, and when that name failed
to produce any response from Andreas, he performed an
exaggerated pantomime—whirling his hands around.

Like he is swinging a staff, Andreas realized. The boy had no
real training, and the technique was raw and unformed, but
clearly he had been watching someone whose skill had made
a deep impression on him. "The Flower Knight sent you?" he
asked.

The boy stopped and nodded. "Feronantus." Back to the
beginning again.

"You can tell me or not," he said with a tiny shake of his
head. "But you will come no closer to our camp."

The boy was shaken by this statement, and his tough mien
threatened to break. He glanced at the woods behind him
and then back at the standard again. When his gaze returned
to Andreas's face, his expression had softened, and some of
the ferocity was gone from his eyes. "Protect…" He pointed at
the standard and then made a circle with his fingers. He held
it over his heart. "Protection?"

The men muttered amongst themselves. "By the Virgin,"
one of them swore, and Andreas kept his expression neutral
as he glanced at the man next to him. "Go fetch Rutger," he
said, using the Northmen tongue the boy did not know. "And
some food," he added, noticing how the boy's ribs pressed
against his ragged shirt.

◆ ◆ ◆

"He said Kim—this *Flower Knight*—sent him?" Rutger continued to pore over both of the messages. They were both written by the same hand, and both were addressed and signed the same. The difference lay in what they actually said.

Andreas nodded. "He said there was only supposed to be one message. Kim told him to deliver both. One would be true, the other false, and we would know which was which."

Rutger looked up and glanced over to where the boy— Hans, as Andreas had managed to learn, finally—was still hungrily working on the wings and thighs of a grouse given to him. "Do you think he knows what the messages say?"

"I don't think so. He said something about a fight. Near the bridge. Between Kim and a couple of bodyguards." He indicated his chest. "He said they were Livonian Knights, but when I asked him how he knew, he said they wore a red cross and sword on their surcoats."

"Shit," Rutger said. "I thought they gave up the cross and sword after they merged with the Teutonic Order. Why are they wearing those colors?" He glanced at the message in his left hand—the note they had decided was the false one. "You think they wrote it?"

"I do," Andreas said. "Why would they be escorting a messenger unless they wanted to make sure we got *this* message?" *Your Brother is dead*, the message said. *I saw the Mongols kill him, after his victory.*

"You think they know something about Haakon?"

"Perhaps," Andreas shrugged. "Maybe not. They could just be stirring up trouble. We won't know until we go down there and find out."

Rutger shook his head. "We can't risk it. That may be exactly the sort of reaction they're hoping to provoke. The boy came here looking for Feronantus, and he knew enough to know you were lying to him. We have to stay here; we have to protect the secret of Feronantus's hunting party."

Andreas made a noncommittal noise in his throat. And when Rutger repeated his last statement, he roused himself as if from a trance. "Yes," he said somewhat curtly, "I know. But these Livonians are another matter, especially if they are wearing the red cross and sword. They aren't hiding in the Teutonic ranks. Who is leading them? Is it someone who truly knows Feronantus on sight? What if they decide to pay us a visit?" He waved a hand at the chapter house behind them. "And what of them? How long can we keep them here, pretending that a few more days of training is all they need to be ready?"

Rutger crumpled up the false message. "I don't know."

"The Khan is going to get bored, if he isn't already," Andreas said, "and he's going to order his army to move on. We can't keep hiding here, waiting for a miracle to happen."

Rutger whirled on him. "What would you have me do?" he snarled, his voice low and harsh. "Throw them all against the horde that outnumbers them ten to one? It's going to happen eventually, so what is the point of waiting any longer, is that it?"

"No," Andreas said quietly. "It is always better to avoid a fight than rush into it. But that does not mean we sit idle." He looked over at Hans. "Kim wants to meet us." He smiled. "From the boy's description, it sounds like he might be one of the Khan's champions. We need to issue a challenge. There are still qualifying fights going on, even if the main arena is closed. We need to draw the Khan's attention to those fights—offer some sort of exhibition bout, even. I'm sure it won't take much to convince the Khan to try another of his fighters against us."

Andreas rolled his shoulders. "Besides, I want to meet this Flower Knight. He sounds like he might be a challenge. I'm getting tired of smacking your charges around."

◆ ◆ ◆

When the guards threw him in the same cage with Zug, the Nipponese man hauled himself off his mat and came to inspect the bruises on Kim's face. "You trusted the wrong man," he grunted as he sat back on his haunches.

Kim rolled onto his back and lay still, staring at the rusty ceiling of their cell. "Yes and no," he said enigmatically. He worked his tongue around his mouth, checking his teeth. The Mongols hadn't roughed him up too much—they had, after all, noticed and appreciated that he had downed two knights from one of Christendom's fighting orders—but they had had to inflict some punishment on him for being so close to the river.

"Was it worth it?" Zug asked.

Kim shrugged. "I'm stuck in here with you now," he said. "I should have given that more thought."

Zug grunted and kicked him lightly as he shuffled back to his mat. His strength was returning, albeit too slowly for his—or Kim's—liking.

Kim ignored Zug, closing his eyes and letting his breathing slow. He had some pain in his lower abdomen and would probably be pissing blood sometime in the next few days, but it would all pass. He could be patient for a while; he had waited long enough.

"Two," he murmured as he started to relax.

"What?" Zug grunted.

"I took down two armored Franks." Kim smiled. "They never touched me. When you're feeling strong enough, maybe I'll show you how it's done." He drifted toward sleep as Zug unleashed an elaborate string of Nihongo curses.

He's definitely getting better...

CHAPTER 25:

THE SUBTLETIES OF WRESTLING

Master Chucai left them, galloping back to Karakorum. Black robes streaming behind, he looked like a giant raven clinging to the horse, its talons digging into the animal's flesh. Lian and Gansukh rode in silence, letting their horses pick their own pace. Neither felt any compelling desire to return to the bustling hive that was the Imperial Court.

"Stop. Look," Lian said as they came in view of the walls. She touched his arm, drawing him out of his maddeningly convoluted reverie, and pointed toward an expansive cluster of colorful tents clustered around the nearest gate. "The traders who have come for the festival. Let us think about something else for a little while." Her lips parted, and Gansukh again caught a flash of her teeth. She snapped her horse's reins. "If you are to face Ögedei, perhaps it would be best to find suitable clothes."

"I have—"

But she was already ahead of him, and he sat on his horse, grinding his teeth. He would never understand her. Her mind was too foreign, too strange in the way it leapt from subject to subject. He couldn't let go of things as readily as she did, and other matters that seemed nonsensical and pointless to him were of paramount importance to her.

The wind, full of her laughter, swirled past him.

He cursed, then wheeled the horse about and tapped it into a trot. *Why not?* he rationalized. *If I'm going to be exiled for failure, I might as well have a clean shirt or two to take with me.* He laughed as he rode after Lian, not sure how else to react to both this insight and the fact that he did understand courtly thinking more than he wanted to admit.

The caravans hadn't bothered to enter the city. The camels and pack animals had come to a stop outside the eastern gate, and the merchants had set up their shops in the middle of the road. Their manner of dress was not familiar to him, and he gawked openly at the men's garish clothing: brightly colored silk pants with tops that didn't match, shirts that billowed at the arms and waist, sweeping body-length coats with high collars. And the women! Some seemed to wear hardly anything, or what they wore was tight and dark or bright, translucent, and swirling. Many of the women were bare-footed and wore heavy ornamental rings or torques on wrists, necks, ankles. Coins like fish-scale mail armor lay in wreaths on their breasts. The men were more likely to dress in white than the women. Small silver bells hung from belts at their waists, and the high, step-rhythmic tinking of jewelry, coins, and bells added a melodic jangle to the raucous atmosphere of the bazaar.

As Gansukh let his horse pick its way through the crowds, he found himself wondering if Lian would ever wear any such adornments.

Somewhere up ahead, in the shadow of the wall, musicians were performing. The strange, loose music sounded an exotic backdrop to the cacophony of shouting and arguing and haggling. The scents were more foreign still, and Gansukh's stomach grumbled as he picked out the greasy scents of boiled mutton and roasting chicken, along with the blood smell of dozens of recently slaughtered sheep—the heady, almost overwhelming miasma of a bazaar. Idly he wondered if his stomach could stand up to any food sold from the makeshift stalls. He had only just become accustomed to the rich food of the court.

"They are Persians." Lian was suddenly at Gansukh's left elbow. She had wound her hair up in a ball at the back of her neck, held in place by a lacquered comb.

"Persians," he grunted. Persia was a vast place. "Where in Persia?"

"From the Khwarezmian Empire," Lian reminded him.

"Ah, yes—the one Genghis defeated."

Lian pursed her lips, but there was laughter in her eyes. "Genghis Khan defeated *many* empires," she said.

"Yes," he shot back, suddenly weary of her constant role of tutor. "And it is sometimes difficult to remember them all." As soon as he said the words, he wanted to take them back.

The humor went out of her eyes, and she spat something at him in her native tongue, a language she knew very well he did not understand. Before he could stop her, she kneed her horse into the crowd. He meant to follow her, but a resounding crash of metal on metal startled his own mount. By the time he worked through the crowd and got his horse under control, Lian had vanished.

He stared glumly in the direction she had gone, hoping to catch a glimpse of her. *Her people belonged to one of those empires.* He sighed and glanced around for the source of the noise that had startled his horse. He needed a distraction; he needed time to let his mind untangle itself from the knots into which it had been tied.

He got down from his horse and led the animal through the crowds, halfheartedly looking for Lian. Mostly he wandered, trying to lose himself in the bazaar—trying to let his mind go blank. Soon enough he was surrounded by dark, grinning faces, with long hooked noses and black desert eyes, offering up jewelry, meats, flagons of wine or beer or *arkhi*.

His stomach had finally decided it could stand a bit of meat, and as Gansukh paused to get his bearings, surrounded by a thick cloud of savory meat smells and spices that now made his mouth water, a vendor caught his eye and waved him over. This one was a more sedentary man, sticking close to his cooking station, also dark-skinned but broad of nose and bushy of beard, and he jabbered at Gansukh, punctuating his words with rapid gestures. The fact that Gansukh had no idea what the man was saying made no difference. Beside him, on a squat stand, was a stone basin filled with fiery coals. Suspended above on a makeshift wire grate were a dozen or so wooden skewers laden with meat, and the entire time he was gabbling—haggling, Gansukh realized—he flipped and rotated the sticks without glancing at them.

The vendor threw up his hand in disgust and waved him off when he tried to purchase only one skewer. His stomach rumbled in disappointment, so Gansukh settled for two. Perhaps he could make himself sick in some sort of penance. *Chicken*, he thought as he plucked off one of the chunks of meat with his fingers, popped it into his mouth, and chewed. *A bit gamey*, he decided. But the spices soon took his thoughts away from the age and toughness of the old bird.

The tingling started on the tip of his tongue, and before he could finish swallowing the first piece, the back of his throat was on fire. When he raised his fingers to his face to wipe his streaming eyes, he realized they had plucked the meat from the stick to begin with—too late. He had spread spice to his lids and cheek, and now he could barely see.

The vendor laughed at him, a wide-mouthed braying that went on and on. Gansukh bared his teeth, wiped his eyes with his sleeve, and boldly tossed another chunk of meat into his mouth. His throat constricted at the sudden shock of more long pepper, but he tightened the muscles in his jaw, chewing and swallowing with the frantic determination of a madman. He was not about to spit it out.

As he led his mount away from the meat vendor, one hand clutching reins, the other the skewer, he turned down a narrow alley and discovered a small square filled with stalls selling all manner of housewares—rugs, cooking utensils, dishes. The materials ranged from reeds used for weaving intricate baskets to brightly polished brass fashioned into all manner of cups and bowls.

His mouth still burning, Gansukh wrapped the reins around his forearm, then bent over to pick up a ridiculously large cup with exotic stones set in the sides. "Water," he gasped, and the slender merchant smiled at the stick of meat held in his left hand and produced a leather skin from beneath his table.

When Gansukh had diluted the fire in his mouth, he tried to return the cup, but the merchant waved him off. Speaking in heavily inflected Mongol, the merchant informed him that the cup belonged to *him* now. He had drunk from it, had he not? Who would want to buy a *used* cup? When Gansukh tried to ignore this and again place the cup on the spread cloth, the merchant's tone grew angry, and his gestures became more animated. Did Gansukh think that just because the Mongols had conquered the known world, they could take what they wanted, whenever they wanted—and not *pay*? Why didn't Gansukh just kill him now and save him the humiliation of being robbed of his life's work? And again, louder still.

Gansukh sighed and dug out a few coins from his pouch. He was out of his depth amongst these shameless hawkers. All at once he was reminded of the vast gulf between life at court and in the towns and life on the steppes, and how he would never truly fit in with the former. *Still, this merchant is no worse than our horse traders...*

Depressed, convinced he should have known better—and now burdened with an enormous metal cup, as well as a stick and a half of spiced meat for which, literally, he might have no further stomach—he tugged with his arm on his horse's reins and headed for the gate to Karakorum.

Passing the pavilion beneath the walls where the musicians were playing, he slowed to watch. Half a dozen men played instruments roughly similar to ones he knew, but these were rounder and taller and had more strings or more pipes than he was accustomed to. Their songs were sinuous and rhythmic, filled with serpentine melodies that reminded him of the wind's song out on the plain. He found himself rooted to the spot and didn't even notice the young woman in light-blue silk pants until she planted her feet boldly, with arms crossed, right in front of his horse. The horse blew out its breath and stopped short, then shook out its mane in irritation.

Having caught Gansukh's attention, the girl now rushed a few steps to stand before him, brought her hands together above her head, bent her arms akimbo, and began to move her hips to the music. The belt around her waist was fitted with silver bells, and Gansukh noted with pleasure that they were the sort of bells he had heard earlier. The musicians, in response to the flick of her hips, quickened the tempo, and she responded in kind, flexing her body and twirling around Gansukh in a flurry of colored silk.

Someone pushed a stool into the back of Gansukh's legs, and he sat down heavily as the crowd around him started to clap in time with the music. The horse chuffed and nickered, its eyes wide, and Gansukh touched its flank with his hand so that it would not kick out and injure someone.

The woman produced a red silk scarf and draped it over Gansukh's left shoulder. Slowly she pulled it back and forth around his neck. She brought her face close to his and drew a long fingernail under his chin. Her eyes were hazel green and lined with a color that matched her blue outfit. She gave him an exaggerated wink and, as Gansukh laughed, raised the red scarf above her head and pulled it tight between both hands. Matching the beat of the music and the crowd, she tilted her hips up and down, left and right, making the silver bells at her waist dance and ring. Gansukh couldn't take his eyes off the woman's slender waist. She smiled knowingly and crooked a finger at him, beckoning him to stand and follow her. Glancing over her shoulder to see that he was still watching her, she began to move toward a small maroon tent set up behind the band.

Gansukh grinned and stood up—and found his way blocked.

"Persian culture is fascinating, isn't it?" Lian's hands were on her hips. Gansukh's grin faltered.

"I…"

"You?"

"She…"

"*She* what?"

Gansukh looked over Lian's head. The woman in blue was standing at the door to the maroon tent. She gave Gansukh a pouty look, pushing out her lower lip, and pulled the tent flap open wide.

"She…has bells."

Lian gave him a withering look. *She has bells?*

With a snap, Gansukh broke eye contact with the dancer. "Bells...which would look better on you." His grin returned.

"Oh, by the heavens." Lian rolled her eyes. "I leave you alone for—"

"I was hungry," Gansukh said, trying to change the subject. Remembering the sticks of meat, he offered her one.

"I can see that." Still the same cold tone.

"I thought you—"

"I did," she snapped.

Gansukh realized she was holding a broad piece of cloth, and when he stared at it uncomprehendingly, she exhaled noisily and hurled it at his feet before storming off into the crowd.

More confused than ever, he looked at the cup and the sticks of meat in his hands, and finally put the meat in the cup so that he could bend down and pick up the cloth.

It was a silk robe, as blue as the summer sky. An intricate pattern of interwoven tree branches, done in red and gold thread, ran down the front. Small birds nested in the tips, and hidden deep within the snarled bramble, he saw the lean faces of wolves.

It was the most beautiful article of clothing he had ever seen.

✦ ✦ ✦

After a night of restless sleep, Gansukh was no closer to understanding any of the puzzles that continued to vex him. He was no closer to comprehending the *Khagan*'s depression and madness, nor how to reach the man who was lost in an alcoholic stupor. Lian was angry with him, and while he knew he shouldn't care what a Chinese slave thought, his brain was constantly churning with confusion and frustration about her.

Not to mention the lacquered box. There had to be a way to open it, and while he could simply crush it with the pommel of his sword, such a solution could destroy what lay inside. It remained a tantalizing mystery—a symbol of his inability to fathom the intricacies of a seemingly simple problem.

He had left the box in his chamber, tucked in the inner pocket of the robe Lian had bought him. Then he had left his room, trying to put both out of his mind. The robe hung behind a paper screen. Hiding all of his secrets.

As he wandered around the compound, Gansukh couldn't shake Master Chucai's parting words from the other day: *You simply need permission, and not from me or the* Khagan.

Who, then? And what sort of permission?

Out on the steppe, he needed no permission from anyone. He was in charge of his own life. Even when he traveled with other clansmen, they each knew how to provide for themselves and those who relied upon them for safety and sustenance. They didn't need to be reminded or commanded. In an *arban*, each man answered to the others in the squad, and their *arban* commander answered to the *jaghun* commander. The *jaghun* commanders answered to the *noyon* of their *minghan*, and so on, up to the *Khagan* himself. It was a simple chain of command—one that had proven itself effective for many a military campaign.

But if he wasn't supposed to follow that chain of command, then who was he supposed to answer to?

It wasn't an impossible riddle. Gansukh couldn't believe that Master Chucai would waste his time playing such games. He wanted Gansukh to discover some insight—one of Lian's constant reminders was that a lesson self-learned was much more likely to be remembered than a lesson taught—and he was sure Chucai had inflicted that same aphorism on her during her own education. These sorts of intellectual jabs were always passed on from master to student, generation to generation.

Who had taught Master Chucai? he wondered. Chucai had been an advisor to Genghis Khan; he had been there when Ögedei Khan's father built the empire. *Who had taught him?* Gansukh wondered, and then another question posed itself: *Whom had Genghis sought permission from?*

He hadn't. But that wasn't the whole answer. He had bound the clans to him. Had he asked their permission? No, they had come to him. *Why?*

As he mulled over that question, he noticed he had wandered close to the quarters of the Day Guard, unconsciously summoned by grunts of exertion and the sound of flesh on flesh and of bodies striking packed earth. The morning wrestling practice. Gansukh had watched them on a few previous occasions; early in his education, Lian had suggested befriending some of the Imperial Guard as a way of helping his standing at court. He hadn't acted upon her idea previously, citing the excuse that having drawn the ire of Munokhoi on several occasions, there was the distinct possibility that seeking out the *Torguud* might be more foolish than wise, but now, with the question of the source of Genghis Khan's leadership in his mind, he reconsidered his standing with the *Torguud.*

Munokhoi might be able to command a certain amount of authority among the Day Guard by virtue of his rank, but given the reaction he'd gotten from the *Khevtuul* (the Night Guard) after the incident in the garden, Gansukh suspected Munokhoi wasn't well liked. Munokhoi's *jaghun* was only a portion of the whole *Torguud,* and it was likely the remainder of the Day Guard might have a similar lack of respect for the cruel commander.

Respect among warriors was hard earned and easily lost. There were only a handful of ways in which a man could win and keep the respect of his peers.

Wrestling was one of them.

The reigning wrestling champion of the Imperial Guard was Namkhai, a tall, heavy-set grappler who—as Gansukh had seen—invariably broke into a chortle and grinned like a demon as his opponent showed any sign of nerves. Some capitulated as soon as he started to smile, knowing they had already shown too much weakness. Others held out longer, until Namkhai caught them in a bear hug and began to cackle in their ears. Gansukh wasn't sure how he would react to Namkhai's gambit, but he wanted to find out. He wanted to find out what it took to change the expression on the wrestler's face.

He wanted to find out what it took to earn the man's respect.

Gansukh was no stranger to wrestling. Chagatai Khan's own personal guard held regular wrestling matches, and he had won a number of bouts. There was a difference in the rules, though, between those observed by Chagatai's guards and by the *Torguud*. On the wrestling field of Karakorum, a fighter could not grab the legs of his opponent. The wrestlers could only grip their opponent's arms or upper body in their efforts to throw the other off balance. A match was lost when a wrestler's upper body, elbow, or knee touched the ground.

Stripped to the waist, Gansukh warily watched Namkhai as the champion took a moment to play to the gathered crowd before entering the marked-off area of the wrestling field. Namkhai approached Gansukh, a tiny sliver of a smile quirking the edge of his lips. Namkhai was both taller and heavier, but his gait was stiff—his hips and thighs moved as one massive column of bone and muscle. Gansukh was faster, more nimble, and when Namkhai tensed his body and threw out his hands, Gansukh only had to flinch to one side to avoid the champion's large grip. He closed, trying to get a headlock.

The champion resisted, and as he pulled back, Gansukh let go and used both hands to push explosively on Namkhai's chest. Namkhai stumbled backward, arms swinging wildly to keep his balance. It would have been so easy to reach down, grab Namkhai by his thighs, and flip him to the ground, but Gansukh held back. This was Ögedei's court; he had to win by the *Torguud*'s rules.

Namkhai's grin faltered, and his hands flexed dangerously as he regained his balance. The champion regarded Gansukh carefully, appraising him more closely. With a tiny nod, Namkhai acknowledged Gansukh's first attack; even if Gansukh lost the fight, they both knew that—if the rules had been different—Gansukh would have won.

Namkhai advanced again, and Gansukh hunched his back slightly, pulling his shoulders in to give the impression that he wasn't going to attack. A submissive pose. *I am on the defensive.* Let Namkhai make the first move. Given the weight difference between them, it was unlikely Gansukh could outmuscle the champion. But he could use Namkhai's assault against him. If the bigger man lunged and grabbed him, Gansukh could twist and manage their fall so Namkhai's shoulders hit the ground first. He turned his hips slightly, letting his left foot slide back a few inches.

Namkhai leaped forward.

A yell rose from the crowd, a wall of sound that rose over and collapsed on Gansukh as Namkhai barreled across the packed dirt. He had seen Namkhai charge other opponents; he had seen the force of Namkhai's assault as it crumpled the defenses of those who, foolishly, thought they could withstand such an impact. But Gansukh didn't try to stop Namkhai.

Instead he met Namkhai's rush with a bear hug, gasping as the full force of the champion's charge slammed into his chest. He was going to fall, and forcefully twisting his upper body, he pushed off the ground with his right foot. Suddenly they were both airborne, nearly perpendicular to the ground. Namkhai's grin vanished as he stared wide-eyed at the sky, amazed at the sudden change of view.

The champion reacted, more by instinct than conscious thought. In mid-fall, he knifed his body against Gansukh and got his feet underneath him. He landed in a deep crouch, with the whole of Gansukh's weight bearing down on his chest. He bellowed as his back arched painfully; growling in frustration, Gansukh squeezed his arms and tried to find enough leverage to push Namkhai even farther. He was stunned Namkhai had found his footing—the man was *inhuman*! They strained against one another, neither one able to shift the other. All Gansukh could hear was the grinding sound of his teeth and the hiss of air escaping from Namkhai's pursed lips.

The crowd had fallen silent.

Their eyes met, and Gansukh realized Namkhai was aware of the silence too.

Gansukh glanced around, and as he became aware of the circle of spectators, he spotted a gap in the crowd. Namkhai saw it too, and without hesitation, they both released their holds on the other and stepped apart.

A space opened in the circle of *Torguud* spectators and quickly filled with a retinue of servants and courtiers, which at the very last parted to form two protective walls. Now appeared the *Khagan* himself, with his most intimate servants and chamberlains. To the *Khagan*'s right, an exceptionally short man hovered, bearing aloft a tray of tiny silver cups.

Ögedei Khan held one cup in his hand and was wiping his mouth with his sleeve. "Don't stop on my account," he said loudly. "Gansukh, you nearly had our champion bested."

Gansukh and Namkhai, having bowed at the sudden appearance of the *Khagan*, now stood awkwardly at the center of the field. Gansukh could barely summon the strength to lift his arms, and his teeth ached from how much he had been grinding them. Namkhai's face gleamed with sweat, and his hair lay matted against his head. His chest heaved, and he looked to be in no rush to start the fight again. Gansukh swiped at his forehead, clearing the sweat that was starting to sting his eyes, then brought his hands together and bowed again to the *Khagan*. He remained bent over, trying to catch Namkhai's attention with a subtle tilt of his head.

Namkhai slapped his hands together and bowed as well.

"No?" Ögedei Khan was jovial with wine and readily dismissed their refusal. "We'll save the rematch for another time. Here"—he motioned to two men on opposite sides of the field—"you two. Fight for me."

Gansukh and Namkhai retired from the field as the two chosen guards bent their knees and began flapping their arms in an imitation of the hawk, the traditional way to start a match. They reached the center, bent at the waist, and brought their arms down into a fighting stance. They then awaited the *Khagan*'s word.

"Go!" Ögedei Khan bellowed.

At the sidelines, jostled by men who slapped his back and shoulders in congratulations at a match well fought, Gansukh fought to catch his breath. While the rest of the men watched the two new combatants, he kept his eye on the *Khagan*.

The short servant adeptly kept the tray in motion, dancing about and rotating it effortlessly with the *Khagan*'s every move, to keep a steady supply of full cups near his reach. Ögedei downed each in one motion, slamming the empty cup upside down on the tray. The servant flinched with each one but kept the tray upright and moving. Gansukh wondered what happened when all the cups were overturned. Would the *Khagan* stop drinking? Judging by his unconscious swaying motion and the strident volume of his humor, that probably wasn't the case. In fact, this was probably not the first tray of cups.

As the *Khagan* snapped his head back again, Gansukh scanned the crowd to see if anyone else was paying attention to the *Khagan*'s drinking, and he was relieved to see everyone's attention was on the wrestling match.

Everyone except Namkhai.

The wrestling champion felt Gansukh's gaze and glanced over his shoulder. His eyes met Gansukh's for a second, and then he turned and rudely shoved his way through the crowd. But it was too late. Gansukh had seen his expression.

The big man had lost his grin, and his face was a mask of disgust and dismay.

The *Khagan* did not seek, or even need, permission from his subjects, but he did need something—respect. Hard earned and easily lost.

A yell rose from the crowd as one of the wrestlers bested the other, sending him sprawling to the ground on his hands and knees. His opponent helped him to his feet as the *Khagan* roared his approval.

"Let us eat and drink tonight!" he shouted. "A feast for our fighters." He staggered as he glanced around the sea of faces, and Gansukh ducked behind a cluster of off-duty guards. His face burned with shame for hiding, but even more for not wanting to be seen beside the *Khagan*.

He was beginning to understand Master Chucai's riddle. It wasn't enough to stop Ögedei's drinking. The whole empire was in danger of being poisoned with loss of respect.

The *Khagan* slammed another tiny cup down on the tray. *How many of those would he consume in one day?* Gansukh wondered, and then an idea struck him.

One cup, he thought. *One instead of dozens.*

It was a preposterous idea, but it could work.

CHAPTER 26:

OVER THE WRECKAGE AND
THROUGH THE RUINS

The walls that encircled Kiev were a wrecked shell, though the Golden Gate retained much of its majesty through sheer bulk, if nothing else. As Raphael rode through it with Percival, Roger, and Illarion, he sensed, if only for a few moments, what the city had been before the coming of the Mongols. Then the gate was behind him and he could see nothing but ruins.

To the east, the Dnieper, winding from north to south, flanked the city. Above it stood a pair of hills, and on the taller of two stood a white-walled structure, obviously religious in purpose, with high arched windows that shone even beneath the gray, overcast skies. To Raphael's eye, it was much in the style of the Byzantine Church, with certain Ruthenian peculiarities.

A street—now just a chute winding among the avalanched rubble of collapsed buildings—stretched before them. Houses had once clustered tightly in the shadow of the old wall, but now only a few rose from the scavenged ruins. The remains of once-proud works of white and gold-tinted stone stood side by side with buildings somehow untouched, as if protected by divine intercession. The building on top of the hill—Raphael suspected that it was the priory of some religious order—was not the only house of God left in Kiev. It was rumored that the Mongols, equally superstitious about all supernatural beings, did not destroy churches if they could avoid it.

The people who remained in this place—he was no longer inclined to call it a city—were likewise a curious mixture of the lost and the enterprising, the shattered and the oblivious. *Even after the passage of the Mongolian Horde*, Raphael mused, *life must go on as best it can.* The scent of boiled cabbage reached his nose, along with the sweet, earthy fragrance of beets. A mouthwatering vapor of onion bread wafted from a stone oven squatting incongruously on a rubble-strewn corner, tended by a burly, sweating baker. The stench of garbage and sewage was also prevalent, but that was familiar to any city dweller and even a sign of revival. Dead cities smelled only of ancient decay and dust. Here, life was evident, even to a blind man, in the odor of unwashed, laboring flesh—mingled with fish that he assumed must have been dragged fairly recently from the Dnieper.

Following Illarion's lead, Raphael guided his horse out of the main path to evade a cadaverous merchant's thudding, grumbling wagon. *It says much*, Raphael reflected, *about the tenacious nature of men that one with wares to sell would be willing to brave such a place.* The profit, it seemed, was small indeed. No doubt much of the money changing hands was ultimately swept into Mongol coffers.

Between the ruins on another street, he caught sight of Feronantus and the rest of their company entering via another gate—no, on second thought, this was a breach in the wall—and heading away in the direction of the riverfront.

The craggy face of the lord of Týrshammar had taken on a more haunted look since Taran's death, and Raphael could not blame him. The loss of their brother was a knife wound that continued to bleed even days after the blade had been withdrawn. Taran had taught several who were numbered among their greatest. His departure was a bitter draught to choke down upon waking each morning—particularly for Feronantus.

And now...another, perhaps even more unexpected disappointment had beset their leader.

"Come," Illarion said, resuming his course in the wake of the wagon. "Pointless dawdling will draw attention."

Illarion had made an impressive recovery, but the absence of his ear impaired his hearing on that side, and the bruising his body had taken under the planks still slowed his movements. Nevertheless, he was a better and more alert guide than Raphael had anticipated. No doubt the Ruthenian, as he looked around him, saw other days, another city—the Kiev of old, in its fabled glory.

Percival rode to Raphael's right, and Roger guarded the rear. The Frank and the Norman made odd friends, Raphael thought, but good ones. Every true heart needed a pragmatic counterweight, and every cynic an idealist to lift his spirits. It was easy to think that Percival was naive if one had just met him, but Raphael had long ago learned that no man was easy or simple, and he had heard enough of the knight's conversations with Taran to know that there was more to him than what first appeared. There was a reason behind every vow, a driving goal and belief behind every action.

The possibility that Percival had received divine grace—or thought he had—made the situation unusually complex, but Raphael found himself strangely untroubled by this. The brute facts of their situation, taken alone, were disheartening. Strange visions might make their way more tortuous but gave Raphael welcome respite from thinking all the time about food, warmth, and rest. In truth, epiphanic episodes fascinated him. How, after all, could something as powerful as God touch so lightly but firmly upon a human frame? Curious circumstance, indeed. Of course, God might be capable of any sort of subtlety...but why Percival? Or, for that matter, Feronantus?

As Raphael mused on these puzzlements, the quartet picked their way into the city's interior, following paths that wound through ruined neighborhoods like the trails of wild game. Hard memories of the Siege of Damietta and other catastrophes in the Holy Land now tugged at Raphael, shouldering aside his loftier speculations about gods and men.

His horse shivered as the ascent became more demanding. *He wants my complete attention here*, Raphael thought, and reluctantly came back to the here and now. The priory at the top of the hill, environed by ascending slopes and tiers of toppled lane walls and burned orchards and vineyards, seemed almost to lean out over them in the wan light of the cloudy day, as if the buildings themselves kept vigil.

Though they were now in the heart of the city, the hillside that rose between them and the foundations of the priory had a wide-open, rural character. Or at least that was the way it seemed to Raphael, accustomed to the densely built cities of the Levant. Blessed with vast lands, the Ruthenians had learned to build in a more expansive style, enclosing broad plots of open ground with rambling fences, growing vegetables and raising livestock close to where they would be consumed. Closer to the summit, the fences were replaced by stone walls, which grew higher and thicker as they circumscribed narrower and narrower rings of territory around the summit. The ones at the top bore the unmistakable look of fortress walls and seemed to have suffered accordingly during the siege.

But they would have to wind their way up several switch-backs and pass through many stiles and gates before they need concern themselves with actual fortifications. The first part of the ascent felt, to Raphael the urbanite, more like a ride through a rural estate than passage through a city.

Riding through the torn-up and burnt remnants of a small vineyard, they encountered a single old man in filthy rags, seemingly the only remaining inhabitant of these heights. He sat in the shade of a small, open-sided, decrepit prayer station, clutching a stem of tiny, moldering grapes and looking blankly at the outer world.

Illarion stopped to address the man in the Ruthenian tongue. The old man regarded them all in silence, as if judging their solidity, their reality, then nodded to himself and replied. Even in his ignorance of the language, Raphael perceived an educated tone and bearing. The man must have once been proud and useful enough to receive some training in speech and letters—a yeoman or vassal, perhaps, who tended the vines and helped supply the priory.

The conversation ended abruptly when the stranger decided enough was enough, brushed his torn kecks, and wandered off down the hill, turning back once to look at them almost in dread.

"I told him we wished to pay a visit on those who live above," Illarion said. "He suggested we leave. He said that they would never open their gates to us and that they would kill us like the others or die trying." Illarion's puzzlement at these cryptic words was so plain on his face that the others—even Percival—could not avoid breaking into shocked laughter.

"Kill us like the other *what?*" Roger asked. "What does the codger take us for—Mongols?"

"Brigands, perhaps," Percival suggested, "for we have an ill-favored look about us."

"Brigands don't ride up to the gate and knock!" Roger returned.

"Then let us go and do just that," said Percival, "and show them that we are not brigands, but men used to plain dealings."

"We would seem to have little choice," Raphael pointed out, "since we have been spotted in any case." He nodded up toward a corner of the priory, where a lookout was peering down at them from an onion-domed cupola.

✦ ✦ ✦

Before they had reached Kiev, Cnán had privately despaired of finding anything of worth or use within the broken walls of the city. She had witnessed the ruinous landscape left in the wake of the Mongolian army, and she knew how the devastation worked its way into the hearts of the survivors, devouring them from within until they were nothing more than hollow shells. She had armored herself against what the sight of Kiev would stir in her—memories, not altogether pleasant, of her mother—but as she and Feronantus and the rest of the party picked their way through the ruins, she was surprised to find that Kiev was not as bereft as she had anticipated.

Not only were there survivors, but they appeared to be building new lives for themselves among the ashes and ruins. Resources were scarce, clearly; one could only build so much with broken timber and shattered stone. Already the people who remained had shifted away from the center of the old Kiev to the banks of the river. The Dnieper.

It flowed all the way to the *Axeinos*, the Unlit Sea, a great snake winding from the north to the south across Rus. In Kiev, the river coiled around the twin hills that housed the holy buildings where Percival and the others had gone. Penitents, making a pilgrimage to hallowed ground.

Feronantus led her, Eleázar, Rædwulf, Istvan, and two horses slowly through the rubble-strewn streets of Kiev. Finn had dismounted after they had passed through the wreckage of the Golden Gate and vanished into the maze of wrecked buildings. Occasionally she would catch a glimpse of him as he scouted their route through the ruins.

Yasper had eschewed his horse as well, though he wasn't nearly as invisible. Or as silent. They could hear him knocking over the charred vestiges of walls, tossing chunks of stone around, and even the sporadic clatter of metal as he rifled through the rare cache of household wares that had not been pilfered.

Cnán was surprised he was finding anything of value at all, which spoke of either the lackadaisical efforts of the survivors or the tenacious inquisitiveness of the Dutchman.

A loud crash startled her horse, and the noise was followed by a chortling yell from Yasper. He danced out from behind a wall, holding a bent and twisted vessel over his head. As she calmed her horse, Cnán stared at the object the Dutchman was carrying, trying to identify what it had been once upon a time.

"It's perfect," he said, in answer to the question that must have been plainly writ on her face. He lashed the oblong vessel to his saddlebags and trotted back to continue his search.

Istvan nudged his horse past Cnán, angling toward Feronantus. "He is making too much noise," the Hungarian bristled.

Feronantus nodded in the direction they had come. "We aren't trying to hide," he said.

On the ridge where they had stood a few scant hours before was a single horse and rider. They were too far to make out any details of the man or animal, but to Cnán's eye, the man seemed too large for his mount, or the horse was too small. *A Mongol,* she thought, and then she realized who he must be. *The one who got away.*

Istvan had come to the same realization, and vituperating in his native language, he reached for his bow.

"Ho, Istvan," Rædwulf said with a smile. "Do you think he will stand still while you ride close enough to put an arrow in his chest?"

"I can track him," Istvan snarled. "Eventually he will stop— to eat or sleep or piss, it doesn't matter. I will put an arrow through his eye while—"

Cnán laughed in spite of the fear that had laid icy fingers on the back of her neck. "Mongols piss from horseback," she said. "They eat and sleep there too."

"That would explain how he kept so close to us," Feronantus noted.

"Who?" Yasper asked, wandering up with a pair of stoppered jugs. He craned his neck to see what they were looking at. "Oh shit," he said as he caught sight of the Mongolian tracker. With surprisingly alacrity, he leaped onto his horse, without losing grip on either jug. "What are we waiting for?" he said.

"You," Feronantus pointed out, with a touch of dry humor. He tapped his horse lightly in the ribs, and in no particular hurry, the animal began to amble toward the river. "He's seen us," he remarked over his shoulder. "My guess is that he knows this area better than we do, so there is nothing to be gained by appearing fearful. The best we can hope to accomplish is to convince him this is our destination. After nightfall, when the others return, we can slip across the river and put some hard distance between us. Let us hope that will be enough."

◆ ◆ ◆

The route to the hilltop became more challenging. Not only because the ground was steeper, but because the path was blocked in some places by heaps of rubble that had tumbled down from damaged sections of wall. In other places, the gaps in the wall were large enough to provide new avenues for their passage, though they had to dismount and lead their horses forward gingerly over difficult footing.

During the increasingly rare stretches when the going was level and easy, Raphael looked up to see that the lookout in the tower had spread news of their coming to several others and that the defenses of the outer wall were becoming crowded with gleaming helmets and spearpoints.

"There may be more knights than monks in this house of God," Illarion remarked.

"Some monks *are* knights," Raphael pointed out, with a glance at Percival.

"You are right and wrong at the same time," Percival said obliquely, "for what you see are not monks."

This game of riddles was interrupted by an exclamation from Roger, who was currently leading the way. The others saw that he had stopped in his tracks to examine, from a wary distance, a form lying full length on the ground in the middle of the path.

During their travels they had crossed many battlefields. To see an actual corpse, lying on the ground fully armored, was unusual. Most armies buried the dead, or burned them, if for no other reasons than to mitigate the stink, prevent disease, and frustrate ravens and carrion dogs. Even in those unusual cases where an army marched on before accomplishing that chore, surviving locals might tend to it once the coast was clear. Any who were so degraded as to leave human bodies lying out in the open would be inclined to strip the corpses for useful or salable loot.

Strange, then, to find a fully armored knight lying dead on the ground, out in the open. That he had been dead for some little while was proved by the number of flies teeming around him. His shirt of mail, and the shape of his helmet and of his shield, identified him as a knight of Christendom—this was no Mongol. He had gone down on his belly, his shield lying flat beneath him. But his head was turned awkwardly to one side and the neck bent back. As they drew closer—though only a *little* closer, given the stink and the number of flies— they got a clue as to why: he had taken a single arrow through the T-slot of his helmet, right into the cheekbone below the right eye, and its nock had struck the ground as he had fallen and wrenched his head around.

Their first instinct, of course, was to look up at the top of the wall and judge the range. They were certainly within bowshot, but far enough away that the archer who had loosed this shaft must have been lucky, or exceptionally good. Several bows were visible along the top of the wall now, and distant creaking noises indicated that some of them were being drawn. Raphael's instinct was to seek cover, but Percival reacted in the opposite manner, turning toward the defenders and holding his hands up, palms out.

"Hold!" he called. "We are knights of Christendom and no enemies of yours."

Raphael winced at the Frank's naïveté. Could it really be that a man of his upbringing would not know of the Fourth Crusade and the atrocities inflicted by Christian knights of the West against their brethren in Zara and Constantinople?

"Before you try our patience with any more such foolish remarks," called back a voice—the voice, Raphael realized, of a woman, speaking in Latin, "pray satisfy your curiosity about the Christian knight who lies at your feet. Ask yourself how he ended up in that estate if he was not our enemy, and then consider the wisdom of drawing any closer to *our* battlements."

Illarion and Raphael exchanged glances, both having heard the woman's stress of the word "our."

"Percival was right," Roger said, "they're not monks." He was staring up at the woman who had been shouting at them. Her femininity was obvious, since she had removed her helmet and tucked it under her arm, but there was something in the postures and the movements of the mailed and helmeted warriors around her suggesting that the priory contained not a single man.

Raphael nodded, somewhat distantly, as he recalled an old story—lore from many centuries past, before the *Ordo Militum Vindicis Intactae* had become Christian. Their first outpost had been Petraathen, high in the mountains between the Danube and the Baltic. Their second was on the island called Týrshammar, and many were the Nordic warriors—Vikings, as some called them—who had learned the way of the sword in that place. Those Northern peoples harbored ancient tales and myths of shieldmaidens—*skjalddis*—which happened to mesh perfectly with the tradition of the virgin warrior that had been promulgated on the crag of Petraathen since ancient days. The women who had become Shield-Maidens at Týrshammar were few compared to the men who became Shield-Brethren, and yet some of them had been present on the Viking ships that, in the later days of the Northmen, had ranged across Rus and down the Dnieper to the Black Sea. Some of them had put down roots here in Kiev, creating a third outpost. According to rumor, they had maintained their traditions, including the peculiar habit of teaching women to fight, even across the religious schism that had later arisen between the churches of the East and the West.

No wonder Percival had wanted to come here so badly.

The Frank had responded to the Shield-Maiden's taunt with a respectful bow and, as directed, turned his attention to the corpse on the trail. The mystery of its lying here, unburied and unlooted, had now been solved: the Shield-Maidens had left it here as a warning. Percival took a step toward it, then another, and then another, each pace slower and shorter than the last. The detail was noticed by the Shield-Maidens, who serenaded him with derisive laughter.

"Why do they hate us so much?" Raphael wondered. "And for that matter, why is she addressing us in Latin?"

"I have no idea," Illarion said, "though I suspect yonder corpse could tell us much if it could speak."

Before going any closer to the dead man, Percival went through a little ceremony of crossing himself and saying a prayer.

Roger, exasperated, cursed and elbowed past Percival and strode directly toward the dead knight, drawing in a deep breath and holding it. He planted a foot on the helmet and spun it around, making the arrow swing up into the air like the hand of a clock. "A face," he announced, "like any other— any other that has been got to by flies and ants, that is."

"Take your foot away," said Raphael, stepping closer in spite of himself, "that we may read the escutcheon on his brow."

Roger began to comply, but the weight of the arrow was wont to spin the head back round to where it had started. He drew out a hatchet and put his head against the fletching of the shaft to hold it in position, then withdrew his foot to reveal the heraldry on the front of the dead man's helmet.

In almost the same moment, he let out a shocked curse.

His three companions stepped forward as one and bent down for a closer look. The design—a red Maltese cross above a red sword, on a background of polished steel—was simple and easy enough to read. They drew in close, not because they hadn't seen it right the first time, but because none of them could quite believe the evidence of their eyes.

CHAPTER 27:

A GIFT FOR THE KHAGAN

Lian watched Gansukh vanish into the press of bodies around the wrestling field. She had arrived with the *Khagan*'s retinue, hanging back in the ranks of servants and concubines who trailed behind the Great Khan. She was pretty sure Gansukh hadn't seen her.

Some of the other concubines were twittering behind their fans about the match between Gansukh and Namkhai, a few casting coy glances in her direction as they wondered what it was like to bed such warriors. She ignored them. Their lives were filled with gossip, a constant stream of whispers back and forth about the sexual prowess of the men at court: who was a splendid lover, who was rough and prone to violence, who was laughably inept and unable to perform. Their constant chatter reminded her of the angry chirping of the blue jays in the garden when they were disturbed. That was all they were—chattering birds.

So much of her life was spent waiting. Waiting for the *Khagan* to decide it was time to leave Karakorum. Waiting until her next meeting with Gansukh. Waiting to answer Chucai's endless questions about the young warrior, about the other men with whom she spent time at court. Waiting patiently until they no longer noticed her and she could escape.

It wasn't difficult to be demure and properly respectful to Chucai; he was her keeper, after all, and there was nothing in their relationship that made it difficult to keep that distinction crystal clear. He appreciated her background and education, and while he still treated her like property, she had, in his eyes, some value.

Gansukh was another matter altogether. She had been mistaken in her original assessment of his character. Even though he still had moments of intolerable insensitivity and brutishness, she could tell that he was trying to change. Not just because he thought his duty required him to be a different person, but also because he knew it brought them closer together.

What would happen to him if she escaped? Would he be blamed? Munokhoi would use the opportunity to discredit him before the *Khagan*. Would her flight ruin his chance at saving the *Khagan*?

Lian shook her head clear of such thoughts. Gansukh was Mongolian. His people had slaughtered and dominated hers. What did she care of the empire? She was not here by choice; she was here as a prisoner. And if this empire—the world of Ögedei Khan's—fell apart, what would become of her?

She knew the answer to that question; she knew what happened to prisoners when new conquerors claimed their spoils.

Nearby, the *Khagan* laughed uproariously and then lurched around his retinue, inviting everyone to join him at the feast that evening. His leering face was dark with drink and his robes soaked through with the sweat induced by the slow poison of the alcohol. The concubines cared little for his appearance—sweat and stink were ever their lot. They squealed with excitement.

During the festival, Lian thought, *they will all be so busy watching the Khagan drown himself in wine no one will be paying attention to me.*

If she dared to dream of escape, wouldn't this be the best time?

✦ ✦ ✦

Gansukh smoothed the front of his new blue robe as he stepped into the large dining hall. It fit him exceptionally well, though he couldn't stop fidgeting with the fine material. He couldn't stop thinking about the fact that *she* had given it to him.

Four large tables dominated most of the room. At the northern end was a low platform on which a round table had been placed. Gansukh glanced at the waiting crowd of nobles and warriors surrounded by servants and concubines, quickly scanning faces for a general idea of who was sitting where. The table to his right was surrounded by *Torguud,* marked by the white fur trimming on their clothing. Several spotted Gansukh by the door and raised cups in greeting. He nodded in return. *Respect earned.* Even though his wrestling match with Namkhai had been a draw, he had performed better than many of them. He pulled at the stiff, wide belt he had wrapped around the robe and nearly dropped the package he held under his left arm. He was already too warm, and he'd be sweating before long.

Suddenly his idea seemed even more preposterous, bordering on ridiculous.

Near the round table, he saw Master Chucai, and though there was a mass of people between them, the tall advisor had little trouble clearing a path to Gansukh.

"Master Gansukh, I have heard stories of your exploits."

Gansukh shrugged. "The match was a draw," he demurred.

Someone shouted at Gansukh from the back of the room, and Chucai's eyes flicked in that direction before returning to Gansukh's face. "Nevertheless, I am heartened by these stories. May I surmise that our conversation earlier today was... insightful?"

"Somewhat," Gansukh admitted. He thought he saw Lian, sitting next to... *Who is that?* He tried to look past Chucai without being rude about it. *Namkhai.*

"You've brought a gift," Master Chucai motioned to the bundle under Gansukh's arm. "Would you like me to present it to the *Khagan?*"

Through the throng, Gansukh couldn't see the pair clearly, and he hesitated, torn between wanting to get a better look and responding to Master Chucai. He sighed, giving up for a moment. Chucai stared at him expectantly. "Yes, of course," he said. "It would be my honor to present it to the *Khagan* personally."

"Of course," Chucai said smoothly, as if that had been the plan all along. Was that a smile creasing the lips of the *Khagan*'s advisor?

"Perhaps you might suggest where it might be best for me to sit at the *Khagan*'s table," Gansukh said. He tapped the package suggestively.

Chucai waved a hand at the table on the platform. "Certainly," he said. Leaning forward, he lowered his voice. "A simple arrangement. Those who can be oblivious to his drunkenness sit close, those who cannot, but still wish to curry favor, sit beside them, and those who feel ashamed, but dare not overtly show it, keep as far away as possible." He smiled grimly. "It is a round table, however, and the *Khagan* likes to circulate and mingle—which makes it very difficult to stay far enough away, I fear."

"I will not overthink my position then," Gansukh said, inclining his head. "I will sit in the first empty chair I find." *And leave the rest up to the whim of the Blue Wolf,* he finished silently.

"A most prudent and wise choice," Chucai said, nodding in return.

Gansukh took his leave, making his way to the head table, where he placed his package on the table in front of a chair to the right of the lavish seat intended for the *Khagan.* He sat down, bending uncomfortably around the belt, before he realized who was sitting directly across from him.

Munokhoi.

He only had a moment to return the *jaghun* commander's glare before a swift drop in the noise level in the long hall signaled the arrival of Ögedei Khan. It took some time for the *Khagan* to make his way through the press of people—during which time Munokhoi continued to stare at him—and as Ögedei approached, Gansukh noted with some relief that his hands were empty. For the moment, he wasn't drinking.

From this vantage point, Gansukh had a better angle on the table where Namkhai sat and tried to see who was sitting next to him. It *was* Lian, and he watched her lean forward in appreciation of what Namkhai was saying. She laughed at his apparent cleverness, and Gansukh frowned. Had she witnessed the wrestling match? He did not dare try to catch her eye—not with Munokhoi watching.

"Gansukh." Ögedei clasped him on the arm, as much to steady himself, Gansukh realized, than as a friendly gesture. His breath stank of wine. "A mighty effort this morning."

"I am humbled, *Khagan,*" Gansukh said, dragging his attention away from Lian. *What do I care, anyway? She isn't any part of what I am here to accomplish.*

"A toast," Ögedei called, gesturing for his short servant with the tray of tiny cups. "A toast to our wrestlers!"

"Please, if I may, a moment, *Khagan*." Gansukh held up a hand to stop the servant's approach. He gulped as all the conversation around them suddenly died, and for a second his courage threatened to depart. *Respect*, he thought, locking his knees. *Demand it. Earn it.*

He picked up the package from the table. "Earlier today," he said, "I saw the *Khagan* drinking from those tiny cups, and I wondered why you bothered. They hold so little wine. They are not worthy of your greatness, your magnitude under the all-covering sky."

Ögedei's eyes seemed even more unfocused than they had been the night Gansukh had visited him in his chambers. His pupils were black holes that might swallow everything—the light, the sound, the very air in the room. His mouth was starting to twist as if he were about to lunge forward and bite at Gansukh's neck.

"I was sent here by your brother," Gansukh continued. "Chagatai wants you to stop drinking—"

He was interrupted by a bray of laughter from across the table. "It's the *little* nursemaid," Munokhoi sneered. "Come to tell us how wine is bad for our health!"

The same suspicion was apparent in Ögedei's face, and Gansukh knew he was perilously close to losing the *Khagan*'s attention, much as he had failed so badly the first day he had arrived in Karakorum. He turned his back, his spine tingling, then tore the paper off his package. With a spin around again that made the chamberlains gasp and the guards shove a step forward, he lifted the object...and revealed his gift to the *Khagan*.

"Chagatai said I should insist that you only drink one cup of wine a day, and here I find you drinking how many? Twenty?

Thirty?" He raised his empty hand, holding the thumb and forefinger close together. "*Tiny* cups. Cups for children and monkeys! Just *this* size. Who brings such cups before the *Khagan* and does not perish of shame?"

He raised the cup—the wide-mouthed, enormous cup he had accidently bought at market the other day—extending it toward Ögedei, and then he slammed it down on the table with a resounding clank. "My duty is to my lord—Chagatai Khan—and the empire. He says one cup a day. I say that the *Khagan* should do as he pleases. You, yourself, told me this when I first came before you: the *Khagan* asks permission of no man. The *Khagan* is beholden only to himself. Drink, if you so desire; it is not for me or your brother or any of these people assembled here to say otherwise. But if you are going to drink, the great *Khagan* must drink from a great cup—a vessel worthy of your vastness, your magnitude, your all-conquering might."

Ögedei's mouth moved like he was chewing a piece of gristly meat. He looked around the table, blearily surveying the faces that turned away from his, and then he spat. And belched.

The utter silence was suddenly broken by the rasping steel hiss of blades being drawn—the guards anticipating violence, eager to carry out the *Khagan*'s fatal bidding.

But a slow rise of Ögedei's arm and a waggle of his thick-fingered hand stayed their punishment. The *Khagan* slowly turned, leaning this way and that, his gaze moving slowly from face to face of the assembled host, all equally enthralled but desperately wishing to move aside, move away, to flee now so as to avoid the wrath they all suspected was about to erupt.

The servant with the tray of tiny cups squirmed, edging away from the *Khagan*. Like an animal that senses weakness in its prey, Ögedei lashed out with a wordless yell. The tray flew out of the little man's hands, spattering the crowd with thick red wine like drops of blood.

The *Khagan* then whirled with surprising and sudden poise on Gansukh, his hands clawing at the warrior's new robe. Gansukh was hauled forward until his face was a mere *aid* from the *Khagan*'s.

Ögedei's face turned as dark as the wine, anger bringing a dangerous flush to his already ruddy cheeks. Suddenly, like a dog, he leaned forward, and his teeth snapped at Gansukh's cheek. "I...*will*...do...as...I...please!" he ground out, spraying spittle on Gansukh, then drew back like a snake, lips curled in an awful, writhing snarl.

Gansukh kept silent, clamping his jaw tightly shut. He had said all that he had come to say. The *Khagan* would either listen or not. In the periphery of his vision, he could see the wide eyes of a few of the faces surrounding them. Flush with fear and excitement, there was no doubt in their minds that the *Khagan*, as soon as he could speak through his overwhelming rage, would order Gansukh to be broken—first the knees and then his ribs—before he would be placed beneath the boards so that horses could be ridden across his fractured body...a slow, suffocating, bone-cracking death for this inexplicable impudence and insult.

He did not look away from the *Khagan*, wordlessly challenging Ögedei to give the order. *It is not a suitable death for a warrior*, he thought. *But that does not make me less of one.*

The corner of Ögedei's left eye began to twitch, and he forcefully shoved Gansukh away, pushing him against the table. "Give me the cup," he snarled. "I will be the judge of whether it is worthy."

Gansukh dropped to his knees, lowering his gaze to look down at the *Khagan*'s feet. "Yes, my Khan," he murmured. His vision blurred, and he swayed, gasping for air. He heard the sound of hooves rattling against wood, and after a moment he realized it was only the echo of his own pounding heart.

Someone pressed the cup into his hands—too fearful, clearly, to give it to the *Khagan* himself. With shaking legs, Gansukh got to his feet and offered the vessel.

Ögedei snatched it from him. "Wine!" he shouted. "Why is there no wine in this cup?" A dozen bodies sprang forward, offering to fill the *Khagan*'s chalice with their own half-filled cups.

With a grunt, Ögedei turned and smashed the cup across Gansukh's face.

Gansukh's eyes filled with tears, and the room became a blur as he spun and fell to his hands and knees. There was blood in his mouth, and it felt like a hot coal had been ground into his cheek.

Something heavy fell against his body, and he stiffened, trying to keep from collapsing entirely to the floor. *Planks.* His hands clenched with panic. But it was only a man, leaning on him, clutching at his shoulders, his hot, stinking breath washing over his bloody cheek. He tried to focus on a glittering object that floated in his field of vision, and blinking through the tears, he realized it was the cup—his gift to Ögedei.

It had fared better than his cheek.

"It is a good cup," the *Khagan* hissed in his ear. "Get out of my sight, young pony, before I change my mind."

CHAPTER 28:

ILL-MET IN KIEV

When they passed around the foot of the hill, they felt the wind on their faces, and while its touch was both light and refreshing, its breath was filled with an unwholesome stink. At first Cnán thought it was the sort of putrescence that was not uncommon in fetid swampland, but the river flowed too freely to allow decaying matter to build up. Glancing at the others, she saw they too were affected by the smell, but unlike her, they appeared more familiar with it.

"Corpse rot," Yasper explained. He rooted around in one of his many satchels until he found a small vial. Carefully unstopping it, he poured a small dollop of the thick liquid onto two fingers, and then he pressed the fingers to both nostrils. Keeping his mouth closed, he inhaled deeply, the sides of his nose indenting. "Ah," he sighed. When he lowered his fingers, he appeared to be no longer in distress from the lingering smell that permeated the air. With a grin, he offered the vial to Cnán.

She stared at him as if he had been taken with a pox fever, and when he waggled the vial at her, she finally took it from his outstretched hand. Somewhat dubiously, she poured a tiny bead onto one of her fingers and sniffed at it cautiously. The smell of mint was overpowering and she jerked her head back in surprise. "What is this?" she asked.

"A tincture of mint oil," he smiled. "My own recipe." He waved his hand about his face as if he were directing more of the revolting stench toward his nostrils.

She put a bead on another finger and, somewhat clumsily, aped his method of applying the oil to her nose. Her eyes watered as she inhaled and the mint vapors speared deep into her head, like tiny icicles. But, she had to admit, it was a pleasant sensation in its own way, and much preferable to the stink of decaying flesh.

Rædwulf chuckled at her expression as he reached over with a long arm and plucked the vial from her fingers. Unlike Yasper, he put drops of the oil in the wide webbing between his thumb and index finger and shoved his hand against his face to smother his nostrils completely.

He passed the vial to Feronantus, who partook before offering it to Istvan. The Hungarian glowered and busied himself with stroking his mustache as if the idea of mint in his beard were too distasteful to contemplate. Finn only sniffed at the vial before shrugging and returning it to Yasper. As if he wasn't quite sure what all the fuss was about or why one would want to mask one's ability to smell.

A little lightheaded from the mint oil, Cnán focused on the tiny shantytown nestled between the hill and the river. Several wooden docks sprawled along the water's edge, and boats were moored to its length by any available means. Makeshift hovels and stalls were arranged in no clear order, seemingly erected wherever two pieces of wood could be leaned together to make the semblance of a wall. The tiny hamlet along the river appeared haphazard and carefree, as if the residents built and crafted what they needed from their surroundings without much worry about permanence or protection from marauders. An attitude, she realized, that wasn't entirely unexpected in the wake of what the residents had survived. What else could the Mongols do that they had not already done? Killing them might even be a blessing.

Without intending to, Cnán fell into a despondency of memory, and her head filled with the scents and sounds of the burning village where, so long ago, she had lost everything. Somewhat dazed, she swayed in her saddle and would have fallen off her horse had someone not placed a hand on her arm. She turned her head, opening her eyes, and flinched when she saw Yasper's concerned expression.

Mistaking her reaction, Yasper let go. "Breathe through your mouth," he said gently. "The scent can be too strong at first. Breathe slowly—not through your nose—until the dizziness passes." He demonstrated.

"I'm fine," she said, more curtly than she had intended, and then, "I am sorry, Yasper. You are only trying to help, and I have spoken rudely."

"It is of no consequence," he grinned. "These are rude times, and the only true incivility is that which is not recognized as such."

"Speaking of which…" Rædwulf interrupted, drawing their attention toward a trio of scruffy natives who were approaching their party. To say the three men were dressed would be to call the scraps of cloth and twine and bits of fur that partially covered their gaunt bodies *clothing*. They shuffled slowly, bent at the waist, their grimy hands raised in supplication. The foremost one, pressed by the other two to be their spokesperson, babbled at them in Ruthenian.

"Cnán," Feronantus called, "do you ken his words?"

She let her horse wander closer, her head cocked to the side as she tried to follow the man's discourse. There was a repetition to his cadence that made it a little easier for her to pick out words she knew. "He's saying the same thing over and over," she reported. "Something about *gifts*, I believe. No, *tribute*." She interrupted him with a few words of Tartaric.

One of the other two men shrieked and fell to his knees, groveling in the dirt. The spokesperson's mouth hung open, but words no longer spilled from his blubbering lips.

"Well now," Yasper opined as he joined Feronantus and Cnán, "that is a mighty invocation. Mayhap you could teach it to the rest of us…"

"I just asked him if he understood what I was saying," Cnán pointed out.

"In the Mongolian tongue," Feronantus reckoned. When Cnán nodded, he squinted at the shantytown, looking for movement among the hovels and detritus. "They're terrified of us," he said. "But we are clearly not Mongols…"

Off to their right, Istvan snorted noisily, and the attention of the three men darted to the Hungarian. His scowling visage only engendered more fear, and the kneeling one tried to press himself even lower against the ground.

"Finn," Feronantus called, not taking his eyes off the shantytown. "We are not alone, are we?"

"Aye," the hunter responded.

Cnán looked around for Finn. He was crouched a ways off, examining the track of the road they were on.

"Horses," he said, pointing at the dirt. "Shod, like ours. Less than a day ago."

✦ ✦ ✦

"The red cross and sword. I thought the Livonians were no more…" was Roger's response upon recognizing the sigil on the dead knight.

"Hell could not hold them," Raphael suggested.

"Or simply found their company tedious," Roger scoffed.

"Whatever their reason for straying into Rus," Illarion said, "it is gratifying to see that one, at least, found the fate he deserved."

"Which leads to the question, are there others?" Raphael said. "For this one is comparatively fresh, and the Shield-Maidens—if my guess is correct as to who yonder women are—seem to be expecting more of them."

The question was an important one and caused all four men to take their eyes from the red cross and sword for the first time since they had seen it. Instinctively they formed up in a loose circle, facing outward, scanning the ruins around them and the jumbled slope below for any signs that they might have been followed. Hands strayed to sword hilts and ax handles. But they saw nothing untoward.

"Brother Raphael speaks correctly," Percival said, "when he says that we must learn—and soon—whether there are other Livonians nearby. But there are only four pairs of eyes among us. Those eyes are peering through burnt vines and rubble piles over a new and unfamiliar landscape. Behind us, many more eyes, used to this place, scan the city from a better vantage point, and so the quickest way for us to learn the answer is simply to approach the gates, state our business, and ask the Shield-Maidens to share what they know."

"Good luck with that," Roger muttered.

"I shall go alone," said Percival. This was an ultimatum, not a suggestion. Again that light seemed to play about his face. Raphael wished it would stop; it was most unsettling. Perhaps it came from a withdrawal of blood from the knight's already pale skin.

Percival removed his sword and scabbard and handed them to Roger, then turned about and began walking directly toward the gates that barred their passage through the inmost and highest of all the priory's walls.

The Shield-Maidens on the battlements above were divided in their response. Nearly all of them were speaking in the local tongue, and so Raphael could not make out what they were saying, but half were merely derisive, while the rest seemed nearly out of their minds with rage. As Percival strode the last hundred paces to the gate, the surrounding rubble heaps suddenly came alive, like a nest of ants disturbed by the blade of a plow, as ordinary persons—mostly wretched sorts, unarmed, not so much clothed as bandaged in improvised swaddlings of gray blankets and rags—scurried out of make-shift shelters that they had erected along the approaches to the priory and abandoned cookfires that they had kindled along the way. Percival turned his head from side to side, observing this curiously, and Raphael sensed from his posture that he was slightly offended by the refugees' obvious fear of him.

"Are they afraid of Percival?" Roger asked. "Or of what is about to happen to him?"

"Either would suffice to make such people get well clear of the man," Illarion said.

Percival found himself standing in a clear space before the gates, gazing directly up at the Latin-speaking woman who had addressed him earlier; she was looking down on him through a crenel on the fortification above the portal. Perhaps feeling that it was not the act of a gentleman to go helmed when he addressed a lady whose own helmet was tucked under her arm, he reached up, lifted his own helmet from his head, bent down, and set it on the ground before his feet, then stood up and raised his chin, tossing his hair back away from his face and gazing directly up at his interlocutor.

All of the ladies went silent for a moment.

"Bastard!" Roger muttered.

The Shield-Maidens' voices were resurgent, not as loud as before, and in a different tone: some of them even more furious, others mock flirting with him, and perhaps a few of them flirting quite sincerely.

Their leader permitted herself a sardonic grin and a little shake of the head. "I am not certain which of your approaches has been more insulting," she said. "You came to us the first time, brimming over with the most insufferable arrogance. 'Well done, girls. Thank you for keeping the place tidy for us. Now open the gates that we can make of it a proper fortress. Vacate your barracks and your bedchambers, plump up our pillows, cook up some vittles, and polish our armor that we may tend to important duties.' When we sent your emissaries away and fought off the inevitable sneak attack that followed, we supposed we'd seen the last of you. But now you are back. And what is your latest stratagem? A handsome face with which to woo the silly girls who hold the keys to the gate. Tell me, are the men skulking behind you as fair to look at?"

"That would be for you and the other Shield-Maidens to decide, my lady," Percival returned.

"You may address me as Sister Vera," said the woman. "I am not a lady, and if I were, I would not be yours."

"Very well, Sister Vera. I am Brother Percival."

"No brother of ours! We have suffered you to draw this close only to tell you, once again, that you and the other Livonians are not welcome in our city," said Vera. "If your friends draw near enough for us to form an opinion of their beauty, they will get arrows in the face just like the one you saw."

"Then it is well that you stayed your hand and held back your flights of arrows until I drew near enough to speak with you and to disabuse you of a grievous but understandable misconception," Percival said. And he stripped his surcoat off over his head, then shed his coat of mail—not easily done, as it weighed as much as some of the women who were aiming arrows at him from above. This occasioned much more bawdy commentary from the Shield-Maidens, which he pretended not to hear. Having dropped his mail on the ground, he unbuttoned his gambeson and stripped off that thick padded garment to reveal a linen shirt beneath, tired and sweat-stained but, given what they had been through, surprisingly clean.

"If your face did not convince us," said the lady above, "then, rest assured, neither will your..."

But then she stopped. And over the course of the next few moments, all of the other catcalls died down as well. For Percival had reached across his body with his left hand, grasped the cuff of his right shirtsleeve, and drawn it back to expose the arm as high as the elbow. In the same gesture he extended his right arm up and outward from his body, rotating his palm up to face the sky, and thus exposing to the Shield-Maidens' view the brawn of his forearm.

Standing behind, Raphael could not see what Percival was showing them, but he hardly needed to, given that the same sigil was marked on his own flesh.

Having seized the Shield-Maidens' attention and silenced them, Percival now let his left hand drop away. The eyes of the women on the battlements tracked the movement carefully. The left hand was curled into a loose fist. He extended it toward them, then straightened his fingers while turning his hand over to display the palm.

There was nothing remarkable about this. And that, to them, was the remarkable thing. For some moments now he remained posed thus, letting them all inspect the marked forearm and the unmarked palm. A change passed through the women on the walls above, like a gust of wind moving over a sea of grass. No order was issued by Vera. But bows creaked as strings were relaxed. Arrows snicked back into their quivers and swords into their scabbards.

"Brother Percival," said Vera, her voice suddenly husky, "we have done you an injustice. You and the other *Skjaldbrædur* are welcome—more than welcome—inside our citadel."

◆ ◆ ◆

Their plan of inquiring after provisions forgotten, the party fell into loose formation: Istvan and Finn (back on his horse) in front, Eleázar bringing up the rear, with Feronantus and Cnán and Yasper and Rædwulf riding in pairs. Once, Cnán would have felt naked and exposed riding in the open, especially without some sort of helm or mail of her own—not that she had ever worn either—but surrounded now by the readied and alert knights of the *Ordo Militum Vindicis Intactae*, she felt...protected.

The sensation was not unlike the one she had felt many weeks ago when she had first entered the Shield-Brethren chapter house for their *Kinyen*. At that time, such a sensation—while new—was not unexpected for being surrounded by the many knights and the stone walls, but she felt both awkward and elated to feel a glimmering of that sensation again when in the company of fewer knights. She tried to not dwell overlong on the source of her emotions.

They rode up the narrow road that ran alongside the river, keeping the winding track of water on their right flank. The gentle slope of the small hill rose on their left, and ahead the road diverged from following the river, dipping down to hug the base of the slope.

The smell of dead flesh was getting stronger. Either that, Cnán realized, or Yasper's mint oil was starting to wear off.

They could see the back side of the hill now. On the crown of the smaller hill stood a dilapidated series of low buildings, hidden by a rough wall of hewn timbers. A narrow path—barely wide enough for a horse, much less a cart—wound precipitously down the slope, where it connected with the larger road not far ahead of them.

What caught their attention was the two men pulling a narrow cart up the hill and the armed company following them.

The company was dressed in mail—from coifs to chausses—and their long surcoats were white. Each carried a shield, along with a plethora of swords, axes, and maces. The insignia painted on a number of the shields was a red cross surmounting a down-turned sword. *Knights*, Cnán realized, like her present company in their armament and in the way they carried themselves. There, however, the similarities ended, for their faces were hard and pitiless, set with grim expressions that told her that these men were of a different breed from her companions. She counted heads. They numbered closer to thrice the number of her present company.

In comparison, the two men pulling the cart seemed almost nonhuman. Both wore filthy and threadbare robes that hung stiffly over their gaunt frames, and the heads that protruded from the robes were topped with tangled masses of hair and beard, so encrusted with dirt and other matter that it was nearly impossible to discern any sort of face. The rickety cart was not much more than a plank nailed to a pair of boards to which rough wheels were awkwardly attached. Piled on the cart was, at first glance, a stack of filthy hides, but Cnán saw a flash of pale movement and realized the bundle was another figure like the two hauling the cart.

Someone spotted the Shield-Brethren and a shout went up from the column of knights.

The company of knights stopped, turning in a block to face Cnán and the Shield-Brethren. The two ragmen began pulling their cart faster. A shriek floated down from the palisade at the top of the hill, more an exhortation of panic than the cry sounded by a bird of prey as it dove on its victim.

One of the knights stood nearly a head taller than the rest of his company, and they parted like water for him as he came down the slope. As he reached the tail of his column, he drew his sword and walked unhurriedly toward them. His men reformed in his wake, like a worm folding back on itself, and fell in behind him.

"Hold," Feronantus said quietly to the other Shield-Brethren. "Let him make his intention clear."

Cnán heard the sound of stretching sinew, and glancing over her shoulder, she saw Rædwulf draw his bowstring back. He appeared unconcerned that he might have to hold that position for some time. Behind him, Eleázar was looping the reins of his horse around the knob of horn mounted on his saddle. He needed both hands to wield his two-handed monstrosity of a sword, she noted, and the only way to control his mount would be with his legs. Should the situation come to that…

She shivered, suddenly chilled, and she wondered if this sensation was what they all felt at the approach of violence. She wanted to vomit.

The tall knight stopped a few horse lengths from them. Tufts of sandy hair curled out from the edge of his coif, and his beard was streaked with red. He laughed, and Cnán caught sight of strong white teeth. "Feronantus," the knight called, "you are far from your rock, old man."

The familiarity with which the man spoke stunned all of them, save Feronantus, who remained unmoved by the man's taunt. If anything, Cnán thought, he was even more like a stone than per usual.

"And you wear the colors of an order that fell ignobly, Kristaps," Feronantus replied.

Kristaps spat. "Schaulen. We were betrayed."

"The only betrayal you faced was that of your master leading you into that trap."

"*Heermeister* Volquin was a great leader, Feronantus, and a better man than you—"

"His leadership is no use to anyone now that he is dead," Feronantus said sadly. "What am I to make of your motley band? Is this all that remains—this sad bunch of deserters— or is there some mischief brewing that requires you to dress ill-informed fools as *real* knights?"

Several of the knights behind Kristaps drew their swords and shuffled back and forth, clearly eager for an order to engage the Shield-Brethren. Istvan's horse snorted and began to fidget, mirroring the Hungarian's own restlessness. Cnán heard the thin creak of Rædwulf's bowstring.

"I wonder the same of you, Feronantus," Kristaps replied, unswayed by the tension between the two groups. "Are you lost?" He raised his hand. "Petraathen lies that way, does it not?" He gestured somewhat aimlessly as if he could not be bothered to make certain of the correct direction. "Though perhaps it will be gone by the time you get back." He showed his teeth. "A long time has passed while you have been *hiding* on the rock, old man. The world has passed your Shield-Brethren by."

Feronantus replied with a humorless smile. "Is this all that is left for you now—wandering far from your home, like mad dogs, rooting for scraps left on the battlefield?"

One of Kristaps's men took a step forward, but the tall knight stopped him with a hand upon the shoulder. "We are God's servants, on a holy mission," he answered.

"'Holy mission?'" Yasper snapped, unable to hold his tongue. "Is that what you call terrorizing the innocent people of this beleaguered city?"

And Cnán inferred what Feronantus and the others had already discerned: the people in the shantytown had mistaken them for men like these and had been trying to appease them with tribute, to forestall some persistent threat of violence.

"There are no innocents before God, only the sinful and the righteous," Kristaps replied with icy calm, as though explaining something as obvious as the rising and setting of the sun.

Feronantus forestalled any reply from Yasper with an upraised hand. "Calm yourself," he said quietly. He stared at Kristaps and the other knights, and Cnán noticed how his gaze lingered upon the sigil marking their surcoats. *It means something to him*, she realized, more than a simple identifying mark like the red rose of the Shield-Brethren. There was something else here that troubled his mind.

"Cowardice suits you. As always." Kristaps's gaze roved across the company, his smile widening slightly as he looked at Cnán. She suppressed a shudder; it had been some time since a man had looked at her in that way.

It was strange, then, when Istvan drew his curved sword and urged his horse forward. She couldn't believe he was reacting to the way Kristaps had looked at her—that was a reaction she would have expected from Percival, after all— but the sudden movement on the Hungarian's part startled and confused her.

Istvan kept a tight grip on his horse's reins and didn't allow the animal to traverse the open ground between the two groups, but his stance was aggressively clear. In contrast to the prancing motion of his mount, the Hungarian was a carved statue—eyes locked on his enemy, knuckles white about his sword hilt.

Kristaps stood easily, his stance that of a man who thought the horseman an amusing diversion more than a credible threat.

"Istvan," Feronantus said, "this is not the time."

Istvan bared his teeth, a feral growl rising from his throat.

"You heard your master, dog," Kristaps hissed. "He calls upon you to heel."

Istvan's eyes bulged in their sockets, and Cnán feared the tall knight had gone too far. The Hungarian was too quick to anger, overly fond of the comfort afforded by his rage. Her head filled with images of the unrestrained glee that had cloaked him when they had fought the Mongols at the farm.

She held her breath, fearing for the worst.

They were outnumbered, more than three to one. An engagement now would surely be their ruin…

CHAPTER 29:

A BROTHER'S SACRIFICE

Gansukh sat on the edge of his sleeping platform, running his fingers over the tiny lacquered box. After a week of toying with the rectangular puzzle, he had been able to discern tiny seams, but the secret of how to manipulate them continued to elude him.

The right side of his face ached. Ögedei had split his cheek with the cup, and Gansukh knew that the wound looked and felt worse than it was; in a few days, it would heal to a scratch and most of the bruising would vanish. Until then, it was a mark to bear proudly, a persistent throbbing ache to be borne without complaint.

But that didn't mean he wanted to dwell on it.

The box was slender, and it fit easily in his palm. The thief, when she had run to him that night out on the steppes, had concealed it inside his *deel*, a desperate sleight of hand. He didn't understand why she had entrusted the box to him; though, given her choice was between him and Munokhoi, he could not fault her. But what was he supposed to do with it? He shook the box, listening to the rattle of the object inside. *Was it the box itself or what was inside that was important?*

When he hunted, the moment of purest feeling came in the instant before he released an arrow. Even though the gut string dug into his fingers and his arm quivered with the exertion of holding the pull, his whole body felt light, like a single fine strand of silk stretched between the arrowhead and the target. He seemed to float, vibrating in the air, and when the target twitched, he felt the motion run through him like a bolt of lightning. And then he let go—breath and fingers acting as one—and he knew, even before the arrow had left his bow, where it would strike.

The arrow flew true only when he knew *himself*, when he knew what must be done and was prepared to act upon that knowledge. Giving the cup to Ögedei and daring him to accept it—as both a gift and as acknowledgement of his madness for drink—had been a moment like that. If he had thought too much about it beforehand, he never would have done it, and now that it was done, there was no reason to not accept it as his fate. The destiny afforded him by the Blue Wolf.

I can discover the secrets of this box.

He held the box gently, his eyes half closed, breath slowing, fingers moving so carefully across its smooth surface. In his mind's eye, he saw the long seam that ran along its length, and as he traced it slowly with his long finger, he imagined drawing his bow, sighting on his target. As he felt the end of the box, he paused, his finger resting lightly on the lacquered surface, his thumb gently caressing the underside. He listened for that moment, that minute quiver wherein his target would begin to suspect its death was approaching, and when he felt *something* shift inside him, he let go.

When he opened his eyes, his hands were empty. The box—rather, the three intricate pieces that it was comprised off—lay on the floor. He pushed aside the pieces to reveal the secret contents of the puzzle box. It took him a moment to make sense of it, in its startling simplicity.

It was a green twig—a sprig cut from a tree. Despite its time in the box, away from soil and light, it was still supple, with tight, youthful bark—and one soft, tiny yellow-green leaf.

He raised the sprig to his nose; it smelled like...the mud along a riverbank in the spring, when the ground was redolent with young sprouts. When he put his fingertip on the leaf, he could almost feel it pulse like a miniature heart.

◆ ◆ ◆

Sleep eluded him.

Opening the box had not solved its mystery, and after an hour of lying on his bed, staring at the sprig, rolling it gently in his fingers, he had wrapped it in a piece of silk and tucked it inside his robe. Hiding it once again, much as the thief had done.

But his mind could not rest; his thoughts buzzed like angry bees swarming from a disturbed nest. The more he tried to get comfortable on his bed, the more aware he became of how small and cramped his room was. The walls were too close; if he threw out his arms, he felt as if he could touch opposite walls. He was like the sprig, rattling around in a tiny box.

How could anything survive in such a box? he thought, throwing a wool-trimmed jacket over his robe. Maybe the sprig only seemed alive *once* he opened the box. Maybe it was rejuvenated by fresh air...

He strode out of the guest quarters, inhaling great draughts of air as he left the confines of the building. *I am not a man of this place,* he reflected, peering up at the night sky. Torches still sputtered and danced along the paths, the fading remnants of the revelry that had filled the palace earlier, and their light made it difficult to see the stars.

A strange cry filled the air, raising the hair on Gansukh's arms. He heard other voices too—men shouting—and he staggered, unable to comprehend how he had been thrown into the past, back to the night when the thief had fled Ögedei's palace and changed everything.

But it wasn't that night. The noise came again, a trumpeting bleat of an angry animal, and when Gansukh reached the corner of the palace, he spied the source of the tumult.

In the square, a majestic beast struggled. Gray and titanic, nearly twice as tall as a man, with ears like tent cloth, great tusks like a boar, and a long snout that curled and uncurled like a snake—a monstrous beast was rearing on tree-trunk hind legs, straining against ropes wrapped around pegs and held by men who were trying to contain it. *As if rope alone could restrain such a creature*, Gansukh thought. *Proof of Heaven's humor.* Its handlers—brown-skinned men with tall wrapped hats—prodded at the beast with long, hooked spears, shouting frantically at each other.

The beast bellowed and trumpeted, stomping the ground with its huge feet, each one as thick as a tent-pole log. As Gansukh watched, both awed and amused that men would try to tame a creature such as this, it reared again. The ropes groaned like men in pain and then tore free of their moorings. The ground shook as the beast came down, and it flung its trunk to the side, smacking a puny handler. The man flew across the square like a child's doll as the other handlers tried—valiantly but hopelessly—to control the beast.

Released from its bonds, the great animal vented a triumphant cry, like a dozen blatting horns, and pounded across the square in a ponderous but unstoppable gallop.

Gansukh shrank against the side of the building as the animal thundered past him. He felt like an insect clinging desperately to a stone shaken by a fierce earthquake. He knew its power by the slow sway of its huge belly and the thick muscles and sinews of its thumping limbs...and by the deep bellows of its lungs pumping a grassy, sour breath.

Why, it's simply a great, snouted bull, with ears like flapping carpets and gray, pitted, wrinkled skin like armor...

Now his mind kicked in. This was not a rhinoceros, whose hide was cut into real armor for royalty, but something like... Its great nose horn softened and lengthened to an obscenely grasping member...and yet that hazel-brown eye, fixing him as it rushed by, deep sunk and frantic, yet intelligent, like the measuring eye of a giant warrior...

And then it was past him, and Gansukh fell away from the wall, sucking in breath. Now the gray beast's handlers ran and pranced by, pointing at him and laughing, but lagging at a safe distance as the warrior bull with the swaying nose pounded and rumbled toward the palace gate. The gate guards, laughing like maniacs, but not at all willing to stand in the way of this living battering ram, hurriedly swung the gate wide to let it pass. The massive animal galloped through, unimpeded in its flight toward the open steppe, and shouts of derision and delight followed. *Better to let it run free until its anger was spent rather than try to stop it.* Gansukh smiled at the thought of such a strange creature roaming free on the plains. There was no doubt in his mind that it would be recaptured eventually, if not hunted down and slaughtered, but for now, it was free to run under the open sky.

As all things should be.

◆ ◆ ◆

Ögedei could never speak of his secret terror. The knot of fear wound tighter and tighter in his gut every year as this day of memory approached. It wasn't remembering Tolui, the youngest of Genghis's four children, that caused him such pain; it was clear to everyone how dear his brother's memory was to the *Khagan*. Nor was it the endless processionals or the interminable ceremonial dinners held in his dead brother's honor throughout the week of the festival. No, what made his guts spasm and ache was the fact that he had to address the court; he had to stand before them and speak of the *importance* of Tolui's sacrifice.

Ögedei paced the length of his chamber like a caged tiger. The great cup stood on a nearby table, half filled. He could not stand to look at it. The smell of the wine followed him. More than once he had wrapped his hands around the cup's stem as if it were a neck he could throttle; if he couldn't snap it in half then at least he could hurl it from his sight. But each time, he would raise the brim to his trembling lips and pour more of its contents into his gasping mouth.

Oh, how he wished the cup were even larger, like a tub, that he might drown in the pool of wine and be released from his burden, freed from the weight of the empire. Each gulp was bitter, but then he only drank more to banish the taste of the previous draught.

Ögedei cursed and slammed the cup down on the table, once more unable to throw it out the window. The young warrior, Gansukh, had stood up to him, in front of all his guests. He should have had him dragged from the room and flogged.

The *Khagan* sneered at his quivering reflection in the surface of the wine. He should have drawn his knife and killed the insolent pup himself. But the fierce expression on the whelp's face had reminded him of Tolui...as had the large cup.

Chagatai, his *older* brother, had chosen this envoy well.

A light knock sounded at the door, and before he could shout at whoever was foolish enough to disturb him, his wife, Toregene, opened the door and entered.

"You should see how many there are," she said, gliding across the floor. She was heavily made up—dressed in layers of yellow and orange silk, her hair freshly braided. "They are all waiting for their glorious and exalted leader." She touched his arm lightly, and he could smell the jasmine and lemongrass oils in her hair.

Ögedei exhaled noisily, his shoulders and chest slumping. He wanted to lie down on one of the couches. Take a short nap. "They should come back tomorrow," he sighed. "Or not at all." His hand edged toward the cup. Even though he refused to look at it, he knew exactly how far away it was. *Just one more gulp,* he thought. *Perhaps that will numb me enough...*

She leaned against him, slipping her arm through his. Her voice floated up to his ear. "They don't want much. Show them your face. Tell them to begin their revels."

"What are they celebrating?" Ögedei snapped. "Master Chucai said this feast would be like nothing seen before under Heaven, but why? To honor my dead brother? To honor..." He stumbled to one side, wrenching her arm loose, and his hand snapped out and grabbed up the cup. He peered over the rim at her as he thrust it against his lips. Wine sloshed and spilled into his beard. "To honor his sacrifice? My brother doesn't care. He's dead. He is gone. *His bones are gone.* A worthless sacrifice to foreign gods."

Toregene kissed him on the cheek, swiping away drips of wine with her thumb. Her soft smile hurt him more than memory. "He died for the glory of the empire," she said, neither chiding nor blaming—merely reminding. "He died for your father's dream. He knew his sacrifice was necessary so the empire would live on."

"How many other sons and brothers have been sacrificed for my father's dream?" Ögedei shouted. "How many more?"

"Tolui was a good man, the best and most noble brother anyone could ever hope to have, but he knew what must be done to keep the empire alive." Toregene gently grasped his cheeks and temples in her warm, dry hands and looked him in the eye. "You are the best of your father's sons. His only worthy successor. Do not shame Tolui's sacrifice by denying what you are."

Ögedei's eyes began to fill with tears. "My brother," he sobbed. "Who else would make such a sacrifice?"

Toregene liberated the cup from Ögedei's slack fingers and set it back on the table. Without a word, she drew him toward the balcony. Under the sky's great blue tent cloth, a host of warriors stood silent, waiting. The sun shone directly overhead, glinting off iron helmets and golden jewelry, and the crowd glimmered like water.

"All of them," she said quietly. "Every last one of them and the thousands who already died in their service—all of them would sacrifice their lives for you, O Great Khan." She wiped his face with her sleeve, clearing away the tears with tender dabs. "Do not deny them."

Ögedei's mouth became firm, and his back straightened. Gently he gathered her hands in his and kissed them. Then, with his own thick finger, he wiped the slight stain of wine from her supple skin and looked up at her from beneath wide brows, his small black eyes sharp. She had this effect on him always, like a tonic, better than any wine, better even than the sight of a fine horse.

When he stepped out onto the balcony, the wind greeted him like an old friend; the horsehair strands of the Spirit

Banner mounted on the railing danced and snapped in the breeze. He could almost hear the wind-borne whinny of anxious, prancing horses, eager to be ridden across the land of grass.

The army assembled below gave one voice, and the sound was like an avalanche falling down a steep mountainside. He let their united voices buffet him, and then, enlivened, rejuvenated by the intensity of their adoration, and smiling like a new father, he raised his arms to silence them and focus their attention.

The sudden expectant quiet of a thousand men seemed to freeze the very air.

"Today," he began, and then started again in a louder voice. "Today we celebrate the sacrifice of my dear brother Tolui."

The knot in his gut gripped him once and then let go, and all the memories that he both cherished and despised flowed back. The time had come. This all meant nothing; it meant everything.

"Nine years ago..."

◆ ◆ ◆

*Nine years ago...*on a night where thick clouds obscured the moon and the air pressed down heavily, threatening rain, Ögedei lay on his deathbed.

His hair was matted to his sweltering skull, and a thin robe clung to his shivering frame. Whenever he had enough strength, he would try to throw off the furs that were damp and rank with his sweat, but the healers would always replace them, ignoring his guttural grunts. Most of the time he simply stared at the wooden lattice supporting the *ger*'s ceiling, watching the smoke curl up and escape through the smoke hole. Shamans, like smoked mummies wrapped in patchwork robes, would appear and disappear like wraiths illuminated by the moon sneaking between clouds. They beat hide drums, droned endless prayers, and made noises like birds and foxes. He was sure one time he would look and they would all be transformed into wolf cubs, panting and whining with fear.

The fever had fallen upon him during the dark of the moon, seizing him like a malevolent demon conjured by his enemies. It grew in him, eating first the strength in his legs and arms, and now it worked on his guts and his lungs. Soon it would crawl up his throat and find a way into his brain, and then he would no longer be Ögedei Khan, but just a sack of pale skin, filled with hot ash.

Riders had gone out, summoning every shaman and healer in the land, and they continued to appear, laboring to drive out the heat demon that infected him. They sang, they danced, they burned incense; some searched for answers in the bubbling, wandering, meaningless words that dribbled from his lips, in the pattern of finger and knuckle bones they shook out on leather maps, in the striations and patterns on charred tortoiseshells.

They all failed to cure him. In defense, they decreed his malady to be a curse, a malediction set upon him by angry gods of the southern kingdoms—vengeance upon the empire that had slaughtered the tribes and despoiled their lands. Some of the shamans tried to communicate with the foreign gods, to seek a sign of what they must do in order to appease their anger. Harsh, dusty winds and sudden lightning storms were the only response.

A life precious to you, the shamans told him, *in return for all those that have been taken. That is the only sacrifice they will accept.*

"Brother..."

Ögedei blearily looked around the smoke-filled tent, try-ing to find the source of the voice that intruded on his fever-ish dreams. Squinting against the firelight, he could make out a tall figure, dressed in yellow and white furs. He tried to raise his arm and beckon the figure closer.

"I rode through the night..." The figure knelt at his bed-side, slender fingers clutching his hot and greasy hand. "The foreign demon has not yet swallowed you," the figure said with a smile.

"Tolui," Ögedei murmured. He wanted to embrace his brother, but the effort required to speak his name had used all of his strength. He tried to turn his hand so that he could squeeze his brother's fingers, but even that was beyond him. "The Blue Wolf is coming for me soon," he whispered. His throat ached, and he could not summon any spit. His mouth was like the southern desert—arid and lifeless. "I... am glad you are here," he managed. "When I pass from this world—"

Tolui put a leather-scented finger to Ögedei's lips, stop-ping him. "You will not die," he said. His face was drawn, and there were dark circles under his eyes, preternaturally aging his youthful face.

"You have found a cure?" Ögedei's voice cracked, break-ing into a dry cough that made his chest ache.

"I have spoken to some of the shamans, and they fear there is no hope. But an old man of the Eagle Hills has told me there is a way..." Tolui's voice fell away, becoming lost in the rhythmic drone of the shamans who still watched over him, chanting and tapping their drums.

"No," Ögedei managed. "I can't allow—"

Tolui shook his head. "Father told me to watch over you, Ögedei. Is that not what I have done? When you forgot your lessons, where was I? When you dozed off, who prodded you awake? Who took care of Father's empire while the tribes squabbled and whined about declaring you *Khagan*? I gave it to you gladly when it was time because I knew you, of all our brothers, to be the wisest and most capable. You were Father's choice, and it has always been—and will always be—my greatest duty and honor to stand by you." His eyes were bright and wet. "If you die, we will be lost. We will be weak and helpless while the tribes gather for the *kuraltai* and pick a successor, like an orphaned child who crawls from its *ger* to find its family devoured by predators."

"It should be you, Tolui. You would make a fine *Khagan*."

"Compared to you?" Tolui shook his head. "The gods fear you, my brother. Look how desperate they are to destroy Father's dream—your dream." He squeezed Ögedei's hand, forestalling any argument. "I have already decided. The shamans will perform the ritual. Let me do this for you. Let me serve my Khan in the best way that I can."

Silence had fallen in the tent, and Ögedei struggled to look around. There were more shamans than he thought the *ger* could hold. They all wore blue robes, and they had traded their drums and divining bones for cups and deer horns and carved wooden rods. He tried to extricate his hand from Tolui's grip, but his younger brother held him fast. He could not sit up; he could not speak. His strength was gone, and he fell back against the sweat-stained furs. They wrapped around him like wet snow, and dark demon patterns danced at the edge of his vision...

The shamans were chanting, and the tent was illuminated by the light from four braziers burning fragrant pinewood. *Had time passed?* Tolui was no longer at the side of his bed, and his hand—the one so recently held by his brother—was cold and cramped. When Ögedei blinked, one of the braziers went out; in quick succession they were extinguished, and great billowing clouds of smoke began to obscure the chanting shamans.

A greasy tendril of smoke passed over his face. He reached out to touch it, but there was nothing there, nothing but a vast emptiness, as if he lay naked on the steppes and the stars had all winked out.

He could smell blood, like a fresh kill, and thought of the deer by the river—the one he had killed with his father so many years ago.

The chanting stopped, and then shamans whooped and yipped, a wolf pack cacophony.

Ögedei could not remember closing his eyes, and opening them was like lifting an iron gate. Little by little, he managed to raise his eyelids, squinting and blinking even though there was little light in the tent.

The shamans were chanting again, muttering and humming under their breath—whispers on the wind. Tolui had returned and he stood at the foot of the bed. His head was lowered, and the sound coming from his throat sounded like the noise of ten men, droning and crying. A wooden cup was passed from shaman to shaman, until it reached his brother, who accepted it, squatted next to Ögedei's feet, and raised it to his lips.

He drank and drank and drank. It seemed as if he would never stop drinking, and Ögedei was about to cry out for him to stop, when he dropped the bowl and fell heavily against the bed. He raised his head, his bright eyes piercing Ögedei. His mouth worked for some time before words came out, and when they did, Ögedei wanted to cry out, to drive them back into his brother's throat as if that would undo what had been done. "Bring greatness to our empire, brother," he whispered.

Ögedei sat up. His spirit was returning in prickly waves running through his limbs. "Tolui," he cried, his voice a hoarse gasp.

Tolui groaned, then doubled over, his hands clutching at nothing. When he looked again at Ögedei, the veins of his brow swelled purple and tight under the sweat-slicked skin. "Brother," he whispered, his voice a ragged hiss, "they *drink* me." All the skin of his face now stretched tight, like the head of a drum, and Ögedei could see *things* moving beneath—like worms burrowing.

"I am drunk," Tolui sighed. He tried to shape one last smile for his older brother, but his muscles failed him and he collapsed in a heap.

Ögedei threw off the furs. Finding he could stand, he rushed to his brother's side.

A shaman stood to one side, half in shadow. "It is done," he pronounced in a hollow, distant voice.

Tolui's eyes were closed, as if he had fallen into a deep sleep. Ögedei hugged him tightly, but there was no life left in his brother's body.

✦ ✦ ✦

"On this day nine years ago, my noble brother sacrificed himself so that I might live. But his sacrifice was not just for me! Tolui...Tolui Khan sacrificed himself so the Mongol Empire would not be denied its leader—or its destiny."

Surrounded by more than a *minghan* of ecstatic and effusive warriors, it was easy to be infected by their enthusiasm, and when the crowd roared in approval following the *Khagan*'s words, Gansukh found himself halfheartedly cheering along.

The courtyard was removed enough from Ögedei's balcony that it was not easy to tell if the *Khagan* had been drinking. Certainly, at this distance, one could not make out any of the telltale details in a man's face that betrayed intoxication, but based on the *Khagan*'s cadence and the way he leaned heavily on the balcony railing while the crowd cheered, Gansukh suspected the *Khagan* was, indeed, besotted.

"We must never forget my dear brother's spirit," Ögedei continued, pulling himself upright again. "His strength is our strength; his spirit is with us still. His name, and the names of all our fallen brothers, are what make us who we are. Those who stand against the empire—those who defy me—defile the memory of our dead brothers."

Ögedei paused dramatically, and as the noise of the crowd filled the courtyard, he raised his arms, urging them to even greater volume. The ground rumbled as men began to stomp rhythmically. This time, when the *Khagan* dropped his hands, silence came slowly.

"It is due to my brother," Ögedei shouted in a ringing voice, "and to your brothers, and all the fallen Mongol brothers, that our empire endures. My father brought the tribes together and set us upon a course that will forever carve a furrow in history. It is our duty—our sacred duty for our brothers who will follow after us—to continue that course."

The crowd's cheers grew louder, more guttural, becoming a war chant. The noise flowed back and forth, beating against the walls of the palace, and above the seething tide of shouting warriors, Ögedei faltered. Gansukh's heart faltered with him. But the crowd did not notice as Ögedei steadied himself, and Gansukh saw someone move behind Ögedei and the sharp shooing motion of his hand as the *Khagan* brushed off any assistance.

The crowd continued its exultation, but Gansukh had seen enough. As Ögedei began to quiet the shouting warriors for one final declamatory exclamation, Gansukh shoved his way through the crowd.

The *Khagan*'s greatness had not departed. The wine addled him, but it had not entirely doused Ögedei's fierce spirit. The *Khagan* could still be saved, but it would require someone like Gansukh—an outsider, a warrior for whom the old ways were still fresh and vital—to show him the path.

Learning the ways of court were a means to an end, much like learning how to read tracks and spoor in order to hunt. A hunter had to know his prey well before he could stalk it, before he could get close enough.

CHAPTER 30:

PILGRIMS' PROGRESS

No place could be less like Jerusalem than the one they were riding into now. Yet as they entered the gates of the priory on the top of the hill in Kiev, Raphael could not help thinking of the day a dozen years earlier when he had ridden into Jerusalem a few lengths behind Frederick II, the Holy Roman Emperor and author of the Sixth Crusade. For Jerusalem too had thrown open her gates without a fight. The martial orders of Christendom—the Teutonic Knights, the Templars, the Hospitallers, and the *Ordo Militum Vindicis Intactae*—had all sent contingents. Buffing their armor, grooming their horses, and unfurling their most glorious banners, they strove to outshine one another in the eyes of the locals—Muslims, Jews, and Christians—who had lined Frederick's route from St. Stephen's Gate to the Church of the Holy Sepulchre.

The Shield-Brethren, who styled themselves after the Spartans, tended to come off quite poorly in such displays, and so had probably made little impression upon the crowd. Which was acceptable—preferable, even—to Raphael and the dozen brothers who had ridden alongside him under the Order's red rose banner. Less attention from the common folk of Zion gave them more leisure to observe the city and the rival orders of Christian knights who were now reoccupying the place after four decades' absence.

The Knights Hospitallers, for one, who had ridden into Jerusalem at the right hand of Frederick II in their black surcoats adorned with silver crosses. After paying their respects at the Holy Sepulchre, they reoccupied the Hospital of St. John, which, in its original conception, had been a hostel for pilgrims who had traveled from the West to visit the tomb of Our Lord. Its martial proprietors had since learned that succoring pilgrims was a complicated business that extended beyond merely giving them food and shelter. For what good were those amenities if they could not travel safely on the roads?

It was impossible for Raphael not to think of that day as he entered the Shield-Maidens' nunnery-cum-fortress and saw the sick and the lame distributed about its courtyard on straw pallets. They were being tended to by the good sisters in their white wimples. These nuns had learned the same lesson as the Crusaders at the Hospital of St. John: protecting the meek required a judicious combination of bandages, simples, and sympathy on the one hand, and brute armed force on the other.

The Shield-Maidens were amply qualified to supply the latter. These were the descendants of Norsewomen who had drawn inspiration from tales of Valkyries and the *skjalddís*. Like all the other Varangians who had migrated down the great rivers of Rus, they had gradually become one with the local population, adopting their Slavic language and their Greek alphabet. But Raphael could plainly see ancient links to his Order in many details of their arms and armor, their movements, and their discipline.

Since they had so much in common, and since Vera and Illarion could both translate freely between Latin and

Ruthenian, conversation flowed easily once they had been formally welcomed, introductions had been made, and they'd been given a tour of the little fortress. Eventually they found themselves seated around a great old table in the keep, quaffing mead and eating coarse black bread dipped in honey.

"This country has fallen under a great mortality, as you have seen plainly enough," Vera explained, reading the astonishment in their faces when the food was brought out. "But bees live, flowers grow, and farmers till their fields, and we are able to sustain ourselves on what they bring us. In exchange, we tend to their sick and offer them some meager protection."

"By what miracle," Illarion asked, "did you escape destruction at the hands of the Mongols?"

"You are almost too shrewd in the way you phrase your question," Vera retorted, giving him a sharp look that made Raphael glad he'd not been on its receiving end.

She was a big-boned woman who in some more fortunate country might have ended up as a strapping, plump milkmaid, blundering about a dairy with heavy buckets yoked to her broad shoulders. Austerity had made her lean and revealed cheekbones that owed more to the steppes than the fjords. A similar tale was told by the color of her eyes and of her hair, which hung just above her shoulders when she swept it back from her head—just the right length to fit under an arming cap but not get tangled between the steel links of an aventail.

"I am not trying to be shrewd," Illarion said, "only to—"

"The wretched people of Kiev, living below in the ruins, are inclined to view it as a miracle, and we see no advantage in telling them otherwise," Vera said, cutting him off. "As you rightly ken, we could not have withstood the Mongols, even had we all fought to the death. Instead we fought them enough to slow their advance and to become an irritant. They had already taken Kiev, and when their strategy is calling them on at a gallop over the sea of grass, it is not their practice to spend months staying in one place to root out every last pocket of resistance. This place looks like a church; they don't like to destroy churches. It is defended by women; in maintaining a long siege, they saw little honor and less glory—as well as danger that they might suffer mockery and humiliation if they were unable to defeat us quickly."

"And so they passed you by," Illarion said, nodding.

Strength was returning to Raphael's body as he ate the bread and honey, and close on its heels came the sorts of feelings that had long been suppressed by cold, dirt, hardship, and the company of men. He began to look at Vera in the timeless manner of men looking at women and saw that smallpox had left a trail of shallow craters in the hollows of her cheeks and extending down the sides of her neck, without really disfiguring her. And it had spared the eyes. Seeming to feel his gaze on her, she turned her head quite deliberately and looked him straight in the eye. It was not a demure look, of course. He'd not have expected any such thing from a Shield-Maiden. Neither was she telling him to drop dead. She was just letting him know that if he looked at her, she would look back. He did the only polite thing, which was to avert his gaze and concede the point with a smile.

"So we were not extirpated," Vera concluded, gesturing at the bread and honey, "and so we have continued to survive. But of communication with the rest of Christendom there has been almost none. Rumors only of great battles, won by the Mongols. What news from your Order? Does Petraathen still stand? Or are you wandering strays, like these others?"

These others. She was talking about the Livonian Knights.

Raphael's mind went back again to Jerusalem. A formation of Teutonic Knights had entered the city just behind the much smaller Shield-Brethren contingent. They were a younger order, but they had fared better in recent decades, being based out of Acre—a city still under Christian dominance—rather than Jerusalem, which had fallen to Saladin forty-two years earlier. They had put on a better show in the parade, making a much stronger impression on the locals than the Shield-Brethren. Their presence in the Holy Land had dwindled soon thereafter as they had moved north to pursue crusades along the eastern border of Europe, where Christianized kingdoms abutted pagan-held lands.

A few years ago, the Teutonic Knights had assimilated the remnants of another crusading order—the Livonian Brothers of the Sword. The Livonians had been scattered by a pagan army, their grandmaster and most of their knights slain. The surviving Livonians had accepted the authority of the Teutonic Knights' grandmaster and discarded their traditional heraldry—a red cross and sword—for the black cross of the Teutonics.

"These strays..." Percival said, leaning forward to grab another slice of the thick bread. "It was our understanding that the Livonian Order was no more. Had we known..."

"You would have ridden to rescue us?"

"Of course not." Percival shook his head, deftly avoiding the trap that lay before him. "We would have sent word."

"If they had been more adroit, we might have let them in the gates and ended up wishing that such a warning had reached us," Vera countered. "As it was, word of their arrogance and vainglory preceded them by several days, and so we knew what to expect. When Kristaps, their leader, presented himself at our doorstep, he spoke true to form. He offered to relieve us of the burden of defending this place and proposed to supply us with duties more befitting the weaker sex."

"I'm sure that went over well," Raphael snorted. Illarion, Roger, and even Percival were barely hiding their amusement.

"From the tone in which he tendered the offer," Vera said, and here she was unable to prevent the corners of her mouth from twitching back, "it was clear he considered the terms to be astoundingly generous. He stood there awaiting our thanks and our admiration. He received neither. When he returned, he spoke less politely, enabling us to see his true nature, as if this were not already obvious."

"Would he be the fellow with the arrow in his eye socket?" Raphael asked hopefully.

Vera shook her head. "That would be pleasing," she said. "That fellow was a knight of lesser rank who made a nuisance of himself." She took a bite of bread and chewed it as the statement sunk in.

She shifted in her chair, facing toward Percival, whom she had identified as the group's leader. "You have shown courtesy," she said, "in expressing brotherly curiosity about our situation. I have not returned it in kind. What brings you all here, and in such a condition? Pardon my frankness, but it's obvious that you have traveled hard for a long time."

Any of them might have answered. Raphael bated because he did not wish to blurt out the truth. Feronantus might later take the Shield-Maidens into his confidence, but it was not for any lesser member of their company to do so. Raphael had seen enough of Vera by now to feel quite certain that, if they simply told her that their errand was none of her business, she would accept it with no pouting or ill feelings.

He was searching for a polite way to say just that when Percival spoke: "It is a quest."

Around the table, Percival's companions were dumbstruck, wondering whether he had spoken sincerely or was making up a lie on the spur of the moment. But supposing that Percival were even capable of telling a lie, he would probably do a miserable job of it. Nothing but sincerity was visible in his face. Vera spent several moments gazing into that face. Raphael, watching her, thought he saw a slight softening, a lowering of the defenses, in her eyes.

"Can you be more specific as to what it is you are questing for?" she finally asked.

"No," Percival responded immediately, "for I do not know."

"Who sent you on this quest? It would have been polite for them to have given you better instructions before sending you such a great distance."

"I hesitate to say it was God, for this would be blasphemous arrogance," Percival said, "but I do believe that some angel or saint passed over me some weeks ago and shone his or her light into my soul and imbued me with a purpose. The nature of that purpose is not yet clear. But I believe that it has drawn me to this place. For what reason I cannot imagine."

Roger was staring at Percival with a mixture of derision and affection that could only stem from long friendship.

Illarion met Raphael's eye briefly, then turned to Vera and asked a question in Ruthenian.

Vera responded in kind; then she said, in Latin, "The hill below us is riddled with caves and catacombs where holy men have lived since Christians first came up this way preaching their Gospel. Any number of saints' bones and artifacts are salted about the place. Of course, it is rumored that buried treasure is also to be found there. Whether the Livonians are here for relics or for treasure is impossible to say—I suspect the latter. But if some holy spirit has sent you to this place in pursuance of a quest, Brother Percival, then I would guess that its object is to be found beneath us."

She nodded at the food on the table. "Once you complete this repast, I would be happy to show you the way."

✦ ✦ ✦

Istvan's horse reared, pawing the air with its hooves.

More of the Livonians drew their weapons, and the sound of steel against steel was like the ringing of bells. Cnán wanted to put her hands over her ears, as if blocking out the sound would forestall what was about to happen next.

Feronantus made no motion toward his sword. "Your quarry is getting away," he said in the hollow emptiness that followed the drawing of swords. His statement elicited confusion among both ranks until Kristaps blinked and turned his head to look up the slope of the hill.

The ragmen and their cart had reached the gate of the monastery. As they all watched, the portal creaked open enough for the two filthy men to drag their burden through, and then it rattled shut.

"How little you truly know, Feronantus," Kristaps laughed.

"I know that, even outnumbering us thrice over, you are not sure that you can defeat us in combat," Feronantus said quietly. "I know that my knight could put a single arrow through two of your men *right now* because they don't know enough to not stand in a row. I know that some of the men on your left flank are terrified of what is going to happen when the knight behind me draws that enormous sword of his. And I know that at least one of your number is going to faint when I say that not only does this man"—he inclined his head toward Istvan—"eat human flesh, but so does his horse…"

Kristaps twitched—only *slightly*—when two of his men fell to the ground. The Livonian tried to hide his loss of composure with a mighty sneer, but to Cnán, his expression looked more pained than fierce. "You and your…degenerate barbarians…are not worth dirtying my steel," he snarled.

"Nor you mine," Feronantus answered. "Run along, Kristaps."

"Next time—"

"Next time, you will be dead before you finish your threat," Feronantus barked, driving Kristaps to silence with the veritable thunder of his voice.

The Livonian snapped his mouth shut, and his lips stretched across his teeth in a grimace. With a jerk of his head, he gave his men the signal to retreat. They milled about, uncertain if they should turn and flee or simply back slowly from the mounted Shield-Brethren. The two men who had fallen were left behind momentarily until Kristaps gestured angrily that they should be collected. Once the Livonians were all moving—the dazed pair being dragged by their arms—they appeared to remember how to conduct themselves and formed a more orderly procession up the slope.

Kristaps lingered, glowering at Feronantus, but when Yasper could no longer hold his amusement in check and let loose a great peal of laughter, the Livonian hurled a final curse at the company and stormed away.

Rædwulf lowered his bow and joined Yasper and Eleázar in boisterous and polyphonic revelry. Istvan stood in his stirrups and mocked the retreating knights loudly, shouting at them as if they were a herd of frightened sheep.

Feronantus did not join in the persiflage of the fleeing Livonians. He watched the retreating knights with a calm intensity, as if there were clues to some mystery that could be gleaned from their departure.

"Who are they?" Cnán asked. Now that the threat of violence was passed, all that remained was a lingering apprehension. How could they expect to undo the might of the Mongolian Horde if the Shield-Brethren's old enemies were sprouting from the earth wherever they traveled?

"The Livonian Brothers of the Sword," Feronantus answered softly. "Though they have not worn that sigil for more than five years. Most of their number were killed in a

battle—at a place called Schaulen. A battle that could have
been avoided. The pitiful few who survived were taken in
by the Teutonic Knights, where they adopted a different
livery."

"Were you there?" Cnán asked, surprised by her own
curiosity.

Feronantus gave her no answer.

"I know him," Eleázar said, joining their vigil. "Years ago I
was witness to the aftermath of his butchery." He leaned over
and spat noisily. "What are they doing here? The Livonians
tried once before to conquer the northern lands and failed.
And they had many more men than now."

"I do not know," Feronantus replied. "This bunch, though
they dress like the Brothers of the Sword, have not worn the
red long…"

The two senseless Livonians had been revived, and the
armed party had managed to form a unit as they snaked up
the narrow path. When they reached the gate, they stumbled
to a clumsy halt, as if they were not quite sure what came next.
Faintly Cnán heard Kristaps's voice, and while he was too distant for her to understand the individual words, it sounded
as if he were announcing his presence and not presenting a
challenge to those who resided within the walls.

In response to his cry, the gate shuddered and then
opened. Keeping their formation, the Livonians proceeded,
disappearing through the gate, which promptly closed once
more behind them.

"I…I thought they were chasing those men," Cnán said,
trying to make sense of what she had seen.

"Apparently not," Yasper offered, scratching his chin.

"Cnán…" Feronantus turned to her. "You are the soft-
est of foot amongst us, as well as the lightest. You and Finn."
He nodded toward the buildings at the peak of the hill. "Set

your eyes upon the interior of that wall and tell us what the Livonians are doing.

"I was the one who suggested they were chasing those beggars, and in doing so, I betrayed our ignorance as to the Livonians' true mission. As much as Kristaps desired to engage us, he had a more urgent matter to contend with. A holy mission, he claimed, and I fear he was not speaking lightly." He waved his hand. "Quickly. We must discern what they are about."

CHAPTER 31:

DANGEROUS BEAUTY

The palace grounds flooded with music, dozens of melodies collapsing into one ear-ringing, chest-pounding sound. There was the constant clash of cymbals and piercing chime of bells, overlaid with the mad piping and bellowing of horns and flutes and the screeching of sinew-stringed fiddles. Singers too, giving voice to so many different songs that one could only catch fragments of verses at a time—heroic epics, songs of praise for the heavens and the mountains and the *Khagan*, short ribald tunes sung in a drunken roister, and low, droning throat singing. And beneath all that the steady beat of great drums, like a heartbeat, like the whole palace had become one giant body and all the revelers were the blood in its veins.

Cups of wine were shoved in Lian's face as she tried to thread her way through the revelers that packed the eastern courtyard to overflowing. Fire pits blazed with such reckless ferocity that she steered well clear, frightened by the way the flames capered and gestured, seductive fingers summoning the drunk and the addled into a fiery embrace. The air was odoriferous with spices, both familiar and exotic, all so mouth-wateringly fragrant that she no longer had the strength to resist when a woman thrust a reed basket filled with warm flatbread at her. Lian dropped a few coins into her hands and accepted a still warm disk in return. She bit into the soft flatbread with relish, savoring the sweet heat of baked onions on her tongue.

She wolfed down the bread, sating a hunger she had refused to acknowledge, and once the bread was gone, she returned her attention to her immediate goal. The celebration was a marvelous spectacle, attracting visitors from across the empire and beyond. It was an endless party that would span many days, and at some point during this chaotic carousal, she might be able to escape.

Slipping out of the palace had been, as always, simple. All she had to do was walk behind any group of concubines or servant girls, or use one of the many unguarded side passages, a trick she had done on occasion when she wished to enjoy some solitude—a threadbare illusion of freedom. Actually escaping the city, however, was much harder.

She had tried to escape once before, very early in her captivity. Naively she had thought it would have been fairly easy to secure passage on a caravan, and once the wagons had left the city, she would vanish. But on the second day of their journey, an *arban* of the *Khagan*'s *Torguud* had surrounded the caravan, demanding her return. Back to the gilded cage of Karakorum.

After that, Master Chucai was much more vigilant. She was a valuable prize, after all, one he had spent considerable time and expense shaping into a useful tool. He could not watch her himself—his duties to the *Khagan* kept him otherwise occupied, of course—but he could keep himself appraised of her activities. She had to report to him every morning and evening, detailing the list of her lessons and engagements since their last meeting; she knew some of the serving staff were his spies within the palace (she took care to figure out which staff were the most likely suspects), and the concubines were altogether too gossipy. On the rare occasion when she was waylaid by an assignation, she found he already knew when she hurried to tell him.

She—like everyone else within the confines of the walls of Karakorum—was supposed to live in constant awareness that Chucai knew *everything* that went on at court. What hope could she have for escape if there was no way that she could move about the palace and its grounds without Chucai knowing? Even if she did manage to slip out of the city, how much of a head start would she get before Chucai sent the *Khagan*'s best trackers after her?

The open steppe wasn't *open* enough to hide her. She needed to utterly vanish. She couldn't rely on some caravan or trader to spirit her away. She had to disappear on her own, at such a time and in such a way that there would be enough confusion about her disappearance that she might get far enough away.

The festival was her chance. If she could use the chaos and confusion of the celebration to muddy her trail, it might be impossible for Master Chucai and his trackers to work out her escape route once they finally realized she was gone.

Part of her wanted to just walk out the front gates of the palace. To take nothing with her. To simply *leave*. But she knew it wouldn't be that easy. She had to have a plan. She had to get a sense of the routines of the guards, of the ebb and flow of the crowds.

Wrapping her thin cloak more tightly around herself, Lian made her way through the crowded courtyard toward the gate. More than once, she wished she were taller. She could barely see the gilded dragons that festooned the top of the faux-Chinese barrier that was her destination. But being taller would also attract attention...

A constant flood of people streamed in, jostling and crowding in their rush to join the revelry in the palace. Lian was pressed against the flow of the crowd, bounced around like a leaf on a river swollen with mountain runoff. Elbows and shoulders poked and slammed her body, and she tried to protect herself as best she could. Some men took advantage of the mob to grope at her, and one of them, big and pale and hairy beneath black furs—Ruthenian, judging by the coarse sound of his words—waggled his bushy eyebrows at her as he *accidentally* pressed his body against her. She turned her head, trying to avoid the stinking cloud of his breath and, in return, sharply elevated her knee as she pushed past him. The Ruthenian doubled over, his breath huffing out, and then the crowd swallowed him as if he had never existed.

An eddy formed in the mob, and enough space opened that she could see the gates clearly. Her heart sank. A trio of guards stood at stiff attention on each side, and the six men scanned the faces of the crowd coming and going with hawk-like intensity. If she put the hood of her cloak up, she would only draw attention to herself and thusly be remembered.

Chucai's eyes were everywhere. *He would know.*

One of the guards looked in her direction and she quickly turned away, her hands tugging at the neck of her cloak—fighting the urge to pull up the hood. Her pulse roared in her ears.

It had been a faint hope that the main gate wouldn't be well guarded, and she hadn't been surprised to see the vigilant guards. She had needed to silence that part of her that dreamed of an easy escape. *It will be difficult,* she thought to herself. *I have to be steadfast. Otherwise I might as well confess everything to Chucai. I might as well give up.*

There had to be other routes—the palace walls, for one. They were not that high. Gansukh—and the thief—had climbed them that night weeks ago; perhaps she could too. She let the next surge in the crowd carry her back toward the palace, slipping away at the first chance into an alley behind a white-painted stone house.

The celebration faded, the crowd's cacophony dulling to persistent grumbling, the wild light of the fire pits dimming to pale flickering tongues of light dancing along the edges of the roof tiles. She leaned against the wall of the house, letting her eyes adjust to the shadow-filled alley. It was three times as wide as she, the stones dusty with accumulated sand, and the wall of the house was plain stone, featureless save for small window slits. There was nothing to help her scale the outer wall here, but as she started to explore the alley, she noticed a small handcart resting against the rear wall of the next house over. If she stood on it, she might be able to grip the top of the palace wall.

As she passed the corner of the first house, a man's boisterous, drunken laughter startled her. She ducked back into the alley and pressed herself against the wall. Once her heart stopped pounding, she sidled up to the corner and peeked around.

There, in a small space between the two houses, squatted a trio of soldiers, rolling knucklebones in the dust and swigging from earthenware bottles. Their faces were weather-beaten and scarred.

One of them glanced in her direction, and she tried to duck back out of sight without being spotted, but she knew, even before she heard him call out to his companions, that she hadn't been successful. "Don't be *shy*," one of the men shouted in wine-fueled good fellowship. "Come on over here." His words were followed by peals of laughter from the others.

Instinct told her to run, but cold, pessimistic reason told her that running would dare them to pursue her. She understood in that instant what men most loved in hunting—the chase. They *wanted* their prey to flee, to show spirit—to challenge their skill. *Their drunken skill...*

Her lips curled and she drew in her breath.

Instead of running, she smoothed her robe, pushed her hair back from her face, and stepped boldly out from her hiding place. She walked toward the men, smiling demurely, but making sure to make firm eye contact—glazed and wandering as all their eyes were—with each of them.

"Well, a pretty Chinese doll," smirked the one who had spotted her. He grinned, yellowed teeth dull in the flickering light.

"What are you doing back here, girl?" asked another. "Something we could assist you with?"

"I was merely taking a shortcut to bypass the crowd," she said.

"A shortcut? Where to?" The first soldier staggered closer, and she feared he might try to grab her robe.

"It is none of your concern." She held her chin high, trying to appear haughty and noble.

"Maybe you don't have any place in mind," suggested the third soldier, a man who looked and smelled as if he never bathed in his life. "Maybe you should stay with us. Tarry a while. Try your luck with the bones. And my bones..." He wiggled his fingers suggestively and laughed—awful and snorting.

"Come on, doll, stay a while. We'll treat you good. Have a drink with us." The second soldier held up one of the reddish-brown bottles. Lian gagged slightly as she imagined what fermented animal sludge might be inside.

"I am not a cheap whore," she said, offering them the obvious in case they were too drunk to notice. "I belong to a rather august person, one who has the *Khagan*'s ear." She intoned each word carefully. There was a way to extricate herself from this situation, if she could find the right gambit. Wasn't she always telling Gansukh something similar? *There is always a solution to any problem.* However, she didn't want to invoke Chucai's name; that would be the equivalent of summoning him.

"Do you think the *Khagan* would be pleased to know you men are not at your posts? That you are gambling in this back alley?" Since she had begun training Gansukh, she found herself starting to think of conversation in terms of combat. It gave her rhetorical victories a certain rousing flair. She snapped the edge of her cloak, as if to suggest their presence was dirtying her, which was not far from the truth.

"Who's to say that we're even on duty?" The second soldier stood up, the humor fading from his face. A scar ran across his chin, and without his open-mouthed grin, he was even uglier. His face, with its wandering, half-sunken eyes, looked like the puffed-up visage of a poorly treated corpse.

"I doubt you even know what duty is," she retorted. A risky response—such flippancy of the tongue—and it might provoke them, but showing fear would invite a response. *Half of combat is causing your opponent to think you are stronger than you are*, Gansukh had told her.

Scarface's expression tightened, making his mouth gape even more. "Sharp tongue," he said, his hand dropping to the hilt of the knife in his sash.

"Sharper than your knife," she retorted, edging a step backward.

"Shall we see?" the man replied, half pulling his knife from its sheath.

"And then what?" she snapped. "Will you gouge out my eyes so that I won't be able to point you out later to the *Khagan*'s Imperial Guard? Or will you just cut my throat and leave me here for the stray dogs to find?"

The man paused, her words cutting through the alcohol-suffused fog in his brain. His tongue poked at the edge of his lips, like a pale worm peeking out of a ragged crack in the ground. He glanced at his companions, who were no longer supporting him with their laughter.

"I can scream very loud," Lian said. She made a show of inhaling deeply.

"Run along, bitch," Scarface spat. He slammed his knife back into its sheath. The others glowered at her, their mood dark, but no longer ugly.

"Very well. I will take my leave of you, then." She bowed slightly, keeping to her masquerade as a highly regarded companion of an important official. "If I pass this way again tonight, I hope I do not see you here." She marched off, her steps a firm, rhythmic mince, miming a purpose she did not feel.

"Better you don't pass this away again," Scarface shouted after her. "Next time, it will *cost* you." The men laughed, prompted by some physical action of Scarface's, but she didn't look to see what it was. She had a fairly good idea.

Let them laugh, she thought as she strode away. *Let them think they got the better of me. Most importantly, let them not remember me.*

The chaos of the festival might make it possible for her to escape, but it had its risks too. An unescorted female might be too much of an allure to drunken men. In the tumult of revelry, it wouldn't matter if she was seen by someone who would tell Chucai. Much worse things could happen to her.

How could she slip out of the city unseen? Every encounter was a potential disaster. She had to figure out a way to vanish without being seen *by anyone.*

Or be in the company of someone who could protect her. Someone who, like her, was running away.

Gansukh.

Could she convince him to flee with her?

CHAPTER 32:

THE SECRET OF THE CAVES

The rough timbers of the monastery wall were aged and warped, and there were numerous gaps and holes in the wood. Covered in pitch, they were a poor defensive barrier, if they had ever been intended as such. Cnán and Finn approached the wood cautiously and dared to peek through the gaps.

Whereupon they discovered the source of the stench.

As they had climbed the rough path, the smell had gotten worse, as if they were climbing through veritable layers of stink. What little breeze there had been had fled, and now, in the torpid stillness of the afternoon, the smell clung to them. It seeped through the seams in her clothing and beneath her hair. Earlier, with the assistance of Yasper's mint tincture, she had kept her stomach in order, but now... Steeling herself against a dangerous loss of her self-control, she leaned toward the stained and warped wall again and put her eye up to a spy hole.

Animal carcasses—so many she couldn't bear to count them—littered the ground as though tossed there by the hands of some immense, thoughtless child. Most had been stripped of their hides and left to rot in the summer heat.

Some of the bodies appeared to squirm and twitch, and she refused to let herself imagine that some of those bloody and flayed bodies might be alive... No, those were maggots and ants at work inside their ribcages.

"Hide workers," Finn muttered, shaking his shaggy head. "Lazy and wasteful." Waddling sideways, he gestured for her to follow him.

She crept along in his wake, breathing through her mouth.

Inside the wall, the one-storied buildings were arranged around a rectangular common. They were simple structures, and there was little art in their construction. *One each for sleeping, eating, and praying*, she thought, counting them. *And one more for their grisly work...* In the open courtyard, there was another structure, a narrow stone well house with a worn wooden door.

Of the Livonians and the ragmen, there was no sign.

"Where...?" Cnán hissed at Finn, who only shrugged in return. She moved a few feet farther along the wall, choosing a different gap to spy through. She squinted, shifting her body from side to side in an effort to see more of the courtyard. But it made no difference. The monastery was deserted.

"Where did they go?" she wondered aloud. It was possible they were inside one of the buildings, but she couldn't fathom an explanation as to why. The gate had been opened readily enough, which meant they had been invited inside and were not—as Feronantus had mistakenly said—chasing the ragged hide workers. *But what was so important in these buildings that they ran away from us?* she wondered.

Finn tapped her on the shoulder and pointed at the top of the wall. He mimed climbing and held out his hands for her to use as a brace. "Oh no," she shook her head, "I'm not touching that wall."

"Would you prefer the front gate?" he asked.

"I would prefer not—"

A clank of metal against stone interrupted her, and they both returned their attention to the monastery.

Two Livonians had suddenly appeared and were standing next to the well house. One had put his shield down, leaning it against the wall. It was the sound of the metal rim scraping against the stone that had alerted them. The Livonians were sullen and angry—not with each other, she realized, but rather with an order they had been given.

"The two who fainted," Finn whispered. "Guard duty."

"Guarding what?"

As if in response to her question, the well house door creaked open to disgorge one of the raggedy monks. The Livonians kept their distance, and the monk jabbered animatedly at them in Ruthenian, stopping only when one of the knights put his hand on his sword hilt. Cackling like a diseased crow—and looking not unlike one as well—the rag-covered man scampered away, ducking into the nearest building.

Cnán eyed the well house. The hut was tiny, and while it *might* hold all three of the men and the well, she couldn't imagine the Livonians tolerating the presence of the foul monk for longer than a heartbeat.

With the monk gone, the Livonians had no one to torment, and their attentiveness gave way to lethargy and boredom. The shieldless one began to cast about, his attention on the nearby ground. *Looking for a place to sit down,* Cnán thought, and she couldn't blame his reticence.

"Caves," Finn said.

"What?"

"Caves," he repeated. "Under this hill." He grabbed her shoulder, pulling her away from the wall. "We must tell Feronantus."

◆ ◆ ◆

"I was surprised when Illarion showed no interest in coming down here," Roger muttered to Raphael. "Now I wish I had thought a little harder about what it signified."

He was a voice from the darkness. During the first part of the expedition—a descent into cellars, subcellars, and crypts of the priory—Vera had lit their way with a torch. The depredations of the Mongols had left fine oils in short supply, and so this consisted of a rag on a stick, soaked in rendered animal fat that was available for purposes of illumination only because it had gone rancid. This had stunk even before she had ignited it and had produced a spreading plume of thick, greasy smoke that they could have followed with their noses even had they not been able to see its fitful yellow light.

After a series of descents into ever deeper, moister, and darker parts of the substructure, they had reached a place where the ceiling had become so low and the ventilation so poor that Vera had been obliged to douse the torch—though not before using it to ignite a pair of crude candles, consisting of the pith of some plant soaked in tallow. By the light of these they crawled through a low opening and thus entered into something that was clearly a natural cave. Chisel marks on the wall proved that it had been widened, and mortared ashlars provided level footing, at least for the first few dozen paces.

Roger's comment was probably a reference to the way the place smelled. It was not well ventilated. Certain notes in the aroma made it obvious that these caves must communicate somewhere with all the gutters of Kiev. That, in and of itself, was hardly unusual. One could not go anywhere near a human habitation without smelling what ran in its gutters. The musty spoor of an uncontrolled rodent population was mixed with it. Too, though, Raphael's nose was detecting an unmistakable smell of dead flesh. Not the unbearable, nausea-inducing ripeness of something that had died recently, but rather the product of a slow decay that had been going on for a long time.

"It is remarkable," Raphael said, "that cities can be so very different in their buildings, their peoples, and their customs—but the catacombs are always the same."

Vera and Percival were several paces ahead of them; the Shield-Maiden knew the way and moved nimbly through the passages, which were becoming rougher and more twisted the deeper they penetrated into the heart of the hill. Percival was carrying their candle and casting a long shadow on the floor in his wake, which Raphael tried to fill in with the feeble light of his own candle. But he was dazzled by the flame directly before his face. The floor was becoming more uneven—the masons had not ventured into this part of the catacombs to lay down pavers. Roger edged in front so that the candle flame would not be shining into his eyes, and Raphael held the candle high to shine the light over Roger's shoulder, to let him find the way and warn him of any hazards.

Raphael's attention wandered. He took note of several niches that had been chiseled into the walls. Some of these were occupied by corpses wrapped up in shrouds. Others were vacant except for jumbled blankets and ragged, dirty furs.

Roger noticed the same thing and turned back, his face incredulous. "People *sleep* down here?"

Raphael made an effort not to laugh. Vera would hear it and be offended. "Perhaps during the worst days of the Mongol siege," he suggested. "But I cannot believe that the good sisters would make a habit of it."

The passage forked from time to time, and whenever it did, Vera led them into what she deemed the correct path, while making some comment to Percival about what exhibits they might have found if they had chosen to go the other way. In most cases, these were holy wonders and relics of various descriptions, but it seemed that some tunnels led off in the direction of churches and monasteries elsewhere in the city.

"Every godly building in this town," he muttered to Roger, "is, it seems, connected by this subterranean network."

"Good thing for them the Mongols never found that out," Roger remarked.

Raphael shuddered. "I doubt they would venture into a place such as this one. No victory would be worth it."

"Which leads to the question…" Roger began, then stifled himself.

"What the hell are we doing here? Going on a quest, of course."

Raphael got the sense that they were approaching some crisis, for the passage had become quite difficult to negotiate, being nothing more than a series of air pockets of varying sizes and shapes, joined by openings that had to be crawled through or climbed up to, with only a few chisel strokes in the slick stone to serve as footholds. Vera had to stop and think for a disturbingly long time at some of the turning points. But then, noting a concentration of scorch marks left by the torches and tapers of pilgrims who had gone before, she finally led them around the curve of a boulder and through a crevice that was invisible until almost the moment they passed through it. They entered into a flat-floored chamber large enough for the four of them to stand comfortably and look about.

The contents of the room were not as interesting, to Raphael, as the faces of his companions: Vera, whose sense of duty and hospitality could not fully hide her impatience; Roger, incredulous that he was down in a place like this when he was supposed to be riding east to kill the Great Khan; both of them looking curiously at Percival, whose face was alert, curious, and avid.

Clearly the chamber was a place of importance. Set into the rock all round were wrought torch brackets, currently vacant; smudges on the stone above them proved that they had once been used to illuminate holy rites of some description. The fainter glow of their candles illuminated carvings along the walls, here visible and there hidden by shadow—painted effigies of figures that Raphael assumed were famed to the place's history. A tall and terrible figure sat in a rigid, dignified posture upon a throne, defied by three figures upon horseback, gleaming swords wavering behind the sheen of hazy torchlight.

"Koschei the Deathless," Vera said, following Raphael's stare. "An evil spirit, a tyrant tsar, vanquished long ago. You stand in the tomb of the one who led his brothers to slay him." She turned to where a marker, chiseled in stone, was set into the wall. The words were nearer Greek than Ruthenian.

"Saint Ilya's grave," Raphael murmured upon deciphering the name on the stone.

"He has held vigil in this place for years uncounted since vanquishing our land's enemies," Vera said, reverently touching the stone. Then she turned to look Raphael in the eye. "There is no safer place for secrets than here."

After a moment, Percival knelt before the marker and crossed himself. "I thank you for your trust in showing us this, Sister Vera. To pay homage at the tomb of such a one is an honor few men receive."

"They called him *Chobotok*," Vera said. "It means 'boot.' For he fought off numerous foes with only his shoe as a weapon."

Raphael's eyes darted to the face of Roger, who was about to burst out into open laughter. He lashed out with his free hand and laid it on Roger's shoulder, giving him a little shake.

Startled, Roger spun away and met his eye. Raphael shook his head minutely, then glanced toward Percival, who was still kneeling and mumbling a Latin prayer.

"Is Saint Ilya speaking to you, Brother?" Raphael asked gently. "For there must be some reason why God has led us to this place."

After a long and agonizing silence, Percival spoke. "Saint Ilya is silent on the matter," he admitted.

✦ ✦ ✦

Trying to catch her breath from the headlong run down the slope—not to mention calm her pounding heart—Cnán let Finn tell Feronantus and the others what they had seen. He seemed annoyed at being asked to speak at length, but after a few sentences, he fell into a surprising loquaciousness.

When they had first departed from Legnica, the hunter's rough version of Latin had been almost incomprehensible to her, but now, after being in his company for nearly two months, she found she could understand him.

"What could they hope to find in these caves?" Feronantus asked when Finn finished.

The hunter shrugged. "There is nothing of value within those walls. What the Livonians want lies elsewhere, but they have to go through the caves to get it. Otherwise they would have brought their horses."

"A raiding party," Eleázar spat.

"But raiding what?" Yasper asked, stroking his beard. He looked at the church on the other hill, the onion-topped domes peeking over the top of the crumbling walls. "The cathedral?"

"Percival…" The name was out of Cnán's mouth before she could stop it, and she mentally kicked herself for the slip of her tongue. It was her heart, she fumed, still beating so hard from the run downhill that had betrayed her.

"Yasper," Feronantus ordered, "stay with Finn and Cnán. Keep a watch on the monastery. If the Livonians return, follow them." He gathered up his reins and snapped them, getting his horse's attention. "The rest of us will ride for the cathedral, to warn our brothers."

Istvan chortled, kicking his horse in the ribs. Clearly the Hungarian was eager for another opportunity to cross paths with the Livonians. His horse sprang forward, and he led the party as they galloped along the road, heading around the hill.

Yasper waved away the dust kicked up by their departing companions, and then he hooked a leg over his saddle and slid to the ground. "Well…" he started, rustling around in his saddlebags, gathering a few oddments and trinkets. "I guess we'd better get started." He grabbed one of the two jugs he had found earlier and forced it and the rest of the items he had selected into a large satchel he hung around his waist.

"Started…?" Cnán asked.

Yasper squinted up at the monastery. "Uh-huh."

"Feronantus said we were to wait and see if they returned. He didn't say anything about going up there."

Yasper shrugged. "He didn't say we shouldn't, either." He toyed with the small vial of mint oil. "Did it really smell that bad?"

Cnán snatched the vial from his hands. "Worse than you can imagine," she said. She smeared the ointment liberally on several fingers and slathered her nose before returning the bottle to the alchemist. "We're just going to keep an eye on them," she said. "From outside the walls."

"Of course," Yasper said nonchalantly, as if she had just commented on the weather or the color of his tunic. He rubbed the ointment into his mustache, twirling the long strands idly with his oily fingers. "Only two?" he asked.

Finn nodded, a wide grin spreading across his face.

Yasper turned his attention to the decrepit wall around the monastery. "Should I bring some rope...?" he offered.

"You think too much," Finn snorted. "Door is weak. Go up, knock it down, fight Livonians."

"I would have thought you a subtler man, Finn." Yasper chuckled.

Finn raised an eyebrow at the alchemist and hefted his boar spear. "Subtlety is for when you are stalking fleet prey. It has no purpose otherwise."

A slow smile spread across Yasper's face as he turned to address Cnán. "How many of those ragged...monks...did you see?"

"Just one, but there must be more," Cnán reluctantly replied. "Unless they went with the Livonians."

What Yasper was suggesting seemed like madness, but she could see some virtue to his plan. They had given no thought to the Livonians' purpose previously, and the raiders had managed to disappear from under their very noses. If they were to follow the Livonians, there might be no other way to catch up to them quickly enough to discern their purpose. "The hide workers," she pointed out, "they skin the animals up there, so I presume they have some tools..."

"Lead us," Yasper said, exchanging a glance with Finn that was half mad excitement, half fear.

Cnán felt the same emotions rising from the pit of her stomach. Was this the infectious spirit of her companions driving her into like-minded madness?

✦ ✦ ✦

"If Saint Ilya offers you no guidance, Brother, then perhaps what...*we*...seek is not down in these caverns, and we should allow Sister Vera to resume her normal duties above," Raphael suggested. "Unless you can supply some meager hint as to what the object of your quest might be."

"Hints, perhaps. I have seen little and been illuminated as to its meaning less," Percival said, getting to his feet. "There is a relic guarded ardently in a secret place. A chalice—searched for by many, protected by the worthy—I had hoped that perhaps it might be found here."

At this, there was silence. Raphael recalled a conversation he'd overheard between Percival and Taran, wherein the late *oplo* had been questioned at length by Percival about cauldron myths from his native Ireland. They'd talked late into the night as Raphael had tossed and turned, wishing they'd shut up. Raphael had thought naught of their conversation until now.

Percival sought the Grail, and he had hoped to find it in Kiev.

"We have protected many things over the march of years," Vera replied. "But the Holy Grail is not amongst them."

Percival gave a respectful nod, though he could not hide the look of disappointment that flashed briefly across his face. "But you do protect something."

Vera said nothing.

"We will help you regardless of whether you divulge your secrets," Percival said quietly. "Know that."

A look of consternation—or was it well-hidden exasperation?—flashed over Vera's face. She had said moments ago that this was a good place to speak of secrets. Clearly—to Raphael, at least—she had been urging Percival to divulge *his* secret. But he had taken it the other way and leapt to the assumption that Vera had something to reveal.

She considered his words in silence, the only sound the faint hissing of the melting tallow in the rushlight that illuminated her face. She looked next at each of them and finally relented. "I will tell you the closest thing we have to a holy secret in this place. According to legend, the grave of Saint Ilya guards the Egg of Koschei the Deathless."

Percival did not try to hide his interest. "Tell us more of this sacred egg."

Roger, unable to contain himself, turned his back on them, stalked to the nearest wall, and pressed his forehead against the cool stone.

"It is not sacred," Vera said. "Rather the opposite—it contains the soul of the evil spirit Koschei, and whoever has it in his possession has Koschei in his power."

"Is it perhaps contained in a sacred relic—something shaped like a goblet or chalice?"

Vera was now looking at Percival very oddly indeed and seemed unwilling to speak plainly for once.

Roger turned to face the center of the chamber and stepped slowly toward Percival. "My brother!" he exclaimed. "How can you not understand her words? *It is not here.* We have come all this way to hear a fairy story about a hobgoblin who keeps his soul in a fucking egg! Whatever purpose led you to steer our path toward Kiev had some other end in mind— some end that is going ignored and untended to while we stand in this sewer prating about Koschei the Deathless."

Another man might have been offended. But no anger was on Percival's face as he locked eyes with Roger. Long was the silence that followed.

It stretched out even longer as first Vera, then Roger, then Percival, and finally Raphael began to glance toward the chamber's exit, distracted by approaching sounds that could not possibly have been made by rats. At first these were human voices, echoing distantly along the intestine twists and bends of the cavern's walls. But as they listened, they began to hear too the metallic clank and jingle of steel—steel worn on the body as armor and steel carried in the hand.

"We are not alone down here," Raphael said.

CHAPTER 33:

AND THEN THERE WAS LIGHT...

The monastery gate was as weak as Finn surmised, the timbers splintering after three strong kicks from Finn's boot. Using his spear as a wedge, he ripped and tore the rotted wood away until there was a large enough hole to pass through. After ducking and looking, he went first, leaping nimbly through the gap. Cnán followed, more readily and eagerly than she had anticipated, and Yasper came close on her heels.

Seeing the slaughtering grounds up close, Cnán was repelled at the number of bodies strewn about the ground. Blood, caked and dried to a black tar, was smeared everywhere, and in some places, it still had a sheen of dampness. Black clouds of flies hovered over carcasses, and some of the bodies wriggled with a false skin of maggots. The noise of the flies was a drone in the air.

Had she been by herself, she would not have been able to compose herself in time to address the approach of the two Livonians guards. However, Finn and Yasper were not as incapacitated, and as the two Livonians charged, the Shield-Brethren were ready.

The first Livonian never reached them. Finn's thrown spear struck him forcefully in the throat, lifting him off his feet. He collapsed, squirming and clutching at the shaft of wood protruding from his neck, his bright blood spattering on the ground.

The second, sensing the sudden disappearance of his comrade, hesitated, and Yasper flung out his left hand. The Livonian cried out, ducking his head as something flew into his eyes. He never saw Yasper's quick sword thrust.

Finn went to retrieve his spear, twisting it slightly to finish his man. "Come," he said. "Let us not tarry to meet the monks who haunt this place." He led them toward the well house.

It seemed almost too easy, and Cnán eyed the monastery buildings with some suspicion as they ran toward the tiny shack. She couldn't help but wonder about the residents. Were there more? Where were they hiding? And were they allies of the Livonians or were they like the rest of the locals—frightened and eager to please?

Finn yanked open the door of the well house and ducked inside. Yasper waited at the door, panting slightly. "Awfully quiet," he said as she reached the well house. The glee he had exhibited earlier was gone, and his face was a mask of shadowed grooves.

In spite of the tense silence in the courtyard, Cnán was gladdened by the Dutchman's concern.

"It's very dark," Finn announced, appearing in the narrow doorway of the well house. "And there is no well."

"Ah yes, in that case, the Virgin has blessed us and our inquiry," Yasper smiled.

Someone screamed, and even though they had heard this voice—this cry—before, they flinched. They were much closer to the throat from which it originated, and the howl was such a blend of human and beast that they could not tell from which type of throat it issued. *It had to come from a man,* Cnán found herself hoping as she caught sight of the black-robed apparition who had emerged from one of the buildings. To believe otherwise would be to believe in monsters.

The scream was a signal, for out of the other buildings poured a host of ragged men. They were more than filthy, their threadbare robes encrusted with shit and blood. Hair and beard were tangled and matted into one another, and their mouths were dark holes. Arms and legs, streaked with raw wounds that looked as if the skin had been flayed off by a ragged whip, poked out of the robes like broken sticks. They carried all manner of implement: knives, sticks, scythes, cudgels, awls, anything that could cut, smash, or tear an enemy's flesh.

"Defilers," the screamer shouted in heavily accented Latin, his voice like the wail of a dozen frightened children. "They must not interfere with God's holy warriors." He raised a long stave; mounted on its end was the horned skull of a ram, doused in some black, slick substance that dripped ichor onto the ground.

"Well," Yasper noted dryly, "I guess that settles—"

From within the building, another monk emerged, a lit torch clutched in his bony hands. He lifted the torch toward the end of the apparition's staff, and with a *whuff,* the ram skull burst into flame.

"Oh," Yasper noted, "how clever."

"Inside," Cnán shouted. "Now!" Grabbing a handful of the alchemist's tunic, she dragged him toward the shack.

Finn was waiting for them inside, and she stumbled as her feet collided with a hard surface. Her eyes adjusted maddeningly slowly to the dimness. Finn had said there was no well, and what she found was a ring of raised stones. Rough steps, hewn out of the rock, led down into nothingness.

Finn pulled the door shut, hiding everything in darkness, and Yasper bumbled into her. "Careful," she snapped as she stumbled again on the edge of the stairwell. "There's a hole."

"Of course there is a hole," he replied, fumbling around in the dark. "How else would the Livonians have slipped away?"

Finn grunted as something slammed against the well house door.

Muttering under his breath, Yasper tripped over the lip of stone and managed to not fall down the stairs. Cnán heard his feet slap against the steps as he began to descend into the utter darkness. "I will see what I can do about light," he called back, his voice floating in the void. "Keep them back as best you can."

"And how are we going to do that?" Cnán grumbled, regretting she had ever acquiesced to their plan.

Finn bumped into her, and his hand found her arm. "Down," he said, his mouth close to her ear. "They can only come a few at a time. Kill enough of them, maybe they leave." He chuckled, low in his throat. "Or maybe not. We'll see, hmm?"

A body slammed against the door again, and Cnán—abruptly aware that Finn was no longer beside the door—let out a tiny cry of despair. But the door remained closed, and Finn had not let go of her. "Down," he said again, tugging at her arm. "There was a beam to block the door. It will hold for a little while."

Mollified, Cnán began to descend the stair, her right hand tracing along the rock wall. The staircase was an impossibly tight spiral, straight down. By the time she thought to count her steps, she had already gone far enough she couldn't remember how many lay above her. Eventually her right hand slipped off the wall, trailing into empty space, and with her heart in her mouth, she took two more steps and found herself on solid ground.

A thin green light bobbled in front of her, and as she stood at the base of the stair, terrified but unable to know which way to run, the glow drew nearer.

It was Yasper, holding a tiny piece of curved glass in his hand. The surface shifted and shimmered as he walked, and the light was bright enough for her to see the nature of the catacombs in which they stood.

The chamber extended farther than the illumination offered by Yasper's witch light. A nearby wall was inset with niches from floor to ceiling, extending endlessly in either direction. Cnán swallowed, seeing in each the bones of the long dead, some beneath cloth so thin as to be transparent under the gleam of Yasper's light. Empty eye sockets stared at her, and skeletal mouths gaped—expressions frozen somewhere between awe and terror.

"Where's Finn?" Yasper asked, peering over Cnán's shoulder.

"He said something about forcing them to attack him one at a time."

"Not on the stairs," Yasper sighed. "Finn," he hissed, trying to catch the hunter's attention, "down here. Where it is flat."

Cnán stared at the liquid in the tiny bowl, trying to ken how it generated light. It was a mystery—one of Yasper's alchemical tricks—and most likely well beyond her knowledge. But staring at the light was more agreeable than gazing upon the staring eyes of the dead.

They heard Finn coming, his feet light and quick against the stone. Yasper grunted and motioned for her to follow. Holding his witch light carefully, he led them deeper into the catacombs.

As they reached an archway, Cnán realized she could see more of the room, and their shadows were stretching, eager to run down the hall before them. She glanced over her shoulder and saw why: the yellow glow of torchlight spilling out of the stairwell.

"Here they come," Finn said, shoving her lightly. "Into the tunnel."

Yasper complied, and they departed the burial chamber. The tunnel ceiling was even lower, and with her head canted forward, Cnán took note of the smoothness of the floor. Worn down by the passage of innumerable feet, over the course of countless years. *How many generations had brought their dead down here?* she wondered.

When they reached the first corner, Finn hung back, ready to face their pursuers.

The first died without a sound, Finn's spear thrust driving through his ragged robe and into his chest. The hunter shoved the monk off his weapon and moved to the right side of the tunnel to await his next victim.

The monk had been carrying a cudgel, and the wooden club lay in the tunnel, not far from Finn's feet. Cnán stared at it, her fear warring with her desperate desire to uphold her Binder vows. But she had killed once already, she reasoned, there was already blood on her hands. Her mind flashed to the slaughtered animals aboveground and the persistent stain of their blood on everything.

At some point, the amount of blood no longer mattered.

The second man came around the corner and took Finn's spear low in the belly. He collapsed in a heap, writhing and moaning, until Finn dispatched him with a quick flick of the spear tip.

Cnán darted forward, snatching up the club. She positioned herself on the other side of the tunnel, ready to bring the weapon down on the head of the first man foolish enough to stick it around the corner.

Behind them, Yasper cursed. Cnán dared to look and saw nothing but shadow. Yasper's tiny light had gone out.

Finn grunted, and she whirled around to stare into the face of one of the filthy monks. His eyes were bulging and his mouth was opening and closing. His breath—*how could it be possible?*—was even worse than the corpse-rot stink of the courtyard. His hands scrabbled feebly at the ash shaft of Finn's spear, protruding from his chest. He grunted and strained, broken Latin spewing from his mouth. Cnán caught a few words—*vengeance* and *reclaiming* among them—and then the breath rattled in his throat.

He was dead, but she hit him on the head anyway. Just to be sure.

The howling monk came next, the flaming skull-crowned staff roaring before him, and Finn hauled Cnán back, blocking the clumsy swing of the flaming staff with the steel tip of his spear. Sweat sprang on his brow and arms, coating him against the heat of the fiery ram skull. The monk swung the staff to and fro, forcing Finn back; he started chanting in time with his swings, an obscene liturgy.

Cnán stumbled down the hall, fleeing the fiery beast on the end of the pole. The tunnel filled with boiling orange light, and the heat—the waves of it, rolling over her—were too much, too much like...

And she was back in the burning house again, eight years old. The fire monster had her mother in its burning clutch, and it snapped and snarled at Cnán as she tugged and pulled at her mother's heavy hand. Her skin blistered as it snorted fire, and her tears sizzled to steam on her face, burning her eyes as she shed them. *Wake up,* she cried, *wake up.*

The monster roared closer. Stark horns protruded from its fiery flesh, and its eyes were a maelstrom of black and red flame. Its mouth yawned open, fire gushing from its empty throat, and she remembered screaming, as if the violence of her cry could force the beast away. But the monster only howled with glee as it devoured her mother, its fiery tongues licking the skin from her face and arms, leaving nothing but black ash.

A shadow interposed itself between her and the flame beast, a phantom that shattered her memory. She came back to the present and found herself sprawled on her ass in the subterranean tunnel. Finn, his hand grabbing at her clothing, was dragging her away from the ragman priest and his fiery stick.

They passed Yasper, who—as soon as they were behind him—threw the fat jug he had scavenged from the ruins. The crazed monk shrieked and waved his flaming skull-crowned stick at them, and he paid no mind to the tumbling jug. It struck the stone floor in front of him and shattered.

The hallway erupted with blue flame, and a concussive wave of superheated air filled the tunnel. Yasper flung himself down on Cnán and Finn, or maybe he was bodily thrown by the wave of force—she wasn't sure of anything after the explosion of light and sound. Fingers of heat crawled across her skin, stroking her cheeks and eyebrows. She didn't dare open her mouth, for fear those hot tendrils would fling themselves into her throat and chest.

And then the tiny sun went out, leaving smoke and shadow and tiny strands of blue and yellow flame in its wake. The stench of burned meat filled the tunnel, and somewhere in the near distance, a pitiful creature mewled and whimpered.

Coughing, Yasper dragged himself off Cnán and leaned against the tunnel wall. His face was streaked with ash and sweat. "Such a waste of good *aqua ardens*," he sighed.

Finn snarled something in his native tongue, and Yasper only nodded absently as he shoved himself upright. "But I didn't kill us," he replied, indicating the burned and smoking heaps in the hall. "The Virgin protects the truly *clever.*" He stamped out several tiny fingers of flame that were dancing on the floor.

The staff with the ram skull lay on the floor, its horned crown still afire, but the flames guttered and shivered as if they were slowing dying. Using his scarf, Yasper beat out the scattered rings of fire that wreathed the pole. Protecting his hands, he lifted the staff and, with its light, illuminated the passage beyond Cnán and Finn.

"*Et facta est lux.*" He grinned. "We'd best hurry before the rest of them find their courage again."

Here Ends
The
Mongoliad:
Book One

ACKNOWLEDGMENTS

ERIK BEAR

Thanks to my family, to my friends, and to everyone who's fought alongside me on this book, both metaphorically and literally. Thanks to all the other writers, especially Mark, for working harder than any one person should. Thanks to my dad and my grandpa, for guiding me down the path of writing.

GREG BEAR

It's been terrific working with all of these fine writers, clashing steel in the mornings under Neal's guidance, then quaffing coffee and breakfasting out of pink boxes of muffins while plotting at a mad pace...watching Mark outline and organize chapters on our blackboard while Joe and Cooper paced and swung and flashed their blades, shooting ideas back and forth with Neal across our writers' table, talking across the continent with Nicole (and wickedly offering her virtual muffins), collaborating with son Erik on both fight strategies and chapters...while we all ventured on foot and horse through untold carnage and across wide plains of rippling grass, straight into the fabulous territories of Harold Lamb, Talbot Mundy, and Robert E. Howard... Thanks to all for the amazing experience!

NICOLE GALLAND

Much gratitude to Mark, Neal, Greg, Cooper, Joe, and Erik for the lively trip we've all taken together—especially for keeping the Skype signal open over the miles, even with all those crickets. A special thank you to Liz Darhansoff. And a nod to everyone involved in the brief, ineffable existence of E.D. deBirmingham.

JOSEPH BRASSEY

To Neal Stephenson, who gave me my shot—I hope I've made you proud. To Mark Teppo, who beat my prose with a stick until it was pretty. To Greg, Erik, Cooper, Nicole, and everyone else at Subutai. To Tinker, who taught me to always add violence and put my feet on the path. To Ken and Rob at Fort Lewis, for opening my mind to new possibilities. To my lovely wife and my patient parents who always supported me. To my little sister and every friend I've had along the way who believed this could happen. Dreams come true. This is for you.

COOPER MOO

Heartfelt thanks to my family for their support: my wife, Mary; our children, Keagan, Connor, and Haven; and my parents, Jan and Greg Moo. A debt of gratitude is owed every member of the writing team, particularly Neal for his leadership and Mark for his editorial guidance. I raise a bowl of *airag* to you all!

NEAL STEPHENSON

Thanks to Mark Teppo, the centripetal force.

MARK TEPPO

This project began when someone asked that eternal question that every storyteller loves to hear: "So what happened next?" I don't think any of us imagined where the answer would take us, but I am exceptionally grateful to have had this creative team—Erik, Greg, Cooper, Nicole, Joseph, and Neal—during this journey. I'd also like to thank Karen Laur, Jason Norgaar, and Neal Von Flue for the character portraits they provided, as well as the entire Mongoliad.com community who ventured into the shiny future with us. Jeremy Bornstein and Lenny Raymond took care of us in that eternally unrecognized way that infrastructure people do; thank you, gentlemen. Fleetwood Robbins provided a keen editorial eye, offering a great perspective on the final arrangement of these words. Also, a nod to Emm, whose constant and unflagging support matters. So very much.

As mentioned in the dedication, Tinker Pierce, Gus Trim, and Guy Windsor provided a great deal of useful insight and instruction as to the Western martial arts. Additionally, Ellis Amdur and Aaron Fields offered fantastic commentary on all matters relating to the martial arts of thirteenth-century Japan. These five gentlemen are true scholars in their fields, and any creative license taken with the arts they study is entirely our own.

ABOUT THE AUTHORS

Neal Stephenson is primarily a fiction author and has received several awards for his works in speculative fiction. His more popular books include *Snow Crash*, *The Diamond Age*, *Cryptonomicon*, *The Baroque Cycle*, and *Anathem*.

Greg Bear is the author of more than thirty books, spanning the thriller, science fiction, and fantasy genres, including *Blood Music*, *Eon*, *The Forge of God*, *Darwin's Radio*, *City at the End of Time*, and *Hull Zero Three*. His books have won numerous international prizes, have been translated into more than twenty-two languages, and have sold millions of copies worldwide.

Nicole Galland is the author of *I, Iago*, as well as *The Fool's Tale*, *Revenge of the Rose*, and *Crossed: A Tale of the Fourth Crusade*. An award-winning screenwriter, she is married to actor Billy Meleady and, unlike all her handsome and talented co-writers, spends no time at all hitting people with sticks in Seattle.

Mark Teppo is the author of the Codex of Souls urban fantasy series as well as the hypertext dream narrative *The Potemkin Mosaic*.

Joseph Brassey lives in the Pacific Northwest with his wife and two cats. He teaches medieval fighting techniques to members of the armed forces. *The Mongoliad* is his first published fiction.

Erik Bear lives and writes in Seattle, Washington. He has written for a bestselling video game and is currently working on several comic book series.

Cooper Moo spent five minutes in Mongolia in 1986 before he had to get back on the train—he never expected to be channeling Mongolian warriors. In 2007 Cooper fought a Chinese long-sword instructor on a Hong Kong rooftop—he never thought the experience would help him write battle scenes. In addition to being a member of the *Mongoliad* writing team, Cooper has written articles for various magazines. His autobiographical piece "Growing Up Black and White," published in the *Seattle Weekly,* was awarded Social Issues Reporting Article of the Year by the Society of Professional Journalists. He lives in Issaquah, Washington, with his wife, three children, and numerous bladed weapons.

Made in the USA
Middletown, DE
17 March 2024

51065110R00262